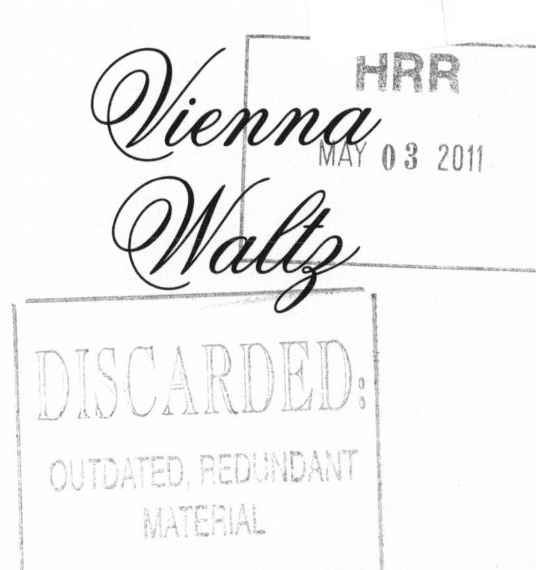
Vienna
Waltz

TERESA GRANT

KENSINGTON BOOKS
www.kensingtonbooks.com

KENSINGTON BOOKS are published by

Kensington Publishing Corp.
119 West 40th Street
New York, NY 10018

All Kensington titles, imprints, and distributed lines are available at special quantity discounts for bulk purchases for sales promotion, premiums, fund-raising, educational, or institutional use.

Special book excerpts or customized printings can also be created to fit specific needs. For details, write or phone the office of the Kensington Special Sales Manager: Kensington Publishing Corp., 119 West 40th Street, New York, NY 10018. Attn. Special Sales Department. Phone: 1-800-221-2647.

ISBN-13: 978-0-7582-5423-8
ISBN-10: 0-7582-5423-7

First Kensington Trade Paperback Printing: April 2011
10 9 8 7 6 5 4 3 2 1

Printed in the United States of America

For Nancy Yost, fabulous agent and friend

My business in this state
Made me a looker-on here in Vienna . . .

—Shakespeare, *Measure for Measure*, Act V, Scene i

ACKNOWLEDGMENTS

Any errors of research or plotting are entirely my responsibility, but I am grateful to a number of people for assistance, support, and inspiration in the writing of this book.

Profound and heartfelt thanks to my agent, Nancy Yost, and my editor, Audrey LaFehr, for believing in this project and helping me polish and shape it. To Kristine Mills-Noble and Judy York for a fabulous cover that beautifully evokes the mood of the book (and actually looks like Suzanne). To Tory Groshong for the careful copy editing. To Paula Reedy for shepherding the book through production. And to Martin Biro and everyone at Kensington Books for their support throughout the publication process.

Thank you to Monica Sevy for the gift of David King's *Vienna 1814*, which inspired me to finally write a book set at the Congress of Vienna. To Tom Stone of the Cypress String Quartet and his children Daniel and Hannah for reminding me that Schubert was in Vienna during the Congress. To Maestro Nicholas McGegan of Philharmonia Baroque Orchestra for advice on Viennese theatres of the time and on Schubert research sources.

To Gregory Paris and jim saliba for creating and updating my Web site. To Greg for filming the wonderful video clips and to jim for the great interview questions.

To Jami Alden, Nyree Bellville, Barbara Freethy, Carol Grace, Anne Mallory, Monica McCarty, Penelope Williamson, and Veronica Wolff for writer lunches and e-mail brainstorming that remind me of what I love about being a writer. And to Veronica for productive (and fun!) writing dates during which large sections of *Vienna Waltz* were written, and to Penny for encouragement, support, and solving the problem of how Suzanne finds the locket.

To Lauren Willig for encouragement, friendship, and wonderful discussions of Napoleonic spies. To Kalen Hughes for answering questions on the intricacies of early-nineteenth-century clothing, and to Candice Hern for the wonderful fashion plates on her Web site. To Miranda Phipps for suggesting via Twitter that having someone get shot makes for a good diversion. To Jayne Davis for the grammar advice. To Melissa Majerol for conversations about Carême. To the History Hoydens for insights, fun, and for being a font of information on period detail. To Tasha Alexander, Deborah Crombie, Catherine Duthie, C. S. Harris, and Deanna Raybourn for their feedback and support.

And to CC, JW, and JJA for the inspiration.

Dramatis Personae

*indicates real historical figures

The British Delegation

Lord Castlereagh, British foreign secretary*
Lady Castlereagh, his wife*
Lord Stewart, British ambassador to Vienna, Lord Castlereagh's half brother*

Malcolm Rannoch, attaché
Suzanne Rannoch, his wife
Colin Rannoch, their son
Aline Dacre-Hammond, Malcolm's cousin
Addison, Malcolm's valet
Blanca, Suzanne's maid

Lord Fitzwilliam Vaughn, attaché
Eithne (Lady Fitzwilliam Vaughn), his wife
The Hon. Thomas Belmont, attaché
Colonel Frederick Radley
Dr. Geoffrey Blackwell

The French Delegation

Prince Talleyrand, French foreign minister*
Dorothée de Talleyrand-Périgord, his hostess and his nephew's wife*
Carême, chef at the French embassy*

The Russian Delegation

Tsar Alexander of Russia*
Tsarina Elisabeth, his wife*

Prince Adam Czartoryski, Polish patriot and adviser to the tsar*
Count Otronsky, adviser to the tsar
Gregory Lindorff, military aide
Count Nesselrode, acting foreign minister*
Grand Duke Constantine, the tsar's brother*

The Austrian Delegation

Prince Metternich, Austrian foreign minister*
Princess Metternich, his wife*
Marie Metternich, their daughter*
Emperor Francis of Austria*
Empress Maria Ludovica, his wife*

Baron Hager, Austrian chief of police*
Friedrich von Genz, Metternich's assistant and secretary to the Congress*

Others

Princess Tatiana Kirsanova, mistress to the tsar
Annina Barbera, her maid

Wilhelmine, Duchess of Sagan, Dorothée's sister, former mistress to Metternich*
Prince Alfred von Windischgrätz, her lover*
Princess Catherine Bagration, mistress to the tsar*
Count Karl Clam-Martinitz, Austrian war hero*
Countess Julie Zichy, Austrian noblewoman*
Baroness Fanny von Arnstein, *salonnière**
Prince de Ligne, former field marshal*

Axel, waiter at the Empress Rose tavern
Heinrich, potboy at the Empress Rose tavern
Margot, his sister, kitchen maid at the Empress Rose tavern

PROLOGUE

Vienna
20 November 1814

Princess Tatiana Kirsanova picked up the tinderbox with fingers that were not quite steady. The flint cut into her palm. She scraped it against steel, harder than was necessary. The first of the three tapers sparked to life, revealing a bit of peeling silver gilt on the candelabrum. She lifted the taper and used it to light the other two. One taper tilted in its base. As she righted it, hot drops of wax spattered against her fingers.

She snatched back her hand, stung, cursing her carelessness. The smell of beeswax filled the room, drowning out the spice and cloves of the potpourri and her carefully applied tuberose perfume, custom blended by her favorite parfumerie in Paris. The trio of flames gleamed against the polished rosewood of the demilune table and was reflected in the curving glass of the bay window. Beyond the window, an autumn moon cast a wash of pale light over the cobbled Schenkengasse. Candlelight sparkled in the windows of the other houses that lined the street. Cool white columns and fanciful rococo balconies glowed in the shadows. She could just glimpse the chancellery where Prince Metternich, Austria's foreign minister, could often be found working late. When he wasn't visiting one of his mistresses. As Tatiana had cause to know.

She set down the tinderbox and stared out at the night sky. Vienna. The city of dreams. The city in which powerful men from the courts of Europe had gathered to carve up Napoleon Bonaparte's empire. But while the official delegates to the Congress of Vienna were men, alongside those men a number of women had come to this glittering city. Women who were perhaps equally powerful, though they had to find more subtle ways to wield their power. The world was being remade in the council chambers and salons of Vienna. And in the bedchambers and boudoirs.

From her first, brutal lesson at the age of eleven, Tatiana had learned to understand and appreciate power. Through intelligence and artifice, deception, calculation, and sheer cunning, she had managed to scrape together a fair amount of it for herself. But tonight, in this city where, every day, borders were redrawn and lovers changed partners as lightly as if they were dancing the waltz, more power than she had ever dreamed possible was at her fingertips. She had only to reach out and grasp it, as she could grip the fluted edge of the table.

If everything fell out as she had designed.

Tatiana touched the cameos round her throat, making sure they still lay at the same precise angle. Then she fingered the thin gold chain of the locket that hung inside the crisscrossed satin bands of her bodice. The locket she always wore. The locket that was the source of everything she was.

She smoothed her shawl over her shoulders. The diamond on her right hand shimmered in the candlelight as her fingers trembled against the silk. It was paisley, a pattern made fashionable years ago when Napoleon had brought it back from Egypt for Josephine. The delicate fabric could slip through one's fingers as easily as carefully laid plans, months in the making. To grasp power required a campaign as intricate as any Napoleon Bonaparte had conducted on the battlefields of Europe. To fall from power could be the matter of a simple misstep. Josephine had fallen. So had Napoleon.

Tatiana tugged the shawl smooth. A quarrel earlier in the evening had distressed her, but that was a minor skirmish, insignificant beside what lay ahead. This was the night that could make her or destroy her. And others along with her. But then she had always found risk headier than the finest champagne.

Beyond the window, a greatcoated, top-hatted figure came into view. Something about the quiet assurance in the way he carried himself was unmistakable. Tatiana's blood quickened. She put a hand up to her hair, making sure the results of her maid's dexterity with the curling tongs were still in place. A fatal mistake to go into battle without all one's armor.

Head held at the angle Jacques-Louis David had immortalized in his portrait of her, she turned from the window and moved to the center of the room to await her visitor.

Elisabeth Alexeievna, Tsarina of Russia, eased open the heavy door. A torch-lit courtyard stretched before her, one of many in the alien maze that was the Hofburg Palace. She pulled the folds of her cloak tighter about her. The sable-lined blue velvet belonged to her lady-in-waiting, who had been seen wearing it going to and from the opera earlier in the evening. Borrowing her lady-in-waiting's cloak was a ploy right out of a comic opera, but so far it had seemed to deceive the footmen and guards she'd passed. She could only hope it deceived any unseen watchers as well.

She waited a moment, but nothing moved in the flickering light. Holding her cloak close, she darted across the cold paving stones, through a door, and then another. The guards by the side door that led to the street were playing dice and sharing a flask. One cast a glance at her and murmured that he'd hate to interfere with a rendezvous. With any luck, it would only be said that one of the tsarina's ladies had a lover. Hardly surprising.

At last she was free of the smothering confines of the Austrian imperial palace. A blast of wind greeted her. She nearly turned and ran back to the palace. But any safety the Hofburg's brilliant splendor offered was merely an illusion. Even in the gleaming white and gold suite allotted to the Russian delegation she found scant refuge. There was no hiding from what she faced now. She pulled her sable-lined hood more firmly over her betraying ash blond hair and stepped into the night air.

As she rounded the side of the four-tower palace, she saw that a distressing amount of moonlight spilled over the street. She walked with her head tilted down, arms tight to her sides beneath the enveloping folds of the cloak. The cobblestones pressed through the kid soles of her ribboned slippers, just as she was sure any watching eyes could cut through the fabric of her cloak.

A carriage clattered by. Light flashed from the flambeaux carried by the footmen who perched behind, turning the pristine white walls beside her a molten orange. It took every ounce of her willpower not to dart into the mouth of the nearest lane. But this meeting had to take place away from the Hofburg.

She clung to the shadows and walked past the limestone and plaster of the palaces of Vienna's elite. Every diamond-bright window seemed to hold unseen watchers. She reminded herself that the dangers in Vienna were more to be found in words whispered behind painted silk fans in candlelit salons than in the dark recesses of moonlit streets. One would think after one-and-twenty years as Alexander's wife, she would have grown used to court intrigue. But she still felt like the wide-eyed girl who had come from Baden to marry the young Russian heir to the throne. Save that that girl, Princess Louise of Baden as she had then been called, had been filled with hope. Had believed that marriage and love went hand in glove. That her bridegroom's dazzling smile held his soul. That vows of fidelity, spoken in a cathedral before the Russian court, rang sterling true. That she and Alexander would live happily ever after and rule over a grateful people. That foreign troops would never breach Russia's borders.

The real language of diplomacy wasn't French. It was lies.

She turned down a narrow side street, grateful for the protection of the close-set buildings, and then down another and another. Twice she was convinced she had lost her way, but at last she ducked beneath a low, crumbling archway into the appointed courtyard.

He was already there, as she had known he would be. In two decades, Adam Czartoryski had never failed her. He detached himself from the shadows and came toward her in three quick strides. The skirts of his greatcoat swirled about him. The moonlight fell on his well-cut features, so achingly familiar, and gleamed against his uncovered dark hair.

"Lisa." He caught her hands in a strong clasp. As clearly as if she had been thrown back in time, she remembered him taking her hands to help her out of a sleigh, snow dusting his hair as it fell over his forehead.

"What is it?" He spoke not in his native Polish nor her German nor the Russian of the country in which they had both lived for so many years but in French, the language of lies and diplomacy and the Russian court. "What was so urgent that we had to meet tonight?"

The impulse to fling herself into his arms was almost overmastering. Were she still the girl who had fallen in love with him, so many years ago, she would have done so.

But she was no longer quite so naïve as the unhappy bride who had first tumbled into Adam's arms. She returned the clasp of his hands and looked up into his eyes. His dark gaze steadied her, though at the same time it was the source of so much temptation. It always had been.

"I've been such a fool, Adam."

He pushed back her hood. His ungloved fingers trembled against her skin for a moment, then slid along the line of her jaw. "You're never foolish, Lisa. Whatever's happened, I'm quite sure you had no choice."

She shuddered, so hard she feared bone and muscle could not contain it. "I've destroyed myself. And I'm terrified I'll destroy you, too."

He reached beneath her hood and curled his hand round the nape of her neck. His touch sent a shiver through her. Though she had known the touch of other lovers since, the brush of his fingers could still affect her like no one else's.

"It can't be that bad, beloved," he said in a steady voice. "Tell me."

She shook her head. "All these years of Alexander's infidelities. All these years of pretending to ignore them and then of trying to learn to play the game. And yet I never guessed she would be the one to destroy me. And everything I care about."

"Who?" Adam's gaze raked her face.

"My husband's mistress." Elisabeth drew a breath that scraped like a dagger against rock. "Tatiana Kirsanova."

Prince Talleyrand eased his clubfoot out before him. He wore embroidered silk slippers rather than the diamond-buckled, red-heeled shoes that were part of his armor on public occasions. His velvet frock coat (a relic of the previous century, carefully reproduced by the Parisian tailor he had frequented through the Revolution, Directoire, Consulate, Empire, and now restored monarchy) lay abandoned over the back of his chair. He sat in his frilled shirt—another relic of a more civilized age—and tapestry waistcoat, though he had not gone so far as to loosen his starched satin cravat. Some standards must be upheld, even in deshabille.

Outside, the wind battered the walls of the Kaunitz Palace. Inside, the coals crackling in the porcelain stove lent a deceptive warmth.

Talleyrand took a sip of calvados, set down the glass, and tented his fingers. His mind was far beyond the red-damask confines of his temporary study. He pictured a Titian-haired woman, housed not so very far away in the Palm Palace. A woman who was here in Vienna partly owing to his design, though he began to think that for once he had dangerously miscalculated.

He had known from the first that Tatiana Kirsanova was a clever woman, with skills that could be molded. He had been sure she could prove useful. She had proved considerably cleverer than he had credited. And far, far more dangerous.

Talleyrand took another sip of calvados, going over his every action since his first meeting with Tatiana so many years ago, searching for where he had gone wrong. His enemies said he rarely admitted to a misstep. But the truth was, he rarely made one. And yet with Tatiana—

The door opened with the faintest stir against the Aubusson carpet. He turned his head nonetheless. He wouldn't have survived this long if he could be approached unawares.

The person he had been expecting closed the door with the same quiet precision and advanced into the room.

"Well?" Talleyrand asked. His breath came more quickly than he would have liked.

"I fear it is as you suspected, m'sieur."

Talleyrand took a sip of calvados. It sat bitter on his tongue. One could not live as many years as he had on the public stage without experiencing the tang of regret. One would think by now he'd have grown accustomed to it. "You're sure?"

"Beyond doubt. It's clear what Princess Tatiana intends. And it's clear how much she knows."

Talleyrand set his glass on the table beside him, careful to keep his hand steady. It was not as though he did not know how to cope with unwelcome developments. He was a survivor. His former protégé, the young general who had risen to rule the Continent, was exiled on the island of Elba, while he was here, helping shape the future of France. A future in which he could allow no interference. "She'll have to be dealt with, then. It's too dangerous to allow her to go on unchecked."

Talleyrand stared down at his ringed fingers. Uncomfortable memories tugged at the edges of his brain. "It's a pity. I've grown quite fond of her."

☙ 1 ☙

Suzanne Rannoch paused on the edge of Schenkengasse. Across the cobbled street, the swinging yellow glare of a street lamp caught the outline of a man, silhouetted against the ink black Vienna sky. Top-hatted, greatcoated, otherwise an undefined blur beneath the wrought iron filigree of the lamppost. He cast a glance up at a bay window in the mansion above. The Palm Palace. The curtains were open. The lit tapers of a candelabrum glittered behind the curved glass. The man stared at the window for a long moment, then looked away as though with an effort. He turned up the collar of his greatcoat and vanished into the night shadows.

From her vantage point in the mouth of an alley on the opposite side of the street, Suzanne willed herself to remain immobile until the man was gone from view. Her silk-gloved hands gripped tight together, she reminded herself that he could have been any of the throng of gentlemen gathered in Vienna for the Congress. Including the most powerful of those men. Prince Metternich. Tsar Alexander. Prince Talleyrand, though then surely he'd have had a walking stick. In the gossip that swirled through Vienna's salons, she had heard them all rumored to be sharing the bed of the occupant of the rooms with the bay window. Of all the women who had come to Vienna for the Congress, that lady was one of the most beautiful and the most talked about. The Russian Diamond. The Eastern Enchantress. The Delilah of the Danube.

Princess Tatiana Kirsanova.

But it wasn't the rumors about Tatiana and the titans of the Congress that chilled Suzanne's soul. It was other talk she had heard. Talk that cut closer to home.

Suzanne pulled the velvet folds of her opera cloak tighter about her shoulders. She could feel the crackle of Princess Tatiana's note where she had tucked it into her glove. Not that she needed to refer to it. The words scrawled on the hot-pressed, violet-scented paper were imprinted on her memory.

> *Madame Rannoch,*
>
> *If you value your husband's safety, you will call upon me tonight, or rather in the early hours of the morning. At three a.m. You are too sensible a woman to fail me.*
>
> *Tatiana Kirsanova*

Precise instructions for how to enter Princess Tatiana's apartments without detection followed on the back of the note. A footman had pressed the note into Suzanne's hand at the opera several hours before, in the midst of the third act of *Idomeneo.*

Suzanne drew an uneven breath. When it came to her husband, Malcolm, the obvious explanation was generally not the correct one. Yet even she had not been able to ignore the talk that he was among the throng of Princess Tatiana's lovers. She had smiled with determination in the face of the rumors. A diplomatic wife learns to practice discretion. She had watched women like Princess Metternich turn it into an art. Suzanne might be only two years married, but she knew the rules of a marriage of convenience.

Not that theirs was precisely a typical marriage of convenience, in which a gentleman gives a lady his name and title and she gives him her dowry and family connections, and they turn a well-bred blind eye to each other's indiscretions. No, what she and Malcolm had exchanged was a bit more complicated. He had rescued her not from the ranks of unmarried young ladies on the sidelines at a ball, but from life on the streets in war-torn Spain. And in exchange she had given him—she couldn't really say what she had given him. Or what lay behind his quixotic offer of his hand and protection. But it had been clear from the start that his heart did not go with his hand. She was supposed to let him go his own way and not make emotional demands.

And now she was breaking the rules. But the alternative was to put Malcolm at risk. She had woken the day before yesterday to find him gone from their bed and a note on the pillow explaining that the foreign secretary had sent him to Pressburg on unexpected business. A spare note, as all his communications were, signed with his initials. He was not expected back for several days, so there was no way she could turn to him for advice on Princess Tatiana's summons. Sometimes, especially since they had come to Vienna, she felt she scarcely knew him. But she could not forget that he had taken her under his protection at a time when she sorely needed it. She had perhaps done him a great wrong in marrying him, but he was her husband and the father of her child.

For a moment, she had a memory, clear as cut glass, of Malcolm and Princess Tatiana standing together on the balcony at the Zichys' reception last week. Suzanne had glimpsed the tableau like a scene from a play, through French windows framed by red velvet curtains. Malcolm's hand had been raised, as though to make a point, his fingers not quite touching Princess Tatiana's white-gloved arm. Something in the angle of his head, tilted down toward Tatiana's own, had radiated tenderness and intimacy. An intimacy Malcolm shared with few people. An intimacy he certainly didn't share with his wife.

Other images followed in quick succession. Malcolm leaning against Princess Tatiana's carriage at the Peace Festival last month. Malcolm bending over Tatiana's hand in her box at the opera. Malcolm tossing Tatiana into the saddle after a picnic in the Austrian countryside.

Suzanne drew a breath, pushed the images to the recesses of her brain, and walked briskly over the cobblestones. A blast of wind cut through the velvet of her cloak and the spider gauze of her gown and settled deep inside her. Fears she would not allow herself to name tightened her throat and squeezed her chest.

When one has suspected a thing for weeks, why is being confronted with stark evidence so much worse?

Three of the most beautiful women at the Congress lodged in the Palm Palace. Wilhelmine, Duchess of Sagan; Princess Catherine Bagration; and Princess Tatiana Kirsanova. The three goddesses, some called them. Though who at the Congress played the role of Paris was anyone's guess. All three were rumored to be or to have been the mistresses of the most powerful men at the Congress. Perhaps at the same time.

So it was no surprise that Princess Tatiana had sent precise instructions for how to enter the palace. She wouldn't wish her visitors to stumble on the Palm Palace's other residents. As instructed, Suzanne went not through the front courtyard but through a wrought iron gate to the side. She found an unlatched side door as indicated and slipped into a narrow passage lit only by a single taper in a wall sconce. The air smelled of beeswax with a faint, lingering whiff of sandalwood. She froze for a moment, one hand on the latch. But Malcolm was not the only man whose shaving soap smelled of sandalwood. She was being the sort of foolish, clinging wife she despised.

Simple pine stairs, of the sort used by servants, led up to the first floor. She climbed them quickly and hesitated outside the green baize door at the top. The instructions had told her not to knock. She turned the handle and opened the door.

The smell slapped her in the face as she stepped over the threshold. Cloying, sickly sweet. Her mind recoiled, even before her gaze took in the sight before her. The images registered in fragments. A single lit candelabrum on a table by the bay window. Shadows. A woman sprawled on the rose and cream carpet in a tangle of bronze-green satin and Titian hair. Blood spilling from a gash in her throat.

A man knelt over the woman, a blur in the shadows. He raised his head, and Suzanne found herself looking at her husband.

Their gazes locked across the room. His gray eyes, so familiar and at the same time so unreadable, were dark with horror.

For a seeming eternity, which might have been minutes or seconds, she was unable to move. Then she took a half step forward and said the words that most needed to be spoken. "Is she dead?"

He stared at her, his eyes like smashed glass. Her controlled husband's gaze glittered with unshed tears.

"Is she dead?" Suzanne said again, her voice a harsh rasp.

"Without question." Malcolm spoke in the flat tone he used when he was holding all feeling at bay. "Perhaps an hour since or a bit more."

Suzanne crossed to his side with quick, jerky steps. Her limbs felt not quite under her control. "You found her like this?"

He looked up at her. It was a moment before he understood. Disbelief filled his eyes, followed by shock and a desperate hurt that cut bone deep. "My God, have we come to this?" His voice was low and rough, like nothing she had ever heard. "How can you ask—"

"How can I not?" She stopped at his side. The folds of her cloak nearly brushed Princess Tatiana's body. Blood had pooled on the carpet, glistening in the candlelight as it began to congeal.

He reached out as though to grip her wrist, then let his hand fall to his side. She recalled, with meticulous clarity, his fingers trailing over her skin three nights ago. The last time they had made love.

"Dear Christ, Suzanne," he said. "We've—"

"Lain in each other's arms. And more." She forced the words from her raw throat. "Though why that's supposed to make two people know each other in any but the carnal sense is beyond me."

His gaze remained steady on her face, imprinted with memories of every intimacy they had shared. "I came into the room less than five minutes ago to find Princess Tatiana like this, with her throat cut."

Air rushed into her lungs. Why his putting it into words reassured her, when there was no way to verify that he spoke the truth, she could not have said. Yet it did. "Did you see any trace of another visitor?"

"No whiff of scent other than her own, no footprints in the carpet, no conveniently dropped objects." His voice turned crisp, falling back on details. "But I think someone searched the room. Look at the escritoire."

Suzanne glanced at the gilt-wood escritoire. The drawer was slightly crooked, as though it had been pushed back into place too quickly. She looked round the rest of the room. Dark splotches that must be blood showed on the carpet. Spatters clung to the watered-silk wall hangings opposite. So much of it. She put a hand to her mouth, forcing down a welling of nausea.

Her eyes growing accustomed to darkness, she saw that one of the splotches was actually a dagger, flung on the floor some two feet from the body. The candlelight sparked off what looked to be rubies and emeralds in the antique gold of the hilt. Blood clung to the blade.

"It was displayed on top of the curio table." Malcolm nodded toward another dark blur a few feet farther off that Suzanne realized was the scabbard. "Easy enough for the killer to snatch it up."

"I saw a man slip out of the palace. Greatcoat, top hat. Indistinguishable. He stopped and looked up at this window, then vanished."

"Suzanne—" This time he caught hold of her hand. "What in God's name are you—"

She looked down at his fingers twisted round her own. Fingers that knew every inch of her body, though the innermost recesses of his mind were closed to her.

Before she could answer, the door swung open behind them and quick footsteps thudded against the carpet. She turned to see a tall, sandy-haired man in an olive-drab greatcoat stride into the room. She had met him many times since they had come to Vienna, but it was a moment before her brain registered that she was looking at Tsar Alexander of Russia.

"Tatiana—" The tsar froze, his gaze on the princess's lifeless body. Beneath his side-whiskers, his face drained of color. He ran forward, then stopped, gaze fixed on Malcolm. "Rannoch. *God in heaven, what have you done?*"

Malcolm pushed himself to his feet in one move. "Your Majesty—"

Alexander's fist slammed into Malcolm's jaw.

Malcolm fell back on the carpet. Suzanne ran between her husband and the tsar. Alexander drew back his fist again. She caught the tsar's arm. He jerked against her hold. For a moment she thought he would strike her as well. Then he went still.

"Madame Rannoch?"

Suzanne looked steadily at the Tsar of all the Russias. "It's a terrible tragedy, Your Majesty. But the princess was dead before Malcolm and I got here."

The tsar's gaze raked her face. "You arrived here together?"

Suzanne met his hot, desperate gaze, aware of nothing save that she was standing before one of the most powerful men in the world, and her husband's life might be at stake. The lie came to her lips without hesitation. "Yes."

Alexander stared down at Malcolm for a moment, then spun away and fell to his knees beside Princess Tatiana. He touched his fingers to her brow, her hair, the line of her jaw. The blue eyes that were a legacy from his grandmother, Catherine the Great, clouded with pain. Womanizer he might be, but whatever he had felt for Princess Tatiana went beyond a fleeting fancy.

"Who could have—What the hell are you doing here, Rannoch?"

Malcolm got to his feet with quiet economy. "I received a message from the princess saying she had something to discuss with me."

Alexander pinned Malcolm with a gaze like a poniard. Malcolm was leaner than the tsar but slightly taller. "What sort of 'something'?"

"I never got the chance to find out."

"Don't expect me to believe that. I know how you felt about her." Alexander's brows drew together. "I thought you'd gone to Pressburg."

"I returned home this evening," Malcolm said without blinking.

"And Madame Rannoch—?" Alexander's gaze slid to Suzanne.

"I insisted on accompanying Malcolm. I'm sure you can appreciate a woman preferring that her husband not pay such a call alone."

The tsar stared at her for a moment. His gaze shot back to Malcolm. "Why the devil—"

Before he could finish, the door from the passage swung open. "Tatiana—" said a light, firm voice.

For the second time in ten minutes, a man stopped short on the threshold, staring down at Princess Tatiana's body. He, too, wore a greatcoat, this one tan. He was shorter and slighter than the tsar, with golden hair that curled round his elegant features. He, too, was unmistakable to anyone at the Congress of Vienna.

It was Austria's foreign minister, Prince Metternich.

❧ 2 ❧

Metternich slammed his hand against his mouth. His gaze went from Tatiana's body to Alexander, and then to Malcolm and Suzanne. Suzanne had never seen such utter bewilderment on the urbane foreign minister's face.

Malcolm stepped toward Metternich. "There's been a terrible tragedy, Prince. Princess Tatiana was murdered, seemingly in the last hour or two."

Metternich, who normally moved with a fencer's grace, crossed to the princess in two jerky strides. The cold reality settled in his eyes, like a wound so painful one's senses refuse to acknowledge it. He lifted his head, his gaze hardening. "What the devil are you doing here, Rannoch?"

"I received a message from Princess Tatiana saying she had information for me."

"And you?" Metternich's gaze snapped to Alexander, who ha pushed himself to his feet. The foreign minister and the tsar regarded each other, incalculable rivalries taut between them. The tension between the two of them at the negotiating table was known throughout Vienna. They had reportedly come close to blows in a private interview a month since. All three of the beautiful women who lodged in the Palm Palace had connections to both men. Princess Tatiana was the tsar's mistress and had been Metternich's lover in the past. Princess Catherine Bagration, also presently assumed to share the tsar's bed, had borne Metternich an illegitimate daughter over a decade ago. And the tsar was commonly assumed to have played a role in the recent spectacular end of Metternich's love affair with the Duchess of Sagan. Now one of those three women they shared lay dead between them.

Suzanne stared at the tableau, struck by the sheer unreality of the situation. A beautiful, brilliant woman sprawled on the floor with her throat cut, and two men who had loved her—three, if one included Malcolm, and she had a desperate, gnawing fear that he should be included—stood over the body. That in itself was strange enough. When one took into account that two of those men represented two of the victorious countries deciding Europe's future at the Congress, and the third man was a diplomat in the employ of yet another triumphant country, the scene was well-nigh fantastical.

In the crossfire of jealousy and recrimination, Tatiana herself had almost been forgotten. Suzanne looked down at the dead princess. Beneath her carefully applied rouge, her skin had a faint bluish tinge. Her eyes, artfully lined with blacking, were frozen open in shock. She had crumpled on the carpet with no sign of a struggle. As though whoever had killed her had taken her unawares. As though it was someone she had trusted. Someone who perhaps had been able to embrace her as a lover.

Metternich drew a breath. The mask of Austria's foreign minister settled over his features. "Did Tatiana ask you to come here?" he asked the tsar.

"How dare you—"

"I mean tonight. Specifically. Or was it just chance that you walked in?"

"I don't see what the devil—"

"Because she sent me a note," Metternich said. "Asking me to call at three in the morning and specifying that I be sure to use the front entrance."

Alexander's eyes widened. "She sent me a note saying the same. Only she said to use the side door."

"Damned odd. Rannoch?"

"She sent me a message asking me to come at a quarter to three," Malcolm said.

Alexander scrubbed his hands over his face. "Are you saying she wanted us all here at once?"

"Or the killer did," Malcolm said.

Metternich met his gaze for a moment. "Precisely."

"Either way," Alexander said, "it makes it clear none of us killed her."

"Not necessarily." Malcolm was still looking at Metternich. His voice was even, but his face was like bleached linen. "Any of us could have killed her and then come back. Or in my case, I suppose, never left."

"Except that I was here with you," Suzanne said. "So we'd have to have killed her together."

Metternich's gaze shifted to her. For a moment she felt he was stripping her bare, cutting through layers of gauze and satin and linen in a way that had nothing to do with amorous intrigues. "I haven't known you long, Madame Rannoch, but you strike me as a very loyal wife. I suspect there's little you wouldn't do for your husband."

"I wouldn't kill for him."

"But would you lie?"

Malcolm moved to Suzanne's side. "Keep my wife out of this, sir. If you have accusations to make, make them to my face."

"Your wife is unfortunately in the middle of it, Rannoch. And I don't know enough to make any accusations. Yet."

"Why the hell would Tatiana have sent for you?" Alexander was staring at Metternich as though they faced each other across a stretch of green with pistols in their hands. "You've had little contact with her in recent months."

"Have I?" Metternich raised his brows. "Who told you that? Tatiana herself?"

"She—" Alexander's cheekbones whitened. For a moment, Suzanne thought he would lunge across the room and seize Metternich by the throat.

Metternich smoothed the cuff of his greatcoat. "And you, Rannoch?"

"The princess is—was—a friend." Malcolm's voice was clipped.

"A word that can cover a multitude of sins."

"You forget, Prince," Suzanne said. "Malcolm came here with his wife."

Metternich regarded her again with that same appraising, razor-sharp gaze. "I forget nothing, Madame Rannoch." He spun away and strode through the door to the front of the house. "Annina!" he called in the voice of one used to command.

Alexander took a step after him but checked himself, perhaps aware of the risks of advertising his presence in Princess Tatiana's rooms. He frowned at the closed door panels, then looked back at the dead princess. A spasm crossed his face, but he seemed unable to look away.

Malcolm's gaze had gone to the murder weapon. Suzanne could see him studying it, analyzing the spatters of blood on the carpet, the angle at which the dagger had fallen, recreating the crime in his mind. Keen appraisal with a weight of grief beneath.

After perhaps five minutes, Metternich returned, holding a chestnut-haired woman by the arm. She wore a linen nightdress with a green damask dressing gown hastily thrown over it, and her hair fell down her back in a long braid. She too froze on the threshold. "Madame." She flung herself down beside Princess Tatiana.

Malcolm moved to the woman's side and put a hand on her shoulder. "I'm so sorry, Annina."

"Monsieur Rannoch?" Annina looked up at Malcolm in bewilderment. She must, Suzanne realized, be Princess Tatiana's maid. And Malcolm was obviously no stranger to her. His fingers tightened on Annina's shoulder. Their gazes met and held for a moment.

"Who's been to see the princess tonight?" Metternich demanded.

"No one." Annina straightened her shoulders and dashed tears from her eyes. She looked to be in her midtwenties, a few years younger than the princess. Her face was delicate, but she had the sharp eyes of a woman who has seen much of the world. Suzanne, who had seen more of the world in her one-and-twenty years than most people knew, recognized the signs. "That is, no one I saw before I retired for the night."

"Which was when?" Metternich asked.

"Just after ten. She said she'd have no further need of me. I read in my room and then went to sleep."

"Was she expecting anyone?" Metternich asked.

"She—" Annina's gaze slid round the room, settled on the tsar for a moment, darted back to Metternich.

"She was dressed for visitors," Suzanne said, looking down at Princess Tatiana's satin and tulle gown, cameo jewelry, and the ringlets and coils of her hair. "Had she been out this evening?"

"No."

Which in itself was unusual. In Vienna these days, quiet nights at home were a rarity. "I saw a man leaving the palace earlier."

Annina fingered a fold of her dressing gown. The green damask edged in black lace looked to be a castoff of the princess's. "I didn't hear the bell. My bedchamber is near the princess's, some distance from the salon. She could have let him in herself. Or he could have entered on his own." As the three men presently in the room had all done.

The tsar had dropped down beside the princess again. "It's gone."

"What?" Metternich's voice was impatient.

"Her necklace."

Tatiana's cameo necklace was half-obscured by blood. "I think—" Suzanne began gently.

"He means her locket." Malcolm was looking down at Tatiana's face, his eyes dark with an emotion Suzanne could not put a name to. "She always wore it, though it was often tucked into her bodice."

Alexander touched the bodice of Tatiana's gown, then snatched his hand back as though burned.

Annina reached inside the tulle-edged satin of Princess Tatiana's bodice. "Yes," she said after a moment. "It's gone. She was wearing it earlier. Monsieur Rannoch is right. She never took it off."

"What was in the locket?" Metternich asked.

"I don't know, Your Highness." The gaze Annina turned to Metternich was as steady and implacable as polished armor. "I never saw it save when it was round her neck."

Metternich gave a quick nod of dismissal. "See that the doors of her rooms are secured and assemble the rest of the staff. I'll speak with you again presently."

Malcolm helped Annina to her feet. Her legs seemed not quite steady, but she held her head high. She fixed Metternich with a gaze like a lancet. "Find who did this."

"I intend to do so," Metternich said. "And I seldom fail."

Annina opened her mouth as though to say more, then gave a quick nod.

Malcolm squeezed her hand and walked to the door with her. He pushed the door shut behind her and rested his palm against the panels for a moment. But when he turned back to the others, his gaze was cool again. "I assume you'll want us all to stay here until we can give a statement to the authorities."

"God in heaven." Alexander's head snapped up from contemplation of his dead mistress. "You can't call in—"

"A common constable?" Metternich surveyed the tsar. "You'd find that inconvenient?"

"A number of us would find it inconvenient." Alexander pushed himself to his feet.

"You'd prefer there be no investigation into the death of a woman you claim to have loved?"

"Of course not." Alexander dug his fingers into his hair. "But—"

Metternich took a step forward. He and the tsar faced each other across the princess's body.

"Might I remind you, Your Majesty, that we are on Austrian soil?" Metternich's voice was soft, but his tone was the tone of a man who had ordered armies across Europe. "Princess Tatiana's murder will be dealt with by the Austrian authorities."

Alexander looked down at Metternich from his superior height. The tsar outranked the foreign minister. Russia had played a more powerful role in vanquishing Napoleon than the vacillating Austria had done. But as Metternich had pointed out, they were presently in Austria, and the machinery of the Austrian government was at Metternich's fingertips.

"Your authority doesn't extend over the Russian delegation," Alexander said. "Or the British delegation, if it comes to that."

"True." Metternich looked from the tsar to Malcolm. "If either of you suspect your compatriots of complicity in Princess Tatiana's murder and attempt to protect them, there is little I can do. You must act according to your consciences. But I will manage the investigation as I see fit."

He moved to the door. "I've learned enough for tonight. I advise you all to return to your quarters."

"You don't wish us to give formal statements?" Malcolm said.

"Not yet." Metternich held the door open. "I know where to find you."

Tsarina Elisabeth closed her door in the Amalia wing of the Hofburg and leaned against the cool, white-painted panels. Her heartbeat thudded in her brain like a Beethoven crescendo. For seconds she was unable to move, afraid that moving would mean thinking, and thinking would mean remembering the events of the evening.

She squeezed her eyes shut, but she could not blot out the images. The memories were even worse than present reality. She opened her eyes and forced herself to look down at the skirt of her gown. Her cloak had fallen back and splotches of crimson showed against the figured ivory silk of her skirt.

She drew a breath that shuddered against the laces of her corset. Then she tugged at the ties on her cloak and cast it aside. She reached for the tapes on her gown, desperate to be free of it. She would strip it off and burn it. But even as she tugged at the first tape, so hard it tore off in her hands, she realized the remnants of pearl-beaded fabric among the ashes would betray her.

Damn this life in which there was no privacy.

She ran to her night table, grabbed the ewer, and poured water on her skirt, heedless of the amount she spilled over the parquet floor. The crimson spread and faded to pink. She tugged up the hem, stiff with pearls and silver embroidery, and rubbed at the spots, crushing the fabric, pulling threads, knocking pearls loose on the floorboards. She seized a cake of lavender soap and scrubbed it over the stains.

They didn't go away. They would never go away. But in the end, when she held her skirt up to the light of the Argand lamp, the stains had faded enough that her maid would not be able to tell precisely what they were. And her maid could not, after all, question what had happened to the gown that had looked so pristine earlier in the evening. There were advantages to being an empress.

Hysterical laughter welled up inside her and spilled from her lips. She pressed her shaking fingers to her mouth. No, the stains on her gown would not betray her.

It was the stains in her mind that would never go away.

3

Suzanne stole a glance at her husband as they walked down the Schenkengasse. His gaze was fixed straight ahead, his generous mouth set in a hard line. Before they had left Princess Tatiana's salon, he'd turned, almost as though under compulsion, and looked back at the dead woman for a long moment. Suzanne had the oddest sense he'd have knelt and closed Tatiana's eyes if Metternich would have permitted it. Instead, he'd held the door open for Suzanne and strode from the room.

Now he walked close beside her, but he'd made no move to offer her his arm. He hadn't touched her since that moment when he'd grabbed her wrist as he knelt by Princess Tatiana's body.

"Do you think Metternich will put Baron Hager in charge of the investigation?" Suzanne asked, in as level a voice as she could manage. Baron Hager was the head of Austria's secret service.

"I expect so." Malcolm didn't pause or turn to look at her. "Hager's agents have bungled some things, but he's an able man. And Metternich knows Hager will understand the need for discretion."

"I still don't understand why Metternich let us leave without giving statements."

"I suspect he wanted a chance to search Tatiana's rooms unobserved."

Suzanne looked up at her husband in the yellow glow of a street lamp. "For what? Love letters?"

"Among other things." A carriage clattered by, bringing the glow of flambeaux and the smell of pitch. Malcolm continued to walk, his gaze shifting over the dark street ahead. The moonlight gleamed blue-black on the cobblestones, but the narrower side streets were in shadows. "We need to get our story straight. We're damned lucky we didn't trip over each other making things up as we went along."

She swallowed a host of emotions that tore at her chest. "It was dangerous to lie to the tsar. I spoke on impulse. I should have thought things through."

"Perhaps." He stopped abruptly and turned his head to look at her. The lamplight bounced off his sharp-boned, Celtic features and the pewter of his eyes. "But your impulsiveness probably saved my liberty and quite possibly my life. To say thank you seems shockingly inadequate. It was a generous thing to do. Particularly given what you think of me."

"Malcolm—" The words caught in her throat. She put out her hand, then let it fall to her side. "I know how much I owe you."

He drew a breath and released it. His dark hair fell over his forehead in that way that gave him the unexpected look of a schoolboy. Save that the ghosts that haunted his gaze made him seem years older. When he spoke, his voice was harsh. "I don't believe in calling in debts. And if you owed me anything, it's been repaid long since. Simply by the fact that you put up with me."

He turned and began walking again, scanning the streets ahead. A carriage had drawn up before a tall house at the corner. Three young men with silk hats decidedly askew stumbled out and clambered up the steps of the house. Attachés, no doubt, home after a night of revelry, though at this distance it was impossible to make out who they were or what country they represented. Of one accord, she and Malcolm fell back in the shadows until the young men had vanished into the house.

"Malcolm," she said as they started forward again. "Were you really in Pressburg?"

They turned down a side street. The overhanging balconies on either side encased them in darkness. "No," he said at last, as though he already half regretted the words. "But I was gone from Vienna from two nights ago until this evening. Castlereagh sent me to rendezvous with a contact who had information about the disposition of Prussian troops in Saxony."

"Did you really receive a note from Princess Tatiana? Or—"

His hand moved to her elbow. He didn't quicken his pace, but he turned his head toward her, his voice conversational. "Don't look round. We're being followed."

Even as he framed the words, she could hear the faint footfalls against the cobblestones behind them. One man. No, two. Moving carefully and almost in unison but with slightly different gaits.

Suzanne had spent part of her life on streets like this. Not the best preparation for a diplomatic wife, but excellent training for other aspects of Malcolm's life. Like her husband, she knew better than to quicken her pace. They turned down another street, lined with shuttered shops and cafés warm with candlelight despite the hour.

"Are they still behind us?" she asked as they passed a brilliantly lit building with fashionably dressed women visible through the windows. Quite definitely a brothel. The strains of a waltz played on the pianoforte spilled out a first-floor window, making it difficult to pick out the sound of the footsteps.

Malcolm nodded. They turned another corner, past three boys roasting chestnuts over a fire in the street. Malcolm pulled her into a shop doorway and into his arms.

His lips were warm. His mouth tasted of wine. She clung to him, with an urgency that took her by surprise, even as she listened for noise from the street behind, heard him fumbling in his pocket, heard the scrape of metal and the jiggle of tumblers.

He pushed the door open and pulled her inside. "Very old ruse," she said. Her voice was just a shade less steady than she would have liked.

"But nearly always effective."

The smell of dust and beeswax and lemon oil engulfed them. The lamplight seeping through the thick, old glass of the windows showed dark rectangular shapes and larger triangular ones with slender tapered legs. They were in a pianoforte maker's. Trust Malcolm to find music even in the midst of an escape.

Malcolm returned his picklocks to his pocket. He and Suzanne threaded their way over the worn floorboards, mindful of the fact that the shop owner probably lived upstairs.

Malcolm paused in the middle of the room and glanced round the darkened shop. "You didn't by any chance think to bring a weapon, did you?" he said in a low voice.

"I could make do with the brooch that fastens my cloak."

"Resourceful as always. But I think we can do better." He scanned the shadowy room. His fingers hovered over the keys of one of the pianofortes, though he didn't dare strike a note.

Suzanne's eye had fallen on another shape, too low and broad to be an upright, too rectangular to be a grand. A worktable. Her eyes growing accustomed to the dark, she found a drawer and tugged it open. "Surely a pianoforte maker would have—" Her fingers closed round them. "Wire clippers."

"That's the woman I married." Malcolm spared her a brief smile, a white gleam in the shadows. He reached inside his coat and pulled out two dark objects. She caught a whiff of sulfur and heard the familiar scrape of a pistol being loaded.

He pressed the loaded pistol into her hand. "If we're attacked, hang back and try to wait until you have a clean shot. But look after yourself. I'll do the same."

She nodded, though she knew perfectly well he wouldn't leave her. It was one of the reasons she'd risked herself and lied to the tsar, and that she'd risk herself again now. She tucked the pistol beneath her cloak and gave him the wire clippers. Their eyes met in the darkness. Something wild and fierce sparked between them, drowning out for the moment all the poisoned questions.

Malcolm bent his head and pressed his lips over hers again in a brief, hard kiss. "I deserve some of the things you think about me, sweetheart. But not nearly all. Try to trust me until we get out of this."

A door at the back of the shop gave onto a cobbled alley. A few lights shone down from first-floor lodgings. Malcolm glanced to either side, then jerked his head to the right, the longer, more shadowy way. They stepped into the alley. A casement was flung open above. They jumped back against the wall just as the contents of a chamberpot spattered onto the cobblestones.

A half dozen paces from the mouth of the alley, two dark forms hurtled at them out of the shadows. Malcolm had a split second to step forward and take the brunt of the attack. The impact sent him crashing into the wall behind him. One man drew back his fist and struck Malcolm a blow to the jaw. The other turned toward Suzanne. She leveled her arm and shot him in the shoulder.

The man screamed, clutched his arm, and stumbled into the street beyond. The shot had made his compatriot cast a quick glance over his shoulder. It was enough opening for Malcolm. Seconds later he had spun the man round and was holding him against his chest, a length of piano wire clamped round the man's throat.

"Who sent you?" Malcolm's soft voice held an edge of naked steel.

"Don't know—"

"I advise you not to trifle with me. I might overlook an attack on myself. But you had the bad sense to attack my wife as well."

"They'll kill me." The man's voice was a harsh whisper.

"So will I. Sooner." Through the darkness, Suzanne saw Malcolm tighten the piano wire round his captive's throat.

The man was stone still in Malcolm's grip, but his gaze shifted to the street. "Fool. You don't know them. You're as good as dead yourself."

"I'm rather good at protecting myself. I can protect you, too, if you'll talk."

The man gave a desperate laugh. "There's no such thing—"

Another shot ripped through the night air, this one from the street beyond. The man went limp in Malcolm's arms. Malcolm staggered, eased his captive to the ground, and put his fingers to the man's throat. He looked up at Suzanne and gave a quick shake of his head. Then he caught her hand and raced to the opposite end of the alley.

He stopped at the house on the corner, gaze on the rococo balcony. "Burgos," he said.

His eyes glittered in the shadows. Suzanne nodded, her memory of their escape from the medieval Spanish city fresh in her mind.

She returned the spent pistol to him. He stuck it in the waistband of his breeches and lifted her in his arms, as though they were dancing a highland reel at a regimental ball. She gripped the balusters. He boosted her higher, and she pulled herself up, grasped the railing, and half levered herself, half fell over the balustrade.

She landed with a thud on the cold, hard stone of the balcony. She stripped off her cloak, twisted it into a rope, and held it down to Malcolm, bracing her feet against the plaster balustrade. Malcolm had shrugged out of his greatcoat and the tightly fitting coat beneath. He caught the end of the cloak and pulled himself up, hand over hand. Her muscles screamed in protest. She tightened her grip.

His fingers scrabbled against the edge of the balcony. She released the cloak and caught his hand. He grasped a baluster and then the railing, got a booted leg over the balustrade, and collapsed beside her on the balcony floor.

"How the devil Romeo ever managed to do that and spout poetry is beyond me," he said in a hoarse voice. "Not to mention that he'd have needed Juliet to haul him up."

"I think it was easier last time we did it," she said. Softly, because the occupants of the house were probably sleeping behind the French windows.

"We were younger last time."

"Speak for yourself. I'm only one-and-twenty." And he was just six years her senior. She forgot sometimes that he was barely twenty-seven.

Malcolm had gone still. Booted footsteps thudded against the cobblestones a street over. "No way to be sure it's our pursuers," he said. "Still, better safe than sorry."

She removed the brooch from her cloak and stuck it to her bodice. He pushed himself to his feet and steadied her as she climbed onto the railing and pulled herself onto the slick, red-tiled roof. The spider gauze of her gown caught on the tiles. Oh well, it wouldn't be the first gown she'd ruined. Or the last, no doubt. She crouched on the edge of the roof and stretched down a hand to help Malcolm up after her.

His shirt tore on the tiles as her gown had done. For a moment they both crouched on their hands and knees, breathing hard. A blast of wind cut against them. Suzanne looked at her husband and found him grinning at her, eyes glinting in the moonlight. She grinned back, laughing with a crazy, wine-sweet rush of exhilaration.

Vienna's old town was spread before them beneath cloud-filtered moonlight. Shiny roof tiles, candlelit windows, glowing street lamps. The gleaming pillars of palaces and the grimy white walls of lodging houses. Winding medieval streets. Columned monuments, broad, tree-lined squares, tiny courtyards. All surrounded by the many-times-rebuilt medieval walls that, according to legend, had originally been constructed with the ransom payment the Austrians exacted for the release of Richard the Lionheart. The glittering city in which the future of Europe was being decided. And in which Tatiana Kirsanova's murderer lurked. Not to mention other unseen enemies.

Their first attacker's crumpled form lay at the other end of the alley. Two shadowy figures bent over him, as though conferring. As she and Malcolm watched from their perch, one man ran back into the street, while the other ran down the alley, directly beneath the balcony they had just climbed. He passed within a few feet of Malcolm's discarded coat and greatcoat, a dark blur against the wall of the house, but he didn't stop to examine them.

She and Malcolm stayed stone still until he had passed, then moved to the darkest part of the roof and crept over the sloping tiles, crouched low. Up the slope and then down and over to the next roof, which was slightly higher. She pulled off her gloves. She scraped her palm on a broken tile, but bare hands gave her better purchase.

They made their way to the next corner, turned and went along another line of roofs, jumped a narrow gap between buildings, turned again.

At last Malcolm paused, gripped her arm, and leaned down over the edge of the roof they were on.

"Where are we?" she asked.

"The Minoritenplatz. The British delegation's lodgings. I hope." He swung his legs down, lowered himself onto another balcony, and reached up to her. She slid down into his arms. His palms were damp when he took her hands. Blood, she realized. He'd scraped his hands raw. She looked down and saw a gash on her own forearm.

Were they at their lodgings? The plaster curlicues over the French window looked familiar, though from this angle she couldn't be sure. Malcolm unlatched the French window with his picklocks and pushed aside the curtains.

An unexpected flare of candlelight greeted them.

"Malcolm, thank goodness you're back." The decisive tones of Lord Castlereagh, the British foreign secretary, came from the room beyond. "We're in the devil of a fix."

4

"Good evening, sir." Malcolm drew aside the curtains and handed Suzanne through the window. "My apologies for the inopportune entrance."

"Never mind about that. I'm used to them. We need—Good God! I thought you'd gone to Baroness Arnstein's after the opera, Suzanne."

Robert Stewart, Viscount Castlereagh, Britain's foreign secretary and representative at the Congress of Vienna, stood by a round table that held a single lit taper, the only illumination in the room other than the coals glowing in the porcelain stove in the corner. His fair hair gleamed smooth, and he wore a dark blue dressing gown beneath which his cravat was still impeccably tied.

"I *was* at Fanny von Arnstein's." Suzanne breathed in the sweet relief of level ground beneath her feet and warm air coming from the stove. "I was called away."

Castlereagh stared at her in the dim light as though he could not make sense of what he was seeing. Suzanne looked down. Her gauze overskirt was in tatters, the satin beneath was torn to reveal her corset and chemise, and in addition to the gash on her arm, she had scrapes on both her hands.

"What in God's name were you doing dragging your wife into this?" Castlereagh asked Malcolm.

"I wouldn't precisely say I dragged her." Malcolm pulled a handkerchief from his breeches pocket and wiped the dirt and blood from his hands, then walked through the shadows to a table with decanters. Suzanne heard the clink of crystal and the slosh of liquid. "Do you mind, sir? I think Suzanne and I are both in need of fortification. It's a bit of a strain having someone try to kill you."

"Someone—" Castlereagh's finely arced brows drew together. "Who the devil tried to kill you?"

"I'm not sure. There were several of them. The man we tried to question was killed himself. After that the first imperative seemed to be to get out of there alive." Malcolm crossed back to Suzanne and gave her one of the glasses. He squeezed her fingers as he put the crystal in her hand.

She took a sip. Cognac, of the best quality, available to the British without the need to resort to smugglers now the war with France had ended. It rushed to her head with welcome warmth. She looked down at the glass and saw blood smeared on the crystal from the cut on Malcolm's hand.

Castlereagh struck a flint against steel. A lamp flared to life. "My dear Suzanne, you must be exhausted after your ordeal. I'm sure you are eager to go down to your room. I fear I need to speak with Malcolm before I can send him after you."

Malcolm took a long drink from his own glass. "She needs to stay for this."

"Rannoch—"

"She knows too much."

Castlereagh fixed Malcolm with a hard gaze. "You're invaluable, Malcolm. But not indispensable. You'd be wise to remember that."

"Believe me, sir, I'm well aware of it. But at the moment we both need each other."

Malcolm's gaze clashed with the foreign secretary's across the room. All the wellborn young men Castlereagh had brought to the Congress of Vienna as attachés were expected to have myriad talents. To make small talk in five languages, to dance the waltz into the small hours, and then return to the embassy and draft the third revision of a white paper before dawn. They were also expected to comb though diplomatic wastebaskets for discarded laundry lists and boot-maker's bills that might be code for something much more serious, and to break those codes and pass them on to the foreign secretary. Every diplomat at the Congress was something of an intelligence agent. But Malcolm's skills were more formidable than most. Though Malcolm and Lord Castlereagh frequently disagreed, Suzanne knew the foreign secretary had a great deal of respect for her husband. He gave him far more latitude than any of his other attachés.

Now Castlereagh inclined his head a fraction of an inch. "Start at the beginning."

Malcolm drew a shield-back chair forward and handed Suzanne into it. Then he paced across the room and leaned against the drinks table. He took another deep swallow from his own glass. "Tatiana Kirsanova is dead."

"I know," Castlereagh said. "Why do you think I said we were in the devil of a fix?"

Malcolm's head snapped up. "My compliments, sir. I didn't realize your sources of information were quite so efficient."

"You're an excellent agent, Malcolm, but not the only one in my employ." Castlereagh dropped into a wing-back chair. "Given Princess Tatiana's role, I'd be remiss if I didn't have a source among her staff. One of the kitchen maids sent the news an hour since. Deuced inconvenient."

Malcolm slammed his glass down on the drinks table. "*She's dead.*"

"And I'm sorry for it. It's still inconvenient."

"God damn it, sir—"

"No time for personal feelings, Malcolm." Castlereagh rested his fair head against the blue velvet of the chair. "How did you learn of it?"

Malcolm reached for his glass. The light bounced off his signet ring. Suzanne, used to reading the signs, knew her husband's fingers were not quite steady. "I discovered the body."

"Good God. The princess—"

"Sent for me tonight." Malcolm stared at a bloodstain on his cuff that might be his own or Princess Tatiana's. "At least the message seemed to come from her. I begin to question if it really did.

She also seemingly sent for Tsar Alexander and Prince Metternich."

"At the same time?"

"Quite. And she sent for Suzanne."

Castlereagh's gaze shot to Suzanne, then back to Malcolm. "You got there first?"

Malcolm nodded. "Her throat had been cut. Seemingly by someone she knew and trusted."

He took another sip of cognac. For a moment, his gaze was raw as an open wound. Suzanne's own glass nearly tumbled from her fingers at the naked pain in her husband's eyes. "I saw a man in the street in front of the house a few minutes later," she said, a little too quickly. "I couldn't make out any more than that he wore a greatcoat and top hat. He looked up at the window of the room in which the princess died. Then he disappeared."

Castlereagh regarded her, his fine-boned face set in harsh lines. "What did the princess write to get you to call on her?"

Suzanne fingered a fold of tattered gauze. "Just that she had something important to tell me."

"All things considered," Malcolm said, his gaze armored again, "we'd better tell Castlereagh the whole truth. We can trust him as far as we can trust anyone."

"Thank you," Castlereagh said in a dry voice.

Suzanne swallowed. "Princess Tatiana wrote that she had something to say to me concerning Malcolm."

Castlereagh grimaced. His gaze moved to Malcolm. "It can't be coincidence. This must be connected to her other activities."

"Probably. The question is how."

"I hate to seem inquisitive," Suzanne said, "but if you want me in this discussion, it would help if I knew what was going on."

Malcolm regarded her. The moment of vulnerability was so completely gone she might have imagined it. Wariness was written in the lean, elegant lines of his body. His white shirt, splotched with blood and soot, gleamed in the shadows. "Princess Tatiana has been supplying us with information."

Suzanne stared at her husband. "Are you saying Princess Tatiana was a spy?"

"She dealt in information," Malcolm said. "Most people at the Congress do, one way or another."

Prince Talleyrand glanced at the porcelain clock on the mantel for the third time in the last five minutes. It went without saying that he wouldn't sleep tonight. He had learned long since that betrayal was a fact of life. But that didn't make it any easier to accept, in others or in himself. Some might consider that a vestige of conscience. He found it damned inconvenient.

He stared at his empty glass of calvados, considered pouring more, decided against it. He needed his wits about him. He drew the folds of his dressing gown closer round his throat. The coals still glowed in the stove, but the room seemed to have grown colder as the night dragged on.

The door opened as soundlessly as it had earlier in the evening. Talleyrand was on his feet before his visitor stepped into the room.

"Well?" The question came out more quickly than Talleyrand intended. "Is it done?"

"Not precisely." His visitor closed the door. "I'm afraid someone else got there first."

❧ 5 ❧

Suzanne looked at her husband. "You were Princess Tatiana's contact?"

Malcolm nodded.

It explained some of his relationship to the princess. It did not begin to explain how far his work as her contact had gone.

"For a long time?" Suzanne asked.

"Off and on for several years." Malcolm turned his glass in his hand. The crystal sparked in the lamplight. "Tatiana spent some months in Spain during the Peninsular War. Before I met you."

Suzanne took a sip of brandy. Her image of her husband's life before she knew him shifted and changed before her eyes, fragments of mosaic forming a picture that remained tantalizingly unfinished. "Was the princess particularly loyal to Britain? Because given her connections to the Russian delegation, not to mention her past connection to Prince Metternich—"

"I think Tatiana decided we paid the best," Malcolm said. "Though I was under no illusions we were the only delegation at the Congress she was supplying with information."

"A welcome admission," Castlereagh said.

Malcolm met the foreign secretary's gaze. "Believe me, sir, I saw Tatiana for what she was."

Castlereagh got to his feet. "My dear boy, you've always been entirely too trusting where she was concerned. But"—his gaze slid briefly to Suzanne—"that's neither here nor there for the moment. What matters is that she was an agent for us, and very likely others as well, and she may well have been killed because of what she knew. We have to learn the truth of what happened. You have to learn the truth, Malcolm."

Malcolm took a sip of brandy. "Baron Hager will launch an official investigation into Tatiana's murder."

"This won't be the first time we've run a parallel investigation. Or the last. Baron Hager is an able man. But I have every confidence in you, Malcolm."

"Your confidence may be misplaced."

"I doubt it. When you let me down it's due to your ideas, not your abilities." Castlereagh walked up to Malcolm and looked him directly in the eye. "I needn't remind you what a dangerous pass we are at, need I? Tsar Alexander has unilaterally handed Saxony over to Prussia and wants to gobble up Poland, the German states can't agree among themselves, no one can agree about the Italian situation. Metternich and Tsar Alexander have seemed ready to come to blows on more than one occasion. And not always about their women. Talleyrand's doing his best to turn France back into a country powerful enough to cause problems for Britain. And if we aren't careful, Tsar Alexander could be more dangerous than Bonaparte ever was. We're one wrong decision away from plunging the Continent back into war. Any incident would be like putting a match to a powder keg. The truth behind Princess Tatiana's death could turn into just such an incident if we don't take appropriate measures. Besides, she was ours. We can't let her death go unanswered. You should understand that better than anyone."

Malcolm scraped a hand through his hair. "I'll learn what I can. I make you no guarantees."

Castlereagh gave a dry smile. "You won't let the matter rest until you've learned the truth. I may not have been in Spain with you, but I know what you're like when solving a problem."

Malcolm tossed off the last of his brandy. "There seems little more to be said. If you'll excuse us, sir? It's been an exceedingly long day."

He took two candles in silver holders from a side table, lit them from the burning taper, and handed one to Suzanne. They went downstairs to their bedchamber in silence. Malcolm set his candle on the chest of drawers. Suzanne eased open the door to the tiny adjoining dressing room. Her candle flickered over the cradle where their seventeen-month-old son, Colin, slept. His eyes were shut, one small fist curled beside his tousled dark hair, the other tucked beneath the blankets. In the shadows beyond, her maid, Blanca, slept on a narrow bed, nearby should Colin wake.

Suzanne pulled the door to and set her own candle on the dressing table. "Malcolm."

He had washed his bloodstained hands in the basin on the dressing table and was drying them with a towel. He looked up at her, his gaze black and questioning. A bruise was rising on his cheekbone from the fight in the alley. The events of the evening must have left emotional bruises that went deeper. Her throat thickened with all the words that could not be spoken.

"I'm so sorry," she said. "Finding her like that must have been brutal."

A muscle tightened along his jaw. "Yes." He glanced away for a moment, drew a harsh breath, then began to undo his frayed shirt cuffs, suppressed violence in the tugs of his fingers. "Though it's hardly the worst sight I've seen. I suppose I should be grateful what I witnessed in Spain didn't completely numb me to brutality." His gaze shifted over her. "Do you need to bandage your hands?"

"I'll be fine. Only minor scrapes." She picked up the ewer, splashed water over her hands, and scrubbed them with rosewater soap, staring at the pinkish brown water in the basin. Her blood and Malcolm's and very likely Princess Tatiana's as well. "I can help you." The words came out quickly, before she could consider a dozen other ways of framing the suggestion.

She turned to look at her husband. He'd pulled his shirt off and was wrapping himself in a wine-colored dressing gown. His fingers stilled on the braid-edged silk. "Suzanne—"

"I've helped you in the past."

"On several occasions I'd have been lost without you. But—"

"You can't claim that this will be more dangerous than what we went through in Spain."

"My God, wasn't tonight danger enough for you?"

"Tonight proves that if people are after you, I'll be in danger in any case. I'll be better able to protect myself if I know what's going on."

He grimaced. "To think I thought Vienna would be a safe assignment."

"And I can be of more help here than I was in Spain. If you want to get at the truth of what's going on in Vienna's salons, you'll have to get a number of ladies to reveal their secrets. They're more likely to confide in me."

He regarded her in silence for a long interval. Then he stepped forward, hesitated a moment, and as though yielding to a compulsion, brushed his fingers against her cheek. "You're an extraordinarily generous woman. After tonight, your help is the last thing I have the right to ask for."

She caught his hand and drew it away from her face, her fingers gripping his own. "Malcolm, there are a great many things we don't know about each other. But whatever I may have blurted out in the moment, I can't believe you killed Princess Tatiana."

His fingers clenched round her own, then went still. "You were asking the obvious question. It's what I'd have asked of you in the same circumstances." For a moment she saw remembered horror smash through his eyes. The brutal shock of finding Princess Tatiana dead, the stark reality that she was gone. He released her hand. "You have the instincts of an investigator."

"Well then. I'd rather be in the midst of the investigation helping you than on the sidelines imagining things." About the dangers he was in. About Princess Tatiana and how deeply her death had shaken him and what she had been to him in life.

A twisted smile played about his lips, though his eyes were dark and raw. "I undoubtedly don't deserve you. But I can't deny this will be easier with your help."

She released a breath she hadn't known she was holding. "You never fail to surprise me, darling. Thank you."

He shook his head. "You're not the one who should be saying thank you."

A dozen questions trembled on her lips. She bit them back, because she had no right to be that sort of wife. And perhaps because she was afraid of the answers. Instead she turned, putting her back to him. "Can you undo my gown? I don't want to wake Blanca."

His fingers shook slightly as he unfastened the tapes and pins that held her gown together, but his touch was as gentle as ever. The brush of his hands sent a current through her as it had from their wedding night, unexpected that first night, now familiar but no less strong. It was scarcely the first time he'd helped her undress, though usually it was the prelude to something they couldn't indulge in tonight. Something he surely wouldn't want to indulge in, though for a moment she knew an impulse to fling herself into his arms and blot out the events of the evening.

"Did Tatiana really send you a note?" he asked as he tugged the last tape loose.

An effective antidote to amorous impulse. She turned round, the tattered gauze and satin of her gown slipping down to her waist. "Asking me to call at three in the morning."

"Do you still have it?"

She hesitated. Easy enough to claim she had lost the note, and deception had become a protective instinct with her. But any evidence might be of help in the investigation. She reached into her corset. She had tucked the note there when she stripped off her gloves during their escape over the roofs.

Malcolm took the much-creased note and stared at it, his face carefully blanked (a trick he only employed, she had learned, when he was being very careful not to reveal anything).

"Is it her handwriting?" Suzanne asked.

"I can't swear to it, but I think so." He folded the note and put it in his dressing-gown pocket. "My apologies. I don't know why

Tatiana summoned you, but I'm sorry you were pulled into the middle of this."

Suzanne removed the brooch from the bodice of her gown and placed it carefully on her dressing table. "As things played out, I'm rather glad I was there."

"It was certainly very fortunate for me."

She stepped out of her gown and put it in the laundry basket beside the dressing table for Blanca to see what she could salvage. "We never did get our story straight."

"No. You received Tatiana's note at the opera?"

She was rather surprised he remembered where she was supposed to have been this evening. "From a footman in the midst of the third act."

"Who was with you at the opera?"

"Fitz and Eithne and Aline." She started on the laces that ran down the front of her corset.

"None of them should make too much trouble." Lord Fitzwilliam Vaughn, one of Malcolm's fellow attachés, and his wife, Eithne, were close friends. Malcolm's cousin Aline was visiting them from England and fiercely loyal to Malcolm. "What did you tell them about the note?"

"That Colin had been fussing earlier, and Blanca had sent word he was safely asleep. We all went on to Fanny von Arnstein's after the opera, but Eithne had a headache and Aline was tired, so Fitz took them home soon after we arrived. I said Tommy Belmont would escort me back to the Minoritenplatz later."

"So we can say I returned from Pressburg and went to Baroness Arnstein's because I knew you'd be there," Malcolm said in a quick, expressionless voice, his gaze armored as though to staunch a welling of shock and pain. "With the press of guests, her footmen will never be able to say for certain if I was there or not. Tatiana's note was delivered to me there. You insisted on accompanying me to call on Tatiana, as you explained to the tsar and Metternich. We came into the Palm Palace through the side entrance just before three to find Tatiana murdered."

"That seems to account for everything." She slipped the unlaced corset from her shoulders and added it to the pile of clothing. "Where *did* you receive Princess Tatiana's note?"

"She sent it after me."

"She knew where to find you?"

He nodded.

While his wife hadn't had the least idea where he was. Of course fellow agents were in many ways more intimate than married couples. Suzanne glanced down at her chemise. Her nightdress was across the room, where Blanca would have left it tucked beneath her pillow. Why on earth should she suddenly feel awkward being naked in front of her husband?

She pulled her chemise over her head, tugging a little too hard. She heard a stitch give way. By the time she emerged from the folds of linen, Malcolm had crossed to the bed to retrieve her nightdress. She undid the string on her drawers with deliberate unconcern, stepped out of them, and took the nightdress from her husband. She could feel his gaze on her, but she couldn't have said what he was thinking or feeling.

She dropped the folds of lawn over her head and did up the ties at the neck. The night air cut through the thin fabric. Or perhaps that was reality sinking in. Malcolm wasn't the only one feeling the cold shock of the night's events.

She sat at the dressing table, removed her pearl earrings and necklace, and began to pull from her hair the pins she hadn't lost in their escape over the roofs. Malcolm draped her dressing gown over her shoulders, then retreated to perch on the edge of the bed.

"Tell me about Princess Tatiana," she said.

She heard him draw a breath. She met his gaze in the looking glass. The barriers were up in his eyes as though what he felt was too raw even to contemplate himself, let alone to share with his wife.

"Darling, I'm sorry," she said, spinning round to look at him directly. "You needn't—"

"No, you're right," he said in the crisp voice he'd use to outline a policy option to the foreign secretary. "You know next to nothing about her background, and you'll need to if you're to help me investigate." He braced his hands on the bed behind him. "Tatiana was the daughter of a minor prince from northern Russia. She came to St. Petersburg at eighteen and married Prince Kirsanov, who was four decades her senior and from a considerably wealthier and more powerful family. She became a fashionable St. Petersburg hostess. Kirsanov died when they had scarcely been married two years. The bulk of his fortune went to his son from a prior marriage, but he left Tatiana enough to set up her own household. She took to spending much of her time in Paris."

Suzanne dropped a handful of hairpins into their porcelain box. If control was what he needed, she could match him. "Did her stepson resent her? Were there other stepchildren?"

"Several, I believe, though Tatiana didn't talk about the family much. Are you suggesting they could have been behind her death?"

"Family often turn out to have the strongest motives when it comes to murder."

"Very true," Malcolm agreed, his voice a model of cool dispassion, "but I don't think Tatiana saw herself as much a part of the Kirsanov family. She even preferred her girlhood style of Princess Tatiana to calling herself Princess Kirsanova. The Kirsanov children had most of the family fortune and seem to have cheerfully ignored her. None of them is in Vienna."

Suzanne pulled a silver comb through her tangled hair and forced herself to view Princess Tatiana simply as the subject of an investigation. "Was she a Bonapartist or a Royalist when she lived in Paris?"

"Tatiana was a Tatiana-ist. She had friends among Bonaparte's court and friends among the Royalists."

"She was dealing in information then?"

Malcolm nodded. "She was an agent for Talleyrand."

Suzanne twisted her head round to stare at her husband. "Princess Tatiana worked for the *French* foreign minister?"

"Off and on for a number of years. Talleyrand's always had excellent sources of information, and Tatiana was connected to powerful people in a number of countries."

"But you said she worked for the British in Spain."

Malcolm leaned back on the bed, resting his weight on his hands. "It was Talleyrand who sent her to us."

"Talleyrand sent an agent to work with the British when they were at war with France?"

"He'd quarreled with Napoleon and resigned as foreign minister. He was still advising Napoleon, but he was afraid Napoleon had overreached himself. Sending Tatiana to us was a sort of peace offering."

"He was talking to you behind Napoleon's back."

"And to the Austrians and the Russians as well, I think. Survival tactics."

"Some would call it treason."

"If he'd got caught. Talleyrand's rather good at not getting caught."

"Was Princess Tatiana working for Talleyrand in Vienna?"

"I think she brought him information occasionally. But for all Talleyrand's efforts, France isn't one of the major power brokers at the Congress. Tatiana thought we could offer her more in terms of money and power."

Suzanne tugged at the comb. The wind had wreaked havoc on her hair during their escape over the roofs. She picked at a snarl that had once been a ringlet, but a knot of dark hair still came away with the comb. "Her affair with Prince Metternich was some time ago, wasn't it? The gossip isn't very specific."

"When he was in Paris for Marie-Louise's marriage to Bonaparte," Malcolm said. If Tatiana's affair with the other man bothered him, he gave no sign of it.

Napoleon Bonaparte's marriage to Austrian Archduchess Marie-Louise had taken place only four years ago, yet that had been a different world, in which Napoleon had ruled a vast empire and Bonapartist France and imperial Austria had been allies. Hard sometimes to remember that Austrian Emperor Francis, host of this Congress to divide up the remnants of Napoleon's empire, was also the father of Napoleon's young second wife, Marie-Louise, and the grandfather of their small son. These days political alliances broke up as quickly as love affairs.

Suzanne dragged the comb through her side curls. Her eye-blacking had smeared beneath her eyes. Or perhaps that was the strain of the evening already showing up. "And when Metternich and Princess Tatiana saw each other again in Vienna at the Congress—?"

"At the moment, Metternich has eyes for no one but the Duchess of Sagan." Metternich's obsession with the beautiful duchess was the talk of Vienna. She had recently broken off their love affair, but Metternich plainly remained besotted. "But it's obvious he's still very fond of Tatiana. As he is of Catherine Bagration."

Princess Catherine Bagration, the Duchess of Sagan, and Princess Tatiana Kirsanova. The three beauties who resided in the Palm Palace, all three linked to both Metternich and Tsar Alexander. "Given the number of women in Vienna," Suzanne said, "one would think Metternich and the tsar could find inamoratas who hadn't shared the other's bed."

In the looking glass, she saw Malcolm's mouth tighten. "I rather suspect that's part of the attraction. Metternich and Alexander compete in everything, whether it's women or who will draw the borders of Poland."

Suzanne set down her comb. "Was Princess Tatiana involved with the tsar before they came to Vienna?"

"Their affair began when Alexander was in Paris last spring at the time of Napoleon's abdication. Though there may have been something between them in Russia years ago."

Malcolm spoke in the same cool tones he had used to describe Princess Tatiana's affair with Metternich. That seemed to be what was enabling him to get through from moment to moment. Suzanne watched him in the glass for a moment, then blew out her candle, moved to the bed, and climbed beneath the coverlet. "Did Princess Tatiana have enemies?"

"Everyone at the Congress has enemies." Malcolm shrugged out of his dressing gown and slid under the covers beside her. Though they were talking about Princess Tatiana, something had eased between them. This, she had learned early in their marriage, was the place they could communicate best, putting their heads together over a shared problem. This and sometimes when they reached for each other in their darkened bed, where words weren't necessary at all.

"Other former lovers?" Suzanne was pleased with how cool she managed to keep her voice.

"A great many, I suspect. But I hadn't heard of any being particularly jealous."

"She never mentioned to you that she was afraid?"

He shook his head, though in the light of the single candle she caught the flash of anger in his eyes. Berating himself for not having seen the danger to the princess coming. "Tatiana was one of the least fearful people I've ever encountered. She had that in common with you."

Suzanne drew her legs up beneath the coverlet and locked her hands about her knees. She wasn't sure what she thought of her husband comparing her with Princess Tatiana. "Her lovers' wives would have had reason to be jealous, though goodness knows both Princess Metternich and Tsarina Elisabeth must be inured to infidelities by now. And Princess Tatiana and Catherine Bagration were rivals for the tsar's affections. Could a woman have killed her, do you think?"

"I'm not sure," he said in the quick, taut tones of an investigator. "I want to get a medical opinion from Geoffrey Blackwell tomorrow. On that and a few other details."

Suzanne stared at the shiny green and gold threads in the silk coverlet. "Do you think she really summoned all of us this evening—you, me, Metternich, the tsar? Or was her killer trying to arrange an incident?"

"To set the tsar and Metternich at each other's throats? It's an interesting possibility. I wish I could have got a look at the handwriting on the notes they received. But the killer snatched up a dagger that was already in the room. Which suggests a crime of impulse rather than something planned."

"Was the dagger an heirloom?" Suzanne conjured up a memory of the antique gold hilt studded with rubies and emeralds. "It looked old but more Spanish than Russian."

"I'm not sure," Malcolm said. "She may have acquired it in the Peninsula."

"The use of the dagger suggests it was a crime of impulse, but someone searched the room where she was killed. She could have been killed because of some piece of information she'd uncovered."

Malcolm nodded. "You might call on Dorothée Périgord and see what you can learn."

"We're going to a dress fitting tomorrow." Dorothée, Comtesse de Périgord, was Prince Talleyrand's niece by marriage and his hostess at the Congress. She was also one of the few true friends Suzanne had made in Vienna.

Malcolm reached out and pinched the candle out between his fingers. "Do you think you can sleep?"

"If I can sleep with gunfire in the distance, you'd think I could manage it now." Suzanne settled back against the pillows. "Malcolm."

"Mmm?"

"Her locket being gone suggests the motive could be personal. Do you know what's in the locket?"

"No." The single word held sterling certainty. But it rang just a shade too bright. Or was she imagining things? For all her skills at reading people, sometimes she couldn't be sure, even with Malcolm. Especially with Malcolm.

"Was the locket a gift from a lover?" she asked.

"Perhaps. It obviously meant a great deal to her."

The bed creaked as Malcolm dropped back against the pillows, inches away from her. She could hear the controlled intake of his breath, but she knew he wasn't sleeping, either. She stared up at the dark frame of the canopy. Her muscles screamed at the night's exertions, but it was her mind that would not be still. Malcolm had agreed to let her help with the investigation. He had answered her questions about Princess Tatiana with every appearance of frankness, had volunteered information of his own, had speculated over the mystery with comforting ease.

And yet she was quite certain that her husband was lying about something.

6

Mouth dry and head throbbing from less than two hours' sleep, Suzanne stepped into the yellow-papered salon Lady Castlereagh had appropriated as the breakfast parlor. The welcome smells of hot coffee and buttered toast greeted her. The room was occupied by two ladies and a gentleman. Eithne Vaughn, wife of one of Malcolm's fellow attachés, was stirring milk into a cup of coffee. Malcolm's cousin, Aline Dacre-Hammond, was, as usual, bent over a notebook of mathematical equations, the frilled cuff of her morning gown dangerously close to a plate of melting butter and toast crumbs. The Honorable Thomas Belmont, another attaché, had a newspaper spread before him, but he was leaning forward to recount a story.

"—heard at least three different versions on my morning ride in the Prater," he was saying as Suzanne opened the door. "A Belgian attaché told me Talleyrand discovered the body when he arrived for a late-night supper with Princess Tatiana. An Austrian guardsman said the Duchess of Sagan and Metternich heard screams and came running into the princess's apartments to see what was the matter, which is interesting because I didn't think Metternich had spent the night with the duchess for some time. And a waiter at the café where I stopped for coffee told me the murderer made his escape through Catherine Bagration's rooms and surprised the tsar there along with Princess Bagration and Julie Zichy, which would horrify poor painfully virtuous Countess Zichy."

"It's dreadful." Eithne turned her gaze to the door. "Suzanne, have you heard? Tatiana Kirsanova has been murdered."

"I can put Tommy's rumors to rest." Suzanne stepped into the room. "Malcolm and I discovered the body."

Eithne dropped her silver coffee spoon to clatter against the Meissen saucer. Tommy sat back in his chair. It was Aline who looked up from her book and spoke first. Her gaze, which usually seemed to be fixed on some distant point only she could see, snapped to Suzanne's face. "Are you all right?"

"Yes, love, but thank you for asking." Suzanne smiled at the younger woman. Aline had come from England a fortnight ago to stay with Malcolm and Suzanne. Of all Malcolm's large and often bewildering family, she was the one Suzanne felt most comfortable with, perhaps because Aline was too eccentric herself to pass judgment on others.

"Unfair." Tommy never lost his equilibrium for long. "We have a firsthand witness to the latest scandal in Vienna within our own delegation. You can't hold out after that, Suzanne. Be reasonable."

"Tommy." Eithne reached for the coffee pot, poured a cup, sloshing a few drops into the saucer, and held it out to Suzanne.

Suzanne sank into one of the shield-back chairs and took a fortifying sip of coffee. Strong and hot, with that rich flavor only Viennese coffee possessed. Cradling the warm porcelain in her hands, she related the version of events she and Malcolm had agreed to. Eithne's blue eyes went wider and wider. Aline listened with an attention she normally gave only to abstruse quadratic equations. Tommy's eyes narrowed, and at one point he let out a whistle. But he gave no sign of disbelief. He was a good test of the story. Tommy was a very clever man and a good agent himself. Not that Suzanne had any doubt of her abilities to dissemble, even on next to no sleep.

"How dreadful." Eithne drew the folds of her Lyons scarf about her shoulders. "To think I saw her in the Prater only yesterday. I never thought Vienna would prove—"

"A danger to life, as opposed to borders and marriages?" Tommy tossed back a swallow of coffee as though he wished it were laced with brandy.

"We're in a civilized country."

"Define civilized," Aline said.

"But who on earth would—"

"Someone driven mad by jealousy or lust or greed." Aline jabbed a loose strand of ash brown hair behind her ear. "All the common motives."

"It's frightening to think there's such a madman running about."

"The most frightening thing is that he's probably very little different from the rest of us." Tommy turned back to Suzanne. "I'd give a monkey to have seen Metternich and the tsar confronting each other. Bold woman, the princess, to invite her lover and her ex-lover at the same time."

Eithne shot him a warning look.

"It's all right," Aline said. "I may be unmarried and not quite twenty, but I'm not easily shocked. You can't be, growing up in our family. I sometimes think we never really progressed beyond the last century. Very Devonshire House. None of us is quite sure who his or her father is."

Eithne's eyes widened again, not at the facts, Suzanne suspected, but at the way Aline had so blithely stated them.

"Excellent training for Vienna." Suzanne speared a piece of toast and began to butter it.

"You're a wonder, Suzanne," Eithne said. "I think I'd have taken to my bed."

"I doubt it. You're much stronger than you admit, even to yourself." Eithne might look like a Dresden shepherdess with her guinea gold ringlets and English rose prettiness, but Suzanne had glimpsed the steel beneath her porcelain façade more than once. It was one of the things that made her likable instead of an annoying paragon.

"This will give Baron Hager an excuse to poke into all our dirty linen," Tommy said. "Without having to try to slip his agents in among the boot boys and dancing girls. As if things weren't complicated enough with the tsar's stubbornness on Poland and Prussian troops in Saxony."

"And as if everyone weren't suspicious enough to begin with," Aline said. "You'd think—"

She broke off at the opening of the door. Lord Fitzwilliam

Vaughn, Eithne's husband, stepped into the room, face drawn with worry. "Belmont—oh, there you are, darling." His gaze softened as it rested on Eithne. "Suzanne. Miss Dacre-Hammond. Forgive me. I'm afraid I have some unfortunate—"

"It's all right, Fitz," Eithne said, "we know. About Princess Tatiana. Suzanne and Malcolm were there last night. They discovered the body."

Fitz darted a quick look at Suzanne. Dark-haired, blue-eyed, and possessed of elegantly boned features, he looked the part of the perfect English gentleman. But in Suzanne's view he had rather more imagination than one generally expected of the type, in addition to a very kind heart and genuine chivalrous impulses.

"The princess had asked Malcolm to call on her," Suzanne said. "It was unfortunate and distressing, but we're both fine."

"Thank heavens you didn't encounter the murderer." Eithne glanced up at her husband. "Do you want some coffee, darling?"

He shook his head. "I'm afraid I can't stay. Castlereagh wants us both in his study, Belmont." Fitz crossed to Eithne's side and bent to touch his fingers to her cheek. Her gaze met his in a moment of wordless communication.

Suzanne stared at the lip rouge–smeared rim of her coffee cup. Some couples could say things with their eyes that she doubted she and Malcolm would ever be able to put into words.

Malcolm made his way down a chestnut-lined avenue in the Prater, the park at the heart of Vienna. Sunlight shot between the thick branches. The weather was still unseasonably warm for November. Leaves of gold and russet and pomegranate red scuttered across the avenue and crunched underfoot. A glorious, gilded world that laughed in the harsh face of oncoming winter. Not a bad metaphor for the Congress itself.

He paused before one of the brightly painted cafés that lined the avenue. A number of people were clustered at the wrought iron tables that spilled out of the café's doors. Attachés in well-cut coats, bonneted ladies with paper-wrapped shopping parcels beside them, students bent over piles of books, soldiers in the brilliant uniforms of several countries, artists with sketch pads. He heard fragments of at least seven languages as he threaded his way between the tables.

Annina Barbera, Tatiana Kirsanova's maid, sat at a table a little to the side. Though it was not yet noon, she had a glass of red wine before her. Her gaze was fixed on the vase of blood red geraniums on the table. Malcolm watched her for a moment, then dropped into a seat across from her.

She looked up with a wintry smile. "You haven't lost your instincts for tracking people."

"I know you rather well. Well enough to know you'd be in need of fortification and a change of scene." And he had met her at this café more than once to pass on messages to Tatiana or receive information from her.

Annina grimaced. There were shadows beneath her eyes, and her lids were swollen. Fatigue, no doubt, but he also suspected she'd been weeping most of the night.

"I'm sorry," he said. The raw pain, sharp as a fresh sword cut, bit him in the throat. "Sorrier than I can say."

"So am I." Annina's fingers tightened round the stem of her wineglass. "She wasn't the easiest mistress, but she was generous. And loyal in her way."

Malcolm signaled a waiter, resisted the pull of wine, and ordered coffee. His head ached and his eyes protested from lack of sleep.

"You look as though you got into a tavern brawl after you left the Palm Palace last night," Annina said when the waiter had moved off.

Malcolm touched his fingers to the bruise on his cheek. "Spot of trouble on our way home."

She stiffened. "Connected to the murder?"

"Almost certainly. The question is how."

"Your wife—"

"Is good at taking care of herself. And me."

Annina gave a faint smile. "I was told to leave the Palm Palace until this afternoon. Baron Hager's men are searching the princess's rooms."

Malcolm went still, his gaze on her face. Hardly unexpected, but he felt his blood chill as though a gust of wind had ripped through the park.

Annina slid a hand into the pocket of her gown. To a casual observer, it would have looked as though she was just arranging her skirts. Malcolm reached beneath the table and took the ribbon-tied packet she was holding out. In Vienna, one never knew when one was being watched. Any seemingly casual passerby who wasn't an agent for Baron Hager was likely to be an agent for one foreign power or another.

"All the letters in your hand that I could find last night before Prince Metternich and Baron Hager got to them," Annina said as he took the papers from her beneath the table. "The princess kept your letters together."

He drew a breath and found the air singularly sweet. "I can't thank you enough."

"You've been a good friend to me. And it's what she would have wanted."

Malcolm slid the papers and their precious, dangerous contents up under his coat. Very nearly all he had left of Tatiana. A life reduced to—No. No time to think on that now. "Did you find anything else?"

"No." Annina twisted her wineglass on the black metal of the table. "She was always careful about burning papers. She had yours tucked in a secret compartment in her dressing table, along with some old love letters from Prince Metternich that I left for Baron Hager to find. Anything else valuable she kept in a box that was hidden in a hole in the floorboards under the carpet in her dressing room. I wasn't supposed to know about it, but it's hard to keep secrets from one's maid." Annina hesitated a moment. "That box is gone."

Malcolm's fingers stilled on the Bath superfine lapel of his coat. "It was taken last night?"

"I'm not sure. I hadn't seen it for a fortnight. I looked for it after I found your letters, while Prince Metternich was still with you and the tsar. It was gone then. The murderer might have taken it. Or the princess might have moved it. If so, Baron Hager's men will find it if it's in her rooms. They're tearing them apart."

Foolish to dwell on what secrets that box might contain and how they might relate to him. "What's to happen to her rooms?"

"The rent's paid through the month. They asked me who her heir was. I said probably her stepson?" She looked at Malcolm in inquiry.

"I expect so." Malcolm laid a silk purse on the table.

Annina stared at it. "I didn't ask for a handout."

"No. But I thought you might accept a gift from a friend. I can help you with a reference as well."

Her shoulders straightened. "I'll manage."

"Very ably, I have no doubt. But the offices of a friend can still prove helpful. There are a number of tiresome things about my family, but my name is rather useful."

Annina gave a half smile of acknowledgment and tucked the purse into her reticule. She was nothing if not practical. As Tatiana had been.

The waiter returned and put a cup of steaming black coffee before Malcolm. He took a sip. Strong and bitter, it went right to the fuzziest part of his brain. He leaned back in his chair and regarded Annina. "I'm not Baron Hager."

"Meaning I can trust you?"

"I want to find out who did this to her, Annina." Rage coursed through him. At the wanton violence that had ended Tatiana's life, at his own inability to stop it. He tightened his grip on the coffee cup. "Tell me what happened last night. What you know of it."

Annina twisted her fingers round the stem of her wineglass. "She was expecting someone. A gentleman."

"She told you?"

"No. But I could tell from the gown and jewels she selected. Your wife pointed out as much last night. The princess had me spread out a half dozen gowns, and she tried on four of them. She changed her jewelry twice. And she had me take all the pins out of her hair and rearrange it three different times."

Malcolm took a sip of coffee. "Tatiana was usually more decisive."

"Last night she seemed—" Annina frowned, searching for the right word. "Distracted."

"As though she was thinking about something else?"

"As though she was worried. Perhaps about whomever she was expecting. Then she told me she wouldn't need me further. She told me to go to my room and on all accounts to remain there for the evening."

"Was that unusual?"

"It depended on—"

"How secret her current love affair was?"

Annina nodded. "She'd taken to dismissing me early more in recent weeks. I didn't know the names of all her lovers. I didn't know the name of—" She bit back the words.

"Of the most recent one?" Malcolm asked.

"You always were too quick."

"Someone besides Tsar Alexander?"

Annina cast a quick glance round the other tables. Strains of violin music wafted from the café. One of the many advantages of the Viennese love of music was that it provided excellent cover. "I think that's the reason it was so secret," she said in a low voice. "It wasn't unusual for her to be juggling two lovers, but the tsar wouldn't have liked it."

"When did this affair start?"

"A month or so ago. Notes began to be delivered that she didn't let me see."

"Do you think she was expecting him last night?"

"I did at first. Until—everything else. Finding her like that, and you and Prince Metternich and the tsar being there. But I still think—She was dressed and in the salon just after ten. You say she hadn't summoned the rest of you until three?"

"Yes."

"It wasn't like her to sit idle for so long. She was expecting someone earlier in the evening."

A quarrel had broken out at a nearby table between an attaché from a German principality—Lichtenstein? Leyen?—and an Austrian lieutenant. Insults rippled across the tables.

"Had Tatiana seemed different in any way lately?" Malcolm asked.

Annina's brows drew together. "No. Yes. That is—there was a sort of tension about her. Like a string for the piano that is wound too tightly."

"Do you think she was afraid?"

"You knew her as well as anyone. She was never afraid. This was the way I've seen her when she was about to wager a great deal at the gaming tables."

A Belgian had rushed into the quarrel between the German and Austrian. Voices rose, all three speaking in their native tongue.

Malcolm curled his hands round his coffee cup. "What do you think she was gambling on?"

Annina shook her head. "You knew more about her work than I did. But whatever it was, the risk and reward were great."

The German attaché pushed back his chair. A wineglass shattered on the pavement.

Malcolm swallowed the last of his coffee. "Thank you, Annina. You need only send word to me in the Minoritenplatz should you remember anything else. Or should you have need of me for any other reason."

She gave a twisted smile. "I can look after myself."

"So could Tatiana." His nails cut into his palm as he set down the cup. "But we're none of us immune to danger. Go carefully."

Annina nodded. But as Malcolm rose to leave, she said, "Your wife. How much does she know?"

Malcolm hesitated. A waiter had rushed forward to sweep up the broken glass. Inside the café, the violinist had changed to a melody in a minor key. Last night in their darkened bed he'd wanted to pull Suzanne to him and bury his anger and loss in the warmth of her body. But it would have been an appalling invasion to use her so thoughtlessly. And God knew he of all people had no right to make such demands on her. "As much as I could afford to tell her."

Annina's eyes widened. "Which means—?"

"Not nearly everything."

"But enough to stop her suspecting?"

"Oh, I doubt it. My wife's a very clever woman." Malcolm drew a breath and tasted the bite of oncoming winter in the air. "But hopefully what she suspects isn't anything near as bad as the truth."

7

Prince Adam Czartoryski slowed his horse to a sedate walk as he reached the wide, chestnut-lined avenue, thick with pedestrians, riders, and all manner of carriages. Chaises, calèches, berlins, coupés. He bowed to the lovely, fragile Empress of Austria, whose high color and translucent skin sadly betrayed her consumption. He exchanged greetings with pretty Julie Zichy and impetuous Alfred von Windischgrätz, agreeing that the news about Princess Tatiana's death was shocking.

He forced himself to nod civilly at Lord Stewart, Castlereagh's half brother, tooling a showy four-in-hand as though his were the only carriage in the avenue. He listened to a catalogue of the latest scandals, including some outrageous speculation on the princess's murder, from the courtly Prince de Ligne. All the while he schooled his features to convey that he was about nothing more than a morning ride. For once he had cause to be grateful for the training of his years in the Russian court. He had become adept at hiding his real feelings.

He glimpsed Malcolm Rannoch on the other side of the avenue, on foot, walking quickly, his face a tight, composed mask. According to some of the rumors, Rannoch had discovered the princess's body. He'd been close to Princess Tatiana. Her lover, some said. Poor devil.

As though aware he was being watched, Rannoch turned, regarded Adam for a moment, and inclined his head. Adam returned the nod. The sunlight shot beneath the curling brim of Rannoch's hat, and Adam noticed a dark bruise on the other man's cheekbone. Surprising that didn't figure in the rumors.

It was as he watched Malcolm Rannoch turn down a side path that Adam finally saw her. In an open calèche of green and white, one of the carriages Emperor Francis had ordered for his royal guests. A coachman in smart new yellow livery (also ordered by the emperor) drove the carriage, and two ladies-in-waiting accompanied her. He guided his horse across the avenue, forcing himself to stop and nod and exchange more greetings along the way.

At last, he drew up beside her calèche. "Your Majesty."

"Prince." Elisabeth's voice was level, but beneath the white satin brim of her bonnet her eyes were blue-shadowed with fatigue and worry. The familiar, impossible impulse to sweep her away from all danger and intrigue swept through him. Twenty years and he was still fool enough to think he could do it.

He bent over her gloved hand in the Austrian fashion and raised it to his lips. An excuse to touch her. And the opportunity to murmur words for her alone. "I'll get them back for you." He could feel the warmth of her hand through the soft kid of the glove. "I swear it. You have nothing to fear."

She leaned forward, and as he lifted his head her gaze met his for a moment. Her mouth curved in a smile that went right to his heart, but her eyes were cold with terror. "You're a loyal man, Adam," she said. "And a shocking liar."

"Monsieur Rannoch." The deep voice rang out across the path Malcolm had taken to escape the crowded avenue. Malcolm turned his head to find himself looking at Baron Hager, Vienna's chief of police.

Hager crossed the path to Malcolm's side. "A fortuitous meeting. I planned to call on you this afternoon."

"Baron." Malcolm inclined his head, wondering just how much a matter of chance the meeting truly was. Had Hager followed him or had him followed? Hopefully he and Annina had managed the exchange of papers adeptly enough. "Of course you'll want to question me about last night."

"Precisely. Perhaps we could sit for a few moments?" Hager gestured toward a wrought iron bench along the path. "I understand you were the first to discover Princess Tatiana's body."

"My wife and I."

"Ah, yes. The charming Madame Rannoch." Hager flicked back the tails of his coat and settled himself on the bench. "A sad pity she had to witness such a sight."

"Quite." Malcolm sat beside the baron on the sun-warmed metal. "Fortunately my wife is an intrepid woman."

"You were paying a social call on the princess?"

"She sent me a note asking me to call on her. I'm sure Prince Metternich told you as much."

"Perhaps he did mention it. There've been a great many details to keep track of," said Baron Hager, quite as though being a master of detail weren't his stock in trade. In addition to the police force, hundreds of agents reported to him, from members of Austria's most powerful families to former slum dwellers now employed as scullery maids and boot boys in the lodgings of various delegations. "Why did the princess wish you to call?" Hager asked.

"I don't know." And the knowledge that he had failed her would live with him forever. "Sadly I never had the opportunity to speak with her."

"But you knew it was a matter of some urgency? Obviously you didn't let it wait until the sun came up."

Malcolm recounted the story he and Suzanne had agreed upon the previous night about Tatiana's message reaching him at Baroness Arnstein's. "Princess Tatiana made it clear she wished us to call last night."

"Both of you?"

Malcolm swallowed. No sense in straying from the agreed-upon story, whatever light it put him in. "Her note was written to me. My wife insisted on accompanying me."

"A great friend of the princess as well, was she?"

"She preferred not to have her husband pay a call on the princess alone late at night. I could scarcely argue with her."

Hager regarded Malcolm through narrowed eyes. "Might I ask how you received that rather spectacular bruise on your cheekbone?"

"Three men attacked my wife and me on our way home from the Palm Palace last night."

Hager's eyes widened. If he had known of the attack, he was an excellent dissembler. But then dissembling was his stock in trade, as it was Malcolm's. "Common footpads?"

"I don't think so. But the one man I tried to question was killed by a confederate before I could learn more. Have you had word of a body in an alley somewhere between the Schenkengasse and the Minoritenplatz?"

Hager shook his head.

Malcolm nodded. "Then his confederates must have moved him."

"You lead an eventful life, Monsieur Rannoch." Hager shifted his position on the bench, perhaps so the angle of the sun gave him a better view of Malcolm's face. "Princess Tatiana supplied information to a number of delegations at the Congress. I assume that was at least part of your connection with her?"

"As a fellow professional, you can hardly expect me to answer that. But I advise you not to jump to conclusions."

Hager crossed one booted leg over the other. "You're a clever man, Rannoch. A fellow professional, as you say. Did you notice anything in particular when you came into Princess Tatiana's salon last night?"

The smell of blood, like a punch to the gut. The pallor of her face, her clouded eyes. The chill of her skin when, against all reason, he had felt desperately for a pulse. "At first merely the obvious. That the princess had been killed in a brutal fashion. Later—Someone else had been in the room."

"Whoever killed her."

"Quite. But that person, or perhaps another party, had gone through the princess's escritoire. I imagine you noted it yourself."

"The room appears to have been searched. Well but rather hastily." Hager leaned against the curving back of the bench. He had been a cavalry officer before a riding accident forced him from the military. For a moment, Malcolm felt as though the point of a cavalry sword pressed against his throat. "I imagine Princess Tatiana could have made things rather difficult for you with your wife."

"You can scarcely expect me to discuss either lady with you. But if that were the case, surely I would have contrived not to bring my wife with me when I called on Princess Tatiana."

"Perhaps. In many ways, it's exceedingly fortunate for you that you did so." Hager adjusted the brim of his hat. "I hear Tsar Alexander has set the funeral for tomorrow. At the Russian embassy chapel. Wants it done quietly, before the rumors flying round the city grow any worse. But I imagine all Vienna will be clamoring to attend. Are you planning to be in attendance, Monsieur Rannoch?"

Malcolm schooled his features not to betray his shock of surprise. Of course Tania's funeral would be planned by others. Of course he would be at best a spectator. "Should space permit, naturally I would like to pay my last respects to the princess."

Hager regarded him in silence for a long moment. "Naturally." The baron flexed his gloved fingers. "Oh, there's one other thing," he added, as though it had just occurred to him, though Malcolm suspected he'd planned every twist of the interview from the outset. "I understand Princess Tatiana was in the habit of always wearing a locket on a gold chain, sometimes tucked into the bodice of her gown. Her maid says the princess was wearing it last night, but we didn't find it on her body. Being such a good friend of the princess, would you have any idea what that locket contained?"

Malcolm looked into Hager's eyes, conscious of the sun falling clear and bright across his face, and put into practice every trick of deception he had learned in his years in intelligence. "None at all, I'm afraid."

Dr. Geoffrey Blackwell adjusted the slide under the microscope, then cursed as the opening of the door sent a draft through the room that ruined his careful alignment. "What the devil—Oh, it's you, Malcolm." Blackwell pushed his chair back and got to his feet. "I'm glad you've come."

"Sorry I disturbed the experiment." Malcolm closed the door.

Blackwell waved a hand. "Thought it was one of the other damned fool attachés wanting patching up after a night's drunken brawl or worried about the French pox." A military doctor, Blackwell was theoretically spending his leave in Vienna, but the British delegation were still quick to call on him for medical attention. "I'm sorry," he said, taking a step toward Malcolm. He cleared his throat. "Sorrier than I can say."

"You've heard about Tatiana?"

"I imagine all Vienna has heard by now." The shock of the news, offered by his landlady's daughter as no more than the latest scandalous gossip, washed over Blackwell again. Damned foolish. This was no time to give way to emotions. Especially when he prided himself on being above them. He moved to one of the frayed tapestry chairs by the stove and waved Malcolm to the chair opposite.

The light from the windows fell across Malcolm's face as he dropped into the chair, revealing a bruise on his cheekbone, shadows beneath his eyes, and a dark wasteland in the eyes themselves. "Suzanne and I found her," he said.

Blackwell drew a sharp breath. He had known Malcolm since the latter was a baby. Blackwell's father was a distant cousin of Malcolm's ducal grandfather, and Blackwell had grown up with Malcolm's mother and aunt. He remained closer to Malcolm's family than to his own, who were baffled by his decision to become a military doctor instead of following his father and brothers into the army itself. Through the years, home on leave, he'd had glimpses of Malcolm's less than idyllic childhood. He knew just how much hurt lay behind that bruised gaze. But he also knew that Malcolm had learned to hold his feelings close. Blackwell did much the same himself. So he simply said, "I'm sorry."

Malcolm nodded. His hands were curled round the chair arms, his gaze fixed on his fingers. "Castlereagh wants me to investigate."

Damn Castlereagh, though Blackwell could understand the foreign secretary's reasoning. And Malcolm might do better with a task. "So you've come to me for information. What did you find when you went into the room?"

For a moment, Malcolm's face held the memory of a glimpse into hell. "Her throat had been cut. With a medieval dagger that she kept in the salon. The cut was left to right."

"So the killer was right-handed. Which doesn't narrow your field much. Though it means Suzanne couldn't have done it."

"Could a woman have done it?"

"I suspect any man or woman with an ordinary degree of strength could have done it." Blackwell shut his mind to a memory of Tatiana the last time he had seen her, champagne glass in her hand, mouth curved with ironic laughter, face glowing with life. A bloody, senseless waste. But Malcolm was desperately trying to hold on to his self-command, and Blackwell wouldn't help the lad if he broke down himself. "How did her skin look?" he asked.

"Blue tinged. And her lips and nails were pale," Malcolm added in a swift, expressionless voice.

"Did her skin blanch to the touch?"

"No."

Blackwell nodded. "Most likely she was killed more than half an hour before you arrived but less than three hours. I'm sorry I can't narrow your field more."

"Anything helps." Malcolm loosed his fingers on the chair arms as though with an effort of will. "The blood had sprayed everywhere. The walls. The carpet. But if the killer stood behind and then dropped her to the ground and flung the dagger away—"

"He—or she—might have managed to avoid the worst of it," Blackwell concluded, matching Malcolm's tone. "Enough to make it home in the dark and then sponge out the evidence."

"And of course if the killer put a greatcoat on after the murder, that would have covered any bloodstains."

Blackwell cast a sharp, sideways glance at his young cousin. "Who was wearing a greatcoat?"

Malcolm kept his gaze on the coals glowing in the stove. "Tsar Alexander and Prince Metternich."

Blackwell sucked in and released a breath. "It seems a bit redundant to tell you to go carefully. But tangling with royalty entails risks even you don't normally run, lad."

"When one is investigating a murder, the lovers of the victim are obvious suspects. Of course, so is the person who discovers the body, which doesn't put me in a very favorable position. I suspect Metternich would have taken me into custody last night if Suzanne hadn't been there to say we'd arrived at the Palm Palace together."

Blackwell noted that Malcolm didn't actually say he and Suzanne had arrived together but made no comment on it. He stretched his legs out toward the warmth of the stove. "How's Suzanne taken it?"

"Intrepid as always. She's insisting on helping me."

"You're a wise man to agree." Blackwell glanced sideways at Malcolm, his distaste for interfering warring with the instincts of affection. "I suspect this is far harder on Suzanne than she's letting you see."

Malcolm started to speak, drew a rough breath, then at last said, "Suzanne and I've found our way to a marriage that works after a fashion. It's a delicate balance. We're both trying to keep it that way."

"Delicate balances have a way of tumbling about one's ears." Blackwell studied Malcolm's face, seeing the awkward, bright-eyed boy with the all-too-keen understanding, overlaid by the scars of the man he had become. "Believe me, I know how difficult and potentially disastrous emotional entanglements can be. God knows I've always steered well clear of them myself. But you've gone this far."

"And I should have the guts to see it through?" Malcolm turned his gaze back to the red-orange glow of the coals. "I look at Fitzwilliam Vaughn and Eithne sometimes. Five years married and still living in each other's pockets. I'd roll my eyes, save that I'm struck by the wonder of being so sure of another person. But then Fitz has a wonderful capacity for believing in things."

"Vaughn's an idealist."

"Fitz is as frustrated by our government's resistance to reform as

I am. But instead of just complaining over the port, he wants to stand for Parliament and try to do something about it. He actually believes he can succeed. And I have just enough of my own ideals left to envy him his certainty."

"You're more of an idealist than you let on, Malcolm. Even to yourself."

Malcolm shook his head. "Believe me, Geoff, I see the world clearly enough. Some truths are sadly inescapable."

"Such as?"

The breath Malcolm drew was like that of a man having a bullet removed without the aid of laudanum. "It was probably a mistake for me to marry Suzanne. But I'll do my best not to let her suffer for it."

8

Dorothée de Talleyrand-Périgord turned on the dais in the fitting room at the modiste's so the seamstress could continue pinning the hem of her white satin gown. "You'd think the war would have inured us to brutality. But this is worse somehow."

Suzanne, seated on a cushioned sofa, looked up from Colin, whom she was bouncing in her lap, and studied her friend. Dorothée's skin was very pale beneath a delicate wash of rouge, but then she was always pale, even without the benefit of a shock. "You must have known Princess Tatiana in Paris."

Dorothée's eyes, so dark a blue they appeared almost black, clouded with memories. "I wouldn't have called her a friend precisely, but we moved in the same circles. My uncle—Talleyrand—had known her for years." There was nothing in Dorothée's tone or expression to indicate she knew Tatiana had been an agent in the employ of her uncle by marriage. But then, though she was only one-and-twenty, Dorothée, like Suzanne herself, was no stranger to the game of diplomatic intrigue. She frequently helped Talleyrand draft letters and dispatches.

"And Princess Tatiana would stand out in any circles." Suzanne detached her garnet beads from Colin's grip and reached into the baby carriage for his rattle.

Dorothée smiled down at Colin. "I do miss my own boys, though I know my mother is taking good care of them." She turned her gaze back to Suzanne. "I don't know that I ever had a proper conversation with Princess Tatiana. I was dreadfully inclined to be shy in company when I first came to Paris as Edmond's bride. Well, I still am."

"You hide it well," Suzanne said. Dorothée was the picture of sophisticated elegance, from her fashionably cropped hair to her perfectly groomed brows. A far cry from the scrawny, uncertain girl she described herself as having been a few years ago.

"I've learned to be good at hiding a number of things." Dorothée glanced down as the seamstress reached for a new paper of pins, but she went on speaking as though the girl weren't there. As the semiroyal daughter of the Duke of Courland, she was used to playing out her life in the presence of servants.

Courland, a duchy on the Baltic, had nominally paid fealty to Poland, when Poland existed as a separate country, and now was a satellite of Russia. Dorothée's family had vast estates that stretched to Sagan in Silesia, only a day's journey from Berlin. Her childhood reminiscences sounded like life at court, with lavish house parties, musicians and singers brought in to entertain, and a resident troupe of actors. She and her sisters had had dowries that could support a small country.

"I remember the first time I met Princess Tatiana," Dorothée continued. "A ball at my uncle's house shortly after I came to Paris. She was wearing a white satin gown with a silver net scarf that somehow turned all the pastel gowns and dark coats and gilded uniforms into a background to set her off. She seemed to have a cluster of gentlemen about her wherever she moved. The way she held her fan was almost a language in itself."

Suzanne picked up the chased-silver rattle Colin had dropped on the floor and returned it to her son. "I noticed that in Vienna. A simple flick of her fan could call any gentleman to her side." Including Malcolm on more than one occasion.

"She had a wonderful laugh. People were always telling me I didn't laugh enough in those days." Dorothée grimaced.

"I'm sorry, madame," the seamstress said.

"It wasn't you." Dorothée smiled at the girl. She might be used to playing out her life in front of servants, but she had a kind heart.

The seamstress finished pinning the gown and left to get the black velvet overdress. Dorothée stepped off the dais, carefully lifting her skirts, stiff with pins. She looked down at the white satin gown. "It does seem dreadfully frivolous to be thinking about a medieval pageant in the midst of all this."

"Pageantry is the stuff of the Congress," Suzanne said. The Carrousel, a re-creation of a medieval tournament, was to take place the day after tomorrow. For weeks, it had been the talk of Vienna, taking equal place with the Saxon question, the future of Poland, and the sensational end of Metternich's love affair with the Duchess of Sagan. At the request of the Festivals Committee, Dorothée had taken a leading role in organizing it.

Dorothée moved a small table, which held a chocolate service, beside the sofa. "I couldn't have done it without you. I'm so glad you agreed to help."

"It's a great honor." Suzanne was the only British lady asked to be one of the *belles d'amour* at the tournament.

"Spoken like a diplomat's wife." Dorothée picked up a silver-rimmed cup and took a sip of chocolate. "When I heard about Princess Tatiana, I wondered if we should cancel the Carrousel."

"Prince Metternich didn't cancel his masked ball this evening." Which was a good thing, Suzanne thought, steadying Colin before he could slip off the sofa. Social events afforded the best opportunities for investigation.

"And the funeral's to be tomorrow. Do you know, when I heard that, my first thought was 'thank goodness it isn't the day of the Carrousel.' Then I thought how horrid I was being to even consider the Carrousel."

"I suspect Tsar Alexander wanted to get it over with as quickly and quietly as possible. So it doesn't become a public spectacle." Admission to the funeral would be by invitation. Would Malcolm be able to attend? Would she? Oddly, she didn't want him to have to go through it alone, though she might be the last person he'd want at his side in such circumstances.

Dorothée wiped a trace of chocolate from the eggshell porcelain of her cup. "Princess Tatiana was everything I'm not. So sure of herself, so ready with the right thing to say. Edmond found her charming, of course."

It was no secret that Dorothée's marriage to Edmond de Talleyrand-Périgord was not a happy one. Dorothée loved books. Edmond, a cavalry officer, was more likely to be found with his horses or at the gaming tables. Or with his mistresses.

"I'm sorry," Suzanne said.

Dorothée set down her chocolate cup. "It's not as though she took him from me. It's not as though he was ever mine to be taken. Or that I ever wanted to keep him. Ours isn't a marriage, it's an alliance. The one good thing I got out of it is my children." She looked down at Colin again. He smiled up at her and held out the rattle.

"I think you've made a conquest," Suzanne said.

"How splendid." Dorothée squeezed Colin's hand, accepted the rattle from him with great ceremony, and returned it to the sofa. "Princess Tatiana could discuss horses and cards with Edmond with every appearance of interest," she said, her gaze still on Colin, "though I daresay they bored her to tears as much as they do me. And then she could dissect Bonaparte's latest maneuver with my uncle or analyze poetry with young Jamie Wilton."

Colin wriggled forward again. "Down," he said, with all the authority Malcolm could muster when he chose to do so.

Suzanne lifted her son to the floor. Colin toddled over to Dorothée, who twitched her skirts out of his way and gave him a biscuit from a plate on the table. "Princess Tatiana dined with us only last week. Good God, it's hard to believe—"

"It takes a while for the reality to sink in."

Colin took a bite of biscuit and toddled over to explore the dais. "I find myself dwelling on the most trivial things," Dorothée said. "That dinner party was one of the challenges I'm learning to surmount as a diplomatic hostess. My sister was also there, and she and Princess Tatiana don't—didn't—like each other very well."

"The duchess?" Everyone at the Congress seemed to be interconnected. Wilhelmine of Sagan, Metternich's adored mistress until recently, was the eldest of Dorothée's three sisters. "Because of Prince Metternich?"

"In part, perhaps. Though in truth I always thought Metternich was more besotted with Wilhelmine than she with him, even when their affair was at its height. And now that it's ended, I know she finds his continued attentions distressing. Willie is much more like Princess Tatiana than I am. They both know how to command a room. They both can fascinate men with a glance, and they enjoy wielding that power. How could they not be rivals? The last time I saw Princess Tatiana was at Willie's two days ago, and they were hardly—"

The sound of Colin plopping down on the dais punctuated the stillness.

"What?" Suzanne asked.

Dorothée frowned. "When I arrived they were quarreling."

"About what?"

"I'm not sure." Dorothée fingered a fold of her satin skirt. "I called on Willie on my way home from a drive in the Prater. I told the footman there was no need to announce me. I could hear Willie saying something about 'exorbitant' through the salon door. I knocked quickly, so they'd know they were being overheard. When I went into the salon, I found Princess Tatiana there as well. It was clear from their expressions that it hadn't been a congenial discussion."

Dorothée cast a sidelong glance at Suzanne. Realizing the possible implications of her sister having recently quarreled with a woman who had then been murdered. Of course, Dorothée didn't know Suzanne was investigating Princess Tatiana's murder.

"I daresay it was something trivial," Suzanne said. "Did you get any sense of what the quarrel was about?"

Dorothée shook her head. "I thought about asking Willie later, but we've never been the sort of sisters to indulge in confidences. She's twelve years my senior. In truth, we've seen more of each other at the Congress than we have in years." She picked up her cup of chocolate and took another sip. "Willie can be a bit of a cynic. I suppose that's what two marriages that end in divorce will do for you. And neither marriage was any more successful than my own. Less, I suppose, since I'm still married, at least in name. We Courlands don't have a great deal of success at finding marital bliss. Of course there seem to be so many considerations other than bliss in choosing a marriage partner."

"Particularly in a family such as yours."

Dorothée gave a twisted smile. "I used to think Paris was a hotbed of scandal, but I swear Vienna is worse. It's you British who take your wedding vows seriously."

For a moment, Suzanne could hear the droning voice of the clergyman in the airless embassy sitting room in which she and Malcolm had been married, and then Malcolm's steady voice as he repeated his vows. "I'm only British by marriage," she said, her voice huskier than she would have liked. "But I think often it's less a case of taking the vows more seriously than of people being more discreet about breaking them."

"Oh, Suzanne. Don't let Vienna turn you into a cynic."

Suzanne looked down at her son. He had picked up a tape measure and was examining it with rapt attention. "I don't think Vienna has made me anything I wasn't already."

"You're fortunate in your husband, *chérie*."

"Malcolm is a very good man." Better, perhaps, than she deserved.

Dorothée shot a quick look at her. "Suzanne—oh dear, I wasn't sure if I should speak, but—Of course I can't help but have heard the rumors about Malcolm and—" She colored beneath her rouge.

"About Malcolm and Princess Tatiana," Suzanne finished for her in a steady voice. "The rumors have been all over Vienna. Gossip is the currency of diplomatic society. I've got quite good at ignoring it."

"Yes, but I can guess how painful the rumors must be, however sure you are of your husband. The thing is, in Malcolm's case, I'm quite sure the rumors aren't true."

Colin had found a pin on the dais. Suzanne hurried over and snatched it from his fingers before he could stick himself. "That's very kind of you, Doro, but—"

"No, listen. One can't seem to take two steps in Vienna without tumbling into some sort of scandal. Last week at the Zichys' reception I went out into the garden for some air. The rooms get so dreadfully hot it might be July, not November. I wandered down one of the gravel paths to have a few moments to myself. I heard—Sounds. From the shrubbery. Unmistakable sounds."

Suzanne gave Colin a length of ivory ribbon in place of the pin. "I've stumbled on the same more than once since we've come to Vienna."

"I won't even mention what I've found in some of our anterooms after we give a ball." Dorothée shuddered. "In any case, I started to retreat, but then I heard footsteps, as though the couple were moving my way. I ducked behind a statue to avoid an encounter that could only embarrass them more than me. Princess Tatiana emerged from the shrubbery a few moments later. Shortly after, she was followed. By Lord Fitzwilliam Vaughn."

The pin tumbled from Suzanne's fingers. "*Fitz?*"

"You see?" Dorothée said. "I don't think Princess Tatiana would have *two* lovers in the British delegation."

Suzanne stared at her friend, seeing Fitz touch Eithne's cheek in the embassy breakfast parlor only that morning.

Dorothée looked back at her, eyes filled with concern. Doro was a clever woman. She might well have meant to soothe Suzanne's fears about Malcolm and Princess Tatiana. But she had also neatly diverted Suzanne's attention from her earlier revelation about her sister's quarrel with Princess Tatiana.

Yet that didn't change the fact that apparently Malcolm's best friend among the British delegation was betraying his wife.

And had a motive to have murdered the princess.

9

Malcolm pushed open the door of Café Hugel, where he had arranged to meet Suzanne at one o'clock. The smell of rich Viennese coffee and bittersweet chocolate wafted toward him. Café Hugel was a favorite haunt of Viennese intellectuals and students. Few members of the aristocracy were to be found within the confines of its faded rose-and-cream-papered walls and slightly tarnished chandeliers, which perhaps accounted for why it was also not a favorite rendezvous for the Congress attendees.

A fair-haired young woman in a blue-sashed white frock was singing "Porgi, amor," accompanied by a serious-faced young man playing the violin. Her voice was a bit thin but sweet, and it caught the song's plaintive pain. A wave of loss and fury washed over him. For a moment the woman singing the song had red-gold hair and a richer voice. How long ago had he last heard Tatiana frame those notes?

He stood stock still for a moment, gaze fixed on a chip in the white-painted cornice, willing his mind back to the present. One step at a time and he could get through this. With a deliberate breath, he moved into the café's quieter back room. Newspapers rustled and pens scratched against paper as he made his way between the tables. He caught the words "Schiller," "Goethe," and "Beethoven," and once he was quite sure he heard Tatiana's name. A name he was now braced to hear. Word of her murder had spread everywhere. Halfway across the room, he glimpsed his wife at a table in the shadows at the back.

His wife. For the longest time after they married, he'd had difficulty framing the words, even to himself. Up until the moment he'd realized the best protection he could offer Suzanne was marriage, he'd been convinced he would never marry anyone. Even now, he would wake to find her beside him, or walk into their rooms to be greeted by her cheerful call of "darling," and be struck anew by the terrifying wonder of it.

Her hands were curled round a cup of *kaffee mit schlag,* her gaze focused on the table before her. She wore a spencer of a shiny rose-colored fabric. Her reticule lay on the table, the sort of frivolous little ribboned thing she loved, though it seemed so at odds with the woman she was beneath the surface. He studied the curve of her neck above the ruffled collar of her spencer, the strands of dark hair escaping her bonnet, the angle of her shoulders. He would know her anywhere. And yet he sometimes felt as though she were an alien creature. A selkie mated to a mortal, Persephone trapped in the underworld.

She looked up as he made his way between the tables. Beneath the white satin brim of her bonnet, her blue-green eyes were dark with disquiet.

He closed the distance between them in two strides and dropped into a chair beside her. "What? What is it?"

Suzanne's fingers tightened round her coffee cup. "According to Dorothée, Fitzwilliam Vaughn was Princess Tatiana's lover."

"Good God." Even in death Tania could take him by surprise.

"You didn't know?" Her gaze moved over his face.

"No." He pushed a hand through his hair. "If I had—" What would he have done? Ordered Tatiana to stop? She'd been an adult. As was Fitz. For some reason, he found himself hearing Fitz four nights ago, arguing passionately about the need to reform the debt laws as they shared a late glass of whisky in the attachés' sitting room. "The damned fool."

"I can't quite believe—" Suzanne took a sip of coffee as though it would steady her.

Malcolm laid his hand over her own and squeezed her fingers. She gave a twisted smile. "After two months in Vienna, you wouldn't think I'd be surprised by the news of any love affair."

Fitz's glowing face when he first announced his betrothal to Eithne flashed into Malcolm's mind. Malcolm had been struck by amazement that anyone could feel that way. And at the same time he'd been conscious of a pang that was akin to jealousy. "It's different when it's your friends."

Her gaze shifted away to focus on the faint remnants of a wine stain on the white tablecloth. "I like Fitz and Eithne. I suppose I liked believing two people could be so happy."

"Scratch the surface of most marriages and one's likely to be surprised by what one finds."

Her hand went still beneath his own. "Sometimes your cynicism surprises me, Malcolm."

"Realism." Images of his mother on the arm of a lover and his father flirting with a mistress came to mind, too commonplace to be shocking. "I don't assume anyone is what they appear to be."

"Nor do I, in theory." She withdrew her hand from his clasp and took a sip of coffee.

"Even in this very public life we lead, it's difficult to really understand what goes on between any two people."

A waiter brought him a cup of coffee. He took a sip that sat bitter on his tongue. "Annina told me Tatiana had begun seeing another lover recently. Someone she was secretive about, probably because of Tsar Alexander's jealousy. It must have been Fitz."

"Was he working with her for Castlereagh, too?" Suzanne spoke in the cool voice of an investigator.

"As far I know, I was the only one in the British delegation dealing with Tatiana."

Her winged brows drew together, dark against her pale skin. "It gives Fitz—"

"A motive. Bloody hell." Fitz, perhaps more than most husbands, would not want to lose his wife's good favor. He cared for Eithne—Malcolm would swear to that. And his political ambitions rested on the influence of Eithne's powerful father, who would not take kindly to his daughter being hurt. "Did you learn anything else from Dorothée?"

"Princess Tatiana and the Duchess of Sagan quarreled two days ago. Dorothée heard her sister say something about 'exorbitant.' Could Princess Tatiana have been blackmailing the duchess?"

Malcolm turned his cup between his hands. "I wouldn't put it past her."

"Meaning she's blackmailed people before?"

"I suspect so." Why, after all that had passed between them, did he feel this perverse loyalty to Tatiana's good name? More loyalty than she'd felt herself, he'd dare swear.

"What did you learn from Annina?"

He briefly recounted their interview, omitting mention of the letters Annina had returned to him.

"Do you think the killer took this box in which the princess kept her secret papers?"

"Perhaps. But it's also possible Tatiana decided to move the box away from her lodgings for safekeeping."

"If Princess Tatiana was blackmailing the duchess, any material she had damaging to the duchess was probably in that box. Blackmail could account for Princess Tatiana acting as though she was making a high-stakes wager."

"Perhaps. But the Duchess of Sagan isn't precisely secretive about her love affairs. It's difficult to imagine what Tatiana might have been blackmailing her about."

Suzanne turned her head toward him. He caught a whiff of her perfume, roses and vanilla and some other scent that remained tantalizingly elusive. "Everyone has secrets," his wife said.

"Especially in Vienna." Malcolm took a sip of coffee. "The duchess should be at the Metternichs' masked ball this evening. Can you contrive to talk to her?"

"I should be able to, though she won't confide in me the way Dorothée does."

"I need to talk to Fitz." Malcolm grimaced at the prospect of the interview. "But I want to call on Talleyrand first."

Suzanne tightened the ribbons on her bonnet. "I'll have our things laid out for the Metternichs' ball."

He stretched a hand across the table but stilled it before his fingers met her own. "You were right last night. Dorothée Périgord would never have confided in me about Fitz and Tatiana's affair."

Suzanne nodded. "I'm trying to muster my wits and courage to face Eithne. I can't imagine what she must—" She made rather too much of a show of tucking a strand of hair beneath the rose-colored velvet and white satin of her bonnet.

"Suzanne—"

She straightened her shoulders.

He knew it would be best not to speak. Far better for her to suspect what she did about his relationship with Tatiana than the truth. Besides, he doubted she'd believe even the most fervent denial. And yet—

"I happen to take vows rather seriously," he said.

"Malcolm, you needn't—"

"I worked with Tatiana. I was fond of her. But I wasn't her lover."

Suzanne's gaze remained on his face, but he couldn't read what she was thinking. Her defenses were as well constructed as his own. "You don't owe me an explanation, darling."

"Do you believe me?"

She took a sip of coffee. "Of course."

He smiled with equal parts affection and regret. He wouldn't have believed a similar denial. "Liar."

She shook her head. "I know what our marriage is, Malcolm. And what it isn't. I don't want to turn into a clinging wife."

He touched her hand, lightly, afraid it was an intrusion. "I don't think you could if you tried."

Her answering smile was sweet and bitter and cut straight to his heart.

"Herr Rannoch?"

The tentative voice came from a short distance away. A slight young man stood a few feet from the table, fingering the brim of the worn top hat he held in his hands. Dark hair curled in disorder about his face and wire-rimmed spectacles shielded his eyes.

Malcolm pushed back his chair. "You have the advantage of me."

The spectacled man stepped closer. He was very young, Malcolm saw, probably still in his teens. "Can you tell me—are the rumors about Princess Tatiana true?"

Malcolm swallowed, his throat scorched. "I'm afraid so."

A spasm of grief crossed the young man's face. Malcolm touched his arm and pressed him into an empty chair. "Sit. It's a shock to everyone."

Tears welled behind the young man's spectacles. He pulled off the spectacles and dashed an impatient hand across his face, then dug in his pocket and tugged out a handkerchief, covered with pencil scratches. Musical notes, Malcolm realized. He pulled out his own handkerchief and put it in the young man's hand instead. "How did you know the princess?" Tatiana's tastes hadn't tended to run to schoolboys, though with Tania one never knew.

"She did me the kindness to take an interest in my music." The young man dried his face with Malcolm's handkerchief and hooked his spectacles back over his ears.

"Ah." Malcolm glanced at the handkerchief with the musical notations, dropped forgotten on the table. "You play the pianoforte? Or the violin?" He signaled a waiter to bring a cup of coffee.

"The pianoforte." The young man stared at the interwoven white threads of the tablecloth, as though looking into a reality he could not accept. "And I compose. When I'm not teaching in my father's school."

"Tatiana loved music." For a moment, Malcolm could feel the warmth of Tania's arm gliding across his own as they played a cross-hand duet.

The waiter brought the coffee. Malcolm stirred a generous amount of sugar into it and put it into the young musician's hand. The boy stared into the steaming cup for a moment, then took a quick swallow. "Last month she attended the premiere of a mass I composed. My first."

"Of course," Malcolm said, the pieces falling into place in his head. "You must be Franz Schubert."

The young man blinked. "How do you know?"

"Tatiana mentioned the mass. She was very moved." Malcolm turned to Suzanne. "My wife, Suzanne."

Schubert inclined his head. "Frau Rannoch."

"Princess Tatiana spoke to you after the mass?" Suzanne asked.

Schubert nodded, flushing. "She said she had little interest in religion, but that the music—that it transported her."

Malcolm smiled. "That sounds very like Tatiana."

The young man looked up with a quick answering smile. "She could say the most outrageous things. And yet she always knew just how to put one at ease. She was one of the kindest people I've ever met."

"Yes, she could be kind," Malcolm said, though it wasn't a word he'd often heard associated with Tania. He could feel Suzanne's gaze on him.

"She asked me if I had any music of a more secular sort, and I brought her some of my songs." Schubert took another fortifying sip of sugar-laced coffee.

Malcolm folded the handkerchief with the musical notes, careful not to smudge the pencil, and handed it back to Schubert. "How did you know I was acquainted with Tatiana?"

"She spoke of you, sir." Schubert tucked the handkerchief into his pocket. "Frequently. She said you were the one man in Vienna she knew she could—" Schubert hesitated. Though he didn't look at Suzanne, Malcolm knew he was wondering at the wisdom of speaking so freely before Tatiana's friend's wife. "The one man in Vienna she knew she could rely upon."

Malcolm leaned back in his chair. "Princess Tatiana was an old friend."

"Of course." Schubert cast a quick glance round the café, then hunched forward. "The last time I saw her she was most anxious for you to return to Vienna, sir."

Malcolm's fingers stilled on his coffee cup. "When was this?"

"The afternoon she—The afternoon of the day she was killed." Schubert tossed down a swallow of coffee so quickly it must have burned his throat. "I'd stopped by the Palm Palace to bring her some new songs. I found her—not in the best humor."

"In a temper, was she?"

Schubert flushed. "There were shards of porcelain on the floor. I think she'd smashed a comfit dish."

"It wouldn't be the first time." And more than once, the smashed objects had been hurled at Malcolm's head. He caught Suzanne's gaze out of the corner of his eye and suspected she'd divined as much.

"I asked her what the trouble was," Schubert said. "I told her I was at her service. She shook her head and said it was just that she'd learned something disquieting. Then she said—" He hesitated again, then spoke in a rush, capturing Tania's accents to the like. "Why the devil does Malcolm have to be gone from Vienna just when I need him most?"

In the quiet precincts of the Johannesgasse, Malcolm rang the bell at the yellow plaster façade of the Kaunitz Palace. Less luxurious than the British delegation's lodgings in the Minoritenplatz but a handsome building all the same. A footman in gray livery took his card and said he would inquire if Prince Talleyrand was at home.

Malcolm waited on a green velvet bench beside one of the stucco-festooned windows in the hall. Whether or not Talleyrand would consent to an interview was an open question. Malcolm was bargaining on the prince's need for the support of the British delegation but also on his own personal history with the French foreign minister.

His first memories of Prince Talleyrand went back to the age of five. He and his brother had been riding in their mother's barouche in Hyde Park, a rare treat. An elegant gentleman leaning on a walking stick stopped to speak with their mother. A cloud of powder rose from his hair as he bent in a courtly bow. Malcolm could still remember how the powder had tickled his nose (powder was becoming a rare sight in London by 1792). Talleyrand kissed their mother's hand. When she introduced the two boys he nodded with a serious acknowledgment adults rarely afforded them.

"I know who you are," Malcolm said, studying this interesting new ac-

quaintance clad in the sort of full-skirted coat his grandfather wore. "You helped overthrow King Louis and Queen Marie Antoinette."

His mother drew a sharp breath, though a hint of laughter showed in her eyes. "Malcolm, that isn't precisely—"

"On the contrary, Arabella. He is a perceptive boy. Just what I would expect from a son of yours." Talleyrand inclined his head toward Malcolm. "You are quite right, Master Rannoch. Though I fear matters have taken a sad turn in France just now. That is why I am enjoying the hospitality of your lovely country."

Talleyrand was nothing if not a survivor. The son of an aristocratic family, he had been unable to follow the family tradition of a military career due to his clubfoot. Instead, his family had sent him into the church. Thanks to their influence, he had quickly risen to become a bishop, though according to Malcolm's mother he had been an atheist even then.

Talleyrand, as Malcolm had pointed out at the age of five, had been a key player in the French Revolution, though he had left France and taken refuge in England and then America during the Reign of Terror. He returned to France, having avoided the most violent days of the Revolution, to play an influential role in the Directoire. As the Directoire collapsed under corruption and infighting, Talleyrand helped guide the young general, Napoleon Bonaparte, to power. He had been France's foreign minister through much of Malcolm's childhood, though eventually he fell out with Bonaparte over the Russian campaign and Bonaparte's dangerous (in Talleyrand's view) ambitions, and retired from official power. Even then, as Malcolm had told Suzanne the previous night, he'd continued to play a role in Napoleon's government, while at the same time talking to Bonaparte's opponents. Now Napoleon Bonaparte was banished to the island of Elba, and his former mentor represented France at the Congress.

The footman returned with the news that the prince had soon to prepare for the Metternich masquerade but would be pleased to accord Monsieur Rannoch an interview. He conducted Malcolm up an imposing limestone staircase to Talleyrand's study. The warmth of a porcelain stove and the scent of eau de cologne greeted him.

Talleyrand sat in a red damask chair, dressed much as he had been when Malcolm first met him twenty-two years ago, in a gray velvet frock coat, a starched satin cravat, and red-heeled, diamond-buckled shoes. The atheist, excommunicated bishop, now possessed of a wife (not to mention a succession of mistresses through the years), was also a former revolutionary who dressed like a pattern card for the *ancien régime*.

Talleyrand closed the book he had been reading. "Ah, Malcolm. A pleasure as always. A glass of calvados? You'll forgive me if I ask you to pour? My foot is a bit troublesome at present, and I think I can make allowances, having known you since you were learning your letters."

Malcolm went to a gilded boulle cabinet and poured two glasses of calvados. With a few easy words, Talleyrand had put the scene on a convivial footing and reminded Malcolm that he had known him since childhood. Which gave Talleyrand the subtle edge of elder statesman and family friend. The man was a master tactician.

"I've been expecting you," Talleyrand said as Malcolm put a glass of calvados into his hand.

Malcolm looked down at the prince. "For how long?"

"Since I got the news about Tatiana." Talleyrand took a sip of calvados. "I'm sorry. I know what she meant to you."

Malcolm's fingers hardened round his own glass. "You were fond of her yourself."

"She was a fascinating and very talented woman."

Malcolm pulled a ladder-back chair up beside the prince. "She was your creature."

"My dear boy, if you believe Tatiana was my mistress—"

"Not your mistress." Malcolm dropped into the chair. "Your agent."

"She worked for me occasionally. She sold information to a number of people. Including you."

"You recruited her."

"I'm more than thirty years your senior, Malcolm. It's not surprising that she worked for me first." Talleyrand leaned against the high back of his chair. "Castlereagh's asked you to learn who killed Tatiana, hasn't he?"

"You're very quick."

"I can still add two and two and get four. If I had to put money on it, I'd wager on your uncovering the truth before Baron Hager. He has the weight of the Austrian state on his side, and he's no fool. But you were quite exceptional, even as a boy."

"You flatter me, sir."

"I don't think so. When I met you, I regretted that your nationality made it unlikely I'd ever be able to employ you. I could see even then what you'd grow into. You'll learn who murdered Tatiana because you'll have the wit to see beyond the obvious. And because you care so much you won't let matters rest until you uncover the truth. It's what you'll do with that truth that interests me."

"Are you saying you know what it is?"

"I'm as much in the dark as anyone. But I can see that the answers won't be pretty, and they may put you in an uncomfortable position. You're remarkably like your mother, Malcolm. A first-rate mind with the ability to understand the need for cool-headed decisions. Sometimes ruthless ones. But you let your emotions get in the way."

Malcolm took a sip of calvados. Delicate and superb—better than Castlereagh's cognac—but it burned his throat. "I appreciate your reputation for omniscience, Prince, but I think you presume to know a bit too much about me."

"Any seeming omniscience I possess is because I'm a keen observer of my fellows. I've had a good many opportunities to observe you these past weeks in Vienna. You're tougher than you were, but not yet tough enough, I think. Becoming emotionally entwined with an agent is a dangerous thing, Malcolm."

"You know damn well—"

"There's more than one way to be entwined. I noticed your wife watching you and Tatiana only last week at the Zichys'. A clever and charming woman, Madame Rannoch. But I don't think she's quite the brittle society wife she manages so artfully to appear."

Malcolm's fingers tightened on the etched crystal. "I don't see any need to bring my wife into this."

"On the contrary. Your wife is very much a part of the equation.

We were discussing the way you're still entwined with Tatiana. Just as Tatiana stayed entwined with Metternich even in the interval when their affair stopped."

Malcolm's senses quickened. "Are you implying her affair with Metternich had resumed?"

Talleyrand took a slow sip of calvados. "Metternich was always more in love with Wilhelmine of Sagan than she with him. Any love affair in which the balance of passion is unequal is bound to run into difficulties. Wilhelmine turned her back on Metternich. Metternich was desperately unhappy. Who else would he turn to for comfort? A woman he had loved, a woman he still cared for."

"A woman who was the tsar's mistress."

"Metternich and the tsar have a way of competing in all things."

Malcolm stared at Talleyrand's sharp-featured face. Equal parts viper and raptor, his aunt had once said. "It was your idea, wasn't it?"

Talleyrand smoothed his sleeve. "What?"

"Tatiana resuming her affair with Metternich. Tatiana becoming the tsar's lover. That's why you wanted her in Vienna."

"You credit me with a farther reach than I possess."

"I can't believe I didn't see it sooner. She was more your creature still than I realized." Malcolm folded his arms across his chest. "She told someone the afternoon of the day she was killed that she'd had disturbing news. She wanted to tell me about it." And he had failed her, as he seemed so often to do.

"Who told you this?"

"A source."

"Perhaps that's what she meant to tell you last night."

"Perhaps. Or were you the one who told her to summon Metternich and the tsar and me?"

Talleyrand's thin mouth relaxed into a smile. "I almost wish I could take credit for such an audacious action. But I can't imagine a logical reason to orchestrate such a meeting. I don't know what Tatiana was thinking of."

"It's possible her killer arranged the whole."

"To create discord? Or spread blame? A bit Byzantine, surely.

Though almost devious enough to be the sort of thing I might think up myself."

Malcolm swallowed the last of his calvados. "My thoughts exactly."

"Of course," Talleyrand added, settling more comfortably into his chair, "given what Tatiana knew about you, you could be said to have an excellent motive yourself. A little more calvados, my boy?"

Malcolm crossed the courtyard of the Kaunitz Palace. Autumn twilight shadows slanted across the street as he turned down the Johannesgasse. He could hear bells chiming from the nearby St. Stephen's Cathedral.

He had a keen memory of the first meeting he had attended with Talleyrand at the Congress. Talleyrand had walked into a room filled with the representatives of Austria, Britain, Prussia, and Russia. The victorious powers who, Talleyrand must have known full well, had been negotiating among themselves for weeks. He examined a protocol they showed him, detailing their plans for how to settle the issues of the Congress. In a voice of exquisite politeness, he inquired about the use of the word *allies*. Allies against whom, he wanted to know. Surely the war was over. If they still considered themselves allies against France, then he had no place at the meeting. Suddenly, Castlereagh and Metternich and the others were protesting and apologizing, and Talleyrand had neatly taken control of the scene. One never would have guessed he represented the defeated power at the table.

He had done much the same just now, turning the focus of the conversation to Malcolm's relationship with Tatiana. And yet he had revealed more than Malcolm had expected. The resumption of Tatiana's affair with Metternich. Talleyrand's own role in orchestrating that affair and her affair with the tsar. Talleyrand only revealed things when he had very good reasons for doing so.

Malcolm turned down an alley that offered a shortcut to the Minoritenplatz. Talleyrand's relationship with Tatiana had been a complicated one. Despite his inside knowledge, Malcolm knew barely a fraction of what had gone on between the wily French foreign minister and—

Tania. She was dead. The reality slammed into him like a fist to the gut. He stopped abruptly, beneath an overhanging balcony, and drew a harsh breath of the cooling air. He had known she was dead for close on eighteen hours, and there had been no time to mourn. Perhaps there never would be. Certainly there was no one with whom he could share his grief. Which shouldn't matter. God knew, he had been used to doing things alone since boyhood.

He pressed his hands over his eyes, forcing back the tears that would help no one, then strode on, more quickly, hoping to outrun his thoughts. His senses caught something—a stir of movement, a whiff of human scent—a split second before a hand closed on his shoulder. Through the fabric of his coat, he felt the cold press of a knife against his ribs.

"I advise you not to turn round, Monsieur Rannoch." It was a man's voice, an expressionless monotone, speaking French, as so many people did in Vienna, with an accent he could not place. "I have a message for you."

"Then you'd best deliver it." Malcolm calculated how much damage the man could do with the knife before he could get in a good blow.

"We want what you have. We are willing to pay handsomely for it."

"I don't—"

"The garden at the Metternich masquerade tonight. By the Temple of Mars. Two a.m." The knifepoint bit through Malcolm's coat. "If you know what's good for you, you won't fail."

10

The flames of the tapers on Suzanne's dressing table swayed as the door opened. In the looking glass she saw her husband step into the room.

He paused, taking in her mantilla, her red satin gown edged in black Spanish lace, the fringed shawl and castanets beside her on the dressing table bench.

"The ladies are asked to come to the ball in regional costume." Suzanne pushed the jet comb that anchored her mantilla more firmly into her hair. "I thought we would do Spain, as it's a bit tricky to work out British regional dress. Lady Castlereagh is wearing Lord Castlereagh's Order of the Garter in her hair."

"Sorry I don't have one to lend you, though I think I prefer the mantilla." His gaze moved over her reflection for a moment. "I've always liked you in them."

She'd worn a white mantilla at their wedding in the stuffy sitting room in the British embassy in Lisbon that had stood in for a chapel. His hand had brushed against the lace as he took her hand to slip a hastily purchased wedding band onto her finger. She'd felt the warmth of his fingers and the cold of the engraved metal and the strange reality of the fact that she had bound her life to the life of this man who was virtually a stranger.

Malcolm stepped into the room and began to unbutton his coat.

"I'm not going as a toreador, am I?" He left it to Suzanne to arrange their masquerade costumes. Masked balls were one of the more popular entertainments at the Congress. There had been so many, beginning with the masked ball at the Hofburg that had marked the start of the Congress, that she could scarcely remember how they had dressed for each.

"A Spanish grandee, circa 1700. Your costume's laid out on the bed."

He stripped off his coat and tossed it over a chairback. "Where's Blanca?"

"Trying to put Colin down."

He went to work on his waistcoat buttons (his valet, Addison, was out interviewing tradesmen Princess Tatiana had dealt with). "I saw Castlereagh on my way in. You and I are to represent the British delegation at Tatiana's funeral tomorrow, along with Lord and Lady Castlereagh."

In the looking glass, Suzanne watched her husband's fingers making precise, controlled work of the waistcoat buttons. "I'm glad we'll be able to be there. I wasn't sure—I know a limited number of people will be allowed to attend."

Malcolm tossed the waistcoat after his coat. "Castlereagh wants me there because he has me investigating the murder."

Or the foreign secretary had included Malcolm because of his relationship to the princess, but that was a topic it would be folly to pursue.

Malcolm began to unwind his cravat. "Speaking of the investigation, this afternoon proved interesting."

Suzanne turned round to look at her husband more closely. His eyes had a glitter that at once signaled trouble and the scent of the chase. "What happened? Was it Talleyrand?"

"No. That is, yes, he had some interesting things to say, but if I look a bit puzzled, it's over what happened later." He tossed the cravat after his coat and waistcoat. "I have a secret rendezvous at the Metternichs' ball in the garden at two. With a mysterious man who stuck a knife in my ribs on my way back from the Kaunitz Palace and informed me he is willing to pay a great deal for what I have to sell."

"What on earth does he think you have to sell?"

"I haven't the least idea. It could be an attempt to buy intelligence about Castlereagh and Britain, but I'd lay odds it's to do with Tatiana."

Suzanne took a sip from the cooling cup of coffee on her dressing table. "Perhaps someone thinks you have the box of papers that Annina told you was missing from the princess's rooms. It's no secret you were close to Princess Tatiana. If she gave it to someone—"

"Yes. They might think she'd trust me with it."

"Malcolm?" Suzanne studied her husband's face as he unfastened his shirt cuffs. Lying next to him last night in the dark, she had been certain he was lying about something. "You don't have it, do you?"

"If I did, and I was bent on keeping it secret from you, I like to think I'd have had the wit not to tell you it was missing."

She watched him as he pulled the shirt over his head. "You're going to keep the rendezvous, aren't you?"

He grinned. She forgot sometimes just how much her serious husband thrived on risk. "How else do we discover what they're after?"

"We?"

"I thought you could hide in the shrubbery and see if you can identify the man. He'll undoubtedly be masked. I'll bluff as long as possible and try to draw him out. You can come to the rescue if necessary."

"That's my Malcolm."

He picked up the frilled shirt of his grandee costume. "Put your pistol in your reticule. Just in case."

The Metternichs' villa was a twenty-minute drive from the heart of Vienna along the Rennweg, a thoroughfare lined with many elegant palaces belonging to Vienna's elite. Masks and dominoes in hand, the British delegation crowded into carriages in the Minoritenplatz. Malcolm and Suzanne shared a carriage with Aline, Tommy Belmont, Fitz, and Eithne. It was the first time Suzanne had seen either of the Vaughns since Dorothée's revelations about Fitz's affair with Princess Tatiana. She watched Fitz hand Eithne into the carriage with his usual solicitude. The cup of coffee she'd swallowed while dressing for the masquerade rose up in her throat.

Seated between Aline and Eithne on the forward-facing seat, which the gentlemen had chivalrously yielded to the ladies, Suzanne reminded herself that she had engaged in far more elaborate deceptions than pretending to be ignorant of an adulterous love affair in front of the man in question and his wife.

Across the carriage, the three men were a study in contrasts. Tommy, costumed as an English jockey, sprawled in the middle with unconcern, white-blond head thrown back against the silk-damask squabs. Malcolm leaned in one corner with an air of reserve that accorded well with his dignified grandee's costume. Fitz, dressed as a gondolier but with none of a gondolier's bonhomie, leaned into the opposite corner, his gaze fixed on the window, though he didn't seem to be focusing on the country estates they passed.

Eithne smoothed the skirt of her Tyrolean peasant dress. "I wonder if Tsar Alexander will be at the ball?"

"Because of Princess Tatiana, you mean?" Aline asked.

"He was threatening not to attend the ball long before the princess was murdered," Tommy said. "Ever since the dustup over Metternich and Castlereagh trying to get Prussia in their corner instead of Russia's. Metternich and the tsar trade their allies back and forth just like their women."

"That's what I like about you, Mr. Belmont," Aline said. "You're so wonderfully direct."

Malcolm ran a finger over the mask he held in his lap. "I suspect he'll be there. Tsar Alexander enjoys the public stage. And whether he likes it or not, tonight the stage is at the Metternichs'."

Midway down the long curving drive to the villa, the press of carriages waiting to let their passengers off stopped their own carriage in its tracks. "Just like a Mayfair ball," Tommy said as they inched over the gravel. "Only more so."

"Better put our masks on," Eithne said. "Fitz? Darling, you've dropped yours."

Fitz picked his mask up with an apologetic smile. Eithne studied him for a moment, a line between her delicate brows, then briskly tied her own mask over her face.

At last their carriage rolled up to the villa, a rambling, columned building in the Italian style. A footman let down the steps and they descended from the carriage, stretching their stiff limbs.

Flambeaux cast a red-orange glow on the wide granite steps that led to the front doors. After the cool night air, the press of heat and bodies in the high-ceilinged entrance hall was stifling. Fortunately, both Suzanne and Malcolm were adept at navigating a crowd. With Aline in tow, they inched through the hall and up the stairs to an equally close-pressed anteroom and then another and then, at last, the ballroom.

Metternich had added the ballroom to the villa for the Congress. The domed pavilion was designed to accommodate above a thousand guests. The crystal chandeliers that ran down the center of the long room sparkled with a fortune in wax tapers. Strings of Murano glass glittered in the columned recesses on either side of the room, as tonight's masquerade had a Venetian theme. Carnival masks in fantastical shapes hung from the pillars that supported the ceiling and brilliant Italian silks draped the walls.

Perfumes and eau de cologne vied with the scent of hothouse flowers and the smell of sweat from energetic dancing in an overcrowded room. The strains of a waltz rose above the cacophony of chattering voices and the clink of crystal.

Aline studied the dancers swirling on the gleaming walnut of the parquet floor. "I suspect there are enough diamonds on that Alsatian peasant dress to feed an entire Alsatian village for a month."

"If not a year." Malcolm stopped a footman and procured three glasses of champagne.

"You can tell who almost everyone is despite the masks," Aline said. "Oh, look." She nodded toward a tall, sandy-haired man in black who stood near the main entrance to the ballroom. "I'm sure that's Tsar Alexander. Weren't all the sovereigns supposed to come in black?"

Suzanne took a sip of champagne. The slender woman beside the tsar was obviously Tsarina Elisabeth. She wore Bavarian dress, the country that had been her home until she went to Russia as the tsar's bride. Beneath her mask her ash blond hair flowed loose over her shoulders in her signature style.

The tsar and tsarina stood for a moment, her hand resting lightly on his arm, accepting the attention of the crowd. Then she released his arm, and they moved in separate directions.

"They do make an exquisite couple," Aline said.

"And as with so much at the Congress, the truth is quite the opposite of the public image," Malcolm replied.

"Glad to see some familiar faces behind the masks." Geoffrey Blackwell joined them, red and white domino billowing over a dark coat. "Came as a British military doctor," he said. "No time to fuss with a costume. Exhausting day. Everyone's talking about Princess Tatiana. They think because I'm a family friend and you discovered the body I must know something. I was stopped four times to listen to theories—each more outlandish than the next—before I even reached the ballroom."

"It's rather fascinating," Aline said. "A problem that can't be solved mathematically."

"At least not without knowing all the variables," Geoffrey replied.

She grinned at him. "Quite. Too many unknowns for a proper equation."

"And impossible to define the constants. Would you care to dance, Aline?"

Aline blinked. "Oh, I don't really—That is, yes. Thank you."

"I'm far from the most dashing gentleman you'll dance with this evening," he said, holding out his arm, "but I think I can promise I'm the safest."

Aline, who often looked uncomfortable with the courtship ritual of dancing, relaxed into a smile and permitted him to lead her onto the dance floor.

Malcolm looked after them, eyes narrowed behind his mask. "I think that's the first time in a good ten years I've seen Geoff dance."

"Aline's far more comfortable with him than with the young attachés," Suzanne said.

Malcolm swallowed the last of his champagne and touched her arm. "You'll do better getting information on your own. As will I. I'll find you just before two."

"Madame Rannoch. May I hope for a dance?"

As Malcolm moved away, a broad-shouldered man bowed over Suzanne's hand. Strongly marked brows and sleek black hair showed above his purple mask. Even before he had spoken, Suzanne easily recognized him as Count Otronsky, one of Tsar Alexander's closest aides. This was not the first time the handsome count had asked her to dance, but she wondered if tonight he was acting on fact-finding orders from the tsar.

"Have you been besieged with a hundred questions about Princess Tatiana?" Otronsky said as he led her into the dance. "Or only a couple of dozen?"

Suzanne looked up at him, her gaze as open and unaffected as she could make it. "No one can talk of anything else. Only yesterday I'd have sworn nothing could supersede Poland and Saxony as topics of debate."

Otronsky twirled her under his arm. "My dear Madame Rannoch, little more remains to be said about either. Our troops have given Saxony to the Prussians, to whom it belongs, and Poland will soon be ours. One way or another."

By possession if not negotiation, his expression implied. Otronsky was one of the most militant of the tsar's advisers. "You mean Poland will be a reconstituted kingdom that pays fealty to Russia," Suzanne said.

"Forgive me, Madame Rannoch. I come from a long line of soldiers and sometimes miss diplomatic niceties. Of course that's what I meant." He swung her forward in the movement of the dance and then back to face him. "Will we see you at Princess Tatiana's funeral at the embassy tomorrow?"

"Lord Castlereagh has asked my husband and me to accompany him and Lady Castlereagh."

"Yes," Otronsky said, "I thought he'd want Rannoch there." He drew their linked hands overhead. "I saw you at Baroness Arnstein's last night, but I don't remember catching sight of your husband."

"Malcolm arrived late in the evening. He returned to Vienna sooner than he expected and came in search of me."

"And you left together to call on Princess Tatiana."

She kept her hand still in his own and her gaze as steady as water on a windless day. "I didn't want Malcolm to go alone."

Otronsky's smile gleamed white but didn't warm his eyes. "I don't know whether you're a clever wife or a very foolish one, Madame Rannoch."

"One never knows that until one sees how events play out, does one, my dear Count?"

Otronsky went on to talk of other things, but Suzanne was now quite sure he had sought her out at the tsar's insistence. Castlereagh wasn't the only one looking into the murder outside official channels. And she and Malcolm remained very much under scrutiny.

"There you are, thank goodness." Dorothée, disarmingly lovely in Carinthian dress, hurried to Suzanne's side when she left the dance floor and Otronsky had moved off. "Masquerades are so exhausting. Gentlemen think a papier-mâché mask gives them license to take all sorts of liberties, quite as though one didn't know perfectly well who most of them are. I must have dodged five sets of wandering hands already. My uncle actually intervened once."

"I wouldn't like to be any young man who angered Prince Talleyrand."

"I've never seen him so fierce. I think he might have laid hands on the gentleman in question if I hadn't stopped him."

"Why did you? It sounds as though the man deserved it."

"Because I wanted to avoid an international incident. It was Lord Stewart."

Suzanne groaned. "Oh dear, I should have seen that coming. My apologies, Doro, on behalf of my husband's country. That man is a menace to diplomacy." Lord Stewart, British ambassador to Vienna and plenipotentiary in the British delegation, was a former soldier ill-suited to his post for a number of reasons, including his drinking, his temper, and his wandering hands. But he was also Lord Castlereagh's half brother, and one of the few people with whom Castlereagh was really at ease.

Dorothée waved her hand. "I've lived in Paris for three years—I've known worse. Better me than some poor débutânte." She snapped her silk fan open and fluttered it against the heat. "In truth, I'd rather not be here at all. I had the most dreadful news just before we left the Kaunitz Palace."

"What?"

"Felix Woyna and young Trautmansdorff have both come down with mumps, of all things. Their doctor expects a full recovery, thank goodness, but they won't be able to take part in the Carrousel."

Four-and-twenty of the best young riders from the cream of the Austro-Hungarian aristocracy had been chosen as the knights of the tournament. The elaborately choreographed plans for the joust rested on having all twenty-four riders take part, matched by the four-and-twenty *belles d'amour*. "There are still two days," Suzanne said. "People have learned *Hamlet* in less time. We'll have to find two more excellent riders."

"But where? I've been racking my brain. If—"

She broke off as Geoffrey returned Aline to Suzanne's side. Aline was pink-cheeked from the exertion of the dance and laughing at something Geoffrey had been saying to her.

"I don't suppose you'd like to be in a tournament, Dr. Blackwell," Dorothée said.

"My dear Comtesse, it's my life's work to patch up the ravages of battle but not to engage in it myself. Even the ceremonial sort. I thought you had all your knights for the Carrousel."

"So did I," Dorothée said, with a sigh that was only partly mock tragic.

Geoffrey's attention was claimed by a military acquaintance, and the three ladies moved into one of the columned recesses that ran the length of the ballroom.

"You seem to have enjoyed your dance," Dorothée said, linking her arm through Aline's.

"So much more agreeable than dancing with the sort of young man who thinks it's his duty to flirt and expects one to flirt back," Aline said. "We actually had a rational conversation."

"A rational conversation while waltzing. My idea of romance." Dorothée leaned her gloved arm against a pillar and flexed a satin-slippered foot.

Aline looked a bit confused at the word "romance," then laughed. "Particularly in Vienna. The young men usually are trying to outdo each other with risqué comments of the undergraduate sort. Though there seem to be rather fewer double entendres tonight. Everyone's talking about Princess Tatiana."

"Tatiana Kirsanova had a way of being the center of attention, even in death." Wilhelmine, Duchess of Sagan, joined them, in Carinthian dress like her younger sister. She smiled at Dorothée. "Maman's diamonds suit you, Doro."

Dorothée touched her necklace, perhaps uncertain how Wilhelmine felt about their mother lending it to her. In the presence of her eldest sister, twelve years her senior, she reverted to the schoolgirl she had been not so very long ago. "It hardly goes with peasant dress."

"No, but it's in keeping with all the other glittering peasant girls in the room. Rather like Marie Antoinette playing at shepherdess. And there are some actual non-aristocrats present. Metternich gave me tickets for my maid Hannchen and her daughters. He even suggested we could switch masks if we liked, but I think that seems a bit too much like something out of a comic opera." Wilhelmine slipped her arm round her sister and squeezed Dorothée's shoulders.

The two made a striking picture. Both were slender and delicately boned, but Dorothée was taller than her petite sister, and where Dorothée's hair was a rich brown, Wilhelmine's curls were as burnished and bright as her antique gold necklace. Dorothée, for all her Paris-fashion-plate gowns and stylishly cropped hair, still had the slightly coltish uncertainty of youth. Wilhelmine was as polished as their mother's diamonds. She had the exquisitely fresh complexion of a débutânte, but the restless eyes of a woman who has seen much of the world and not found it up to her expectations.

"Willie." Dorothée fingered the border of her spangled scarf.

"You are being careful, aren't you? I mean, your rooms are only a few paces away from Princess Tatiana's."

Wilhelmine removed the scarf from Dorothée's nervous fingers and settled it over her younger sister's shoulders. "I doubt Princess Tatiana was killed by a random madman, Doro. Horrible as it is, I suspect this murder was carefully planned."

"Why?" Aline asked.

"One can't live the sort of life Princess Tatiana lived without making enemies. I should know. I live much the same life myself."

"Precisely what I mean." Dorothée sent her sister a meaningful glance.

Wilhelmine gave a peal of laughter like the tinkling glass keys of the harmonium at the British delegation's lodgings. "If you mean Prince Metternich, dearest, I assure you I can handle him. His refusal to recognize when a love affair has run its course is tiresome but not anything I haven't coped with before."

"Princess Tatiana may have thought the same thing."

"Doro." Wilhelmine flipped open a silk fan painted with a Carinthian scene. "You can't think Prince Metternich had anything to do with the murder."

"You said yourself it was probably someone she knew," Dorothée said. "Which means someone we know."

A shadow of unease crossed Wilhelmine's face, but she shook her head. "I'm more cautious than the princess, Doro. And perhaps more ruthless. I don't let my guard down."

"You always say that, Willie, but—"

"Talking about Princess Tatiana, I see." A white-haired man in an elaborate pink and gold mask stepped into the alcove. Even were pink not known to be his signature color, the Prince de Ligne was easily recognized. The seventy-nine-year-old former field marshal carried himself with an air that would stand out in any crowd.

"How did you know, Prince?" Suzanne asked.

"I might as well ask how you recognized me, Madame Rannoch," the prince said, bowing over her hand. "Or how I recognized you. The insouciance with which you hold your fan is unmistakable, even without the clue of your Spanish dress. We're all sadly predictable, I fear. Just as it's predictable that everyone in the ballroom and the antechambers and the salons and the garden and anywhere else in the villa is discussing Princess Tatiana."

"Vienna feeds on scandal," Wilhelmine said. "And what could be more scandalous than a murder?"

"What indeed?" said the prince, who had been an intimate of both Voltaire and Casanova. "Especially when the victim happens to have been entangled with so very many illustrious personages. People are clamoring to be on the guest list for her funeral, as though it were a court ball. Though there are rather fewer spaces available."

"And one can only hope there won't be as many uninvited guests slipping in as there have been at most balls at the Hofburg." Wilhelmine stirred the air with her fan. "It's amazing how many people I've heard claim the princess as a great friend tonight."

"Just so," said the prince. "I hear her spoken of with considerably more approbation than when she was alive." He turned back to Suzanne. "You're a generous woman, Madame Rannoch. You appear genuinely distressed by the princess's death."

Suzanne summoned a smile that had all the sweetness of lemon ice. "I didn't know the princess well, but how could I not be horrified by what happened to her?"

"You have the makings of a diplomat, *chère* madame."

"She lived life on her own terms," Aline said. "One can't help but admire that."

"Princess Tatiana was an enterprising woman," the prince murmured. "She'd even found a way to turn the ruins of the empire to her advantage."

Suzanne looked at him in inquiry, as did Dorothée. Wilhelmine raised her brows.

"What on earth do you mean?" Aline asked.

The prince regarded each of them in turn, savoring his audience. "My dear ladies, it's no secret that Bonaparte and his soldiers had—ah—liberated numerous art treasures in the course of their conquests. We hear a great deal about the collection in the Louvre, but a number of treasures also remain in private hands. There's considerable squabbling about whether these treasures will be returned to their rightful owners, not to mention just who those rightful owners happen to be."

"And Princess Tatiana—?" Dorothée asked.

"Princess Tatiana had come into possession of several of these treasures," the prince said. He paused a moment, smoothing the shiny silk of his domino. "But she didn't seem overly concerned with identifying the rightful owners. She was selling them. To the highest bidder."

☙ 11 ☙

A shout of laughter and a flirtatious giggle from the ballroom echoed through the suddenly silent alcove. "Good God," Aline said. "How do you know?"

The Prince de Ligne flicked open an enamel snuffbox and took a pinch of snuff. "Because I bought a piece from her myself." He sneezed behind a lace-frill-covered hand. "She drove a hard bargain."

"How did Princess Tatiana come to be in possession of these art treasures?" Suzanne asked.

"I never inquired," the prince said, "and I doubt she'd have told me. Or if she had, I doubt it would have been the truth. But just as Bonaparte helped himself to the treasures of the countries he conquered, a number of his soldiers helped themselves to them as well."

"And sometimes they fell into the hands of the opposing army," Aline said. "Only think of Vitoria." The Bonapartist Spanish government had been fleeing Spain with a number of treasures, including the Spanish crown, when the British and French armies met at Vitoria. In the chaos after the British victory, British soldiers had looted the French baggage wagons. A number of soldiers had made a tidy fortune that day.

The Prince de Ligne inclined his head. "Just so, mam'selle. And in the course of her eventful life, Princess Tatiana had formed close acquaintances with a number of gentlemen who fought on various sides. I can only imagine such gentlemen put these treasures in her hands. Or she took it upon herself to liberate the treasures from them."

"I wonder if that has anything to do with why she was killed?" Aline said. "There are fierce quarrels about who rightfully should end up with what."

Suzanne saw Dorothée dart a quick glance at her sister. Dorothée had said she'd heard Wilhelmine use the word "exorbitant" in her quarrel with Princess Tatiana.

"Oh, look," Wilhelmine said in a crisp, bright voice. "I think it's time to go in to supper."

They joined the throng moving toward the stairs to the supper room below. "Not that we're likely to get food any time soon," Dorothée murmured as they inched forward.

The supper room was really a spacious hall, which was fortunate with something approaching fifteen hundred guests. Buffet tables ringed the vast room while supper tables bedecked with carnival masks were set up in the middle. As at the Metternichs' Peace Ball the previous month, the ladies sat at the tables while the gentlemen fetched them delicacies from the buffet. Wilhelmine quickly disappeared on the arm of her lover, Alfred von Windischgrätz, but Suzanne, Dorothée, and Aline shared a table. Malcolm materialized out of the crowd, juggling a plate of oysters and three glasses of champagne, then slipped off as they were besieged by young attachés from the French embassy paying court to Dorothée.

"Aren't the sovereigns supposed to be supping in their own room?" Aline said. "I swear that's Tsar Alexander and the King of Prussia moving between the tables."

Dorothée surveyed the two gentlemen in black dominoes. "Not losing a chance to flirt. I rather hope they don't come over here."

After supper, the orchestra seemed to play at a faster tempo. Breathless and laughing—though it was very hard to carry on any sort of useful interrogation while dancing so quickly—Suzanne found herself relieved when it was time for the polonaise. The long formal dance had, along with the waltz, become the signature dance of the Congress.

Geoffrey Blackwell arrived to claim her for the dance, while Tommy Belmont partnered Aline. The orchestra struck up the stately notes of the polonaise. At least it was usually stately. Tonight the line was already wavering as Suzanne took her place beside Geoffrey. The freedom of the masked ball was at odds with formality. Several couples had their arms entwined as though they were waltzing. She saw one couple actually steal a kiss while another gentleman's hand strayed beneath the laced bodice of his partner's dirndl.

"Rather less stuffy than an event at the Hofburg," Geoffrey murmured as they began to move forward. His gaze went to Tommy and Aline ahead of them. Tommy could be an outrageous flirt, but he was holding Aline's hand in a very correct clasp.

The dance was supposed to be an elegant progress, led by the sovereigns, but the long, unwieldy column swayed even with the first steps. Two couples got tangled up and bumped into a pillar, sending a vase of roses crashing to the floor. Water, flowers, and broken glass spilled over the walnut parquet. The dancers dodged out of the way, falling out of line.

As they wound through the salons, Suzanne lost sight of either end of the column. Suddenly, the dancers came to such an abrupt halt in front of her she nearly stumbled. Shouts and laughter cut the air.

"I think the head and tail of the column have collided," Geoffrey said, tightening his grip on her arm to keep her from falling.

Ladies tripped over their trains. Their partners steadied them and took advantage of the excuse for touching. A man with rumpled white hair collapsed on a sofa, doubled over with laughter.

"I think that's the King of Denmark," Suzanne said to Geoffrey. Across the room she saw Lady Castlereagh also overcome with laughter, her husband's Order of the Garter slipping dangerously to one side.

The formal dance had dissolved into chaos. Tommy returned Aline to Suzanne's side and went off in search of the Hungarian countess who was his latest flirt. The salon was still crowded with dancers—laughing, retrieving fallen reticules and hair ornaments, shaking out crushed skirts. Suzanne anchored her mantilla, which had begun to slither backward.

"Suzanne," Aline said, "there's a man watching you."

Suzanne tugged the mantilla smooth and turned to find a tall, fair-haired man with his gaze fixed on her. He was dressed as a Cossack, his face covered by a black and silver half mask, but she would know the proud line of his shoulders and the arrogant tilt of his head anywhere.

He gave a smile that sent a chill to the toes of her Córdoba slippers. "Mrs. Rannoch." He crossed to them in three easy strides. "What a delightful surprise. I should have realized you'd be in Vienna. I swear I'd know you anywhere, mask or no."

Suzanne smiled into the blue eyes of the man who could bring her fragile life tumbling down about her ears. "Captain Radley—No, it's Colonel now, isn't it? My congratulations. I didn't realize you were in Vienna."

Colonel Frederick Radley bowed over her hand. "I arrived this afternoon. Wellington sent me from Paris with dispatches for Castlereagh." Beneath the half mask, his skin was paler than she remembered, no longer tanned by the constant Spanish sun. "I'll call round on Castlereagh tomorrow. I'm staying with Lord Stewart."

"Of course," Suzanne said. "You knew him in the Peninsula. I can quite see how you'd be friends." Radley had a great deal in common with Castlereagh's half brother, from military courage to wandering hands and a tendency to lose his temper.

"We fought together at Busaco and Talavera. Stewart's a capital fellow." Radley turned to Geoffrey. "Unless I've lost my skill at looking behind masks, you're Blackwell. The last time we met you were putting my arm in a sling."

"Hunting's a dangerous sport."

"But what else is one to do, confined to quarters all winter?" Radley's gaze moved on to Aline. "Won't you present me to your charming companion, Mrs. Rannoch?"

Even now Suzanne could not deny the force of his smile. "Colonel Radley, Aline. My husband's niece, Miss Dacre-Hammond."

"You must have known Malcolm and Suzanne in Spain," Aline said as Radley bowed over her hand. She seemed blessedly unaffected by his charms, but then Aline was hardly a typical young lady.

"So I did. But separately, as it happens." Radley's gaze returned to Suzanne, cutting neatly through the satin and lace of her gown. "You look very much at home as a diplomatic wife."

"I'm fortunate in my life."

"Fascinating how these things have a way of working out. We must reminisce sometime."

Suzanne's fingers dug into her gloved arms. Fear squeezed her chest as though her corset laces had been pulled beyond bearing. She'd always known the past would catch up with her sooner or later. But the fear had settled into a constant, nagging presence, like the ache of an old wound that one learns to ignore because it is the only way to get on with one's life. These last few days, discovery had been the furthest thing from her mind. While she'd been agonizing over Malcolm and Princess Tatiana, her own ghosts had been waiting to pounce.

Julie Zichy drew Radley away, though Suzanne suspected she would see him again all too soon. Aline looked after him. "Judith will be so jealous," she said, referring to her fifteen-year-old sister. "She has a box of clippings about his exploits on the Peninsula. Especially his commendations after Vitoria."

"A good soldier, Radley," Geoffrey murmured. "One can't deny him that."

"I don't think Malcolm would have cared for the way he was looking at Suzanne," Aline said. "Though Malcolm isn't the sort to get jealous. And he knows you can take care of yourself."

"Thank you, dearest." For a moment Suzanne could hear the cries of wounded men, see blood congealing on cobblestones, taste the cold bite of terror.

"Suzanne?" Aline said. "Are you all right?"

"Of course, love. Just caught up in memories."

Geoffrey touched Aline's arm. "A lot of ugliness happens in war.

A lot of ugliness happened on the Peninsula in particular. It's hard to reconcile the memories with our current spun-sugar environment."

"Quite," Suzanne said. She straightened her shoulders and flicked open her fan. She could only hope Aline's confidence in her ability to handle Radley was not misplaced.

For she had learned that the most insidious dangers could not be faced down with a pistol or a knife.

Tsarina Elisabeth turned her back on the crowd for a moment and pressed her fingers to her temples. Above the jeweled border of her mask, her head was pounding. Even when her face was uncovered, she always wore a mask in public. Tonight should be easier, with a stiff creation of papier-mâché actually covering her face, but she felt as vulnerable as she had as a fourteen-year-old bride. Last night's events had slashed her carefully cultivated ability to dissemble, as surely as Princess Tatiana's throat had been slashed by the murderer's dagger.

"A waltz, Your Majesty?"

The voice washed over her with comfort, even before his fingers brushed her arm. She turned round. Though his familiar features were covered by a half mask, Adam's eyes were the same, and their warmth steadied her. She stepped into his arms, grateful beyond measure for this dance that allowed human contact and the chance for whispered confidences.

"Courage." He spoke into her ear, the way in the past he had whispered across her pillow. "I have an idea about where to look. Trust me, Lisa. In this, at least."

She looked up into his eyes. "I've always trusted you, Adam. It's the world that's conspired against us."

"But we've grown more deft at conspiracy ourselves, through the years."

She shook her head. "I don't deserve you, Adam. I should never—"

"Shush," he said. "The past doesn't matter."

"Oh, Adam," she said, as they circled in the pattern of the dance. "The past is all round us."

* * *

Three dances—with Princess Thérèse Esterhazy, Princess Catherine Bagration, and young Marie Metternich—a turn round the crowded supper room, and half an hour in the salon that had been given over to smoking had exposed Malcolm to a great deal of speculation about Tatiana and her death but nothing useful in the way of new information.

He emerged from the brandy fumes and choking smoke—he'd never cared for cigars, they put him in mind of his father—and had started down the corridor to the ballroom when he saw Fitzwilliam Vaughn duck through a door. The library, if he remembered the floor plan of the villa correctly. Malcolm bit back a bitter laugh. Usually he was the one to take refuge in the library at entertainments. When the call of diplomacy, espionage, or investigation didn't require him to circulate, he was happier with a book than making conversation in an overheated room. Since their marriage, Suzanne had more than once come in search of him and pulled him back to the ballroom to be sociable.

He opened the door onto the light of two candelabra and the smells of ink and leather. No sense in wasting a chance for private conversation. It might be more easily come by here than in the Minoritenplatz. "An odd reversal of roles for me to find you ducking into the library."

Fitz turned with a start of surprise. He had crossed to a cabinet that held a set of decanters. "There must be above a thousand people here. Difficult to manage anything approaching rational conversation. And I find I'm not in the mood for frivolity. Brandy?"

"Thanks. I imagine we could both do with a drink."

"It's been a difficult day." Fitz poured brandy into a glass, splashing a bit onto the Chinese lacquer of the cabinet. "I couldn't believe it when Castlereagh called us in this morning—"

"That was the first you heard of Princess Tatiana's death?" Malcolm felt the faint, telltale catch in his throat when he framed the words.

"Yes." Fitz reached for a second glass.

"It must have been especially hard for you."

Fitz lifted his head.

Malcolm met his friend's gaze. From their undergraduate days at Oxford, Fitzwilliam Vaughn had been one of the few people he trusted without question. "I know, Fitz. About you and Tatiana."

The crystal stopper fell from Fitz's fingers to clatter against the decanter. For a seeming eternity he and Malcolm stared at each other across the paneled length of the library.

"Dorothée Périgord saw you at the Zichys' reception," Malcolm said. "She told Suzanne."

"Dear God." Fitz pressed his hands to his face. "Does—"

"Eithne doesn't know. At least not from us."

Fitz dropped his hands and gave a quick nod.

A friend would go to Fitz's side and clap him on the shoulder. But Malcolm wasn't a friend in this. Not first and foremost. "Your private life is your own business," he said. "Or would be if your mistress hadn't been murdered."

"But you think I'm a rutting bastard and wonder how the devil I could do this to the woman I love."

A bitter acknowledgment of his own shortcomings echoed through Malcolm's head. "I wouldn't presume to know what's inside anyone's marriage. Though I confess I always thought you were singularly blessed."

Fitz took a quick turn about the room, like a caged lion at the Royal Exchange. "I thought I was the luckiest man in the world when Eithne accepted me. I still remember the first time I saw her—at Almack's, of all places. I was home on leave from the Peninsula, doing my duty squiring my sister Sophia and regretting an evening of tepid punch and matchmaking mamas. I came off the dance floor and saw Eithne talking with two other girls. She was wearing a white gown with a yellow sash, and she had pearls in her hair. She took my breath away. I was sure I'd never look at another woman again. I never thought I'd be the sort of husband who—You know. We see it all round, here and at home. The Devonshire House set. Lord and Lady Cowper. Prince Metternich. Tsar Alexander."

"My own parents," Malcolm said, images etched sharp in his memory. "It's one reason I never thought to marry."

"My father and stepmother, truth to tell. My older brothers.

And my married sisters, I suspect." Fitz grimaced, stalked back to the drinks cabinet, picked up one of the brandies and took a long swallow. "I was so smugly certain I could never be like my father and brothers. I never bargained on—"

"Growing bored?"

"No. That is—" Fitz stared into his brandy glass. "I suppose inevitably it becomes less intense. Surely you find that yourself."

Malcolm considered his own marriage. Except for a few unguarded moments, he kept his feelings carefully in check. But he could hardly say the intensity had dissipated. Quite the reverse, in fact. For a moment his consciousness of his wife was so vivid he could almost feel the brush of her hair between his fingers and smell the scent of her skin. "I don't think I've been married long enough to judge."

"Perhaps not." Fitz rubbed his hand over his eyes. "I could blame it on the familiarity of five years of marriage. On this city, where one can't seem to turn round without stumbling over a romantic intrigue. On the mad hours we're keeping. But the truth is, I looked at Tatiana and I felt—does it sound mad to say bewitched?"

"Not mad." Malcolm moved to the drinks cabinet and picked up the second brandy. "Though if you're implying the blame is hers—"

"Of course not. I take full responsibility." Fitz turned his glass in his hand, studying the play of the candlelight on the crystal. "My love for Eithne was as sweet and safe as sugared rose petals. With Tatiana it was quite the opposite. Crazy, insane, a fever that fed on itself. I was dazzled the moment I first saw her, but I never thought she'd look twice at me."

"You underrate yourself."

Fitz shook his head, started to speak, took a swallow of brandy. "It was on one of those expeditions we all took to the countryside in October when the weather was so glorious. To the Klosterneuburg abbey."

"I remember," Malcolm said. "Suzanne and I stayed in Vienna and took Colin to the Augarten."

"Eithne stayed for a dress fitting. Castlereagh particularly asked me to go on the expedition as Otronsky and Humboldt and the King of Denmark were in the party, and he wanted a British presence. My horse cast a shoe on the way home. Tatiana offered me a seat in her carriage. We stopped at an inn for a glass of wine, and—You can guess the rest." He began to pace again. "The horrible thing is, I wasn't sorry. She was fascinating. She could talk about anything, and she had the most remarkable knack for listening."

"She could make any man think he was the center of her world."

"You felt it, too." Fitz shot him a quick glance. "Did—"

"No," Malcolm said, a little more firmly than necessary. "Though I don't expect you to believe me any more than Suzanne did."

Fitz opened his mouth as though to voice a denial, then shook his head. "I knew I wasn't her only lover. But I suppose I flattered myself that I was the only one who wasn't political. I even had mad thoughts about giving up everything and running off with her. Though as soon as I was with Eithne I knew I could never do that. God help me, Lord Beverston will kill me if he finds out what I did to his daughter. Rightly so."

"Which wouldn't do your political prospects any good."

Fitz flushed but didn't look away from Malcolm's gaze. "Without his support, I'd have little chance of achieving anything. For Eithne's sake he wouldn't let me be ruined, but he'd never make me his protégé knowing how badly I'd hurt his daughter. And my own father would only back me if I turned Tory, which would rather defeat the purpose. Not that any of that signifies beside Eithne. I know her. She'd stand by me. She wouldn't reproach me. But it would never be the same."

Malcolm took a swallow of brandy. "Fitz. Where were you last night?"

It was a moment before Fitz made sense of the words. "Good God. You can't think—"

"I'm endeavoring to be objective."

Their gazes met, like the clash of fencing foils. Memories hung between them, echoing back to their first meeting on the sun-splashed flagstones of an Oxford terrace, when Malcolm had been in his first year and Fitz in his last. Poring over lecture notes, correcting essays, debating in coffee houses. Drafting diplomatic communiqués over guttering candles, sharing wine in Spanish farmhouses, going cross-eyed as they drew up tables to decode documents.

"I was at the opera," Fitz said. "I escorted Eithne and Suzanne and Aline."

"And then?"

"We went on to Baroness Arnstein's. But Eithne had a headache and Aline was tired, so I took them home soon after we arrived. You must have found Suzanne at the Arnsteins'?"

"Yes," Malcolm said. "And you?"

"Eithne went to bed when we returned to the Minoritenplatz. I sat up drafting a paper for Castlereagh on possible responses to Russia's actions in Saxony."

"Alone?"

"Yes."

"When did you last see Tatiana?"

"The night before last." Fitz flushed again. "I looked in at the Duchess of Sagan's reception and then ducked round to Tatiana's through the side entrance."

"Did she appear concerned about anything?"

Fitz frowned. "She seemed—distracted. I asked her if something was wrong. She laughed and said 'on the contrary.'"

"Anything else?"

Fitz hesitated. "There was something odd in the way she kissed me when I left. For a moment I was afraid it was a . . . a farewell."

Malcolm studied his friend, knowing the bleak loss in Fitz's gaze was the twin of his own. "Who do you think killed her?"

Fitz shook his head. "The tsar would have been furious if he'd known of our affair. If we were seen at the Zichys'—"

"I doubt Dorothée Périgord would have told the tsar. But yes, it's difficult to keep a secret in Vienna. On the other hand, the tsar also believed I was her lover."

"Women were jealous of her. Men wanted her. But I can't imagine anyone—"

"Nor can I. But someone did."

Fitz met Malcolm's gaze. "I know Castlereagh's asked you to investigate—"

"I won't reveal your involvement with her unless it becomes necessary. But it may become necessary."

"That isn't what I meant." In the candlelight, Fitz's gaze was dark and direct. "I want to know who did this to her, Malcolm. I want the bastard to pay."

"Yes," said Malcolm. "So do I."

❧ 12 ❧

The vast quiet of the book-filled library, normally Malcolm's favorite sort of sanctuary, suddenly felt as suffocating as an overcrowded ballroom. Judging by Fitz's expression he felt the same. Without speaking, they left the library and made their way down the corridor to the ballroom. Walking side by side as they had a score of times in the past.

"Monsieur Rannoch. Lord Fitzwilliam." Dorothée Périgord fell upon them as they entered the ballroom. "I have just hit upon the most perfect solution to my dire plight. You two must be chivalrous and save me. Chivalrous being the operative word."

"We are of course at your service, Madame la Comtesse," Malcolm said. "But—"

"Splendid." Dorothée gripped his hand and squeezed Fitz's hand as well. "Everyone says you're the best riders in the British delegation. I'm in desperate need of two knights for the Carrousel. You won't fail me, will you? It's perfect because you're such good friends."

The Meissen clock over the mantel in the side salon where Suzanne was talking with Aline, Geoffrey, and the Princess von Thurn und Taxis showed ten minutes to two. She excused herself and started for the French windows to the garden. A few paces from the door, a hand touched her arm. She froze, sure it was Radley.

"Suzanne? What is it?" Malcolm's voice spoke in her ear.

"Nothing." *Sacrebleu,* her wits were deserting her along with her finely honed abilities at deception.

"I talked to Fitz," he said, as he opened one of the French windows onto the garden. "I'll brief you later. Dorothée just waylaid us on our way back into the ballroom. She wants Fitz and me to replace the two knights she lost in the Carrousel. Was that your idea?"

"No. I thought she was looking for Austro-Hungarians."

"I think at the moment she'll settle for good riders. Someone told her Fitz and I are halfway decent."

"Someone no doubt told her you're brilliant horsemen. You agreed?"

"It would have been difficult to say no," Malcolm said as they descended the terrace steps. "She's going to change round the favors so I can be your cavalier."

Suzanne cast a surprised glance at him. "Doesn't it violate some rule of social etiquette for a husband and wife to be so in each other's pockets?"

"Dorothée must realize how unconventional we are."

Moonlight and a soft glow from strings of Venetian glass lanterns washed over the garden. On the night of Metternich's Peace Ball a month since, the garden had been crowded with dancers, musicians, and performers. Tonight, in the cooler weather, it was empty save for a few intrepid couples, walking arm in arm or standing with their heads close together. Malcolm took Suzanne's hand so they'd blend in, and they made their way down a gravel walk to the Temple of Mars, its gray stone splashed blood red by the light of a crimson glass lamp.

Before they reached the temple, Suzanne gave Malcolm a flirtatious kiss, as though she were leaving him to serious business, and turned back toward the villa. When she reached some nice, concealing shadows she slipped down a side path, senses tuned to watchers, and circled back to the temple. She came up behind a topiary hedge that had served to conceal an orchestra at the Peace Ball. She drew the folds of her mantilla over her shoulders against the night air and settled where she had a good view through the interlaced leaves. Just in case, she eased open the clasp on her reticule and gripped her pistol.

Malcolm leaned against the temple. After a few minutes a figure emerged, swathed in one of the red and white dominoes Metternich had instructed those not in costume to wear. He came not from the direction of the villa but down one of the side gravel walks.

"You're punctual. That's good." The man spoke French, but in a flat voice that didn't sound native yet was impossible to place. He was not overly tall, and beneath the folds of the domino he appeared to be slightly built. A red mask covered his face. "Just in case you have any rash thoughts in mind, Monsieur Rannoch, I am holding a loaded pistol. Did you bring what I asked for?"

Malcolm turned toward the man with leisurely care. "Surely you don't imagine I'd be fool enough to bring such valuable goods to a preliminary negotiation?"

"Who said anything about preliminary?"

"You have yet to even make an offer." Malcolm continued to lean against the statue with an ease that suggested he found the discussion less than urgent. "I'm waiting."

"Ten thousand," Red Mask said in a crisp voice. "In English pounds or whatever currency you name."

Dear God, it was a small fortune. What on earth did these people think Malcolm had?

"A handsome offer." Malcolm set his shoulders against the temple and crossed his legs at the ankle. "But who's to say I'm in the mood to sell?"

"You'll be safer without it. Your wife will be safer."

"So you were behind the attack on my wife and me last night?" An edge of steel crept into Malcolm's voice.

"I didn't say that. A number of people want what you possess. You and your family will be far safer once you've relinquished it."

"Or perhaps we'll become expendable because I've lost my bargaining chip."

"I think not. I advise you—"

A branch creaked, though the air was still. Not a branch in Suzanne's hedge. From across the garden. Red Mask spun round, then whirled back to Malcolm, his pistol leveled. "Damn it, Rannoch, what have you done?"

"Nothing but what instructed."

"You're a fool or a liar." Red Mask backed away, still holding the pistol leveled, then turned and ran toward the ballroom.

Malcolm lurched into the shrubbery. A scuffle followed, a few thuds, a sharp cry.

Suzanne stayed where she was, though she pulled her pistol from her reticule. A few moments later, her husband emerged from the shrubbery, dragging a man who wore another red and white domino and a black mask. Malcolm had his own pistol pressed to the man's side.

"It's all right, Rannoch." The man spoke quietly, in French. His voice was familiar, though Suzanne could not immediately place it. "Now that I know you're in possession of the papers, I'm prepared to negotiate."

"I'm pleased to hear it," Malcolm said. "But—"

The man tugged at the strings on his mask and pulled it from his face. The light of the Venetian lanterns revealed the well-cut features of Prince Adam Czartoryski. "I'll pay you twice what your friend offered," he said.

"Czartoryski." Malcolm studied the prince. "How can you even be sure that I possess what you want?"

"I wasn't. But I'd begun to suspect you were the one person she might have given them to."

"Princess Tatiana?"

"Of course. When I saw you leave the ballroom just now, I followed. What I overheard confirmed my suspicions. You have them and you're willing to sell them." A faint undertone of distaste crept into Czartoryski's voice. "I will top any other offer you may receive."

"Look, Czartoryski." Malcolm hesitated. Echoes from the negotiating table reverberated through the small patch of garden. Adam Czartoryski was an adviser to Tsar Alexander. Tensions between the British and Russian delegations ran high just now, quite apart from the fact that the tsar had as good as accused Malcolm of murder. Yet Suzanne knew her husband admired Czartoryski as a man of integrity. She could see Malcolm weighing his options, debating how much to reveal. Sometimes one had to give out information to gain the information one was seeking.

Malcolm untied his own mask and pulled it from his face. "I'm afraid you're under a quite understandable misapprehension. I don't have what you are looking for."

"But—"

"Just now you saw me endeavoring to bluff in an effort to acquire information. My wife was listening. Suzanne?"

Suzanne stepped from behind her hedge shield. "Good evening, Prince."

Czartoryski looked from Malcolm to Suzanne. "I don't—"

"I suspect," Malcolm said, "that we may be able to help each other by pooling information. We'll tell you our side of the story first, and then I hope you'll be persuaded to confide in us."

Czartoryski gave a slow nod.

"As you must have heard, Suzanne and I discovered Princess Tatiana's body last night," Malcolm continued. "On our way home from the Palm Palace, we were attacked by two armed men. When I captured one and tried to get him to talk, he was shot by a third. This afternoon, the man in the red mask stuck a knife in my ribs and said he was prepared to buy what I had to sell. I think he meant papers that had been in Princess Tatiana's possession. I'll hazard a guess that you are also looking for papers that Princess Tatiana possessed?"

Czartoryski was silent for a long moment. The moonlight and the glow of the lamps slanted over his still, tense features. At last, he nodded.

"And I'll hazard a further guess that these papers have something to do with Tsarina Elisabeth?"

Czartoryski's dark gaze widened. "How—?" He bit back the words. His face went as closed as if he were still masked.

"I saw you talking to her in the Prater this morning," Malcolm said. "I saw the look on your face. I've seen enough of you to suspect that were your concern about these papers because of information they contained about yourself, you wouldn't be so desperate. In fact, I can think of few things that would make a man like you as desperate as a threat to the woman he loves."

Czartoryski shook his head. "You're an uncanny judge of your fellows, Rannoch."

"Hardly. But sometimes I have good instincts."

Czartoryski's gaze flickered from Malcolm to Suzanne. Making the same calculations Malcolm had done about the risks and rewards of trusting and taking on allies.

"Prince Czartoryski?" Suzanne said, going on instinct. "Were you at Princess Tatiana's last night?"

His gaze whipped to her face.

"Because of these papers?" Suzanne pressed her advantage.

Czartoryski spun away and gripped the stone side of the temple for a moment, then turned back to face her. "I went to ask the princess to return papers that rightfully belong to no one but the tsarina. When I got there Princess Tatiana was already dead. I don't expect you to believe that—"

"What time?" Malcolm asked.

"About two-thirty."

"Was her skin blue-tinged?"

Adam met Malcolm's gaze. "Yes. From what I know of dead bodies, she had been killed at least half an hour before. Once I had determined there was nothing I could do for her, I searched for the tsarina's papers."

"You were efficient."

He gave a bitter smile. "I've played this game for some time." He straightened his shoulders with military precision. "I know I should in honor have reported the crime. But that would not have helped the princess and might have done irreparable harm to Lis—to the tsarina."

"So you left."

"So I left." His mouth curled with self-reproach. "I feared the tsarina's papers had fallen into the hands of Princess Tatiana's killer. But then I realized the killer might well not even have known of the papers' existence. I tried to think where they might be if they hadn't been in her rooms. I heard you had been the one to discover the princess's body. I glimpsed you in the Prater this morning. It occurred to me that if Princess Tatiana had given the papers to someone she trusted, you were the obvious candidate."

"So you watched me this evening, and when you saw me go into the garden, you followed."

"I had recognized you and Madame Rannoch when you arrived." Czartoryski inclined his head to Suzanne. "You're a striking pair."

"Princess Tatiana kept her most secret papers in a box in a hiding place in her rooms," Malcolm said. "According to her maid, that box has disappeared."

"You trust her maid?"

"I consider her a friend."

Czartoryski raised his brows but did not comment, as many would have done, on considering a servant a friend. "Do you think Princess Tatiana's killer is in possession of this box?"

"Not necessarily. It's entirely possible Tatiana herself hid it in recent days. But she didn't hide it with me."

"And yet a number of people think you have it."

"Quite. Possibly even the killer."

"So if we find the papers, we may find the killer."

"Perhaps."

Czartoryski looked from Malcolm to Suzanne. "What can I do to help you? I will give you any assistance that is in my power."

Malcolm and Suzanne returned to the villa through the French windows that opened onto one of the side salons. They found a small crowd gathered on the chairs and settees. All eyes were focused on the corner of the room where Princess Catherine Bagration stood, one hand resting on a pillar that held a statue of Cupid and Psyche. She had removed her mask, but even had she still worn it she was easily recognized. The light of the chandelier gilded her blond ringlets and shot through the gauzy fabric of her Ukrainian peasant dress, outlining the shapely legs beneath the muslin.

She cast the briefest glance at Malcolm and Suzanne as they

stepped into the room, then continued with what she had been saying. "I know one shouldn't speak ill of the dead. And goodness knows I'm as horrified by what happened to Princess Tatiana as anyone. More so, perhaps, since I live in the Palm Palace. I keep wishing I'd been able to do something to save her. But—well—" Princess Bagration shrugged her elegant shoulders. Her gauze scarf slithered down, baring her low-cut laced bodice. "There's no ignoring the facts just because someone has died."

"What facts?" the Prince de Ligne inquired. He was reclining in an armchair, gaze fixed on the princess with the appreciation of a connoisseur. Gossip was to him what brandy or first editions were to some.

Princess Bagration turned her pale blue gaze on the prince. "I made some inquiries. I'm not sure why, save that something about Princess Tatiana has never quite rung true to me. These past weeks were the first time I'd been much in her company, as she spent most of the last decade in Paris." Her gaze moved to Malcolm and Suzanne. "You knew her... well, Monsieur Rannoch. Did she ever talk about her past?"

"Not her childhood," Malcolm said. Suzanne suspected her husband's voice would sound easy to anyone but her.

"Perhaps I was the only one who was suspicious. Of course we were both Russian. Or so I thought."

"Thought?" Dorothée asked. She was perched on a settee beside Julie Zichy.

"Princess Tatiana's history was cleverly documented. I can quite see how Prince Kirsanov was taken in when he married her. But I found one of the servants from the school she attended. Supposedly attended. The school—"

"Catherine." A tall, brown-haired figure in a black domino appeared in the doorway from the ballroom. Tsar Alexander.

Princess Bagration lifted her chin and regarded the man who was acknowledged to be her lover just as he was acknowledged to have been the lover of Princess Tatiana. "I'm only revealing what I've learned to be fact, Your Majesty. The school Princess Tatiana supposedly attended burned down years ago, but this woman told me that the one little daughter of Prince and Princess Sarasov,

Princess Tatiana's supposed parents, died of a fever at the age of nine. Princess Tatiana quite cleverly appropriated this poor child's identity."

Princess Bagration paused, letting her words sink in. Suzanne resisted the impulse to look at Malcolm and see how he was taking the revelation.

Count Otronsky cast a quick glance at Alexander, then looked back at Catherine Bagration. "Are you saying Princess Tatiana wasn't the daughter of Prince and Princess Sarasov? Then who the devil was she?"

"I haven't the least idea." Princess Bagration extended a gold-sandaled foot. "For all I know she wasn't even Russian. But it's quite clear Princess Tatiana was a fraud."

13

Elisabeth touched her fingers to the jeweled edge of her mask. A number of the guests had switched masks at midnight, adding to the usual masquerade mischief. She wished she had managed to do so herself, though she doubted that a simple change of mask would have given her anonymity.

Candles burned low in the chandeliers and gilded sconces, but she could still hear the strains of "Mon Grandpère" from the ballroom. The dance from the last century was a traditional close to Metternich entertainments. Some intrepid souls continued to dance, while others milled about the stairs and the entrance hall, waiting for their carriages. The guttering candlelight gleamed against brightly colored silk and glinted off jeweled masks and diamond-stitched peasant skirts.

As she was about to step from an anteroom onto the stairs, she turned and met a familiar gaze. He had changed his black mask for a harlequin design, but she still knew Adam at once. He jerked his head to the side. The slightest gesture, but they'd learned to read each other's smallest signals years ago. The knowledge was ingrained in her, like a pattern etched in glass.

He disappeared, and a moment later she followed him, through another anteroom into a salon that had been given over to cards but was now deserted. The remains of a game of écarté lay on the baize-covered table, and the air smelled of snuff and champagne and a mélange of perfumes.

Meeting Adam's gaze, she knew at once what had happened, despite his mask. "You weren't successful."

"No." He took her hands in his strong clasp. "But we now have allies."

"Allies?" She drew back in alarm. In the Russian court, one learned not to trust oneself to allies.

Adam's mouth lifted in a smile. "Sometimes one must learn to take help where it is possible, Lisa." He told her about his arrangement with Malcolm Rannoch and his wife.

Fear thrummed through her like a shock from fire-warmed metal. "We scarcely know them."

"I've been in numerous meetings with Rannoch and talked to him on more than one occasion. He has a good understanding, and he strikes me as a man of honor. I've been impressed with his willingness to stand up to Castlereagh when he disagrees."

"This isn't a border dispute, Adam."

"One learns a lot about a man over border disputes. To own the truth, I was surprised and disappointed when I thought Rannoch was selling Princess Tatiana's papers. His subsequent explanation confirmed my earlier opinion of him."

"Though he was apparently betraying his wife with Princess Tatiana."

"There are all sorts of betrayals, Lisa, for all sorts of reasons. Whatever else is between them, Rannoch and his wife clearly work well together."

Elisabeth twitched her skirt away from a patch of spilled champagne on the floor. She had spoken with Suzanne Rannoch once or twice at various events and had met her in the Prater, walking with her young son. She had an image of Madame Rannoch holding the little boy up to look at the Chinese pavilion, heedless of the way the child crushed her frogged pelisse. "I like Suzanne Rannoch." She drew a breath. "You're right, we must be practical. I've made my mistakes. It's folly to lament over the dangers in trying to fix them. This man who wanted to buy the papers from Monsieur Rannoch tonight. He knows about my letters?"

"Not necessarily." Adam's fingers tightened over her own. "We don't know what else Princess Tatiana had in her possession. But he'll almost certainly approach Rannoch again. If we can entrap him, we can learn more."

She lifted a hand and smoothed his thick hair back from his mask. "Be careful, Adam."

"If I weren't careful I'd have been dead long since."

"Don't joke. I have enough on my conscience as it is." She let her fingers linger against his temple. "Did you hear about the accusations Catherine Bagration made? That Princess Tatiana was a fraud?"

"The talk spread like wildfire. Whether or not it's true is another matter."

"To play a part for so many years—"

Adam gave a bleak smile. "Isn't that what we've all done, one way and another?"

"But not with assumed identities. Why would she have pretended to be someone else?"

He shook his head. "We can't know that until we discover who she really was."

"Adam." She put her hands on his shoulders. "You didn't tell the Rannochs *what* was in my missing papers, did you?"

"Need you ask it? Of course not."

Their gazes held. Below the mask, she saw that Adam had a small cut on his chin from shaving and that the lines beside his mouth were deeper than she remembered. How well she knew that mouth. Teasing against the corner of her own, lingering at the hollow of her throat. Hot with urgency and yet always filled with a desperate tenderness.

The candlelight seemed brighter, but she felt the chill of the night air through the muslin and lace of her Bavarian gown. Adam stared down at her for a long moment. Then, as though yielding to a compulsion, he bent his head, and for the first time in years, pressed his mouth to hers.

Dorothée leaned her head against the Italian silk squabs and studied her uncle by marriage across the lamp-lit interior of the carriage. "Did you know? That Princess Tatiana wasn't who she claimed to be?"

Talleyrand opened his heavy-lidded eyes and smiled at her. "My dear child, are you accusing me of perpetrating a fraud upon society all these years?"

"Of course not," Dorothée said, though she knew her husband's uncle was capable of doing just that if he thought it necessary to achieve his objectives. "But I can quite see you wouldn't have wanted to expose someone you thought of as a friend."

"Princess Tatiana is hardly the only one in society to lie about her origins." Wilhelmine, who was sharing their carriage on the drive back to Vienna, looked up from contemplation of the mask lying on the seat beside her. "Though I must say, to adopt the identity of the daughter of a real noble family was quite brazen."

"Safer in a way than making up an identity out of whole cloth," Talleyrand said. "She had a real family history to back her up. There were no close Sarasov connections in St. Petersburg or Moscow. And once she'd married Prince Kirsanov, few would have thought to question her. It probably helped that she didn't live much in Russia."

Wilhelmine adjusted the gold silk folds of her domino. "Very enterprising of Catherine Bagration to have learned the truth. Though it smacks a bit of desperation. I always thought Catherine was afraid Tatiana outranked her in the tsar's affections."

Dorothée's gaze flew to her sister's face. "You don't think—"

"That Catherine Bagration murdered Tatiana Kirsanova in a fit of jealousy? I can imagine less likely scenarios."

Talleyrand crossed his clubfoot over his good leg. "Catherine Bagration is certainly cold-blooded enough to commit murder. But I think she'd need a stronger motive. Jealousy over the tsar's attentions might pique her vanity enough she'd look for reason to discredit her rival. But I don't think she takes any man so seriously as to kill for him. Much like you, my dear Wilhelmine."

Wilhelmine returned Talleyrand's smile with one every bit as dangerous. For a moment Dorothée felt as though she were watching a play without knowing quite what had happened in the first act. "Thank you, Prince," Wilhelmine said. "But I think you forget that for women such as Catherine Bagration and Princess Tatiana and me, the way to power lies through men. Surely you of all people understand the seduction of power."

"I do indeed." Years of events that had occurred before Dorothée was born drifted through Talleyrand's shrewd blue eyes. "Though I wouldn't think a woman as addicted to power as you claim to be would have given up Prince Metternich."

Wilhelmine shrugged her shoulders. There was something so elegant about her every movement. Dorothée always felt hopelessly gawky beside her. "It may not be in your makeup to realize this, Prince Talleyrand, but as seductive as power can be, some things are even more so. I didn't mean to fall back in love with Alfred von Windischgrätz, but—well, that's just it, isn't it? Love isn't something you plan. Besides, Metternich's adoration was growing smothering."

Talleyrand twitched a frilled cuff smooth. "Prince Metternich has yet to learn that love should never be allowed to interfere with politics. Though even after my long and varied career, I confess that that is often more easily said than done."

"Metternich didn't seem to pester you too badly this evening, Willie," Dorothée said.

"No. He's stopped the mad, desperate pleas. But he still follows me round the room with that intense gaze." Wilhelmine threw up her gloved hands, her sapphire bracelet flashing in the light of the interior lamps. "Oh, the devil. I sound heartless. I am sorry for him. But you'd think by his age he'd have learned to let a love affair die a graceful death."

"Anyone would think you didn't believe in love, Willie," Dorothée said, and then wondered at her own words, because she wasn't at all sure she believed in it herself.

Wilhelmine gripped the carriage strap as they rounded a corner. "Oh, *chérie*, of course I believe in it. I just don't expect it to last."

In an odd way, Dorothée found this idea even more disturbing. Silly. She wasn't as far removed as she'd like to think from the idealistic schoolgirl she'd been a few years ago. She wound the strings of her mask through her gloved fingers, and returned to the most dramatic events of the evening. "Tsar Alexander was furious at

Catherine Bagration when she told the story about Princess Tatiana's origins. I almost thought he was going to storm across the room and strike her."

"He can't abide being made a fool of." Wilhelmine adjusted the links of her bracelet.

"He has the temper of a man used to supreme power," Talleyrand said. "You'd be wise to remember that, Wilhelmine."

"I can look after myself. Though Tsar Alexander's temper is hardly any concern of mine."

"Is it not?" Talleyrand asked in a soft, polite voice.

The lamplight bounced off Talleyrand's hard gaze and Wilhelmine's defiant one as they jolted over a rut in the road. Dorothée studied her sister. She knew the tsar had called on Willie several times recently, often at the hour of eleven o'clock in the morning, which Willie had once reserved exclusively for Metternich. She had heard the rumors that her sister's relationship with the tsar had gone further. Some even whispered that the tsar had pressured Wilhelmine to end her affair with Metternich.

"Willie—" Dorothée said.

Wilhelmine let out a peal of laughter. "Oh, Doro, I always thought the good thing about your bookish side was that you were above listening to silly gossip. Tsar Alexander has a bevy of mistresses in Vienna, including Catherine Bagration and poor Princess Tatiana. But I'm not among their number."

Dorothée gripped the carriage strap. "That isn't why—"

"Why I quarreled with Princess Tatiana two days ago?" Wilhelmine flicked a glance at Talleyrand. "Doro walked in on Princess Tatiana and me being less than civil. No, that was about something else entirely, *ma chère*."

"Did it have to do with Tatiana's trade in art treasures?" Talleyrand inquired.

Wilhelmine's brows lifted, then she gave a faint smile. "Your store of knowledge still surprises me. I suppose there's no need to keep it secret, now that the Prince de Ligne blurted it out. I'd learned Princess Tatiana had come into possession of a casket that had belonged to our family for generations."

Dorothée's fingers froze on the carriage strap. "Princess Tatiana had the Courland casket?"

"Apparently." Wilhelmine's gaze flickered back to Talleyrand. "It was fashioned by Cellini. Legend has it that he created it for an Italian noblewoman called Maddalena Verano who helped him when he was imprisoned in the Castel Sant'Angelo."

"Supposedly for embezzling jewels from the pope's tiara," Dorothée put in, picking up the story long familiar from childhood. "Cellini claimed the charges were false."

"And when he eventually was freed, he gave the casket to Contessa Verano in gratitude," Wilhelmine said. "She later became the mistress of Gotthard von Kettler, the first Duke of Courland, and gave him the casket. It's been in our family ever since. Until it was lost in the wars."

"How on earth did Princess Tatiana end up with it?" Dorothée asked.

"I don't know." Wilhelmine smoothed the folds of her domino. "I made her what I thought a very handsome offer for it by any standards. She refused me. Needless to say, I was annoyed because the casket belongs back in the family. But I was hardly so annoyed I'd have killed the princess."

Dorothée sighed, relieved, and yet also troubled because Willie could have told her all this earlier. Why hadn't she? "And Tsar Alexander—?" Dorothée asked.

"I find him useful at the moment." Wilhelmine whipped the domino closed over her Carinthian costume. "For my own reasons."

Dorothée met her sister's armored gaze for a moment, then looked away to find that Talleyrand was watching Willie as well, his eyes narrowed. Dorothée knew the calculations that went on behind that gaze of her uncle's. Wilhelmine was hiding something. And Talleyrand knew it.

There was something unusually brittle in Wilhelmine's manner tonight. The tension of being Metternich's guest might account for some of it, but Willie had been in company with Prince Metternich a score of times since their love affair had ended. Was Wilhelmine's quarrel with Princess Tatiana as simple as an argument over purchasing back the Courland Cellini casket? And why on earth did Willie, who was fabulously wealthy and had her pick of men, need Tsar Alexander?

Dorothée rubbed her elbows. Even in her earliest memories, Wilhelmine had seemed thoroughly grown up, though thinking back, Willie would only have been a young teenager. They had never been close, but they had spent more time together these past weeks in Vienna. For the first time, Dorothée could almost think of her eldest sister as a friend. And yet in many ways she didn't know Wilhelmine at all.

Dorothée looked up to find Talleyrand's gaze had shifted to her. The appraising expression was gone from his eyes. They rested on her with a look that was carefully veiled. Yet behind that veil lay—She couldn't say what, precisely, save that it was something very different from the usual chess master's calculation in his eyes.

Confused, for reasons she didn't entirely understand, she smiled back, a little uncertain, and turned her gaze to the dark glass of the window.

This time it was Malcolm who opened the dressing room door to look in on their sleeping son. He stepped into the room, moving with the quiet that was second nature to him in his intelligence work, twitched the blanket smooth, touched his fingers lightly to Colin's forehead.

Suzanne watched from the doorway, her throat gone tight. Whatever uncertainties she had about Malcolm's feelings for her, his love for Colin was absolute. She moved to the dressing table and began to remove her gloves. As she peeled down the finely knitted silk, she recalled the pressure of Frederick Radley's hand on her own. Her gaze went back to the dressing room, her husband bending over their son. Despite the coals glowing in the porcelain stove, a chill shot through her at the cold reality of everything she had to lose.

Malcolm returned to their bedchamber and gave a crooked smile. "There's something about danger. I always need to reassure myself that he's all right."

"So do I." She moved Malcolm's shaving kit to the chest of drawers to make room on the dressing table. "Given the life we lead, that means we need to reassure ourselves pretty much every night."

She pulled out the comb that anchored her mantilla and folded the lace into careful squares. Malcolm went to the chest of drawers, picked up the bottle atop it that held the whisky he'd brought from Britain, and poured them each a glass.

She took a sip when he put the glass in her hand. The smoky bite took her back to her first visit to Scotland the previous summer. Granite cliffs, salt-tinged air, Malcolm at home in a way she had never seen before.

While he helped her undress, he told her about his talk with Fitz. Suzanne was grateful to be busy with tapes and laces and hairpins. Much easier not to meet her husband's gaze as they discussed the infidelity in the marriage of two of their closest friends.

"In the end, all I can really say is that Fitz doesn't have an alibi for the time of Tatiana's murder," Malcolm finished.

Suzanne wrapped her dressing gown over her nightdress and took a sip of whisky. "Princess Tatiana could have destroyed his marriage and his political prospects by revealing the affair. But why would she have done so?"

"Quite. But with Tatiana one can never be certain. Or they could have had a lover's quarrel."

"Malcolm, do you really think Fitz—"

"I don't. But I didn't suspect he was Tatiana's lover, either."

Suzanne perched on the edge of the bed, one arm curled round the bedpost, while Malcolm finished removing his grandee costume. "What do you think is in the papers Princess Tatiana had that Adam Czartoryski is desperate to recover? Love letters he wrote to Tsarina Elisabeth?"

"I suspect it's more than that." Malcolm tossed his coat over a chairback. "I've heard stories from Michael Langley, who was stationed in Russia in those days. Czartoryski's love affair with the tsarina was a fairly open secret twenty years ago. In essence, Czartoryski had been sent to the Russian court as a hostage. He was the main voice calling for Polish independence, and the Russian government feared he'd inspire an uprising if he returned home."

"This was before Alexander became tsar?"

"His grandmother, Catherine the Great, was still on the throne." Malcolm tossed his frilled shirt after the coat. "She died a year later, and Alexander's father, Paul, became tsar. Paul was a temperamental man with a violent streak. Alexander was a rebellious heir apparent. Czartoryski's idealism appealed to the side of Alexander that sees himself as a liberal reformer. The two became close friends."

"Until Czartoryski's affair with Elisabeth?"

"No, that's the interesting thing. Alexander was seeking consolation elsewhere and by all accounts didn't object to his young wife doing likewise."

Suzanne found herself remembering Frederick Radley's mocking gaze in the Metternichs' salon this evening. "Surprisingly broad-minded of him."

Malcolm stepped out of his breeches and reached for his nightshirt. "The affair went on for three years. Then Elisabeth gave birth to a baby girl. Her first child. At the christening, Tsar Paul commented on the wonder of two light-haired people producing a child with such dark hair and eyes."

Suzanne's fingers closed on the silk folds of her dressing gown. "And that ended Prince Czartoryski's residence at the Russian court?"

"He was packed off as ambassador to Sardinia." Malcolm shrugged his dressing gown on over his nightshirt. "As Michael Langley describes it, Alexander appeared to miss Czartoryski as much as Elisabeth did. Czartoryski returned to Russia two years later, when Alexander ascended to the throne. Before long he became chief minister. Langley worked closely with him, as Czartoryski's policies were anti-French and favored an alliance with Britain."

"And the affair with Elisabeth?"

"The tsarina is said to have been seeking consolation elsewhere by then. Czartoryski and the tsar did fall out, but over the Prussian policy, not the tsarina. And Czartoryski still advises Alexander."

Suzanne curled her feet up under her. She had seen a wide variety of marital relationships, but this triangle of the tsar, his best friend, and the tsarina was difficult to grasp. "What happened to the dark-haired child?"

"She died young, as did Alexander and Elisabeth's only other child."

Suzanne cast an involuntary glance at the closed dressing room door behind which Colin slept. "Tsarina Elisabeth has had a difficult life."

Malcolm's gaze flickered after her own. "Yes."

"And her relationship with Prince Czartoryski now?"

Malcolm picked up his whisky glass and looked thoughtfully into it for a moment. "I know no more than what is revealed by his gaze when he looks at her. Whatever the state of their relationship, his feelings are deeply engaged."

"But whatever secret these papers contain may have nothing to do with Czartoryski."

"Perhaps not." Malcolm moved to the bed and dropped down beside her, draping his arm round her shoulders.

She leaned into him, warmed by more than just the heat of his body. "I like Adam Czartoryski, Malcolm. He's always struck me as a decent man. But if he killed Princess Tatiana—Working with us would be a clever feint."

"I thought about that." His fingers moved against her shoulder. "But I can't see him killing Tatiana when she was the only one who could tell him where the tsarina's papers were."

"No, you're right, it doesn't make sense." Suzanne slid her own arm round him, the silk of his dressing gown soft beneath her fingers. "Count Otronsky asked me to waltz and posed some not too subtle questions about our arrival at Princess Tatiana's last night. I suspect the tsar sent him."

Malcolm's fingers stilled against her arm. "I wouldn't doubt it for a minute. The tsar seems to rely on Otronsky more than any of his other advisers these days."

"Malcolm." Her husband's heartbeat reassuringly steady beneath her ear, Suzanne sought for the best way to frame her next question. "Did you know Princess Tatiana wasn't really the daughter of Prince and Princess Sarasov?"

She felt his sharp intake of breath and the tension that ran across his shoulder blades. "No. Perhaps the one thing I never questioned about Tatiana's life was her origins."

Suzanne lifted her head from her husband's shoulder and studied him beneath the shadows of the canopy. Whatever Princess Tatiana had been to him, he made no secret of having cared for her. Surely to learn she hadn't been what he had thought could not but cause him distress. Yet his face was even more carefully armored than usual. A sign, perhaps, of just how deep his feelings ran. "Do you think Talleyrand arranged Princess Tatiana's new identity?" she asked. "Could she have been his agent even then?"

"It's possible." His voice was cool and appraising, but he kept his arm round her, which was oddly reassuring. "Tatiana would certainly have needed the help of someone as powerful—and wily—as he is."

"It seems a bit odd for him to arrange all that to get her into the Russian court, only to have her end up spending most of her time in Paris. But perhaps his objectives changed."

"And it would have been easier for her to infiltrate French society as a foreigner than with a counterfeit French identity."

Suzanne took a sip of whisky. "Do you think Princess Tatiana was really French?"

"Difficult to say. She was damnably skilled at accents. She could sound convincingly as though she came from a host of countries."

"Like you."

"And you." He lifted his hand from her shoulder and brushed his fingers against her cheek. Odd how his slightest touch could stir her. He leaned forward. She felt the warmth of his breath and caught the scent of whisky. For a moment she was sure he was going to kiss her. Instead, he drew back and asked, "What else did you learn tonight?"

She suppressed a sigh, unsure if it was the fact that they still had things to discuss or something else that had stopped him. "According to the Prince de Ligne, Princess Tatiana was selling looted art treasures."

Malcolm's eyes widened. "Good God."

"I think Wilhelmine of Sagan was negotiating to buy a piece

from Princess Tatiana. It seems almost insignificant next to everything else we've discovered—"

"But it's the seemingly insignificant things that may be vital clues. What—"

A discreet rap at the door made them both jump. Malcolm tied the sash on his dressing gown and went to the door. His valet, Addison, stood outside.

"I'm sorry, sir. Madam. But I thought you'd want to hear this at once."

"Of course." Malcolm stepped aside to allow Addison into the room.

Addison's normally immaculate shirt collar was limp and tinged gray, his pale blond hair fell over his forehead in uncharacteristic disarray, and he wore a corduroy jacket instead of one of his exquisitely cut coats. His costume for a night of information gathering.

"I spent most of the night—and the early morning—in a tavern with three footmen employed at houses near the Palm Palace," he explained.

Malcolm's eyes narrowed. "Yes?"

"There was a great deal of speculation. One of them saw a gentleman go in through the side entrance about three in the morning, who must have been Tsar Alexander or you, sir. Another saw a cloaked lady arrive, and swore it was just before the clock struck three. I assume that was Mrs. Rannoch."

Suzanne nodded.

Addison drew a breath, a rare sign of unease. "But the third footman says he saw a gentleman go into the house much earlier in the evening. About twelve-thirty."

Malcolm cast a glance at Suzanne. Too early even to be Adam Czartoryski.

"The gentleman stopped beneath a street lamp, and the footman got a glimpse of his face. Apparently he'd seen the man go up the side stairs to Princess Tatiana's room before." Addison hesitated. A shadow of concern flickered over his usually impassive face. "The footman swears it was Lord Fitzwilliam Vaughn."

❧ 14 ❧

One advantage of being at an international peace conference where the fate of nations hangs in the balance is that no one looks askance if one bangs on doors in the middle of the night. Malcolm rapped on the door of Fitz and Eithne's room. Not as hard as he would have liked, but hard enough to wake any sleepers.

Fitz opened the door, dressing gown open over his nightshirt, eyes wide with confusion. "What's happened?"

"We need to talk." Malcolm jerked his head down the passage.

Fitz gave a quick nod. "It's all right, darling, go back to sleep," he called over his shoulder to Eithne.

Malcolm strode down the passage to the sitting room appropriated by the attachés. A litter of papers covered the desk in the center of the room and the smells of ink and brandy hung in the air. He set his candle down on a table near the door. Then he grabbed Fitz by the throat and slammed his friend against the door panels.

"Did you kill her?"

"Of course not." Fitz's voice was a choked rasp. "I told you—"

"You lied to me."

"I didn't—"

"You bastard." Malcolm tightened his grip. "You were seen going into Tatiana's rooms last night."

Fitz's shoulders went slack beneath Malcolm's hands. "God in heaven."

"Do you deny it?"

In the flickering light of the single candle, Fitz's gaze held not fear or anger but sick horror. "What's the use?" He sounded more exhausted than a soldier after a fortnight's siege.

Malcolm loosed his grip and took a step back. "What happened?"

Fitz scraped his hands over his face but made no attempt to move away from the door. "I did come home and go to work on a white paper on the Saxon situation. In this room." He cast a glance round the sitting room. "I was sitting at that desk, drinking a pot of coffee I'd sent for to counteract a night of brandy and champagne, when the footman brought in her note."

"Don't tell me she wanted you to call at three in the morning along with the rest of us."

"No. She just said she needed to see me at once." His gaze went to the flowered porcelain stove in the corner. "I burned the letter and ground up the ashes. I wish—" A spasm of pain gripped his eyes. "That was the last letter I had from her."

"And then?" Malcolm kept his gaze trained on his friend's face.

Fitz drew a harsh breath. "When I got to the Palm Palace Tatiana was—distressed."

"About?"

"Look, Malcolm—" Fitz moved away from the door, paced over to the desk, turned back to face Malcolm. "I know my lying to you is unconscionable. But the truth is, I didn't want to have to tell you this." His hand clenched on the desktop. "After everything else that happened, I couldn't bear to tarnish her memory."

"Christ, Fitz. Tatiana was one of the most pragmatic people I've ever met. She'd care more about us discovering who killed her than she would for her reputation."

Fitz cast a glance at the sheets of scribbled-over, hot-pressed paper on the desk, as though they held the answer to how to frame his story. "Tatiana was—I don't think Kirsanov left her very comfortably situated."

"Not given the circles in which she moved."

"Quite. A woman like Wilhelmine of Sagan could purchase a country with the wave of her hand. It can't have been easy for Tatiana to make her way in that world. If you look at her actions in that light—"

"Fitz, are you trying to tell me Tatiana was selling looted art treasures?"

Fitz's widened eyes gleamed white in the blue-black shadows. "What have you heard?"

"Rumors."

Fitz picked up a tinderbox from the desktop. It took three tries of his shaky hands to light one of the tapers in the candelabrum on the desk. "Tatiana had come into possession of a number of valuable pieces."

"Where did she get them?"

"I didn't ask." Fitz lit the second taper. "But I assume—"

"From various of her lovers."

The third taper flamed to life. "You don't seem surprised."

"I had no notion it was going on until I heard the rumors tonight. But I'm not surprised Tatiana would do such a thing."

The candle flame flared in Fitz's eyes. "You wrong her."

"Hardly, since it seems it's precisely what she was doing. Tatiana was very good at looking after herself." Malcolm strode forward so the angle of the candlelight gave him a better view of Fitz's face. "When did you learn of it?"

"The night she died." Fitz passed a hand over his eyes. "God, was it only last night?"

"What made her tell you?"

"When I got to the Palm Palace she was upset. She'd just had a terrible scene with the Duchess of Sagan."

"Relating to the art treasures?"

"Apparently Tatiana had a silver casket that had belonged to the Courland family. Wilhelmine of Sagan had learned somehow that it was in Tatiana's possession and tried to buy it from her."

"They couldn't agree on a price?"

"Tatiana didn't want to sell it."

"She thought she could get more for it elsewhere?"

"She said she wouldn't part with it under any circumstances.

She said it had value to her beyond mere coin." Fitz stared at the candle flame. "I can only assume the value had to do with whoever had given it to her."

"She didn't tell you who that was?"

"No. And it seemed indelicate to ask. Apparently the Duchess of Sagan had tried to buy it from her the day before, and they'd quarreled. Dorothée Périgord arrived and cut the scene short. Last night, Wilhelmine of Sagan called on Tatiana and demanded she hand over the piece. Tatiana said they had a dreadful quarrel. I'd never seen her so shaken."

"What time did you leave?"

"A bit after one. I heard the clock striking a quarter after when I returned to the Minoritenplatz. I'd have stayed longer, but she told me it was too risky. If only I had stayed—"

"I suspect she sent you away on purpose."

"Because she'd summoned the rest of you at three in the morning?"

Malcolm nodded.

"And in the interval between my leaving and your arrival someone killed her."

"So it seems."

"You mean, assuming I'm telling the truth." Fitz met Malcolm's gaze. Perhaps it was a trick of the flickering light, but his face looked sharper and harder than usual. "I told myself I kept it secret to protect Tatiana's memory. But the truth is, I knew what you'd think if you knew I'd been with her last night."

"You assumed I'd rush to judgment."

"You've already twice accused me of killing her, Malcolm."

Their gazes locked. Friendships were delicate things, built slowly, carefully nurtured through the years, shaped into something precious. And like fine crystal, they could be smashed in an instant.

Suzanne helped herself to a pastry from the sideboard, mostly to keep her hands busy. She hadn't seemed to be hungry for the past two days, though she knew from experience the necessity of continuing to eat.

Behind her, she heard the rhythmic click of a spoon against a cup as Eithne, the only other occupant of the breakfast parlor, stirred her coffee. Suzanne stared down at the pink-flowered porcelain of her plate, searching for small talk to get them through the meal.

"I must have had a dozen people commiserate with me at the ball last night on not being among those invited to Princess Tatiana's funeral," Eithne said. "As though it were the social event of the season."

"It's rather ghoulish. But not unexpected." Suzanne added a dollop of currant preserves to her plate.

"I own to a craven relief you and Malcolm are going instead of Fitz and me."

Suzanne reached for the butter, feeling the weight of the coming event press on her shoulders. "I can't say I'm precisely looking forward to it."

"You know, don't you?" Eithne said.

Suzanne set down the butter dish and spun around. "I beg your pardon?"

Eithne returned her spoon to the gilt-rimmed saucer. "That Fitz was Princess Tatiana's lover."

Suzanne, who prided herself on her skill at dissembling, stared into her friend's seemingly guileless Wedgwood blue eyes. "Eithne—"

Eithne lifted her cup and took a careful, precise sip of coffee. "As soon as I knew you and Malcolm were looking into the murder, I was sure you'd learn the truth. Poor Fitz should have realized it as well."

Suzanne moved to the table. "Dearest—How long—"

"Almost from the beginning." Eithne returned the cup to its saucer. The porcelain barely rattled, but her knuckles were white.

Words, which usually sprang easily to Suzanne's lips, seemed to have quite deserted her. She had seen her family killed, had nursed dying soldiers, had confronted her husband over the body of the woman who might be his mistress. But the bleak despair in her friend's gaze was uncharted territory.

She dropped into a chair across the table from Eithne. "I'm so sorry—"

"It was the day of the expedition to the Klosterneuburg abbey," Eithne said. "I stayed in town for a dress fitting—God, how the most trivial detail can come back to haunt one. When Fitz came home that evening, I could tell something was different. I could almost feel it in his lips when he kissed me." She put a hand to her mouth. "A little too insistent and yet at the same time surprisingly detached. Strange how much one can tell from a kiss."

"It's one way couples communicate." For a moment, Suzanne had an intense memory of Malcolm's lips against her own in the pianoforte maker's darkened shop.

"And one way couples lie," Eithne said, with a cynicism Suzanne had never before heard in her friend's dulcet voice. "When I watched Fitz kiss Princess Tatiana's hand at a ball at the Hofburg two nights later, I was sure."

Suzanne reached across the table and laid her hand over Eithne's own. Her friend's skin was ice-cold.

"I used to think we were safe." Eithne's voice cracked, like a pianoforte when a wire snaps. "I remember watching Princess Metternich's face while Prince Metternich waltzed with the Duchess of Sagan and thinking how dreadful her situation was. I was so secure in my own marriage, I could be magnanimous with my pity. Oh, I knew things had changed a bit between us through the years. I told myself one couldn't live in that mad, passionate state forever. He had his work to focus on, I had the children. He's been thinking so much about standing for Parliament. I actually thought Vienna would be good for us. I knew he'd be busy, but with Will and Bella at home, I thought we'd have more time for each other. A sort of second honeymoon. Dear God, I'm a fool."

"Eithne." Suzanne tightened her grip on her friend's hand. "Fitz is the one who committed the betrayal. You have nothing to reproach yourself with."

"And yet I can't stop going over every detail and wondering where we went wrong. In some deep corner of my mind I suppose I always knew it was a possibility. How could you live in our world and not?"

"Does Fitz—?"

"I don't think he has the least idea I know. Men are frequently ten steps behind their wives when it comes to understanding these things." Eithne studied Suzanne, her gaze flat and cold and at the same time filled with pain. "A wife always knows, don't you find?"

"I'm not sure." Suzanne's chest tightened as though a knife had cut through her corset to twist between her ribs. "Perhaps I don't have your instincts. Or perhaps I don't know Malcolm as well as you know Fitz."

"Or perhaps you haven't had to face betrayal."

Yet. The unspoken word hung in the air between them. "Betrayal rather depends on one's expectations going into the marriage. Malcolm and I made a bargain. You and Fitz made a love match."

Eithne twisted the heavy gold of her wedding band round her finger. "I thought so. But that was when I believed in love. Or believed it was something permanent. Fitz must have loved Princess Tatiana. He's not a man who'd stray without that. Do you know what's odd? When I heard she'd been killed, my first thought was 'poor Fitz, this will be beastly for him.'"

"You still love him."

"A part of me remembers the time I did." Eithne picked up her coffee cup, then set it down untasted. "I said I thought we were safe, but the truth is, there's no such thing as a marriage that's safe. I'm not sure there's such a thing as a marriage that's happy. Not under the surface. When it comes down to it, they're all bargains, even if dressed up in roses and lace veils and cakes from Gunter's."

Suzanne swallowed. Why, when she prided herself on her lack of illusions, did Eithne's words send a chill to her soul?

"You can't help but wonder, of course," Eithne added. "I knew that the moment I learned Princess Tatiana had been killed."

"Wonder?"

"If Fitz killed her." Eithne reached for her cup again and this time took a sip with careful deliberation. "Or if I did."

15

Annina looked up at Malcolm as he slid into a chair across from her at a table in the back room of Café Hugel. "You must have just come from the funeral."

"Yes." The image of the open casket was burned in his memory.

Annina rubbed at a lip-rouge smear on her cup of mocha. "I couldn't go. Admission by invitation only, and all the spots saved for dignitaries."

"It wasn't about Tatiana." Malcolm could still feel the artificial press of the hot air in the room. "Not the real Tatiana. She was gone the night before last. This was a public show. People were there to speculate about Tania and gape at those close to her. Though that didn't stop Tsar Alexander from weeping. I think Metternich did as well, though less openly."

"Did you?" Annina asked.

"Not at the funeral."

Annina met his eyes in a moment of understanding. Her own were still red. "You didn't ask me here to talk about the funeral. What have you learned?"

A waiter set a cup of coffee before Malcolm. He took a measured sip. "Did you know Tatiana was selling looted art treasures?"

Her dark blue eyes widened. "I'd have told you."

"Would you?"

"Why keep it secret now?"

"Perhaps because you wanted to sell them yourself."

Annina gave a harsh laugh. "I might have done, at that. If I'd known about them. But that's a secret she'd have thought too dangerous to share with me." She jabbed a strand of hair behind her ear. "Where did she get these art treasures?"

"I was hoping you could tell me. From one of her lovers? Or more than one?"

Annina took a sip from her cup of mocha. "The tsar and Prince Metternich gave her the occasional bit of jewelry, but I can't see them giving her art treasures to sell off, no matter how besotted they were."

"Surely there were others. What about before her involvement with the tsar last spring?"

"I told you, I didn't know the name of every—" She broke off, gaze appraising. "Gregory Lindorff."

"From the Russian delegation?"

"He came to Paris with Tsar Alexander, as a military aide. I heard him boasting one night about the riches he'd seen as the Russian army moved across the Continent."

Malcolm had caught a brief glimpse of Lindorff at the funeral. His normally carefree face had seemed uncharacteristically gaunt. "He was Tatiana's lover?"

"I think so. In Paris, last spring. Before her affair with the tsar began. She was having difficulties with her creditors at about that time, and then suddenly she paid them all off and ordered a new wardrobe. So the timing would fit." Annina cast a quick glance round the café. The back room was mostly empty, but she leaned closer to him. "Do you think someone is looking for these bits of art?"

"Why?"

"I woke last night, and I was sure I could hear someone moving about in the princess's bedchamber. I got up and went to look—" She caught Malcolm's frown. "Yes, I know. But I took a knife with me. In any case, by the time I got to her room it was empty. So were her boudoir and the rest of the apartments. But the latch on the bedchamber window wasn't secured, and I'd swear I'd checked it before I went to bed."

"Was anything taken?"

"I don't think so."

"Did you notice any unusual paintings or sculptures or other artwork in the last few months? Or anything she had locked up?"

Annina fingered a fold of her shawl, a fringed blue silk that had once belonged to Tatiana. "She was always adding new bits and pieces to her rooms and then changing things about when a new decorating style came into vogue. Remember when she had everything Egyptian? One of the times you paid us a secret visit in Paris. And then it was all Greek or Roman or something a bit later. But there were some paintings last spring that didn't seem the sort of thing she'd normally have chosen. I remember one in particular. A man and a woman with a small child. They wore dark, old-fashioned clothes. The lady had full skirts and a ruff that stood up at the back and the gentleman had a plumed hat. I kept staring at the way the light fell across their faces. The fabric of their clothes seemed to shimmer."

It sounded very like a Rubens.

Annina reached for her cup. "She took them down or got rid of them before we came to Vienna."

"Anything she might have kept hidden?"

"Not that I know of."

"Did you ever see a silver casket?"

Annina frowned. "No, nothing like that."

"And her box of secret papers. Where might she have hidden that?"

Annina shook her head.

"At least one person thinks I'm in possession of it."

"Who?" Annina set her cup down with a clatter.

Malcolm drew a breath of the coffee-scented air. "That's what I'm trying to discover."

The smell of sweat hung in the air as Malcolm stepped into the Fogelmann's Fencing Academy. A foil clanged against another. A lithe, agile man with tawny hair showing beneath his fencer's mask parried his opponent's attack, disengaged his blade with a whir and scrape, and danced to the side. He moved with controlled violence. Fighting off the emotions stirred by Tatiana's funeral? As his opponent moved in for a fresh attack, the tawny-haired man darted under his guard and touched him on the chest, just over his heart.

"My point, I think. Good match, Esterhazy." The tawny-haired man tugged off his mask to reveal the angular features of Count Gregory Lindorff. He strolled to the edge of the floor and grabbed a towel to drape round his neck.

"My compliments," Malcolm said. "That was neatly done."

"Rannoch." Lindorff returned his blade to a waiting attendant and regarded Malcolm with raised brows. "Don't usually see you here. Heard you were going to take part in the Carrousel tomorrow. But that's lances, not rapiers."

"Still hand-eye coordination. But I came in search of you, as it happens. Could I have a word?"

Lindorff's eyes narrowed, but he merely said, "There's a tavern across the way. I don't know about you, but I could do with a glass of beer."

Lindorff said little more until he had donned his coat and they had crossed the street and were settled on oak benches in the tavern with tankards of Bavarian beer. The sound of a zither playing a ländler filled the air. Music was everywhere in Vienna, even taverns.

Lindorff took a long swallow and regarded Malcolm over the rim of his tankard. "I can guess why you're here, of course."

Malcolm took a drink from his own tankard. Lindorff had always struck him as one of the quickest of the Russian delegation. "Why?"

"Tatiana. What else can any of us think or talk or even dream about these last two days?"

"I hadn't known," Malcolm said.

"About Tatiana and me?" Lindorff leaned back against the slats of the bench. "No, I flatter myself we were reasonably discreet. Who told you?"

"Annina."

"Difficult to hide one's dalliances from a maid or valet." Lindorff's voice was light, but for a moment the sunlight slanting through the thick glass of the tavern windows caught a weight of grief in his eyes. "It was never very serious. It was never meant to be very serious. But she was an extraordinary woman."

"And you took it more seriously than you intended?"

"Probably." Lindorff reached for his tankard and stared into the depths. "Perhaps it's as well the tsar took an interest in her before I could make a complete fool of myself. And you?"

The look in Lindorff's eyes brought Tatiana vividly to life. For a moment Malcolm almost fancied he could smell the tuberose of her scent over the sour beer and fried sausages that filled the tavern's air. "Tatiana meant a great deal to me."

"Words that cover a multitude of sins."

And when it came to Tatiana, his sins would live with him forever, as would his memories. Malcolm took a swallow of beer and decided a bold feint was the only way to force his opponent out from under cover. "You must have cared for her a great deal yourself. You passed a fortune on to her."

"A fortune?" Lindorff threw back his head with a shout of laughter. "My dear Rannoch, I'm a third son of a family who are still considered Swedish upstarts by people like the Otronskys, even if we have lived in Russia and served the tsars for three generations. Three generations with a weakness for gaming and bad luck at the tables. I don't have a fortune myself, let alone one to pass on to a lover, however cherished."

"I was referring to the art treasures you acquired in the Russian army's advance on Paris."

Lindorff pushed back his bench, scraping it against the floorboards. "How the devil do you know about that?" His voice was as taut as a rapier blade.

"My dear Lindorff, you weren't the only one to profit from looting. I have little interest in exposing your actions, and I'd look the worst sort of hypocrite, given the number of my countrymen who made off with loot at Vitoria."

Lindorff's gaze skimmed over his face, as though scanning enemy terrain for snipers. "Why bring it up, then?"

"You cared for Tatiana, that's plain. I would think you'd want to learn who killed her."

"You think this is connected to who killed her?"

"Anything Tatiana was involved in may be connected to the reason she was murdered."

Lindorff cast a quick glance round the tavern and leaned across the table. "To own the truth, I wasn't sure what to do with them. Tatiana knew. How to sell them discreetly. At least she told me she knew. Dear Christ, do you really think that's why she was killed?"

"Even if it was, it doesn't make it your fault. Guilt isn't good for problem solving. How many art pieces were there?"

"I don't remember exactly. A dozen. Fifteen perhaps. Some small paintings and statues. Jeweled snuff boxes. Nothing very large."

"Where did she keep them?"

"In her rooms. Some of the paintings and statues she had out in plain sight."

"A medieval Spanish dagger that she kept in her salon?"

"Yes, that was one of the pieces, she—Oh God." Horror shot through Lindorff's gaze. "Was that—"

"If it hadn't been in her salon, the murderer would have made use of something else."

Lindorff turned his tankard between his hands. "One can't but wonder."

Malcolm shut his mind to his own memories of congealing blood and cold flesh. "There was a silver casket that had belonged to the Courland family."

"That—" Lindorff bit back whatever he had been going to say. "I remember it."

"Do you have any idea why Tatiana would have refused to sell it?"

Lindorff shook his head. "Not unless the price was too low."

"Wilhelmine of Sagan offered her a great deal for it. Tatiana refused to sell at any price."

"Odd. She wasn't a sentimental type."

"Could it have had a special meaning for her?"

"What sort of meaning?"

"Perhaps it was one of the last of the treasures left?"

"You mean as a remembrance of me?" Lindorff gave a laugh sharp with irony. "It's an appealing thought. But—No."

"You sound very sure."

Lindorff looked up at Malcolm as though to give a quick denial, then took a drink, his gaze on the beer-stained wood of the table.

"There's something special about that piece, isn't there?" Malcolm said.

Lindorff glanced round the tavern again, as though to reassure himself that the other occupants were busy with dice and newspapers and conversation. Then he spoke quickly in a lowered voice. "That particular piece didn't come from me. If she treasured it as a memory of a lover, it was a memory of a different man."

"Who?"

"You don't know?" Lindorff scanned his face for a moment. "Odd. I thought of all her lovers she shared the most with you." He wiped a trace of condensation from the side of his tankard. "I only had a brief time with Tatiana, snatched between her liaisons with two great men. If I hadn't caught her at the right moment, I doubt she'd have looked twice at me."

"You said your liaison with her ended because of the tsar. And before you met her—"

Lindorff looked up and met his gaze. "Before she became entangled with me, Tatiana had been the lover of Napoleon Bonaparte."

❧ 16 ❧

The sweet strains of the zither echoed in Malcolm's head, like an insistent fact he should have seen. Bloody hell. Even from beyond the grave Tania's secrets could chill him to the bone.

Lindorff's gaze glinted with mockery. "Don't look so shocked, Rannoch. Knowing Tatiana, can you be surprised she caught Bonaparte's eye?"

"Hardly. But surprised that—"

"She didn't tell you?" A smile curved Lindorff's mouth. "She was a woman of secrets. If it's any comfort, I don't imagine a lot of people knew this one. Bonaparte was very concerned not to cause any ripples in his marriage to Marie-Louise at the time."

"But Tatiana confided in you?"

"I was rather in a position to be confided in at the time the affair ended. The new person who happens to be across the pillow usually is."

A dozen questions raced through Malcolm's mind, most of which he couldn't put to Lindorff. "Why did the affair end?"

"It would have been difficult for it to continue with Bonaparte on Elba and Tatiana in Paris."

"So they were lovers up until Napoleon's abdication and exile?"

"As Tatiana tells—told—it." Grief shot through Lindorff's eyes at the reminder she was gone.

"And she told you straight out that Bonaparte gave her the Courland casket?"

"With no prevarication. It was the one keepsake she had of him. Come to think of it, it was after she showed it to me that I told her about the trifles I'd—er—acquired during the war. She quite adroitly put the idea in my head. Damned clever woman."

"Did she display the Courland casket openly?"

"No, she kept it in a chest in her rooms. I suspect she knew even then the sort of fuss the Duchess of Sagan would kick up if she knew Tatiana had it."

"So I can imagine."

Lindorff stared at him for a moment. "See here, Rannoch. Wilhelmine of Sagan's a strong-minded woman who doesn't like to crossed. But surely you don't think she'd kill over a bit of silver, however long it had been in her family."

Malcolm drained the last of his tankard. "Who's to say why anyone kills? Armies regularly do so over a little patch of ground."

"And then a final curtsy." Dorothée observed the *belles d'amour* as they completed the minuet that was to open the ball after the Carrousel. "Perfect. Suzanne? How does it look from the left?"

"Lovely," Suzanne said from her vantage point across the room. "Marie, you're in the lead. Make sure you signal with your arm a bit to cue the other ladies."

Marie Metternich, Prince Metternich's pretty, bright-eyed seventeen-year-old daughter, nodded as though the Carrousel was the most important matter at hand. Which, at the moment, it was.

"Be sure to return your veils to the attendants," Dorothée said. "You should all have your gowns by now. Let me know if there have been any difficulties." She crossed to Suzanne and her sister Wilhelmine. "I need to check on how the gentlemen are progressing in the riding school. Wait for me? I'll need reassurance when this is over."

As the other ladies milled about, returning their veils to attendants and exchanging comments about the performance tomorrow night, Suzanne and Wilhelmine of Sagan moved into an anteroom that had been set aside with refreshments.

"Poor Doro. She's quite brilliant at this. Far more organized than I am. But I'm afraid she's going to make herself ill." Wilhelmine moved to a table that held a decanter of pale gold wine. "A glass of wine, Madame Rannoch? I think we've earned it."

"Thank you." Suzanne sank down upon a tapestry settee. "In truth, I've been hoping for a moment to converse with you."

"For reasons that aren't entirely social, I imagine."

"What makes you think that?"

The duchess poured two glasses of wine. "My dear Madame Rannoch. I may not have the best sources of information at the Congress, but I would be a sad failure if I didn't know your husband is investigating Princess Tatiana's murder."

Suzanne plumped the settee cushions. "Baron Hager is investigating Princess Tatiana's murder."

"Officially."

"You can scarcely expect me to comment on anything unofficial."

"You're a good diplomatic wife, Madame Rannoch." Wilhelmine crossed the room in a stir of muslin and Valenciennes lace and put a glass of wine into Suzanne's hand.

Suzanne took a sip. From Alsace. Light, fruity, yet dry. Airy and elegant, like the duchess. But the duchess's defenses were so well constructed that her gauzy gown and sarcenet spencer and filmy scarf might have been plate armor. Suzanne decided on an attack direct. "I know you quarreled with Princess Tatiana over the Courland casket."

Wilhelmine of Sagan sank into a chair across from Suzanne, her own glass held negligently between two fingers. "Oh dear. I should have known it wouldn't remain secret. I know poor Doro overheard us, though I don't think she realized what the subject was. Quarrels are so vulgar. You'd think I'd have learned not to lose my temper."

"Her refusal must have been very provoking."

"Exceedingly. The casket is a Courland heirloom. I was quite prepared to pay her for it, though I'm sure she didn't come by it honestly."

"And so you went back to demand it of her again the night she died."

Wilhelmine went still. "Who told you that?"

"Someone the princess confided in later that evening."

"So you know the princess was alive when I left her rooms."

"I never suggested otherwise."

Wilhelmine took a sip of wine. "Dorothée had cut our discussion short. I thought I could reason with the princess."

"But she still refused."

"She said nothing would compel her to give up the casket."

Suzanne took a sip from her own glass. "Was Princess Tatiana wearing her locket when you saw her?"

"Her locket?" The duchess blinked at this turn of the conversation. "She had a cameo necklace on—"

"Earlier in the evening she was wearing a gold locket as well, perhaps tucked into the bodice of her gown. Apparently she always wore it. But it was missing when we found her after the murder."

Wilhelmine frowned. "I can't be sure—No, I do remember something gold round her throat. It glinted when she stood by the candles. I was surprised because she was wearing the cameos." The duchess shook her head. "Odd to remember that when I was in such a temper."

"It must have been particularly trying to have her refuse your offer when she was quite prepared to sell other pieces. I can understand why you lost your temper."

Wilhelmine settled back in her chair. "But now, of course, you're wondering if I went back that night and killed her over it."

"That would be a rather extreme reaction."

"Someone had an extreme reaction to something Princess Tatiana did. And if I read your husband correctly, he won't let the matter rest until he discovers the truth." The duchess regarded Suzanne, her head tilted to one side, her dark gold ringlets falling with artful abandon about her face. "It can't have been easy watching him with Princess Tatiana. The intimacy was obvious."

Suzanne took another sip of wine, holding her fingers steady.

"I'm hardly the only woman in Vienna whose husband demonstrates intimacy with another woman."

The duchess shook her head. "My dear child. You're really very young, aren't you? And I suspect you care for your husband far more than you'll admit, perhaps even to yourself."

"There are all sorts of caring. And all sorts of marriages."

The duchess gave a dry laugh. "I should know, I've had two of them. Louis de Rohan married me for my dowry and was quite content to live on my money until I decided it would be less expensive to get rid of him. You'd think I'd have learned my lesson, but after the divorce I made the same mistake with Prince Troubetskoi. So handsome, but he proves all the clichés about Russians being grim and depressing. Divorces are shockingly expensive. I've finally learned that it's much more sensible to simply take lovers."

"A luxury not all women can afford."

"True. I'm blessed with a substantial fortune of my own. You, I believe, were not in a similar position when you married."

"No." Suzanne slammed the shutters closed on a host of memories. "I lost my family in the war in Spain."

"I'm sorry for it." Compassion, warm and seemingly genuine, flashed in the duchess's dark eyes. "I can well imagine how you'd have accepted any marriage offer made to you in such a situation. But you appear to believe in your husband as only a young romantic can."

"Believe me, Duchess, I went into my marriage with my eyes open."

Wilhelmine twirled the fluted stem of her wineglass between her fingers. "Have you seen Mozart's *Così fan tutte*? That aria of Dorabella's, 'È amore un ladroncello.' Calling love a thief is perhaps the most accurate description I've ever heard."

"*Così* rather questions whether love exists at all," Suzanne said. "Something I've done myself on more than one occasion."

"On the contrary. *Così* acknowledges that love is delightful, so long as one doesn't take it too seriously. Or make the fatal mistake of expecting it to last."

The duchess's light words nicked beneath the lacing of Suzanne's corset. Wilhelmine of Sagan was a master of verbal fencing. It was past time to deflect the attack. "Is that what happened between you and Prince Metternich? Boredom?"

Wilhelmine shrugged. "Adoration sounds delightful, but it can become smothering. People change."

"And yet you left him to return to an old lover."

For a moment the worldly ennui in Wilhelmine's eyes softened. Her mouth curved in a rueful smile. "I never claimed to be consistent. I suppose I never properly got over Alfred von Windischgrätz. Which is odd, because so often as soon as one achieves the object of one's affections, the attraction begins to pall."

"And the tsar?"

Wilhelmine pulled the sky blue folds of her scarf about her shoulders. "Tsar Alexander is not my lover. But he's a prime example of a man who grows bored once the conquest has been achieved. Princess Bagration is learning that. Princess Tatiana would have learned it soon enough." The duchess regarded Suzanne for a moment, her gaze sharp but not unkind. "I suspect part of the reason your husband continues to fascinate you is that you've never been entirely sure of his affections."

Suzanne took a sip of wine, a little too quickly. "My husband never made me any promises."

"Which only makes him all the more elusive and intriguing. Falling in love with a spouse is dangerous. When one happens to be married to the object of one's affections, one is rather compelled to wallow in the ashes after the fire burns out."

"That assumes the fire was there to begin with."

"Oh, I think I've observed you with your husband enough to be confident of that."

Suzanne fixed her gaze on the pale wine in her glass. Clever fingers teasing her skin, the heat of his mouth meeting her own, the ragged scrape of his breath. Whatever her marriage was, she couldn't claim it was cold.

"I applaud your good sense in helping him with his investigation of Princess Tatiana's murder," Wilhelmine continued. "A lesser woman would have turned shrewish."

Suzanne forced her fingers not to tighten on her glass. "Like

Malcolm, I want to learn the truth of what happened to Princess Tatiana."

"Truth's a difficult commodity to come by in Vienna. Though at least you've managed to learn the rather prosaic reason for my quarrel with the princess."

Suzanne stared down at the tufted silk cushions. "To own the truth, I'm wondering if there's more to it."

"You don't think Princess Tatiana's intransigence is enough to explain our quarrel? I told you I have a tendency to lose my temper."

Suzanne leaned forward, her gaze fixed on the duchess's own. "I know you have no cause to confide in me. But would it change things if I told you we have reason to believe a box of Princess Tatiana's private papers is missing from her lodgings?"

Wilhelmine of Sagan's glass tumbled from her fingers and shattered on the Turkey carpet at her feet.

"I thought so," Suzanne said. "She was in possession of information that concerns you? Letters?"

"I said nothing of the sort." Wilhelmine brushed her hand over the spilled wine on her skirt.

"Not in so many words." Suzanne set her glass down on a porcelain-tiled side table. "Duchess—My husband has every intention of finding this box of papers. Knowing Malcolm, he is likely to succeed. I can be of more assistance to you if I know what you're afraid of."

"Why should you wish to be of assistance to me?"

"I don't like the idea of anyone's private miseries being used as capital."

The duchess's laugh was like the snap of crystal. "Private miseries are the coin of the realm in Vienna. In most European courts. Surely you've learned that?"

"I don't have to agree with it. Nor does Malcolm."

"Your husband wouldn't have survived this long in the diplomatic corps if he hadn't learned to put information to use." Wilhelmine reached down to pick up the pieces of broken crystal, then muttered a curse. Blood spurted from her finger.

Suzanne crossed the room and dropped down beside Wilhelmine's chair. She pressed her handkerchief into the duchess's hand. "The sooner we learn why Princess Tatiana was killed, the sooner people will stop asking questions."

Wilhelmine stared at the handkerchief for a moment as though she could not make sense of what to do with it, then wrapped it round her finger with an almost vicious tug. "You're either hopelessly naïve or a bare-faced liar, Madame Rannoch. Some questions never go away. And some truths are more destructive than cannon fire."

Malcolm had two hours to observe Prince Talleyrand across the conference table during a meeting at the Austrian chancellery about the Polish situation. Adam Czartoryski, speaking for the tsar, reiterated Russia's determination to turn the majority of Polish territory into a kingdom of Poland. A kingdom that, naturally, would pay fealty to Russia. Czartoryski was less arrogant than Tsar Alexander or Count Otronsky, but that only made him seem more implacable. Not by so much as a flicker of an eye did he betray the alliance he had made with Malcolm, who sat beside Castlereagh, busily taking notes.

When the official meeting broke up and Castlereagh was talking with Metternich and Prussian chancellor Hardenberg, it was a simple matter for Malcolm to meet Talleyrand's gaze and glance toward the pedimented white door to an anteroom. It was more of a surprise that Talleyrand followed him.

Malcolm closed the anteroom door and regarded the French foreign minister, the man who had served Napoleon Bonaparte and now served the French king, the man he had known since he was a child. "Did you set Tatiana to seduce Napoleon Bonaparte?"

Talleyrand's strong brows lifted. "My dear Malcolm. Your imagination is beginning to run away with you."

"Which part is imaginary?"

Talleyrand's walking stick thudded against the parquet floor. He moved to a high-backed chair and sank into it without haste. "If you think I had any control over Tatiana in recent years, let alone over whom she took as a lover—"

"So you admit Bonaparte was her lover?" Malcolm moved away from the door to face Talleyrand.

"Why should it be up to me to admit it? You seemed very sure in your initial accusation."

"You were in Paris. You'd have seen them together. You can't tell me you wouldn't have known."

Talleyrand smoothed his frilled cuff. "The wonder is that she didn't catch Bonaparte's eye sooner. But then there was Marie Waleska and Mademoiselle Georges, and the quarrels and reconciliations with Josephine. At last I suppose the timing was right. Marie-Louise threw a tantrum over his continued visits to Josephine, and her jealousy was enough to make his eye wander elsewhere."

"It would have been a convenient time for you to have a source close to Bonaparte."

"Because I wasn't in his favor myself at the time? Yes, I suppose it would. It would have been quite clever. If I'd thought of it."

"Did Tatiana communicate with Bonaparte after he was sent to Elba?"

Talleyrand leaned against the chairback, his ringed fingers relaxed on the arms. "You know as well as I do how carefully Bonaparte's communications are monitored."

"And who better than a mistress to smuggle secret information to him."

"My dear boy." Talleyrand's voice was bland as cambric tea, but his gaze turned even more hawk-like than usual. "What you're accusing me of would be treason."

"Damn it, sir, you've been playing all sides of every question since before I was born."

"And knowing me as you do, you can't possibly have expected me to answer this particular question. So why ask it?"

"Because I wanted to observe your reaction."

Talleyrand regarded him from beneath hooded lids. "What did my reaction tell you?"

"That I was a great deal nearer the mark than I realized."

17

Dorothée paused on her way upstairs at the Kaunitz Palace. The door to Talleyrand's study was closed, but she'd grown accustomed to looking in when she returned from an outing. He seemed to appreciate it, no matter how busy he was, and she found herself looking forward to these brief snatches of conversation. She moved to the door, rapped once, and opened it without waiting for a response.

Talleyrand lifted his gaze from the papers strewn on the desk before him. A smile crossed his face. "My dear. You're a refreshing sight on a dreary afternoon."

"I was at the riding school rehearsing all afternoon. Willie and Suzanne Rannoch had to ply me with wine and convince me all will be well tomorrow. I'm just on my way upstairs to dress for the opera." But something in his gaze instead drew her into the room. She crossed to stand beside his desk. "I'm looking forward to it. I like *The Marriage of Figaro*."

"A charming blend of realism and romance."

"I hope you can enjoy it." Dorothée perched on the edge of Talleyrand's desk, breathing in the familiar smells of fresh ink and eau de cologne and hair powder. She looked down to study his face. The shadows beneath his eyes seemed more strongly marked than usual. "You look as though you've been brooding."

Talleyrand gave a wry laugh and tossed the pen he was holding onto a sheet of cream laid paper. It left a jagged black line. "I can't imagine why. It's merely that Russia's refusing to budge on Poland, and Prussian troops are in Saxony, while Tsar Alexander and Metternich circle each other like a pair of prize gamecocks, and Castlereagh dances round trying to break up the fight without throwing his lot entirely in with France."

Dorothée touched his ringed hand where it lay on the ink blotter. "No progress at today's meetings?"

"None." His voice was unusually clipped and flat.

She left her hand resting on his own. "It's as though Tsar Alexander is two different people. He can be quite charming and agreeable and talk with the greatest seeming sincerity about enlightened principles, and then he turns into an autocrat who's quite ready to impose his will by force. He reminds me of my little boys in that he can switch from one mood to the other in the blink of an eye. Only he's much more dangerous when crossed."

"Astute as always, my dear."

"I saw him talking to Count Otronsky quite intently at the Metternich masquerade."

"I'm afraid Alexander listens to Otronsky all too much these days." Talleyrand returned the pressure of her hand, forced a smile to his face, and looked up at her for a moment. "Dorothée—How did the rehearsal go?"

She thought perhaps that wasn't what he had originally intended to ask, but then as much as she was coming to know him she was never quite sure what Talleyrand was thinking. "Well, all things considered. Malcolm Rannoch and Fitzwilliam Vaughn have learned their parts admirably in a very short time. Though Malcolm had to hurry off to a meeting at the chancellery."

"Yes, I saw him there. You'd never have guessed he was about to take part in a joust. He's clever at juggling multiple activities."

"He and Lord Fitzwilliam have quite saved the Carrousel. And I don't think I could have managed to organize it all without Suzanne Rannoch. She's splendid at details and she has a wonderful sense of the theatrical."

"You've become quite good friends with her."

"She's one of the few people I've met in Vienna to whom I can really talk."

"She strikes me as a very clever woman."

"That's one of the things I like about her."

Talleyrand picked up a jade-handled penknife and turned it over in his hands. "And her husband?"

Dorothée tugged at a fold of her French silk walking dress. "I like Malcolm Rannoch."

"But—?" Talleyrand's shrewd gaze darted over her face.

"I'm not sure what to make—"

"Of his attentions to Princess Tatiana?"

Dorothée fingered the embroidered cuff of her spencer. "I'm the last person to make an issue of fidelity between husband and wife. But I can tell that Monsieur Rannoch's attentions to Princess Tatiana hurt Suzanne, even though she denies it. Perhaps especially because she denies it."

"Princess Tatiana was a difficult woman for any man to ignore."

"And yet at times I'll catch Malcolm Rannoch looking at Suzanne, and I'll swear he cares for her. With startling depth. But if he does, I don't see how he can let her be so hurt."

"Motives are rarely simple. Just because Malcolm Rannoch cares for his wife doesn't mean he didn't also care for Princess Tatiana. And while I can't claim to understand his motives, I think he rarely does anything for purely personal reasons. Any more than I do."

Dorothée looked into the eyes that could be so kind and at the same time so inscrutable. In the ease of sharing a moment like this or working on a communiqué or laughing together over some nonsense in the newspapers, she forgot that he had been manipulating the fate of nations for forty years before she was born.

He looked back at her with a steady gaze that made her glance away. She twisted her gold bracelet round her wrist. "Malcolm is going to partner Suzanne in the Carrousel. I thought it might help. I tried to reassure her. I told her—" She bit back the words. In Vienna, one learned to be careful with secrets, even with someone one trusted.

"Yes?" Talleyrand said.

Dorothée clasped her hands in her lap. Talleyrand negotiated with England. The information might help him. "That Princess Tatiana was the mistress of Lord Fitzwilliam Vaughn."

Rare surprise flickered through his gaze. "Ah. I didn't realize."

"I didn't think Princess Tatiana would have been involved with both Lord Fitzwilliam and Malcolm Rannoch. I thought it would calm Suzanne's fears."

Talleyrand reached up to push a curl behind her ear. "My dear child, in many ways you're still quite an innocent. It's most refreshing."

His touch was merely the lightest brush of fingertips against her cheek. He dropped his hand back to the desktop at once, but she could still feel the imprint against her skin. Odd. Gentlemen touched her more intimately simply in the course of dancing the waltz. She found herself staring fixedly at the chased-silver inkpot and the row of pen nibs. "You think Princess Tatiana might have been having affairs with two members of the British delegation at the same time? I thought—"

"That she targeted her interests more neatly? So she did in general. But I certainly wouldn't put it past her to juggle two lovers who happened to be colleagues, if she saw a reason for it. Or if she simply found it amusing."

Dorothée forced her gaze back to her uncle. Her uncle by marriage. They weren't blood relatives at all. "Most people in Vienna seem to treat love as a game. But it's a game that causes a great deal of bitterness."

"Perhaps because it's difficult to take it as lightly as one should."

For a moment, Dorothée had a vivid memory of how ardently Talleyrand had once looked at her mother. For some unaccountable reason she shivered. "Why all the questions about Malcolm Rannoch? You knew him as a boy. I thought you understood him better than most of the British delegation."

"So did I." Talleyrand reached for the penknife. "But I begin to think Malcolm may be a great deal more dangerous than I anticipated."

* * *

Malcolm stepped into his bedchamber at the Minoritenplatz to find his wife sitting on the floor, the skirts of her evening dress spread about her in a tangle of ivory lace and pearl-beaded champagne silk, rolling a red ball to their son.

"Dada." Colin jumped up and toddled across the room to fling his arms round his father's knees.

"Good show, old chap." Malcolm swung his son up in his arms. "You'll be on the cricket pitch before we know it." He looked at Suzanne. "I'm not sure Blanca would approve your recklessness with your evening gowns."

Suzanne twitched her crumpled skirts out from under her. "It isn't nearly so dangerous now Colin's past the stage where he's likely to be sick at a moment's notice. Do you remember the embassy dinner for Wellington in Lisbon?"

"It's forever imprinted on my memory." He'd had to help her strategically pin her scarf after Colin threw up down the back of her gown. He pressed his lips to Colin's forehead and studied his wife over their son's tousled hair. He knew that look of taut excitement. "From the glint in your eyes, the game's afoot."

"You received a letter, darling. Plain paper, no crest on the seal. I'm afraid I was a shockingly prying wife."

"You opened it?"

"And decoded it. A substitution code. Not very difficult."

He found himself grinning. For all they were still strangers in so many ways, sometimes he was shocked by how similarly their minds worked. "And?"

> *"The anteroom off the grand salon at the opera, ten o'clock. On all accounts come alone. Bring the materials in question. I will bring payment."*

"So our friend from last night still wants the papers. I'm relieved."

"How do you think he'll conceal his identity?" Suzanne said. "Come masked?"

"It will be interesting to see."

"It will also be more difficult to spy upon the scene in the anteroom off the grand salon than it was in the Metternichs' garden."

"So our mysterious friend has apparently decided. I'll alert Czartoryski at the opera. If we can't determine the man's identity at the time, we can follow him. We'll need fake papers."

Suzanne nodded toward the escritoire. A bundle of papers lay atop it, tied with pink silk ribbon. "Not enough time for my best work, and obviously they won't pass a close inspection, but I think they're convincing enough to buy you time to draw the man out."

Malcolm moved to his wife's side and reached down a hand to brush his fingers against her cheek. "Have I ever told you you're remarkable?"

"Usually under the oddest circumstances."

Colin wriggled in Malcolm's arms. "Ball."

Malcolm set Colin on the floor and dropped down cross-legged in a triangle with his wife and son. "I can dress quickly," he said, glancing from Suzanne to the clock on the chest of drawers.

Suzanne rolled the ball to Colin. "You've learned something as well."

"Tatiana continues to surprise me." Malcolm reached out to catch the ball as Colin rolled it slightly off track. "Apparently she was Bonaparte's mistress in the months just before he abdicated and was exiled to Elba."

"*Sacrebleu.*" He heard the scrape of Suzanne's indrawn breath. "You didn't know?"

"I didn't know a great deal about Tatiana. More even than I realized." He kept thinking he'd have to ask her to explain things, only to be hit by the hard reality that he'd never speak to her again.

"Was she—"

"I think Talleyrand was behind it." Malcolm bounced the ball to Colin. Colin gave a cry of delight. "After our meeting at the chancellery this afternoon I accused him of using Tatiana to communicate with Bonaparte after he was sent to Elba. From Talleyrand's reaction, I think I was closer to the mark than I realized."

Out of the corner of his eye, he saw Suzanne go still. Napoleon Bonaparte's empire might be reduced to the few rocky miles of the island of Elba, but his shadow hung over the Congress. Many throughout his former empire were still loyal to him and would welcome his return.

Colin picked up the ball and dropped it in an effort at a bounce. It thudded to a standstill. Suzanne reached for it and pushed it back to their son. "Why do you think Talleyrand was communicating with Bonaparte?"

"Talleyrand likes to keep a foot in all camps. He could simply want to keep an eye on Bonaparte. Or—"

"It could be more serious. Would Talleyrand try to restore Bonaparte?"

"I wouldn't have thought so. It's true that at first Talleyrand didn't do as well with the restored king as he'd have liked, but he's currently France's foreign minister. I would think he'd see a return of Bonaparte as destructive. But the one thing I know about Talleyrand is that one can never be sure what he'll do. Or why." Malcolm pushed the ball to Suzanne.

Her fingers tightened for a moment on the red leather. "If Princess Tatiana was communicating with Bonaparte—could letters from him be among the papers the man who sent the coded message is so desperate to recover?"

"Along with whatever papers of Tsarina Elisabeth's Adam Czartoryski is bent on retrieving? It's an interesting possibility."

"Me," Colin said. The ball was now lying neglected between his parents.

"Sorry, old chap." Malcolm pushed the ball back to his son. His throat tightened for a moment as he watched the concentration with which Colin caught the ball and the triumph on his face as he pushed it back to Suzanne.

It will change you. He could hear Tatiana's voice when he'd told her he was going to have a child, light with familiar mockery and yet with an undertone that was uncharacteristically serious. She'd been sitting at a tavern table, a glass of wine in one hand, head tilted to the side, hair escaping its pins. *Whatever the terms of this marriage and whyever you've gone into it, you won't be able to take it lightly, Malcolm. Certainly not when you have a child. I know you.*

Tatiana had had a damnable ability to see beneath his defenses.

A trait, oddly enough, that Suzanne shared. Or would if he allowed her to get close enough.

He watched as Suzanne leaned forward, her carefully arranged ringlets falling against her cheek, and pushed the ball to Colin. Tatiana had been right. Being a husband and father had changed him. Among other things, it now mattered whether he lived or died. Which could be a damnable complication.

"What about the art treasures?" Suzanne asked. "Did Annina help you figure out how the princess acquired them?"

Malcolm told her about Gregory Lindorff. "According to Lindorff, Bonaparte gave her the Courland casket."

"That would explain Princess Tatiana's attachment to it. Although—" Suzanne's gaze moved from Colin to Malcolm as they rolled the ball back and forth. "Malcolm, I don't think Wilhelmine of Sagan's quarrel with Princess Tatiana was entirely about the casket."

She described the conversation she had had with the Duchess of Sagan after the Carrousel rehearsal. "It was as though the scene went into an entirely different key the moment I mentioned papers. Wilhelmine of Sagan is terrified of some secret Princess Tatiana knew about her. It's as though she kept secrets about everyone."

"A form of insurance."

Her gaze skimmed over his face. "I've heard you say you abhor blackmail."

Malcolm tossed the ball in the air and caught it. Colin giggled. "Tatiana had had to make her own way in the world for a long time. Perhaps longer than we realize, now we know her childhood may not have been what she claimed. I can understand her wanting insurance. That doesn't mean I sympathize with the methods."

Suzanne watched him a moment longer. "We keep coming back to Princess Tatiana's papers."

"I can only hope our rendezvous tonight reveals something."

Suzanne got to her feet. "If you don't start shaving, we'll never be ready. Come here, darling, sit with Mummy." She scooped Colin into her arms and perched on the bed.

Malcolm went to the dressing table and stirred shaving soap into a lather.

"Eithne knew about Fitz's affair with the princess," Suzanne said.

He met her gaze in the looking glass. "For how long?"

"She says she suspected almost from the first."

How many hours had he spent with Eithne in the past weeks and not noticed? To have been blind to the pain she must have been suffering seemed even more egregious than failing to notice the affair. "How did Eithne seem?"

"Bitter." Suzanne was playing pat-a-cake with Colin. "Angry. Partly at herself for not seeing the possibility Fitz could stray. Or perhaps for being foolish enough to believe in love."

Malcolm grimaced.

Suzanne pressed her palms against Colin's. "Darling, I know it sounds insane, but—"

"Yes, I know." Malcolm picked up his razor and drew it down the line of his jaw, harder than he'd intended. Drops of blood spurted against the metal. "This means Eithne has a motive as well."

Adam Czartoryski took a sip of champagne and glanced round the jostling crowd in the grand salon at the Kärntnertortheater. His face betrayed no hint of the information Malcolm had just relayed to him. "Your rendezvous with this man who wants to buy the papers won't tell us where the papers really are," he murmured.

"No. But any information about them may help us determine where they're hidden. You'll assist us?"

Czartoryski gave a soldier's nod. "Of course. I don't go back on my word."

Malcolm nodded across the room at Julie Zichy. "We'll get the papers back one way or another," he said. "And I'll see you have what it is you seek. I know you have no reason to believe me—"

"But oddly I find I do." Czartoryski sketched a half bow to Catherine Bagration. "You're a man of honor, Rannoch. Which is a rare commodity in Vienna."

"You're very kind."

"Perceptive, I think. I suspect—" Czartoryski broke off as Tsar Alexander materialized from the crowd round the bar, a champagne glass in hand. Hardly a surprise to find the Tsar of all the Russias mingling freely and getting his own drink. He was known to stroll into Vienna's taverns and order himself a glass of beer, to the despair of Baron Hager's security forces.

"Rannoch." The tsar's gaze settled on Malcolm's face like a sword point. "I hear you've been asking questions about Tatiana."

"I want to see her killer brought to justice. As I know you do, Your Majesty."

"If I knew the man's identity, I'd kill him with my bare hands." Alexander's gaze remained on Malcolm's face.

"You assume it was a man."

"You think it might have been a woman?"

"At this point it might have been any one of us."

"How very true." The tsar stared at Malcolm a moment longer, then jerked his head at Czartoryski. "Adam. Walk to my box with me."

"Sir." Czartoryski followed the tsar, with an apologetic lift of his brows at Malcolm.

Malcolm turned toward the bar and heard his name called.

"Rannoch." A tall man in the gleaming dress uniform of a British cavalry officer strode toward him, hand extended.

A face from the past that took Malcolm back to card parties at the British embassy in Lisbon and dinners in the officers' mess.

Frederick Radley.

18

Malcolm shook Frederick Radley's proffered hand. Colonel Radley now. Radley had been two years ahead of him at Harrow, a hero on the cricket pitch who deemed bookish boys two years his junior quite beneath his notice. While the young Malcolm had had little time for someone who couldn't tell Cicero from Catullus. But Radley had been in Lisbon a good deal when Malcolm was first stationed there. He was in the same regiment as Fitz's stepbrother Christopher, so they'd all ended up dining together more than they might otherwise have done.

"I saw Castlereagh earlier today, but you were out," Radley said. "Keeps you busy running his errands, does he?"

"The true life of an attaché. Glorified errand boy."

"Hardly. As I hear tell, you lot are exposing secrets right and left and saving the Continent from a fate worse than Bonaparte. Besides, you never were just an attaché, Rannoch. I saw that in Spain."

"Praise indeed from the hero of Vitoria."

Radley gave a self-deprecating smile that was just a shade too calculated. Or perhaps, Malcolm thought, he was being unfair. Radley's perfection had always grated on him.

"I didn't know you were on such good terms with Adam Czartoryski," Radley said. "Or is that the result of secrets too deep to be shared?"

"Nothing so interesting. I've got to know him a bit round the negotiating table."

Radley glanced toward the door through which Czartoryski and the tsar had vanished. "I've heard Adam Czartoryski called the most dangerous man in the Russian delegation."

"I suspect he has the keenest understanding. But that can be an asset in one's opposite number."

"So he's an opponent?" Radley dug his scarlet shoulder into the paneled wall.

"He's a Polish patriot. From his perspective, a restored Poland under Russia may be the best he can do. From our perspective, a Russia with Poland in its control has a bit too much power for comfort. As with so much of diplomacy, it's a matter of balancing perspectives."

"Not quite the excitement of Spain, is it? Still, I understand Vienna offers many diversions." Radley's gaze roamed round the jeweled ladies who thronged the salon. "I hear I'm to felicitate you." His gaze settled on where Suzanne stood with Aline and Dorothée Périgord. "My compliments. Mrs. Rannoch is a charming woman."

Malcolm would have said Radley held few surprises. He'd have been wrong. "I didn't realize you knew my wife."

Radley's gaze remained on Suzanne. Her head was turned to the side, dark ringlets stirring about her face, diamond earrings glinting in the candlelight as she laughed at something Dorothée was saying. "I had the privilege of meeting Suz—Mrs. Rannoch—in Spain before your marriage."

"When her parents were still alive."

"Quite. Dreadful tragedy, the way they were lost. It's good to see her looking so well. You're a fortunate man. I trust you appreciate her as she deserves."

"Believe me, Radley, I'm well aware of my wife's worth."

"She appears to be carrying off her role with aplomb. But I imagine Vienna has been an adjustment after Spain." After only the briefest pause, Radley added, "I heard about Princess Tatiana. I'm sorry."

"It's a great tragedy."

"She was a remarkable woman." Radley's gaze flickered to Suzanne again. "I don't suppose the lovely Mrs. Rannoch knows about you and Tatiana."

The boyhood longing to plant Radley a facer swept through Malcolm with surprising force. "My wife's a very clever woman. She discerns a great deal."

"Learned to be the perfect diplomatic wife, has she?" Radley gave one of the lazy grins that had grated so across the commons at Harrow. "Still, I don't expect she knows it all."

"You'd have to ask her."

"Oh no, old man. I wouldn't do that to you." Radley clapped him on the shoulder. "You may not be a soldier, but we did fight on the same side."

Dorothée looked across the grand salon. "Odd to think I was madly in love with him once."

Suzanne glanced round the room. "Who?"

"Adam Czartoryski. Of course, to him I'm sure I was just a gawky girl scarcely out of the schoolroom, but I had my heart set on marrying him."

Prince Czartoryski and Tsar Alexander were making their way toward the door. A few moments ago Czartoryski had been talking to Malcolm. Malcolm, Suzanne saw, was now talking with a man in brilliant regimental dress. Frederick Radley. She tightened her grip on her champagne glass.

"Prince Czartoryski *is* very handsome," Aline said in the tone of one who didn't generally pay much attention to such things.

"And brilliant." Dorothée's voice softened the way it does when one talks of a first love. "And a patriot with ideals, which are a precious commodity these days. When I was fifteen he seemed to me to embody every romantic virtue a man should have."

Suzanne took a drink of champagne, a deeper drink than she'd intended. "Your family opposed the match?"

"Thanks to my uncle," Dorothée said. "My future husband's uncle, that is. Talleyrand wanted me for Edmond. He got the tsar to exert his influence on my mother."

Aline wrinkled her nose. "At least we don't have the prince regent interfering in our marriages. How disagreeable."

"The life of a Courland." A trace of her eldest sister's cynicism crept into Dorothée's voice. "Not that I expect I'd have been much happier with Prince Czartoryski. Oh, I think he's a much better man than Edmond. But I don't think he's ever got over Tsarina Elisabeth. And I'd have loved him. Better a loveless marriage than to love someone and—"

"And not be loved in return," Suzanne said. She could feel Radley and Malcolm both looking at her.

Dorothée bit her lip and took a sip of champagne. "Besides, if I hadn't married Edmond, I wouldn't have got to know—I wouldn't be here."

"You rate Vienna highly," Aline said.

"Not just Vienna. Being at the Congress. Helping Talleyrand. Being able to—"

"Use your mind?" Suzanne asked.

"Precisely."

"Being a wife can interfere with using one's mind if one isn't careful," Aline said. "It's one reason I don't expect I'll ever marry."

Dorothée touched her arm. "You say that now, *chérie,* but in time—"

"I doubt it," Aline said. "I have my own fortune, and my mother won't fuss. And I'm not the falling in love sort."

Suzanne smiled at her husband's cousin. Aline was only two years her junior, yet a gulf of experience separated them. "Love has a way of catching one by surprise."

"I thought I was quite done with it," Dorothée said. "And yet—"

"Yes?" Suzanne asked.

"More things seem possible now." Dorothée glanced round the room as though seeking distraction. "Goodness, is that Colonel Radley? Talking to Malcolm."

"You know him?" Suzanne asked. "Of course. He's been stationed in Paris."

"With Wellington and the allied army. In fact, I think I first met him at Princess Tatiana's."

Suzanne took a sip of champagne to cover her surprise. "I didn't realize Radley and Princess Tatiana were acquainted."

"I got the sense they'd known each other in the past," Dorothée said.

Aline groaned. "Is there a man in Vienna who wasn't her lover at some point?"

"I don't think Radley was her lover actually." Dorothée's brows drew together as she puzzled over the past. "There was something between them, but not a love affair, I think, even a past one. Of course I may have entirely misjudged the matter."

Suzanne turned her gaze back to Radley and Malcolm. Damn and double damn. She wanted nothing more than to stay as far away from Radley as possible. A connection between him and Princess Tatiana would force her to do quite the opposite.

Tsar Alexander strode down the corridor toward the Russian box. "I've never liked him."

"Rannoch?" Adam Czartoryski made his voice light as he kept pace at the tsar's side. He had known Alexander for nearly two decades and had learned to tread lightly when the tsar's eyes had the restless glitter they currently possessed. "He strikes me as a decent man."

"He found Tatiana's body. He and his wife."

"Dreadful. Particularly for Madame Rannoch."

"Given her husband's relationship with Tatiana. The impertinent puppy was in love with her himself." Alexander stopped before the gilded door to his box. A bewigged footman at once stepped forward and opened it.

"You can hardly suspect his motives the night of the murder, given that he had his wife with him," Adam said as he followed Alexander into the box's anteroom.

"Assuming they really did arrive at the Palm Palace together. There was something damned suspicious about the whole thing. I had Otronsky talk to Madame Rannoch at the Metternich masquerade. He agrees their story is dubious, though he couldn't catch her in a falsehood."

Adam grimaced. He deplored Count Otronsky's rising influence with the tsar. Otronsky's combination of belligerence and romanticized dreams of Russian grandeur seemed calculated to push Alexander in precisely the wrong direction at the Congress.

Alexander paused, one hand on the crimson curtains to the box itself. "I loved Tatiana, Adam."

Adam touched the tsar's arm. For all that had passed between them, for all the layers of disagreements and betrayals, personal and political, at times Alexander was still the friend of his youth. When Adam had been a young man exiled to an alien court and Alexander an heir to the throne with an increasingly unstable father, it had often seemed they had no one but each other. They'd sat up late at night in the darkened recesses of the palace, poring over Voltaire and Locke, dreaming of a Russia with its own constitution, designed on the finest liberal principles. They'd been going to remake the world. "I know."

"You heard Catherine Bagration's accusations last night? That Tatiana was an impostor?"

"I heard of them."

"Do you believe them?" Alexander's voice was rough and raw, the voice of twenty years ago. Once he had relied on Adam's opinion in nearly everything. These days he asked for it less and less in personal matters.

"I don't know enough to determine what to believe or disbelieve. But even if she was born with a different name to different parents in a different country, she was still the woman you loved."

"If she lied about her birth, what else might she—" Alexander shook his head. "Catherine's always been jealous. And when she's jealous she can be spiteful. She's done her best to turn me against the Duchess of Sagan."

"Without success."

"I don't listen to lies," Alexander said, almost defensively.

Even in the days before his own love for Elisabeth—so difficult to remember those days—Alexander's love affairs had baffled Adam.

To love more than one woman at a time seemed—unnecessary. Overcomplicated. And a contradiction to the word "love."

"Wilhelmine of Sagan has won your confidence," Adam said.

"She is in need of assistance. I am endeavoring to render it to her."

"And your association with her angers Prince Metternich," Adam added, perhaps unwisely.

"Metternich's an arrogant fool. If he wasn't man enough to keep Wilhelmine, that's his problem."

Adam studied Alexander's face, trying to remember when it had grown so hard. "He sent Baron Hager to question you about the night Princess Tatiana was killed?"

Alexander gave a curt nod. "I told him the truth, of course. I have nothing to hide."

"Alex—" Adam took an impulsive step forward. "Sir, do you have any idea why Princess Tatiana asked you to call on her that night?"

"None," Alexander said in a flat voice. "It wasn't particularly unusual for me to call on her at that hour. Naturally I suspected nothing."

Adam returned the gaze of the man he had once felt he knew better than anyone. "Naturally."

Wilhelmine of Sagan lifted her opera glasses and willed her heart to still. It had been beating a mad staccato ever since her interview with Suzanne Rannoch at the rehearsal for the Carrousel that afternoon.

"I've been remembering my youthful madness." Dorothée slipped into the seat beside her.

Wilhelmine raised her brows.

"Adam Czartoryski," Dorothée said.

Wilhelmine trained her opera glasses on the box across the theatre where Tsar Alexander was taking his place beside Tsarina Elisabeth. Adam Czartoryski sat in the row behind. "You're a married woman whose husband is far away, Doro. You're in a far better position to amuse yourself with Prince Czartoryski now than you were as an unmarried girl."

Dorothée shook her head. "I don't think Adam Czartoryski is the type for amusements. More important, I don't think I should like to *be* an amusement."

Wilhelmine studied her younger sister. She forgot, sometimes, what a child Dorothée still was. And yet her sister's expression stirred an unexpected welling of envy. Envy of something she could scarcely remember. If she had ever known it at all. "Oh, Doro. You always expected too much. It will doom you to disappointment."

The thud of a walking stick signaled Talleyrand's arrival in the box. A few moments later, the first notes of the overture sounded, almost as though Talleyrand had cued the start of the performance. Wilhelmine wouldn't put it past him for a moment.

The first act passed in a blur. She was in no mood for the tangled love lives of fictional characters. Figaro and Susanna were fools to think marriage would bring them happiness. Count Almaviva was doing what all husbands did. At least they hadn't got to the long-suffering countess yet. If the woman were sensible, she'd stop bewailing her lost love and take Cherubino to her bed and have some fun. God knows he'd have more stamina than her husband.

Guests began to pour into the box almost the moment the curtain fell on the first act. Dorothée was besieged by adoring young attachés, and Talleyrand's attention was claimed by Baron Hardenberg. Wilhelmine started to get to her feet when someone dropped into a chair beside her.

Without so much as turning her head, she knew who it was. She would know the smell of his shaving soap and the starch he used in his shirts anywhere. She stiffened. "Prince Metternich."

"That bad?" he said in a dry voice. "I assure you, I have no intention of importuning you with any more tiresome pleas. I merely wished—"

"What?" Impatience tinged her voice.

"To assure you that all will be well."

Wilhelmine turned to look at the face she had so often seen across her pillow. Even now she could not deny his good looks, from the golden curls falling over his forehead to the finely molded lines of his mouth. He returned her gaze, his own hot with memories.

For a moment she, too, was caught by the past. The way his fingers had toyed with her garter and slid up her leg, the brush of flesh against flesh as she pulled his shirt over his head, the roughness of his breath as his mouth claimed her breast. Had she ever loved him? Or had she merely enjoyed basking in his adoration? "I don't know what you mean."

His gaze remained steady on her own. "I know you have little use for me. But let me at least render you this service."

The look in his eyes took her back to the time she could have taken comfort in his arms. And yet he had made her promises in the past that he hadn't been able to keep. "You can't—"

Something in Metternich's expression stopped her. She turned and saw that Alfred von Windischgrätz had come into the box. "Alfred." Wilhelmine extended her hand to her current lover.

"Windischgrätz." Metternich rose and sketched a quick bow in his direction. "Duchess. I trust you will enjoy the rest of the opera."

"My love?" Alfred kept hold of her hand but glared after Metternich with the gaze of a soldier who has spotted the enemy on his terrain. "Was he plaguing you?"

"No. Merely paying his respects." Wilhelmine got to her feet and unfurled her fan. She loved Alfred, but she couldn't trust even him with her current predicament. Besides, Alfred thought like the brilliant cavalry officer he was, and a saber cut could not solve this problem. Violence had already made the situation infinitely worse. She suppressed a shudder and slid her hand through his arm. "Shall we find some champagne, darling?"

"Herr Rannoch."

The voice stopped Malcolm as he followed Suzanne and Aline down the corridor that ran behind the boxes. He turned to see Franz Schubert making his way through the press of people.

Malcolm shook the young man's hand and presented Aline, who said, "You compose? How splendid. There's something quite magical in turning numbers into sound."

Schubert flushed. "Thank you, fraulein. The kapellmeister—Herr Salieri—gave me private lessons when I was in the imperial choir, and he's been kind enough to continue my instruction now I've left."

"Salieri is much talked of at the Congress," Aline said. "When I arrived in Vienna people were still agog at the concert he organized with the hundred pianos. And—" She bit back what she had been about to say. Malcolm caught the appalled look in his young cousin's eyes. Aline was not one to gossip, but the hothouse atmosphere in Vienna affected everyone.

"I know." Schubert met Aline's gaze directly. "There are still rumors about Herr Salieri regarding Mozart's death."

"Vienna is full of rumors," Aline said. "The more scandalous, the wider currency they seem to receive. Though I must say, the ones about Salieri and Mozart strike me as excessive enough to be worthy of the plot of a particularly improbable opera."

"Quite." Schubert grinned at her, in a moment of youthful camaraderie. Then his gaze moved back to Malcolm. "I saw you in your box during the first act. Princess Tatiana meant to be here tonight."

"She loved Mozart," Malcolm said. Tatiana's voice giving a mocking rendition of "Voi che sapete" echoed in his head.

"We were talking about the opera that last day I saw her. My mind wasn't working properly when I met you yesterday—I was in shock. But seeing the opera brought it back."

"Yes?" Malcolm drew Schubert a little to one side, into a gap between a pier table and a pillar. Suzanne and Aline followed.

"It was after she told me she'd discovered something disquieting. She recovered her composure, I gave her the music I'd brought, and we were talking about the opera tonight. She knew how I was looking forward to it. She said as a girl she wanted to be Susanna and in recent years she fancied herself as the countess, but now she thought she identified more with Figaro. I asked if that was because he was so clever. She said perhaps. Then she bent down and picked up a piece of the comfit dish she'd smashed and said she could understand Figaro's rage when he learns the count is plotting to take Susanna. He'd thought the count was his friend and ally and look how he repays him." Schubert's gaze moved over Malcolm's face. "Could that have been the disquieting news? That she realized she couldn't trust someone she'd thought she could rely upon?"

A dozen possible scenarios raced through Malcolm's head. "It could indeed. Thank you, Schubert."

Schubert gave a shy smile. "The second act will be starting. You should return to your box."

"We have a spare seat," Aline said. "Do join us."

"Oh no, I couldn't—"

"Excellent idea." Malcolm put a hand on Schubert's shoulder. "It's the least we can do."

They made their way back to the box. Malcolm pulled the door of the box to, about to follow Suzanne, Aline, and Schubert through the curtains from the anteroom to the box itself, when he felt someone grasp the door handle from the corridor behind him.

"Rannoch." The voice, coming through the crack in the door, was low and urgent. Not the voice from the garden last night, though he couldn't place it otherwise. "Listen." The man spoke French with a good accent, though not that of a true native. "There isn't much time."

"Who—"

"Who I am doesn't matter. You're looking in the wrong place."

"For—"

"Don't play dumb. It's not who killed Princess Tatiana that's important, it's what she was about to discover."

"Which is what?"

"You have to ask the right questions. Why did Princess Tatiana go to the Empress Rose tavern the day she died?"

"Why—"

"Take the gifts you're offered, Rannoch. Don't be greedy. I risk a great deal simply to tell you this much."

"If—"

"Trust no one. You can't be sure who in Vienna may be involved in this. Tatiana learned that to her cost."

* * *

Malcolm reached out and squeezed Suzanne's hand. Her fingers twined round his for a moment. She was behind the curtains of the windows that ran along one side of the grand salon, empty now as the waiters had taken a break during the second act. The door to the anteroom was a few feet off. Adam Czartoryski was in a convenient niche in the corridor, watching the door that opened from the corridor onto the anteroom. Whichever door the mysterious man seeking Tatiana's papers used, they should have a view of him and would be able to follow him when he left. Malcolm released his wife's hand and pushed open the door to the anteroom.

It was in darkness, startling after the brilliant candlelight of the grand salon. Malcolm pushed the door shut to protect Suzanne. Even as he paused to get his bearings, he sensed a presence in the shadows.

"I have a pistol drawn, Rannoch."

"So do I."

"But mine is pointed at your head. I had a glimpse of you as you opened the door. Turn to the wall. Tilt your pistol to the ground. I'm not taking any chances after last time."

Malcolm complied. It was the voice from the Metternichs' garden—definitely different from the man who had spoken to him in the box just now—but he still couldn't place the accent.

A flint scraped against steel. A single candle flared to life. "You have the papers?" the clipped voice asked.

"You have the payment? I'm willing to humor your desire for secrecy, but should you try to take the papers without payment, I'm a very quick shot. And quite accurate, even when I fire while whirling round."

Paper slapped against a demilune table to Malcolm's right. Out of the corner of his eye, he saw a stack of British banknotes.

"Put the papers beside them," the uninflected voice said. "Then you can pick up the banknotes."

Malcolm pulled Suzanne's dummy papers from inside his evening coat without haste, held them out so Uninflected Voice could see they were letters, and then set them on the polished wood of the table. Keeping in character, he reached for the bundle of banknotes and began to count them.

Uninflected Voice gave a harsh laugh. “Trusting, aren’t you?”

“Is anyone in Vienna fool enough to be trusting?”

“You have a point. Count the money if you will but don’t turn round. I still have my pistol trained on you.”

Footsteps sounded against the parquet floor. A hand shot into Malcolm’s peripheral vision, reaching for the dummy letters. At the same moment, the door from the grand salon swung open.

“Just in time, I see,” said a deep voice. “If you hand those over to me, this will be much simpler.”

Malcolm spun round to see a man in the doorway from the grand salon, a black silk scarf tied over his face. In one hand he held a pistol. His other arm was wrapped round Suzanne, a knife at her throat.

☙ 19 ☙

Suzanne's gaze flickered toward Malcolm with warning and apology. The knife was just above her collarbone. Fear and anger scalded Malcolm's throat.

"The papers," the masked man said again. He wore a gleaming black evening coat over an ivory and gold brocade waistcoat, and thick, dark hair showed above the scarf that covered his face. He spoke French, though it did not seem to be his native tongue any more than it was that of Uninflected Voice or the man who had spoken to him in the box earlier. "Put them in my pocket. And drop your guns. Both of you."

Malcolm let go of his pistol, gaze trained on Suzanne. Uninflected Voice, revealed to be a stocky, brown-haired man, lowered his hand, as though to do the same, then brought it up in a lightning motion and fired.

The masked man staggered and cried out. Suzanne spun away from him. Blood spurted from her shoulder. Malcolm caught her in his arms, dropping the banknotes.

Uninflected Voice grabbed the letters from the table, snatched up the banknotes, lurched across the room, and flung his shoulder against the window. At his second try, the frame gave way and the glass cracked. He sprang out of the window in a hail of broken glass and splintered wood. Masked Man raced after him, just as the door from the corridor burst open. Adam Czartoryski stepped into the room and froze on the threshold.

Suzanne pulled out of Malcolm's arms and darted to the window. Malcolm ran after her to see Masked Man push himself to his feet on the cobblestones below. Uninflected Voice was almost out of sight on the lamplit street. Masked Man staggered after him, dodging through the crowd who were running out of cafés to stare up at the broken window.

Malcolm pulled his wife back from the window as a gust of cold wind cut through the broken glass.

"Malcolm—" Suzanne protested.

"No chance of catching them." He pushed her into the nearest chair and pulled out his handkerchief.

Czartoryski was at the window. "I got a glimpse of the brown-haired man going into the anteroom, but I didn't recognize him. What in God's name—"

"The first man was an Austrian, I think. I'd swear I've seen him round the chancellery." Malcolm pushed Suzanne's lace and silk puff of a sleeve down off her shoulder.

"He only winged me," she said. "I was stupid."

"We weren't expecting someone else to show up in search of the papers," Malcolm said. Thankfully she spoke the truth about her wound. The bullet had hit a blood vessel, but the blood was already starting to clot. He bound his handkerchief tight round her shoulder.

"It was just like Prince Czartoryski interrupting the first meeting. This man was very quiet coming into the grand salon, but I heard the opening of the door," Suzanne said, as Malcolm tied the ends of the handkerchief. "Of course I just thought it was an opera-goer in search of a drink, so I stayed still behind the curtains. He had the pistol trained on me by the time I realized what was happening. A few years ago, I'd have tried to get away. Before I had Colin."

"Thank God for our son's influence." Malcolm pulled her gold-braid-edged sleeve up over his makeshift bandage.

"Who the devil was he?" Czartoryski asked.

"I couldn't hear enough to place the accent," Malcolm said. "Suzanne?"

She shook her head. "I confess I was distracted."

"You think the first man worked for Metternich?" Czartoryski asked.

"So, it appears if I'm right about seeing him at the chancellery, though at the Congress one can never be sure who's working for whom."

"But why would Metternich be after—"

"The papers you want to recover for the tsarina? I doubt that's what he's interested in. I suspect Tatiana also had papers of interest to Prince Metternich."

"Or perhaps to the Duchess of Sagan," Suzanne said.

Czartoryski cast a glance out the broken window as though he would wrest answers from the wreckage. "We're no nearer to finding where any of the papers are."

"No, but we know Metternich didn't get them the night of the murder." Malcolm looked down at Suzanne, relieved to see some color returning to her face. "When Metternich went out of the room to summon Annina, I think he'd have had time to send word to one of his agents."

"And you think the agent orchestrated the attack on us on the way home from the Palm Palace?" Suzanne asked. "Metternich thought you had Tatiana's papers?"

"If Metternich knew where she hid them, he'd have had time to check the secret compartment. If he saw the papers were missing, it would be a logical assumption that I might have taken them. When we eluded his thugs that night, he decided it would be safer to buy them."

"And now he knows you tried to trick him. Or he'll realize it when his agent brings him the fake letters."

"Assuming the masked man doesn't get them away from him."

"Who the devil is the masked man?" Adam asked. "Someone after yet another secret Princess Tatiana was keeping? What sort of game was she playing?"

"Tatiana's games tended to be rather Byzantine. But she always had an endgame in mind. Do you know how she got the tsarina's papers?"

"I don't—"

"Damn it, Czartoryski." Malcolm strode toward him. "I trusted you with my wife's and my safety."

"The tsarina thinks Princess Tatiana took them herself on a visit to the Hofburg, though she isn't sure precisely how."

Suzanne's gown rustled as she got to her feet. "If Prince Metternich didn't take the papers the night of the murder, either the killer took them or Princess Tatiana hid them somewhere other than in her rooms."

"And if the killer took them, he or she doesn't seem to have used them for blackmail," Malcolm said. "At least not yet."

"But if Tatiana did hide them—"

"What?" Malcolm studied his wife's face. He knew the look she wore when she was piecing together bits of information.

Suzanne pulled her shawl up to cover her bandaged shoulder. "I was thinking of a place a woman can go without comment, and yet in which she tends to place all her trust."

"Where?" Czartoryski asked.

"Her dressmaker's."

"I'm ten times a fool." Malcolm struck a flint to the tapers on the dressing table in their bedchamber. The smell of beeswax filled the night air.

Suzanne twisted round on the dressing table bench to look at her husband. Her dressing gown, which she was half wearing, leaving her injured shoulder bare, slithered down on the bench about her. "You weren't the one who had someone sneak up behind you with a drawn pistol."

"No, I was engaged in a charade in the next room while someone put a knife to my wife's throat." He pulled a brandy flask and a clean handkerchief from a drawer in the dressing table.

"Malcolm, I'll never forgive you if you turn into a Hotspur or a Brutus. Not now."

"At least Hotspur and Brutus weren't so wantonly careless with their wives." He doused the handkerchief with brandy and pressed it to her shoulder.

She winced at the touch of the alcohol against her torn skin. "It's barely a scratch."

"You could have been killed."

"So could you. Tonight, last night. Most nights I've known you."

Malcolm opened another drawer and took out the brass-bound box where she kept her medical supplies. Usually she was the one patching him up. Geoffrey Blackwell had trained her well. "I chose this life."

"And you think I didn't?" She stared up at him. In the flickering light from the tapers, his face was unusually grim, all sharp angles and intense eyes. "Darling, I knew what you did when I married you. I knew I'd never be able to bear being your wife if it meant sitting on the sidelines or waiting like Penelope to see if you came back alive. If you wanted that sort of wife you shouldn't have married me, however strong your chivalrous impulses."

He flipped open the lid of the medical box and clipped off a length of lint. "When I married you—" He gave an unexpected smile. "I hadn't the least idea what I was getting into."

"We barely knew each other." She saw them the night he proposed, on a moonlit balcony overlooking the Tagus River. A romantic setting for a very unromantic scene. Malcolm had explained what he was offering her with all the precision with which he'd outline a policy option to Lord Castlereagh, pointing out that his parents had given him a bad impression of marriage, that he'd never thought to marry, and that he feared he wouldn't be very good at it. Not so very long ago, yet when she recalled the scene the two people standing on that balcony seemed so very young. "Marriage has a way of opening the eyes."

"So they say." He pressed a pad of lint against her shoulder. "Though in many ways—"

"We're still strangers?"

"We haven't had time. For much of anything."

"Beyond strategizing our next move."

"This isn't a game, Suzanne." He took her hand and put it over the lint. "Hold this."

She pressed the pad of lint against her shoulder. "Oh, darling, the whole Congress is a game. But the stakes are the fate of countries, and lives hang in the balance. That's why I won't be left on the sidelines."

Malcolm began to unwind a length of linen. "I know you have the heart of a lion, Suzanne. But I sometimes think—"

"What?"

He snapped the scissors on the linen. "That marrying you was the most selfish thing I've ever done."

For a moment, her blood went ice-cold. "That's ridiculous, Malcolm. Marrying me was an act of kindness. We both know that."

He turned to look down at her, his gaze night black. "Is that what you think?"

She returned his gaze, her own steady. "I know the man you are. I know what I owe you."

"For God's sake, don't—"

"I don't ask a lot. Only not to be wrapped in cotton wool while you go off on your adventures."

He bound the linen round her shoulder with deft, precise fingers. "When have I ever tried to wrap you in cotton wool?"

"Just now. It's the one thing—the *only* thing—I won't tolerate from you, Malcolm."

"Damn it, Suzanne, if you think—"

"What?"

He pulled her to her feet and caught her in his arms with unexpected force. His fingers sank into her hair. His mouth came down hard on her own.

She clung to him without hesitation, parting her lips, clutching the fabric of his coat, pulling him closer.

He was the one who drew back abruptly. "I'm sorry. I—"

"No." She dragged him back to her with a hunger that matched his own.

This at least was real between them. His fingers sliding into her hair, the smooth super fineness of his coat beneath her hands, the ragged warmth of his breath on her skin, his mouth hot and desperate against her own.

He kissed her as though he could keep her safe. She held him to her as though she could strip away his mask and find the truth of who he was. Brand him with recognition of what was between them.

When he raised his head, it was only to lift her in his arms. He carried her to their bed and she lost herself in the familiarity of his hands and the tantalizing mystery of his lips against her own.

Later, lying against his shoulder, she said, "What else did you learn tonight?"

"Mmm?" Malcolm had his head turned to the side, his lips against her hair.

"Before you came back to the box after the first interval. Something happened."

His fingers tangled in her hair. "You don't just have witchcraft in your lips, Suzanne. It's in the workings of your mind."

"Simple, everyday observation. I looked round and saw your face when you came into the box."

"And to think I flatter myself on my acting abilities."

"Don't worry, darling. At least half the time I haven't the least idea what's going through your head."

He pushed himself up on one elbow and looked down at her. The candlelight slid over his smooth skin and outlined the muscles she had traced with her lips. "I'm not such a mystery."

She stared into his eyes, deceptively open at the moment. He'd made love to her with startling intensity. As though seeking to lose himself in oblivion. His memories of Princess Tatiana must still be raw. "Oh, dearest. You could rival the most elaborate cipher."

"Easily enough said, given your skills at code breaking."

"Not when it comes to you."

"You just said marriage was supposed to end the mystery."

"In some cases it only deepens it." She reached up and pushed his hair off his forehead, indulging herself by letting her fingers linger against his temple. These were the moments when she could almost believe the illusion that he was hers.

She dropped her hand back to the tangled sheets. "But despite all your brilliant efforts at diversion, I do know something happened tonight at the end of the first interval."

He seemed almost relieved at the subject change. "It's going to sound mad, but someone else approached me in secret."

Suzanne pushed herself up against the pillows so she could get a better look at her husband's face. "About Princess Tatiana's papers?"

"No. To tell me I was asking the wrong questions."

"About her death?"

"He said I should be asking not who killed Tatiana but what she had discovered. He implied she uncovered a plot just before she was killed."

Suzanne sat up in bed and wrapped her arms round her knees, bare beneath the cool sheet. "The disquieting news she told Schubert about?"

"Very likely. The unseen man who told me this said she went to the Empress Rose tavern the day she died."

"It could be a trap."

"Possibly." He rolled onto his back and sat up beside her. "But we know from Schubert that she'd discovered something. It's worth investigating. I'll take Addison."

"Take me."

He swung his gaze to her. "Sweetheart, it's not wrapping you in cotton wool to—"

"I can say I'm looking for information about my sister. It's a more innocuous approach. It will take them by surprise."

"I thought you were going to call on Tatiana's dressmaker to see if she hid the papers there."

"I'll send Blanca. A maid will more easily be able to do it without rousing suspicion."

"Suzanne—"

"And if there's a trap waiting for you at the Empress Rose, they won't be expecting you to have a woman with you. It will throw off suspicion."

His indrawn breath scraped through the still air. "Castlereagh ought to take you to meetings. We could use some arguments that are impossible to refute."

"I've had your example for two years. Do you have a likeness of Princess Tatiana?"

"Why—"

"It would help in making inquiries. I could do a sketch or we could probably find a portrait in a print shop; her likeness was much copied. But I thought you might have a miniature."

His gaze shifted to the hills and valleys of light and shadow made by the sheet. "Yes, actually. She gave it me years ago."

"Good," Suzanne said with determination. "It will be helpful. What else did this man say?"

"To trust no one. That anyone in Vienna might be in on the plot. So you see the risk I'm taking in trusting you."

She pleated a fold of sheet between her fingers. "I'm flattered, dearest."

"Of course, we don't know what the devil the plot is, which makes it a bit difficult to judge who may be behind it."

"Malcolm." Suzanne stared at the shadow patterns her fingers made on the white sheet. "Princess Tatiana seems to have been amassing a blackmail dossier against a number of powerful people. It makes me wonder if—"

"If?"

She could feel the pressure of Malcolm's gaze on her face. "If she was striking out on her own. Making a bid to amass power herself."

One of the candles on the dressing table sputtered in its silver holder. Malcolm lit a taper on the bedside table, then got to his feet and went to the dressing table. "Tatiana was—I knew her less of late." He brought the candlesnuffer down over the sputtering tapers. "To begin with she was loyal to Talleyrand, but she'd branched into working for whoever paid the most. I think she saw safety in power."

"We don't know what country she actually came from, do we? She might have been working in the interests of her real country."

"Not Tatiana." Malcolm snuffed the brace of candles on the table by the door. An acrid smell drifted through the air. "I never knew her to think in terms of countries."

"But you've just admitted you knew her less well of late." Suzanne studied the angles of her husband's bare back. She'd swear he was seeing Tatiana Kirsanova's face in the smoke guttering from the extinguished candles. "For all you know, she could have been secretly working for her real country even when she was supposedly working for Talleyrand."

He turned round and stared at her. "My God, Suzanne. You have a devious mind."

"Thank you."

"But whether she was working for herself or for someone else, the question is, was it random chance that she acquired information about these particular people—Tsarina Elisabeth, the Duchess of Sagan—or was there a specific endgame in mind?"

"Would Metternich change the course of Austrian policy to protect the duchess?"

Malcolm returned to the bed and pulled the covers over both of them. "He's certainly given every sign of being a man desperately in love. The tsar, on the other hand, has hardly shown himself protective of the tsarina."

"But if whatever these papers contain would bring embarrassment to him and his family—"

Malcolm nodded, unseen ghosts in his eyes.

"Someone with a hold on both Metternich and the tsar could achieve a great deal at the Congress."

"They could indeed." His hand clenched on the embroidered silk coverlet.

"It's as though she was two different women," Suzanne said. "The schemer amassing blackmail information and the agent uncovering a plot."

"Being two different people would be positively straightforward for Tatiana." Frustration edged his voice, and something like regret. He leaned back against the pillows. "Speaking of surprises, I didn't realize you knew Frederick Radley in Spain."

Her breath froze in her throat. How odd that after a night of knives and gunshots, the most terrifying moment came now. Sitting naked beneath the covers, her arm brushing her husband's own, her body still warm from their lovemaking. "He was near my family's home on a mission."

It was a bare half-truth, but Malcolm merely nodded.

Then, because it might be important, she added, "Dorothée says she met Colonel Radley at Princess Tatiana's in Paris."

"Does she?" Malcolm's eyes narrowed. "Not that it's necessarily surprising. Still, any connection to Tatiana—"

"Doro said there seemed to be something between them, but she didn't think it was a love affair, even a past one. Doro's a good judge of people."

"Interesting."

"Did you know Radley well in the Peninsula?" Better not to mention Radley at all, but she couldn't resist asking.

"Not particularly, but we were thrown together a fair amount when he was stationed in Lisbon. Fitz's stepbrother was in his regiment, and Fitz would take me along when he went to dine with Christopher."

She cast a sidelong glance at him. "You didn't like Radley?"

He gave a sheepish grin. "Soldiers tend to dismiss diplomats as frippery talkers rather than doers, and diplomats tend to categorize soldiers as quicker with a pistol than a thought. So Radley and I weren't exactly set up to be blood brothers."

"You have friends who are soldiers. Fitzroy Somerset, Alexander Gordon, Lord March. Radley wasn't an exception to the rule?"

"Radley always struck me more as defining the rule. Sorry, I expect to you he was quite charming."

"On the surface." Again, it was a half-truth.

Malcolm laughed and let his head slide into the pillows.

Suzanne settled into the linen beside him. He flung a warm arm round her and she turned her head into the hollow of his shoulder, but a cold knot lurked in the pit of her stomach. Malcolm gave every indication of believing her. She'd diverted any suspicions he might have, for now.

The sad, uncomforting truth was that she was quite adept at lying to her husband.

20

The sour, pungent smell of beer seemed to have leached into the rafters and the floorboards of the Empress Rose tavern. Smoke from pipes and cigars, forbidden in most of Vienna's more elegant cafés, hung thick in the air. Suzanne stepped through the door that Malcolm was holding open for her. Guessing Princess Tatiana would have costumed herself for the venue, Suzanne had dressed in a simple poplin covered by a scarlet wool cloak. A deep-brimmed cottage bonnet covered her hair, which was in turn covered by a blond wig.

Malcolm, garbed in a sturdy wool coat that might belong to a middling tradesman, followed her into the tavern. Heads turned in their direction. Though several women were present, their gaudy, low-cut gowns and bright hair dyed in shades of gold and red suggested that they were there in search of custom. It was just past eleven o'clock, but a number of men filled the tables as well. Tradesmen and clerks, judging by the cut and fabric of their clothes. And some, with flashy coats and spotted handkerchiefs in place of cravats, who Suzanne suspected were cardsharps or even thieves or fences. The smattering of accents that assailed her ears as talk resumed came from a variety of classes and districts, and she caught fragments of French, Dutch, and Italian layered in with the German.

Malcolm took her arm and steered her to an empty table. Ostentatiously in the middle of the room. Today they wanted not to hide but to observe those about them. When a waiter appeared, Malcolm ordered two glasses of beer but made no effort to ask questions. Safer to settle in first.

Suzanne untied her cloak and let it fall over the rough-cut slats of the chairback. She felt a crossfire of curious gazes shot their way. Hostility from several of the women, frank appraisal from a number of the men. Her gown had a modest neckline but clung to the curves of her body and the blond wig had luxuriant ringlets that fell over her face for added protection. She caught a negotiation over terms, in progress at a nearby table between a lady with bright gold hair and a stout, red-faced gentleman. Fragments of other conversations drifted through the air—the rise in the price of candles and laundry soap during the Congress (a lot of dirty linen to be washed, one man joked), the money to be made if one had rooms to let, and the gullibility of foreigners. In particular the English, if she heard correctly. Malcolm must have heard the same, for she saw a grin reflected in his eyes.

Their waiter returned and set two foaming glasses of pilsner before them. Suzanne looked up at him, her gaze turned beseeching. "If I could ask you—You see, we didn't just happen to come into this tavern." She hesitated, eyes downcast, as though modesty forbade her to frame what she needed to say next.

"My wife is in search of her sister," Malcolm said.

The waiter, a thin young man with straw-colored hair and sharp blue eyes, looked between them. "Ladies don't come here often." He cast a glance round the tavern, indicating that he would not class the other women present as ladies.

"That's just it," Suzanne said. "Constanze ran away." She put a hand to her face.

"*Meine liebe,* you're getting it all muddled." Malcolm gripped her hand and drew it down to the table. "My wife's sister ran off with a scoun—A man of whom the family did not approve. I fear it wasn't the first—" He coughed. "That is neither here nor there. We have been searching for my sister-in-law in vain for some weeks—"

"You didn't *try* hard enough." Suzanne pulled a handkerchief from her felt reticule and blew her nose.

"*Liebling*, as I've told you many times, I want her safely home as much as anyone. The scandal isn't good for business."

"You and your wretched shop." She wadded up the handkerchief and threw it on the table.

Malcolm spared her a brief, quelling glance. "Suffice it to say, we had no luck in discovering my wife's sister's whereabouts until yesterday. Someone reported seeing Constanze come into this tavern three days ago."

Suzanne reached into her reticule again and drew out a pewter-framed miniature. A Titian-haired young woman, loose curls falling about her face, a gauzy white muslin gown slipping from her shoulders. When Malcolm had first shown it to her, she'd been startled by how young Princess Tatiana looked. Young and unexpectedly artless, though worldly wisdom still glinted in her eyes. Suzanne suspected the princess had had that from childhood.

The simplicity of her gown and hairstyle fit well with their charade. The fair-haired waiter took the picture and held it to the light from the windows, raised his brows, frowned, then shook his head. "I was here three days ago, from opening until closing. I saw no one resembling this lady. More's the pity."

"She might have disguised herself," Suzanne said. "Changed the color of her hair perhaps."

"Believe me, I'd have remembered this lady. Whatever her hair color."

"She might even have been dressed as a man," Malcolm suggested.

"*Mein schatz*—" Suzanne protested.

"God knows what your sister might get up to."

The waiter grinned, then shook his head again. "Even dressed as a man, she'd have stood out."

Suzanne studied him with wide, pleading eyes. "Could you ask the others who might have been working that day?"

"They won't remember differently."

Malcolm took a sip from his glass of beer. "I'm sure I need hardly say how highly we would value news of my sister-in-law."

He reached into his pocket and pulled out a purse. He slid out a handful of banknotes. "Very highly."

Something flickered in the waiter's eyes for a moment. Then he gave a reluctant grin. "Sorry. I'd like to. But I'd have to fabricate a story."

That smile was just a bit too practiced. Suzanne's blood quickened. She didn't risk a glance at Malcolm, but she knew he had sensed it as well. The waiter was lying.

"All the same," Malcolm said, "if we could talk to the others who were working that day. I fear my wife will give me no peace if we do not pursue all possible avenues."

Wariness settled in the waiter's eyes for an instant. Then he inclined his head. "Of course."

Two other waiters, a kitchen maid, and a potboy returned the same negative answers. One of the waiters made appreciative noises over Tatiana's picture. The other answered in monosyllables. The kitchen maid fidgeted with the tie on her apron. The potboy stared fixedly at the worn toes of his shoes. His eyes widened at the sight of Tatiana's picture. For an instant Suzanne thought he was about to tell them something. Then he cast a sidelong glance at the fair-haired waiter and went silent.

Malcolm and Suzanne lingered at their table for a time in case any of the staff tried to approach them on their own, or any of the tavern's regulars who had overheard them (they had taken care to speak in tones that carried) offered information, but no one came forward. At length they wrapped themselves in their outer garments and left, their glasses of beer still half-full.

A light rain was falling when they left the tavern and an autumn chill had settled in the air. The unseasonable warmth was at last giving way to the promise of winter. Malcolm gave her his arm, and they proceeded down the street at a slow pace.

A whistle sounded as they passed an alley on the left. "*Mein herr.*" The voice was low, fierce, and high-pitched.

It was the potboy. Heinrich. He was a thin child of perhaps ten or eleven, with brown hair in want of trimming and a smattering of freckles across his pale skin. Malcolm stepped quickly into the alley, bringing Suzanne with him, so the skirts of his greatcoat and the folds of her cloak shielded Heinrich from view.

The boy's wary gaze shot between them. "I wanted to tell you. But I knew I'd get a whipping. If they find out—" He cast a nervous glance in the direction of the tavern.

"There's no need for them to find out," Malcolm said.

Heinrich gave a quick nod. He looked at Suzanne. "The lady with the red hair—she's your sister? She's in trouble?"

"We fear so," Suzanne said. "Did you see her?"

"Three days ago. She must have dyed her hair or been wearing a wig like you said, sir. Her hair was dark as boot blacking. But I remember her face. Her smile—it was kind."

"Was anyone with her?" Malcolm asked. "Or did she meet anyone at the tavern?"

"No. She came in alone. And she wasn't meeting anyone. She wanted information."

"About?" Malcolm asked. Suzanne heard the edge of tension in her husband's voice.

Heinrich scraped his foot against the cobblestones. "She wanted to know if a group of men met in the tavern."

"And do they?" Malcolm's voice was gentle and steady.

The boy gave a quick nod. "In a room above the taproom."

"Who are they?"

Heinrich dug at a loose cobblestone with the worn toe of his shoe. "Gentlemen, from their coats and linen. Here for the Congress."

"How do you know?"

"They speak German with an accent. And when they're alone in the room, they speak another language. I don't know which."

Malcolm cast a glance at Suzanne. "Was it this?" He offered a phrase in French. "Or this?" He tried Italian, Spanish, Russian, Polish, Dutch, Swedish.

Heinrich listened, brows drawn with concentration, but shook his head. "I never heard more than vague sounds through the door. The few times I was sent into the room with a pot of ale or a plate of food they stopped talking. They always spoke to me in German."

"When did they start coming to the tavern?"

He frowned, knocking the loose cobblestone against its fellows. "A month since, perhaps. They come about once a week, sometimes twice. Not always on the same night. And sometimes they don't come at night at all. The last time was a week ago yesterday."

"You told the lady about them?"

"Axel did. The waiter you first talked to. But then later a man came to the tavern and spoke with him for a long time and with Herr Franck, who owns the tavern. Afterward Axel said we were to say no more about the men. When I asked a question he cuffed me."

"You're very brave." Malcolm reached into his pocket and drew out the purse he had offered to Axel.

Heinrich stared at it, then lifted his gaze to Malcolm, his shoulders straightening with pride. "I didn't ask for money."

"No, but you've rendered us a great service, at considerable risk to yourself. I hope you'll allow us to show our gratitude. It will help ease our consciences from the fear that we've brought danger upon you."

The boy hesitated a moment longer, then gave a quick, shy smile and accepted the banknotes Malcolm pressed into his hand. "Is the lady with the red hair in danger?"

"Not anymore," Malcolm said. "And your information will help us ensure no one else is put in danger. Do you know Café Hugel?"

Heinrich nodded.

"If you discover anything further or if your situation at the Empress Rose becomes difficult, go there and ask for Lisl. She'll know how to find me."

Heinrich gave a grave nod, pleased to be treated as an adult and equal. He inclined his head to Suzanne, then darted down the alley.

Malcolm put up an umbrella and gave Suzanne his arm as they moved back into the street, quiet now as most had gone inside for the midday meal. The rain was falling harder, tumbling in sheets off the overhanging roofs, washing the street with gray and obscuring the view.

"Who do you think these men are?" Suzanne asked.

"They could be anyone, from the boy's description. Damnation." Malcolm stared at the sodden cobblestones. "If only I'd been in Vienna those last days."

"Do you think—"

She broke off as a carriage rumbled down the street, at a speed only allowed by the lack of traffic. Wheels rattled, horse hooves pounded against the rain-slick cobblestones, sending up sprays of water. They drew to the side. The carriage veered, thundering straight toward them.

Malcolm half threw her into a doorway. She stumbled and caught her hand against the doorjamb, just as a hoof struck Malcolm, and he fell on top of her.

His body slammed into her own and crushed the breath from her chest. Pain shot through her injured shoulder. A broken spoke of the umbrella jabbed her near the eye.

"Malcolm?" She pushed side the wreckage of the umbrella, slid out from under Malcolm, and shook her unresponsive husband. His eyes were closed, his hat knocked from his head. She pulled him into her lap, carefully, tugged off her gloves, and felt sticky blood on the back of his head. "Darling?"

She put her fingers to his throat and found a pulse that sent a wave of relief coursing through her. She slid her fingers into his hair and explored his scalp gently, seeking for how bad his injuries were.

He jerked away from her touch and lifted his head with a sound of protest.

Air rushed into her lungs.

He sought for purchase on the rain-splashed stone, trying to push himself up. "What the devil—"

"A carriage tried to run us down. Do you remember?"

"Got hit. Stupid—"

"Hardly stupid. You got me out of the way and managed not to get yourself killed. For both of which I'm exceedingly grateful."

"Should have been quicker."

"You're the one always saying not to waste time on regrets. Hold still a moment, darling. Your head's bleeding."

Malcolm might be too hard on himself, but at least he wasn't foolhardy. He stayed still while she finished examining his scalp. Though blood matted his hair, it had stopped flowing and the wound did not appear serious. She helped him sit up. "Are you dizzy?"

"No."

"Liar." She retrieved his beaver hat, which had rolled into the corner by the door, brushed it off, and returned it to him. "Do you think they were trying to kill us or just scare us?"

"I don't know, but we certainly could have been killed." He settled his hat on his head. "Either way, it could have been a trap by the man who spoke to me last night and sent us to the tavern, but why—"

"Send us somewhere we could obtain real information."

"Quite. I think it's more likely Axel sent word after we spoke with him. There would have been time to arrange for the carriage while we were interviewing the others and then talking to Heinrich." He pushed himself to his feet, almost steadily if one didn't look too closely, and reached down to help her up. He tucked her hand through his arm, but she wasn't the one he spoke to. "Tania, what the *hell* had you stumbled into?"

21

"You think Tatiana Kirsanova discovered some sort of secret conspiracy that threatens the Congress?" Lord Castlereagh stood at the desk in his study, drumming his fingers on the polished mahogany.

"That's what the evidence suggests."

Castlereagh fixed Malcolm with the stare he used across the council table. "The evidence is that Princess Tatiana visited a tavern in a less than savory part of town and asked questions about a group of men meeting there."

"Foreign men meeting about something so secret someone tried to kill Suzanne and me when we got too close to it."

"The carriage could have been an accident."

"Believe me, sir, I know the difference."

Castlereagh strode to the windows and stared out across the rain-drenched square at the lodgings of his half brother, Lord Stewart, Britain's official ambassador to Vienna. "These men could be dealers in stolen artifacts. We know Princess Tatiana was one herself." He turned and regarded Malcolm, the gray light from the window at his back. "We have matters to consider that are weightier than personal feelings. But I'm not insensible of the strain the princess's death has placed upon you."

"Believe me, sir, I'm perfectly capable—"

"For God's sake, Malcolm." Castlereagh took two impatient steps toward him. "Suzanne isn't here. We can stop pretending. I know what Tatiana Kirsanova was to you. I won't say I approve your relationship with her. But I wouldn't be human did I not make allowances for your feelings for her." Castlereagh, notorious through Vienna for his surprising fidelity to his wife, tugged a crisp shirt cuff smooth beneath the well-cut superfine of his coat. "And I believe I am human, whatever some of my detractors in the House of Commons may say."

"Sir." Malcolm clasped his hands behind his back. "I learned long since to put my personal feelings aside when it comes to matters of policy."

"My dear boy, you're desperate to believe there was some good in Princess Tatiana, and that she thought more of you than of all the others she played against one another." Castlereagh crossed to Malcolm and gripped his shoulders. "Desperate enough that you'll grasp hold of any shred of evidence. Desperate enough that you'll overlook the fact that Tatiana Kirsanova was an unscrupulous adventuress who lived by her wits. Who took a string of men to her bed, including Napoleon Bonaparte. Who occasionally gave us worthwhile information but was no more loyal to us than to anyone else and had the morals of a—"

Malcolm jerked away from Castlereagh's hold. He stopped himself, hand raised, a split second before he struck the foreign secretary a blow to the jaw.

Castlereagh regarded him steadily. "Point taken, I believe."

"Your pardon, sir," Malcolm said, appalled. "I—"

"It's all right, Malcolm. I provoked you to it. Deliberately."

"And proved your point to admirable effect." Malcolm rubbed his hand. "But granted I'm not the most clear-sighted person where Tatiana is concerned, of all the people we have access to, I best understand the workings of her mind. You ordered me to discover who killed her."

"I'm beginning to question my judgment." Castlereagh moved back to the desk and folded the London-couriered copy of the *Morning Post* that lay atop it into neat quarters. "You've been talking to Adam Czartoryski."

"I thought talking to our fellow diplomats was the point of the incessant round of entertainments we endure in Vienna," Malcolm said, mindful of the secrecy he owed Czartoryski.

Castlereagh set the newspaper aside and aligned the papers on his ink blotter. "I should have known Czartoryski's veneer of liberal principles would draw you in."

"I think it's more than a veneer."

"That's exactly what I mean." Castlereagh spun round to face Malcolm. "If Czartoryski has his way, we'll be facing a Russian empire that reaches its tentacles west through Poland."

"Czartoryski wants freedom for his country, with its own constitution. In our concern about Russian influence, we've rather lost sight of what the Poles want."

"Dear God, you sound like the Opposition talking at home. Czartoryski was trained in intrigue in the court of Catherine the Great. He can be as ruthless as anyone in Vienna, and he's pushing Tsar Alexander in a ruinous direction."

"With all due respect, I'm more worried about Count Otronsky and his dreams of Russian empire."

"That's because Otronsky doesn't pull the wool over your eyes by going about quoting Locke and Paine."

Malcolm gave a short laugh. "You seem to think I've lost perspective about more than just Tatiana."

"Not entirely. You're still the best brain I have at my disposal. Just try to remember the truth may take you places you don't wish to go."

Malcolm drew a breath. The air smelled of damp and candle smoke. "If Tatiana did stumble upon a plot, I presume you want to learn what the plot was. Unless—"

"Yes?"

The sound of rain lashing the window echoed through the room, punctuated by a faint hiss from the porcelain stove.

Malcolm stared at the blue tiles of the stove and the flickering flame within. He turned his gaze back to the foreign secretary. "Unless, of course, you already knew of this plot."

"What the devil—"

"My mysterious source warned me to trust no one."

Castlereagh's lips whitened with an anger he had not displayed when Malcolm nearly struck him. "You'd trust your mysterious source over me?"

"My dear sir, you've always said you value my tendency to question everything."

Eithne's maid was setting a Vaughn family tiara on her mistress's head when Fitz came into the room. At the sight of his reflection in the looking glass, every muscle in Eithne's body tensed.

"That will be all, Mary," she said, as the weight of her tiara settled against her scalp.

Mary, who had grown up on Eithne's father's estate and had been with Eithne since she was a bride, smoothed the lace at the neck of Eithne's gown and twitched her sash straight, then curtsied and withdrew.

Eithne sat very still, conscious of Fitz's gaze upon her in the mirror.

"You look lovely," he said. "I'm sorry, I know I'm late."

"Your costume for the Carrousel was sent round this afternoon."

"I'll dress quickly."

"Fitz." Eithne turned round on the dressing table bench, smoothing her heavy embroidered skirts. "I don't know if this makes it easier or harder for you. But I know."

"Know?" His gaze moved over her face.

"That you were Tatiana Kirsanova's lover."

He went as still and cold as an image carved in ice. Then he took a half step forward. "Darling—"

"Don't."

"Oh, Eithne." He seemed frozen to the spot. "I never meant to hurt you."

"Which doesn't alter the fact that you did." She got to her feet, conscious of Fitz's mother's sapphires heavy round her throat and the matching earrings swinging from her ears. "I still remember the day we met. That evening at Almack's. I'd had my toes trod upon by one too many recent undergraduates, and then I turned round and saw you coming across the room toward me. I thought you were the most handsome man I'd ever seen."

"Eithne—" Her name was a harsh rasp upon his lips.

"But that wasn't when I fell in love with you." She picked up one of her embroidered evening gloves from the dressing table and began to pull it on. The French kid was smooth and cool against her skin. "A fortnight or so later my brother and I met you riding in the park. Johnny hung back to allow us time to talk. You told me you'd taken up fishing to give you something to share with your stepbrother. So many people resent intrusions into their family, and here you were, looking for a way to make it easier for him. I thought then that you weren't just the handsomest man I'd ever met but quite possibly the kindest. I wrote in my diary that night that I was sure I'd love you forever." She reached for her second glove. "It's amazing how long I went on believing that."

She saw Fitz swallow, saw the thoughts chase themselves through his brain. "And now?"

"I can't believe I was ever so naïve as to believe love existed."

He took a step toward her, then checked himself. "I have no right to ask anything of you. Least of all that you believe I speak the truth when I say I can't imagine a life without you."

She tugged her gloves smooth. "You're used to me, and change is difficult, particularly for men."

"Don't, Eithne." His voice slammed against the silk-hung walls with sudden force. "Call me any names you will but don't cheapen what I feel for you."

"Why not? You've already cheapened it yourself."

He strode forward and stopped, a handsbreadth from her dressing table. "My God, do you really think that of me?"

"I think you cared deeply for Tatiana Kirsanova. Perhaps I'm giving you too much credit, but I'd like to believe you wouldn't have acted as you did if your feelings weren't engaged."

Fitz scraped a hand through his hair. "I did love her. Or I thought I did. But it was entirely different from—"

"The comfortable, prosaic, domestic love you feel for me?" The words were like acid on her tongue.

"Of course not. But there's no denying we've—"

"Grown used to each other." The unaccustomed rage drained from her body, leaving her winded. Perhaps this was how prizefighters felt after sparring. She dropped back on the dressing table bench. "Even all the time you were in the Peninsula, it never occurred to me that you would—Perhaps it should have done."

"No." He crouched down beside her, his gaze level with her own. "There wasn't anyone else. Though I don't expect you to believe me."

His eyes had that expression that always tugged at her heart. She was disgusted to find that it was still so. And at the same time oddly relieved. "I do, though I fear I'm being a fool." She reached out and pushed his hair off his forehead, then pulled her hand back.

"Never that, Eithne." He reached for her hand, then he, too, let his own fall to his side. "I'm the one who wasn't worthy of your trust."

She plucked at the satin of her gown. "It must be horrible for you. Losing her."

"I—Yes." He drew a rough breath. "Thank you for understanding."

"I seem to be able to hate you and yet at the same time—" She shook her head. "I told Suzanne I knew about the affair."

His gaze shot to her face.

"Oh, I'd worked out that they'd already discovered the truth. I knew they were bound to do so. You should have realized that, Fitz. You can be far too naïve."

"Malcolm suspects—" Pain swept over his face. "I never thought one of my closest friends could think such a thing of me."

"How could he not?"

Fitz's gaze froze on her face. Cold horror filled his eyes. "You aren't sure, are you?"

She looked back at him. The man she had loved and trusted without question now seemed as much an illusion as a prince in the fairy tales she read to her children. "How *could* I be sure? I've been so willfully blind in so many ways."

"But you must know I'd never—"

"I can't finish that sentence anymore."

He pushed himself to his feet. "I never wanted to turn you into—"

"A cynic? More a realist. My dear, are you really sure you can say with confidence that you don't suspect me?"

Blanca adjusted the diamond clasps on Suzanne's black velvet overdress, then twitched her slashed sleeves so they fell to show a glimpse of the white satin beneath. "You look like a princess."

Suzanne laughed. "I'll look more like a lady-in-waiting when I'm in company with all the other *belles d'amour*."

Colin, sitting on the carpet with his wooden blocks, stretched up his arms to Suzanne. "Pretty."

"Thank you, darling." Suzanne scooped him up. A twinge ran through her shoulder, though it was already much improved since last night. She pressed a kiss to her son's forehead. "I'm glad you appreciate all the time it takes to create an elaborate toilette. It's an excellent quality in a gentleman." She glanced at the clock on the escritoire. "I'd best get Malcolm. The carriage will be round soon."

Malcolm had dressed first and then gone to the attachés' sitting room to review some papers while Blanca helped her into her Carrousel finery. Suzanne gave Colin to Blanca, picked up her long veil, and made her way down the passage to the sitting room. She turned the handle without knocking, but as she started to push the door panels open, a sound turned her blood to ice. A cry of naked anguish, sharper than a sob.

She eased the door shut and waited the length of several heartbeats, her mouth dry and her chest tight with bitter acknowledgment. At last she drew a steadying breath and rapped loudly on the door panels. "Malcolm? I'm dressed at last. The carriage will be round in a few minutes."

She waited another second or so, then pushed open the door. Her husband was sitting at the desk, his hands flat on the ink blotter, as though through an effort of will. The candlelight glittered against telltale traces of damp on his cheeks, though she might not have noticed if she hadn't known to look.

He got to his feet. "You look beautiful."

She had completely forgot for a moment about her Carrousel costume. She looked into his eyes. His smile was kind, his gaze a world away from her. "Thank you. You make a very handsome knight yourself."

He reached for the candlesnuffer and began to put out the tapers. "I've been reading David's latest update from the House of Commons. More Whig criticism of Castlereagh's lack of concern for the self-determination rights of everyone from the Poles to the Genoese. Much of which I find it hard to argue with."

"Remember you're a diplomat, darling." She subdued every impulse to go to his side and touch him. "That includes being diplomatic with your own foreign secretary."

He grimaced and she wondered just what had transpired at his interview with Castlereagh this afternoon. "Sometimes one of my greatest challenges."

"Well, tonight for a change you can journey back a few hundred years and tilt at your opponents."

"Instead of at windmills, as I usually do?" He moved to her side and offered her his arm.

"Nonsense, darling." She tucked her arm through his own, curling her fingers lightly round his velvet sleeve. "I'm sure you can tell a windmill from a handsaw."

His eyes glinted, though their depths were still opaque. "At least when the wind is southerly."

They moved into the candlelit passage. That cry of anguish might have been a figment of her imagination. But she knew it had not been. That broken, desperate sound would echo in her memory forever.

She kept her fingers steady on her husband's arm and her gaze fixed straight ahead. She had known Tatiana Kirsanova meant a great deal to Malcolm. She had been almost sure they were lovers. But until now she hadn't realized how very strong the bond between them had been.

22

Dorothée fingered the end of the long veil draped over her arm. "I couldn't sleep last night. I kept going over and over all the things that might go wrong."

"Dearest, it's probably inevitable that something will go wrong." Suzanne squeezed her friend's shoulders, careful not to crush the black velvet of Dorothée's overdress. "The trick is carrying it off when something does." Just as one could maintain a bright tone when one's husband's grief over another woman still reverberated in one's ears.

Dorothée gave her a quick, dazzling smile. "You're a splendid friend, Suzanne. And I think you must be the perfect diplomat's wife."

"Hardly. I'm still learning the language. It isn't my native tongue."

Dorothée cast a glance round the twenty-two other women gathered in this anteroom outside the Spanish Riding School's arena. Their gleaming velvet and satin gowns, in the style of the early seventeenth century, divided them into groups representing four countries. Hungarian green, Polish crimson, Austrian blue, and French black. "I do think the costumes turned out well."

"The fabric should be splendid beneath the lights." Suzanne smoothed her full Louis XIII skirts. Like Dorothée, she was in black French dress. *After all*, Dorothée had said, *you are half French.*

You'd have grown up there if it weren't for the Revolution. Which was more or less true. Suzanne's father had been French, her mother Spanish. That much of Malcolm's knowledge of her past was accurate.

"Thérèse Esterhazy always forgets her place in line," Dorothée said. "I keep worrying we should have had one more rehearsal—"

"It's a pageant, Doro, not Shakespeare." Wilhelmine of Sagan joined them in a swirl of green velvet and white satin, sparkling with diamonds. "Do you think Tsar Alexander is really ill, or is he boycotting the Carrousel for reasons of his own?"

"You'd have more reason to know than any of us," Dorothée said.

Wilhelmine lifted her chin. "He's called on me a few times. I can hardly claim to be in his confidence."

"He looks at you as though it's more than that."

"Looks can be deceiving."

"I don't think we'll lack for an audience," Suzanne said.

Wilhelmine adjusted her jeweled toque. "Metternich isn't here, either."

"Relieved or sorry?" Dorothée asked.

Wilhelmine shrugged, fluttering her green velvet oversleeves and the embroidered white satin beneath. "It's his name day today. I sent him a new candlestick yesterday to replace the one on his writing table and he wrote me quite a civil note of thanks."

"Civil or impassioned?" Dorothée asked.

Wilhelmine smoothed the veil draped over her arm. "I'd have thought he'd have come tonight to see Marie. Whatever his failings, he's a devoted father."

Dorothée cast a sidelong glance at her sister. "He probably couldn't bear watching Alfred von Windischgrätz act as your champion."

Wilhelmine's gaze was on Marie Metternich, who was practicing a step of the minuet. "I never desired to make anyone unhappy."

"But it seems to happen regardless," Dorothée said.

"I don't believe I've ever worn quite so many jewels at once." Suzanne stepped between the Courland sisters, literally and metaphorically. A pearl-and-diamond necklace, on loan from

Aline's mother, hung heavy round her throat, and the diamond earrings Malcolm had given her for her recent birthday (reparations for their life in Vienna, she often thought) swayed from her ears. "I feel positively weighted down."

"I think we're wearing every pearl and diamond to be found in Hungary, Bohemia, and Austria," Dorothée said. "I still can't believe you broke up Metternich's Order of the Golden Fleece to trim your gown, Willie."

Wilhelmine glanced down at her jewel-encrusted bodice. "Yes, well, we were on better terms when I started work on the costume, and you made such a point of wanting everything to be lavish. Besides, I loaned out some of my own jewels. I even offered Laure Metternich the choice of my emeralds or sapphires." Wilhelmine cast a glance round the antechamber. "One could fund a small kingdom with the jewels in this room alone."

Dorothée twitched a fold of her skirt smooth. "The Festivals Committee want this to be the most dazzling event of the Congress."

"I wasn't criticizing the event, Doro. I daresay it will be a great triumph. You're quite right, at the Congress nothing succeeds like excesses."

Sisters. They always knew just how to wound. Suzanne touched Dorothée's arm. "It's a marvel, Doro. You should be very proud." She felt Wilhelmine give her a sidelong glance and suspected a good part of the duchess's sharpness was due to the aftereffects of their conversation the previous day.

A side door opened and the thud of boots and jangle of spurs announced the arrival of the knights. They wore velvet doublets and plumed hats, six each in green, crimson, blue, and black to match the ladies. Malcolm crossed to Suzanne's side and swept his hat from his head.

"You do know that knights dressed in these clothes would have been cut to ribbons at Agincourt, don't you?" he said.

Looking into those mocking, ironic eyes, one would never guess he'd been lost in grief a mere hour ago. "Oh, what it is to have a husband who read history at Balliol." Suzanne took the scarf she'd been holding along with her veil and tied it near Malcolm's sword hand. The other *belles d'amour* were doing the same with their cavaliers. "We aren't recreating a proper medieval tournament, we're recreating the days when young men played at recreating the mythical days of chivalry. Very appropriate. You're supposed to put on a good show, not really go about bashing each other."

Malcolm looked down at the bow of gold-embroidered fabric. "Doesn't it rather defeat the idea of a favor that you've given us all such similar scarves?"

"Don't be difficult, dearest."

A man in a harlequin-patterned tunic hurried into the anteroom and bowed to Dorothée. "It lacks but two minutes to eight, Madame la Comtesse."

Dorothée straightened her spine, an actress about to step onto the stage. She draped her gossamer veil over her head and signaled to the other ladies to do likewise. The twenty-four *belles d'amour* and their cavaliers lined up in their predetermined order. A bouquet of lustrous velvet, brilliant white satin, and sparkling gems. A trumpet fanfare sounded from the arena, just as two footmen in tunics and hose pulled open the double doors. They stepped through into the glare of candlelight.

A multitude of crystal chandeliers blazed down on them. A roar went up from the crowd. The galleries on either side of the riding school were packed. Though Suzanne had known the crowd would be huge, somehow rehearsals had not prepared her for the sight. The golden light gleamed indiscriminately off ancestral tiaras and gifts from current lovers, gold braid on dress uniforms and coats encrusted with medals and decorations.

They passed the British delegation and she caught a glimpse of Eithne's pale face, Tommy Belmont's appreciative gaze, Aline's bright eyes. In the gallery reserved for ambassadors and dignitaries, she saw Castlereagh, austere and elegant in black, and Lady Castlereagh, once again wearing her husband's Order of the Garter in her hair.

Hammered metal armor flashed on the Corinthian columns that supported the vaulted ceiling, and she glimpsed the mottoes of the knights who were to compete in the tourney (many of which she and Doro had invented while poring through books of medieval legends over glasses of Rhenish wine).

The knights escorted the *belles d'amour* to a brocade-draped stand at one end of the hall. The ladies sank into their seats with a unison that should make Dorothée proud, gossamer veils swirling about them. The knights bowed and withdrew.

Another trumpet fanfare signaled the entrance of the sovereigns. The spectators rose to their feet, and the *belles d'amour* did likewise. Dorothée lifted her hand. At her signal the ladies pulled their veils from their heads. A cheer went up from the crowd. Suzanne didn't want to ruin the picture by glancing round, but it seemed no one's headdress had tumbled to the ground. So far so good.

The sovereigns occupied the stand at the opposite end of the hall from that of the *belles d'amour*. Tsar Alexander was a notable absence, but Tsarina Elisabeth was there, lovely in white satin and diamonds, a tiara glinting on her white-blond hair. The Emperor of Austria moved to the gold velvet chair in the center of the stand, his wife and Tsarina Elisabeth on either side of him. The other sovereigns and princes regnant took their places according to their precedence.

"Thank God they didn't get tangled up," Dorothée murmured to Suzanne as they dropped back into their seats.

"You'd think after nearly two months in Vienna they'd be clear about precedence," Suzanne replied, settling her full skirts. "Especially considering they agreed to go by order of age."

"I imagine they could disagree about that if they put their minds to it," Dorothée murmured.

A military fanfare echoed through the hall, announcing the arrival of the knights. Hooves thudded against the ground. Bridles jangled. Twenty-four page boys entered the arena first, carrying banners that rippled as they walked. The knights followed riding coal black Hungarian horses, whose glossy coats gleamed in the warm candlelight. Their squires, dressed in the Spanish fashion—*Why do Hungarian, Polish, Austrian, and French knights have Spanish squires?* Malcolm had asked—brought up the rear.

The pages and squires lined up on either side of the arena. The knights, two abreast, advanced to the sovereigns' stand and lowered their lances in a salute. Tsarina Elisabeth and Empress Maria Ludovica waved, and the other ladies in the stand followed suit.

The knights wheeled round and rode to the opposite end of the arena where they bowed to the *belles d'amour*. The crowd rose to their feet again with a roar of approval.

Dorothée and Wilhelmine stood to greet the knights, and the other ladies followed their example. Dorothée's cavalier, handsome young Count Karl Clam-Martinitz, lifted her hand to his lips. She blushed like a schoolgirl. Wilhelmine tugged playfully at the feather in Alfred von Windischgrätz's hat.

Malcolm edged his horse up to the stand near Suzanne. His eyes held an ironic glint. "Of all the roles I ever thought to find us playing, this seems the least likely," he murmured in English.

"But one must still play one's part with conviction." On impulse, she pulled her handkerchief from her sleeve and fastened it to his shoulder with a pin.

"You already gave me a favor," he said.

"But this one is unique and really comes from me."

He grinned and then, to her surprise, lifted her hand and pressed it to his lips. He held it for a moment, and the shock of the contact ran through her.

The knights turned their horses and circled the arena twice to the delight of the crowd. The heralds blew a fanfare echoed by the orchestras situated above the stands at either end of the arena. The rich sound reverberated off the high ceiling and washed over the hall. Then the thunder of horses' hooves shook the ladies' balcony as the first six knights to compete rode into the arena, accompanied by their pages and squires.

The tournament began with the *pas de lance*, the knights riding at a gallop and removing on their lance point one of the rings hung from ribbons before the sovereigns' stand. "You can scarcely tell Monsieur Rannoch and Lord Fitzwilliam from the Austro-Hungarians," Dorothée murmured to Suzanne. Given the value Austro-Hungarians placed on riding skills, it was praise indeed.

They proceeded to tossing javelins at models of Saracen heads. Suzanne turned her head away in cold shame. Dorothée cast an anxious glance at her and squeezed her hand. Suzanne had argued strenuously for not including this particular game in the tournament, putting diplomacy and good taste ahead of historical accuracy. Goodness knows they were bending historical accuracy in a number of other ways. Doro had listened, but the Festivals Committee had held firm. She could only wonder what some of the dignitaries present, such as the turbaned Pasha of Widdin and Prince Manug, Bey of Murza, made of the distressing spectacle. Malcolm flung his javelin wide of the mark. She doubted it was an accident.

The less troubling game of cutting at apples dangling from the ceiling followed. At last they progressed to jousting, a parody (supposedly safe, like stage combat) of a medieval joust. The rules of attack and defense had been carefully laid out, and the heralds of arms intervened the moment they saw the faintest move out-of-bounds. Suzanne had seen greater aggression in a tennis match, let alone a real battle.

Then in the midst of a charge, the Prince of Lichtenstein's horse reared, and the prince thudded to the ground. A murmur of concern rose from the crowd as the illusion of the pageant was rent by the reality of physical hurt. Squires rushed forward and carried the fallen prince from the arena.

Dorothée rose to her feet, her hand to her mouth. Wilhelmine pulled her back into her chair. "I saw him move his hand, Doro. He'll be fine. He's probably suffered worse on a morning ride in the Prater."

The crowd settled back and the tournament resumed.

Malcolm and Fitz faced each other in the next-to-last joust. For a moment Suzanne forgot Fitz's deception, Princess Tatiana, Eithne's pain, and the poisoned gulf between her husband and his friend, in the sheer pleasure of admiring Malcolm's and Fitz's skill. Dust rose as their horses thundered over the sand-strewn ground. Lances crashed against shields. They wheeled and rode at each other again, lances glinting into the candlelight. Metal met metal in another resounding crash.

And Fitz tumbled to the ground.

Malcolm caught Fitz's horse by the reins and brought it to a standstill before it could trample its fallen rider. Then he swung down from the saddle and knelt beside his friend. Where the Prince of Lichtenstein had shown no sign of hurt, the candlelight gleamed against blood spilling from Fitz's head, staining the sand crimson. Dorothée gave a stifled cry and gripped Suzanne's hand.

In the gallery where the British delegation sat, a fair-haired woman in white had risen to her feet. Eithne. Suzanne cursed that she was so far away. A slender figure in yellow rose and put her arm round Eithne. Aline.

The squires hurried out with another stretcher and carefully lifted Fitz onto it. Malcolm followed them from the field, fear and self-recrimination in the taut set of his shoulders.

Dorothée's fingers bit into Suzanne's hand like an iron shackle. "God in heaven. What have we done?"

Count Clam-Martinitz knelt opposite Malcolm across the stretcher where Fitz lay. "What the devil happened?"

"Someone tampered with his horse." Malcolm picked up Fitz's hand and drew a breath of relief when he felt the blood pulsing through Fitz's wrist. "Find Geoffrey Blackwell. He'll be with the British delegation."

"I'm here." Blackwell strode into the room, Aline and Eithne behind him.

Malcolm moved aside to give Geoffrey his place beside Fitz. Eithne hung back, gaze fastened on Fitz as though her world had shrunk down to his each indrawn breath. Malcolm went to her side and squeezed her hand. "His pulse is strong."

Fitz's eyes were still closed. Geoffrey examined the wound on his head with brisk, methodical care. "Nasty looking, but with luck it won't leave him with more than a headache."

It was, Malcolm thought, a hideous echo of his and Suzanne's encounter with the carriage outside the Empress Rose earlier in the day. For the first time he understood what Suzanne had gone through as he lay unconscious. But he had recovered consciousness far more quickly than this.

Fitz stirred. Eithne dropped down beside him and took his hand.

Fitz stared at his wife, then looked round in confusion. "What—?"

"I'm afraid I unhorsed you." Malcolm knelt beside Eithne. "Your horse had a shoe loosened."

"Why—"

"Never mind about that now." Geoffrey pressed a brandy-soaked cloth to Fitz's wound. "You're a fortunate man, Vaughn. Head injuries can be exceedingly dangerous. Don't move too quickly."

Fitz's gaze focused on his wife. "Eithne. Shouldn't—"

"Hush, love. It's all right." Eithne folded his hand between both her own.

While Blackwell wound lint round Fitz's head, Malcolm got to his feet and addressed Count Clam-Martinitz. "Who had access to the horses?"

Clam-Martinitz frowned at the implications. "Almost anyone. The stables weren't locked. But why—"

"For want of a nail—The nails on one of the shoes of Fitz's horse had been loosened. It was only a matter of time until the shoe came loose, and one could predict Fitz would suffer an accident. It was clear who would ride which horse, from our last rehearsal."

"Good God." Clam-Martinitz stared at him. "You think someone wanted to harm Vaughn?"

Malcolm glanced at his friend. Fitz's head was now swathed in folds of lint. Blackwell was snipping off the ends, while Eithne stroked Fitz's hair. "It very much looks that way."

"In God's name, why?"

"That," Malcolm said, his gaze still on Fitz, "would seem to be the question."

23

"Champagne, Your Majesty?" Adam Czartoryski bowed to Elisabeth, a crystal champagne glass held steady in one hand.

"How kind of you, Prince." Elisabeth accepted the glass and smiled at Adam, remembering him opening a bottle of champagne during a stolen interlude in an abandoned gardener's cottage nearly two decades ago. Remembering, too, the warmth of the log fire he'd kindled, the slither of blankets on their bare skin, the pounding of rain on the roof. And the flash of lightning reflected in his eyes as he'd lowered his body to hers.

A betraying wave of heat shot through her. She felt the pressure of myriad inevitable gazes turned in their direction, but no one could take exception to Adam bringing her a glass of champagne. Harp music from wandering minstrels cascaded through the supper rooms, masking their conversation. "Have you heard how Lord Fitzwilliam does?" Elisabeth asked.

Adam shook his head. "I think he's been taken back to the Minoritenplatz."

Elisabeth stared at the frothy bubbles in her glass. "I saw his wife's face when he was carried from the field. As though her whole world had been destroyed. It made me realize—"

"How you'd feel if it had been Alexander?" Adam asked.

Elisabeth looked up at him. She saw concern in his gaze and something else beneath. He masked it well, but she had long since learned to read every nuance of his expression. The embers she saw in his eyes now were jealousy. An absurd, traitorous triumph rushed through her, headier than if she had downed the entire glass of champagne.

"No." She scanned his face, marveling at the power that lay in knowing one was loved. "How I'd feel if it had been you."

"You think Fitz was deliberately targeted?" Suzanne regarded Malcolm over the rim of her champagne glass. All about them jewels flashed in the candlelight, satin slippers and kid shoes pattered against the floor, crystal glasses clinked. The smell of oranges and cloves and cinnamon hung in the air. Thank goodness she and Dorothée had arranged for wandering minstrels to entertain at the ball following the Carrousel. The music (much of it authentic, at least from the sixteenth century, they had spent hours looking for it) washed over the room and prevented conversations from carrying.

"I don't see any other explanation," her husband said.

"Because of something Princess Tatiana had told him? Or something he knew about her?"

"The implication is unmistakable, but if so it's something he's been keeping secret."

"Dear God." Dorothée joined them in a rustle of satin and velvet. Lines of strain bracketed her mouth. "It seems this evening will never end. With all the things I lay awake worrying could go wrong, it never occurred to me someone would be hurt. What a criminal fool I've been."

"Doro, no." Suzanne put her arm round her friend, heedless of crushing their gowns. "You couldn't have foreseen this."

"Believe me, Madame la Comtesse," Malcolm said, "I've seen enough death to know that guilt is the inevitable sequel and to realize how fruitless it is. And in this case, quite misplaced. Lord Fitzwilliam's horse was tampered with."

Dorothée stared at him. "But who on earth—" Her eyes narrowed. "Because of his relationship with Princess Tatiana?"

"Perhaps." Malcolm's gaze skimmed over Dorothée's face. "Besides Suzanne, who else had you told about Fitz's affair with Princess Tatiana?"

"No one. That is—" Dorothée fingered the full sleeve of her gown. "I mentioned it to my uncle, but—"

"When?" Malcolm asked.

"Yesterday after the rehearsal. Monsieur Rannoch, surely you can't think—"

She broke off, her gaze fixed unseeing on a juggler in green and red who was passing through the crowd.

Malcolm touched her arm. "Any number of people may have known of the affair. Gossip has a way of spreading in Vienna."

"There you are. It takes half an hour just to cross a ballroom in Vienna." Geoffrey Blackwell joined them, Aline at his side.

"Lord Fitzwilliam?" Dorothée scanned Geoffrey's face with anxious eyes.

"Back to the Minoritenplatz with Lady Fitzwilliam. He shows reassuring clarity of mind. I've instructed Lady Fitzwilliam to keep him awake for at least three hours and to send for me if he shows any signs of confusion."

"Thank God." Dorothée gave a heartfelt sigh. "He'll recover fully?"

"If there aren't complications." Geoffrey was not one to sugar-coat matters, but he smiled at Dorothée with reassurance as he said it.

"He kept telling Eithne he loved her," Aline said. "It's enough to make one lose one's cynicism about marriage."

Dorothée shook her head. "I knew Vienna was dangerous. But I never thought the dangers would be so—"

"Bloody?" Aline asked.

"Frowning, Madame la Comtesse?" Count Clam-Martinitz joined them. "You should be enjoying your night of triumph."

"It doesn't feel very triumphant."

Clam-Martinitz smiled down at her. "What happened to Vaughn was terrible, but I hear he will make a full recovery. The near tragedy doesn't lessen your achievement. Dance with me."

"I can't—"

Suzanne squeezed Dorothée's shoulder. "He's right. No help will come from dwelling on it."

Dorothée hesitated, as though teetering on an unseen precipice. Then her face relaxed into a smile, and she took the count's arm. Geoffrey offered his arm to Aline, who took it with less surprise than she had shown when he asked her to dance at the Metternich masquerade.

"Leaving us free to speculate," Malcolm said, "though there seems little more to be said."

Suzanne took a sip of champagne, remembering the bottle they'd shared on their wedding night. Some of it had ended up spilled on the sheets. "Do you think it could really be resolved so simply?"

"What?"

"Fitz and Eithne. Could a moment of danger wipe away all the bitterness?"

"No," Malcolm said in a flat voice. "She'll never again see him as the man she thought he was. But perhaps with time she'll come to—"

"Appreciate the man he is? Darling, coming from you that sounds positively romantic."

"There's a great deal to be said for realism."

"Then we're exceedingly fortunate." She meant the words to be light, but they held an edge like smashed crystal.

He watched her for a moment, his gaze unreadable, then held out his hand. "Shall we—"

"Still a pattern card of courtly love. You'd look right at home at the court of Louis XIII." Count Otronsky, in the dark Russian uniform Tsar Alexander also affected, medals glittering on his chest, stopped before them and swept a bow. "You both gave superb performances this evening."

"Thank you, Count." Suzanne gave him her hand. His gaze seemed to slice through the velvet and satin of her gown, but unlike many gentlemen he seemed to be probing for the secrets of her mind, not her body. "But I merely sat in the stands and danced the minuet to open the ball."

"Don't underestimate the value of evoking a mood, madame.

Rannoch, I knew you British were good at putting your horses over fences in pursuit of foxes, but I didn't realize you were so adroit at the more elegant maneuvers."

Malcolm shook Otronsky's hand. "We have more finesse than our Continental friends sometimes credit."

"Believe me, Rannoch, I never make the mistake of underestimating the British." Otronsky's gaze locked with Malcolm's own for a moment. "I understand Vaughn has recovered consciousness?"

"And Dr. Blackwell is hopeful of a full recovery."

"A tragic accident."

"Tragic, yes. But not an accident. His horse was tampered with."

Otronsky frowned. "Vaughn is one of the last people in Vienna I'd have thought to find the victim of a plot. Perhaps he's more like you than I realized."

"Are you implying my husband has enemies, Count?" Suzanne asked, masking her words with a playful smile.

"Merely that your husband is a man of secrets, madame."

Suzanne followed Otronsky with her gaze when he moved off. "Tsar Alexander still has him watching us."

"I wouldn't be surprised if Tsar Alexander has him investigating Tatiana's murder. I can only hope he hasn't learned about the tsarina's papers."

"Champagne?" A young man—a boy really, he could not have been more than sixteen—appeared beside them with a tray of glasses.

Suzanne shook her head. Her glass was still more than half-full.

The footman inclined his head. But instead of moving off, he pressed a sealed paper into Malcolm's hand. "I was to give this to you tonight, sir. The lady was most specific."

"Lady?" Malcolm asked.

"With the red hair. She said if she didn't tell me otherwise before, I was to give you this letter at the Carrousel."

Malcolm's fingers closed on the paper. "When did she give it to you?"

"Three days since."

Malcolm gave the waiter a coin, and he moved off. Suzanne

stared at the paper in her husband's hand. It was sealed with a lavender wafer, impressed with an unadorned button. Malcolm slit it open. A series of nonsense letters stared up at them. A code.

"Tatiana?" Suzanne asked.

"Tatiana."

Three days ago, she would have laughed in bitter mockery at the suggestion that she would ever be relieved to see her husband receive a communication from Tatiana Kirsanova. But evidence was evidence. Not that that stilled the lurch in her chest as she watched Malcolm run his fingers over the paper.

Quickly as it had come, the tenderness in his eyes was gone. He tucked the paper into his sleeve, his diplomat's mask well in place. "We'll draw comment if we leave too early. Everyone seems to be dancing. We might as well—"

"Rannoch. Mrs. Rannoch." Colonel Frederick Radley materialized soundlessly out of the shifting crowd. A prince of cats. "My compliments, Mrs. Rannoch. The evening was a triumph."

"A triumph marred by tragedy."

"That's a bit strong, surely. Sad about Vaughn, but I understand he's expected to recover."

"It looks that way," Malcolm said. "It's too early to be sure."

Radley regarded Malcolm. "Must have been difficult coming so close to killing your best friend in battle. One would have thought that sort of thing went out with Palamon and Arcite."

"It was hell," Malcolm said in an even voice. "Though as it turns out, someone tampered with Vaughn's horse."

"Good God. Plots within plots. Of all the men in the British delegation, Vaughn's the last I'd have thought would have an unseen enemy. But then perhaps Vienna's changed him."

"Or perhaps he was an unwitting victim."

"So many unanswered questions." Radley turned to Suzanne. "But we can't allow them to mar Mrs. Rannoch's triumph. Would you honor me with a dance?"

Suzanne hesitated, gaze instinctively going to Malcolm. But Malcolm merely smiled and inclined his head. "By all means do, my dear. I need to speak to Count Nesselrode."

There was nothing for it. She allowed Radley to lead her

through an archway into the ballroom as a new waltz began. A smooth, gloved hand clasped her own as they stepped into the promenade that began the dance. Then his other arm encircled her waist. She could feel the warmth of his fingers on her back through the kid of his glove and the layers of her velvet gown and satin underdress and the corset and chemise beneath. Or perhaps the warmth came from memory.

"I always knew you had formidable talents," Radley said, his breath stirring her hair. "But I confess I never envisioned you orchestrating a tournament."

"Dorothée Périgord orchestrated it."

"As I hear tell, you were a great help. The Comtesse de Périgord says so herself. I suppose I shouldn't be surprised. I always knew you were a consummate actress." His gaze shifted over her face. "You still teach torches to burn bright."

Bile rose up in her throat. Shakespeare was Malcolm's code for talking to her. For Radley to use it seemed a desecration. "Rank flattery, Colonel."

He swung her to the side. He led in the dance as he did in other things, with a casual assurance that his partner would follow. "Your husband's an obliging fellow. If you were my wife, I don't think I'd send you off so lightly to dance in another man's arms."

They were positioned facing in opposite directions. His hipbone jutted against her own. "My dear Colonel, if you had a wife, I suspect you'd be so busy pursuing your latest flirtation that you wouldn't have the least idea with whom she was dancing."

"Touché. You know me well." His smile still dazzled like diamonds in firelight. His arm settled with confidence across the front of her gown, where her fitted bodice met her full gathered skirts. "But then I expect your husband has his own interests as well. I understand he was very close to poor Princess Tatiana."

"That seems to be the general impression." She curved her arm across the braid and gold buttons of his coat.

He caught her free hand and drew it overhead, so their clasped arms made a half circle above them. "In fact I think the most warmth I've ever seen Malcolm Rannoch display was when he looked at the princess."

Head turned to the side, she kept her gaze steady on his own as the dance required. "You saw them together in Spain?"

"Oh yes. Malcolm told you he knew Princess Tatiana in the Peninsula?"

"Of course," she said, gaze locked with his own. "What I didn't realize until recently was that you had known the princess there." *There was something between them,* Dorothée had said, *but not a love affair, even a past one.*

Radley's fingers tensed ever so slightly on her own. "Our paths crossed."

"Princess Tatiana was working for British intelligence in the Peninsula."

"Malcolm has told you a great deal, hasn't he?" He spun her forward into his arms. "But of course intelligence missions were his business, not mine."

"Yet you crossed paths with the princess."

His eyes glinted down at her. "My dear Suzanne, are you jealous? I danced with her once or twice at regimental balls—she was using an alias, of course—but for what it's worth she never shared my bed. As I said, Malcolm was the one who knew her."

"They were friends."

"Such an interesting word. In French you can't tell whether it means friend or lover."

"And yet lovers can just as easily be enemies."

The tempo increased. Radley slid his arms round her, holding both her hands prisoner behind her back. "Relieved to have your husband off your hands? Or jealous? I can't imagine you don't feel at least a bit of pique."

"Your imagination, Colonel, has its limits."

"So that's how the wind lies. It makes sense you'd take to a Continental marriage. Enjoy being able to cast your own eye about?" He spun her faster, circling after the other couples. "You know, I find myself deluged by memories."

"So do I," said Suzanne, in a tone that indicated the nature of those memories.

"My darling. I have no desire to interfere with the agreeable life you've built for yourself."

The words should have been comforting. But then she knew just how little she could rely on Radley's word.

"But," he continued, "I find I cannot contemplate another man's ring on your finger without feeling my own twinge of—"

"Pique?"

He pulled her closer and looked straight down into her eyes. She felt the warmth of his breath on her skin. "Jealousy."

Aline stared at Colonel Radley twirling Suzanne beneath his arm. Her foot came down on Geoffrey Blackwell's toe. "Damnation." She looked up at him. "Sorry."

His mouth twitched. "I won't tell your mother."

"Mama could hardly complain about my using a word I learned from her. I think when she received billets-doux from three different lovers with her morning chocolate, all appointing rendezvous at the same ball. I meant sorry for treading on your toes."

"I didn't notice."

"You're a very kind man, Dr. Blackwell."

"You're clearer sighted than that, Aline. I have a reputation as a curmudgeon."

"Which serves very well to get you out of things like squiring débutântes through dances. It's kind of you to dance with me."

"My dear girl. I don't do it to be kind."

"Chivalry lies in action more than words. And I don't mean tilting with lances or throwing javelins at ghastly models of Saracen heads." Aline cast a sideways glance down the circle of dancers. "I suspect you're much more chivalrous than Colonel Radley."

Dr. Blackwell followed the direction of her gaze. Perhaps it was her imagination, but she thought she felt his fingers tighten for a moment on her hand. "I shouldn't worry about Suzanne. She's better equipped to look after herself than most soldiers of my acquaintance."

"You don't like Radley."

Blackwell twirled her to the side and pulled her back to a very correct six inches away from him. He was a surprisingly good dancer. He made her quite forget about minding her steps. "Radley's fearless on the battlefield. He lacks the imagination to really appreciate danger."

"And?"

He grimaced. "His behavior toward the Spaniards didn't help the reputation of the British army."

She regarded him with the candor of Frances Dacre-Hammond's daughter. "How many girls did he seduce?"

Blackwell's mouth tightened. "Thank God I don't know. He left at least two with child."

"The Peninsula sounds very like Vienna."

"Some things don't change the world over."

"Vienna rather does it to excess, though. The society here reminds me of Mama's stories about Paris before the French Revolution."

"A number of people at the Congress would like to turn the clock back to the *ancien régime*."

"And the romantic intriguing goes along with the reactionary politics?" Aline glanced at the couples circling the dance floor, then looked up at Blackwell. She had known him her whole life, but he had never been part of the particular intrigues that her mother and so many of her mother's friends indulged in. "You never really tried to play their games, did you?"

"Whose?"

"Mama and her set."

"My dear Aline, I was hardly in that league."

"Because you're far too sensible." She studied his familiar features. The intense eyes, the strong nose, the flexible mouth. Odd to think that he had once been her age and perhaps as bemused by her mother's set as she was herself. "When I was seven I was passing round tea after dinner at one of Mama's parties. I was horrid at passing tea, I always sloshed it into the cups. But I had to do it. Mama wouldn't let me hide in the schoolroom or the library all the time. That day as I handed round the teacups, I heard one of the ladies say, 'She takes after her mother, which is a mercy. No telling who her father is.'"

This time his arm definitely did tighten round her. "I'm sorry, Allie."

"Don't be." She looked up at him with a laugh. "I didn't really mind, even then. It explained the odd way Papa sometimes looked at me. It was vaguely interesting, but after a bit I gave up speculating on who my father might be and decided it really didn't matter. As I grew older I was quite grateful for Papa's benign neglect and the fact that Mama allowed me to be myself, though I think she often hasn't the least idea what to make of me. But then I can't imagine living a life like Mama or the Duchess of Sagan. It seems exhausting."

"So I've always thought. Your mother says it means I lead a sadly dull life."

"Yes, I don't suppose Mama's life is dull. Or that Aunt Arabella's was." Aline thought of Malcolm's mother. For a moment she could see the restless glitter in Arabella Rannoch's eyes and hear her brittle laugh. "But at least in Aunt Arabella's case, it doesn't seem to have made her very happy."

Blackwell's gaze clouded. Though Aline could never recall seeing him engage in the flirtation that was so common in her mother's drawing room, she had a distant memory of seeing his gaze rest on her Aunt Arabella with startling tenderness. Even at the age of seven she'd felt a shock of surprise at the softness in his eyes. There was no mistaking the pain in his usually cool gaze now. "I don't think much of anything made Arabella happy," Blackwell said. "She spent her life looking for distraction. Not very comfortable for her children, I'm afraid."

"I sometimes think that's why Malcolm takes his responsibilities so seriously. Because neither of his parents was particularly responsible." Aline saw her cousin's stricken face as he knelt over Fitzwilliam Vaughn. "What happened to Lord Fitzwilliam—it could easily have been worse, couldn't it?"

"Much." Blackwell's voice turned grim. "If he'd hit his head differently or landed on his neck. Or if the horse had struck him."

Aline frowned at the top mother-of-pearl button on Blackwell's waistcoat. "Malcolm would never have forgiven himself. I'm afraid he's going to have a hard time forgiving himself as it is."

* * *

Eithne met Suzanne and Malcolm at the door of her and Fitz's bedchamber when they returned from the ball, wrapped in a dressing gown, hair tumbling down her back. "He's sleeping. Dr. Blackwell just looked in. He says Fitz's breathing and pulse are good. And Fitz hasn't reported any headache."

Despite the shadows of fatigue on her face, the tension was gone from about her mouth, and her eyes had a glow that Suzanne hadn't seen of late.

Malcolm pressed Eithne's hand. "I can't tell you how relieved I am to hear it. You will try to sleep yourself? You'll be little good to Fitz if you drop from exhaustion."

Eithne smiled. "I think I'm actually calm enough I might manage to."

Suzanne hugged her friend. "Wake me if you need anything. Even just the reassurance of someone to talk to."

"Malcolm," Eithne said, as they started to move off.

Malcolm turned back to her. "You'll find who did this?" Eithne asked. "Tampered with Fitz's horse?"

"I'll make every effort to do so."

She nodded. "Whoever was riding against him would have knocked him from his horse, you know."

"It's kind of you to say so, Eithne. But the devil of it is, I can't help replaying every moment of the joust. I'm only glad no permanent harm was done."

Suzanne and Malcolm went down the passage to their own bedchamber in silence. At last Malcolm was able to pull Tatiana's note from his shirt cuff. Suzanne lit the tapers on the escritoire, and he spread the note on its polished surface. Block capitals, all run together with no spaces between words.

"Get the Shakespeare, will you?" Malcolm said. "*Hamlet,* Act I, scene iii."

Suzanne took the leather-bound volume from a shelf against the wall. Shakespeare was one of the first things she and Malcolm had shared. It shouldn't be surprising that he had shared the Bard with Princess Tatiana as well. With determination she opened the book to the appropriate scene and perched on the edge of the escritoire while he took a sheet of writing paper from a drawer, dipped a pen in the inkpot, and began to write, stopping every so often to refer to the page of Shakespeare that held the key to the code. He had Aline's gift for numbers and patterns, a gift inherited from his mother.

> *Malcolm,*
>
> *I hope you never receive this. I hope I can give you the information myself. But I am learning caution. I found a fragment of paper in the grate after my reception the night before last. In code. From what I could decipher, it referred to a plot. No clue to who the plotters were or whom they plotted against, but it was clear the substance of their plot was assassination. Of a person of importance. I also found the name of the Empress Rose tavern. I visited it and determined that a group of foreign gentlemen have been meeting there. I still don't know their nationality or whom they plot against. But I have every expectation that I will have more information for you by the time I see you. In the event that I don't, you will at least know what I know.*
>
> *Always,*
>
> *T.*

24

For a moment, both Malcolm and Suzanne sat absolutely still. The smell of fresh ink hung in the air. In the circle of light cast by the single taper, the black letters glistened on the cream laid paper. Malcolm's handwriting bringing Tatiana Kirsanova back to life. Simple words that changed everything.

Suzanne stared down at her husband. The candlelight turned him into a creature of shadows, sharpened the lines of his face, caught the weight of horror in his gaze. He ran his finger over the still-damp ink. "Oh, Tania. You always had a knack for sniffing out the worst dangers. What a damnable time for me to have been gone from Vienna."

Suzanne touched her husband's shoulder. "Even if you'd been here, even if she'd been able to tell you this in person, there's no guarantee you'd have been able to prevent her murder."

His muscles tensed beneath her touch, but he didn't pull away as she half expected him to do. "Perhaps not. We'll never know. In any case, there's nothing to be done about it now." His voice was clipped and matter-of-fact. His gaze said he would never stop wondering.

Suzanne squeezed his shoulder, then drew her hand back. To do more seemed an intrusion. "Word of her visit to the Empress Rose must have got back to the conspirators. Young Heinrich told us someone talked to Axel and the tavern's owner, and after that the tavern staff were told not to say anything. Presumably the conspirators paid them off."

"And so Axel arranged for the carriage to run us down."

The horror of those moments when Malcolm had lain unconscious coursed through her. "If they were willing to kill us—"

"They could well have killed Tatiana because of what she'd discovered." Rage flashed white-hot in Malcolm's gaze. "And if they'd seen Fitz leaving her rooms the night of the murder and guessed he was her lover, they might have worried about what she'd told him. Us turning up making inquiries could have pushed them into thinking they should deal with Fitz."

Malcolm rubbed at the smeared ink on his fingers with more force than was necessary. A torrent of emotions raged behind the iron control in his gaze. Still-raw anger at Tatiana's death. Bitter guilt at his inability to save her. But also, Suzanne thought, a measure of relief. They had spent the first part of the investigation uncovering sordid details about Tatiana's life. Now Tatiana the blackmailer and dealer in stolen artifacts had become Tatiana the heroine who had uncovered a conspiracy that threatened to shake all Vienna.

As always in their marriage, what lay beneath the surface was not to be discussed, so she fell back on practicalities. "There's also the man who approached you at the opera and sent you to the Empress Rose," she said. "One of the conspirators who had second thoughts but was afraid to openly betray his confederates?"

Malcolm wiped a trail of ink from the side of the inkpot. "That seems the likeliest explanation."

A question not yet voiced hung in the air. A question with implications far beyond Tatiana Kirsanova's violent death. "Who do you think is the target of the plot?"

Malcolm shook his head. "The assassination of just about anyone could wreak havoc on the Congress. And just about every delegation might have reason to want someone in another delegation dead. In some cases there are probably competing views within delegations."

Suzanne frowned down at Malcolm's deciphered text of Princess

Tatiana's note. "Malcolm. Princess Tatiana was an experienced agent. Yet there was no sign that she had struggled with her killer. Whoever it was had been able to get so close as to be practically embracing her."

She saw the flinch in Malcolm's eyes at the image, but he regarded her with a steady gaze. "Meaning that perhaps the killer wasn't one of these conspirators? Or—"

"That perhaps one of the conspirators was someone she knew and trusted."

Their gazes locked.

"It's a compelling scenario," Malcolm said. "Though of course there's no proof."

"You don't think Prince Metternich—?" Suzanne asked. "Or the tsar—"

"Would be behind a plot to assassinate someone? One may smile, and smile, and be a villain. Not that there's been that much smiling across the council table. I wouldn't discount anything. Tsar Alexander came to the throne after his father was assassinated. There are rumors he may have been involved in the plot."

"And then there's Talleyrand."

Malcolm lined up the pen and penknife on the ink blotter. "We know Dorothée told him about Fitz's affair with Tania. But oddly enough, I'm less inclined to suspect him. Not because of his morals. Because he's less rash than Metternich or the tsar. He'd know an assassination would unleash a chain of events he couldn't control, no matter how much he wanted to get rid of the target."

"There are other people Princess Tatiana trusted. Count Lindorff. Fitz."

"Fitz involved in a secret plot? I can hardly say that's impossible. But it would be a bit far-fetched for him to have staged the accident at the tournament tonight. There's also Radley. Did you learn anything dancing with him?"

The question sounded entirely casual. But Malcolm would sound just like that if he was trying to mask his suspicions. Difficult being married to a master of deception. Not that she was precisely a novice at it herself. "Just that his compliments are as fulsome as ever."

Malcolm gave a wry grin. "The things we do in this line of work. Well, I suspect you'll have further chances. Radley has an eye for you."

He didn't sound remotely jealous. He never did. She should be grateful to have a husband not susceptible to the green-eyed monster. Really, it made life so much easier.

So why did his casual tone cut her to the bone?

Castlereagh stared across his dressing room at Malcolm. "God in heaven."

"I rather suspect a more earthly power is behind the conspiracy, sir."

Castlereagh grimaced and reached for his tea. Malcolm had rapped at the door of the Castlereaghs' suite at the earliest hour he thought remotely appropriate. Castlereagh, already awake, had murmured an explanation to Lady Castlereagh and summoned Malcolm into his dressing room where a tea service was set out. Perfectly brewed, with a milk jug and wedges of lemon. Castlereagh had insisted the British delegation hire their own staff to avoid Baron Hager planting spies among the servants. He'd also made sure the kitchen help could brew a proper pot of tea.

Now he took a long swallow and regarded Malcolm over the rim of the Meissen cup. "You believe her."

"I see no reason not to."

"For God's sake, lad, Princess Tatiana—"

"Played all sides. But I fail to see why even Tatiana would have fabricated a plot and sent me evidence in a coded letter that was only to be delivered to me in the event some mischance befell her. What would have been the point?"

Castlereagh drew a breath that fairly scraped with frustration. "With that woman God knows what the point was of anything."

"You weren't so quick to dismiss her information in the past."

Castlereagh returned his cup to its saucer. "That was before I knew she'd been Napoleon Bonaparte's mistress, and you yourself think she was still in communication with him."

"To keep tabs on him for Talleyrand."

"And that's supposed to make me trust her intelligence?"

Malcolm reached for his own tea and tossed down a swallow that burned his throat. Even after he and Suzanne had finally retired to bed, he'd had trouble sleeping. His head throbbed and his nerves felt as though they'd been stripped raw. "The most valuable intelligence doesn't usually come from our friends but from people we have cause to be wary of. The trick is to weigh it and sift it and not reject anything out of hand. Sir, you have to at least acknowledge the possibility that Tatiana's warning about an assassination plot might be true. And if it is true—"

"We're in the devil of a mess." Castlereagh let out a sigh and dropped into the dressing table chair. "It was always the risk in bringing so many dignitaries together. Not just the diplomats but the sovereigns. I don't know when we've had so much royalty assembled in one city. There was that plot against the Austrian emperor last summer, but Hager nipped it in the bud before it became serious. Since then we've seemed safe."

"And you'd like to believe we still are."

Castlereagh shot him a sidelong look. "Are you accusing me of not wanting to believe Princess Tatiana's intelligence because it's inconvenient?"

"Of course not, sir."

"Impertinent puppy." Castlereagh took another sip of tea. "You're right. We can't ignore the possibility."

Malcolm leaned against the dressing table beside his employer. "Do we take this to the other delegations?"

"Has your brain stopped working, Malcolm?" Castlereagh clunked his cup back in its saucer, spattering tea over the blue and white tray. "Of course not. If we knew the target, we could warn them. But something this vague would only instill panic and accusation and rumors and counter rumors."

"Sir—"

"Your mission remains the same, Malcolm. Find out who's behind this plot and who is the target. And who killed Princess Tatiana."

"We have to at least tell Baron Hager."

Castlereagh frowned.

"He has a network of informants," Malcolm said. "Far more extensive than our own. As you pointed out, he and his people ably uncovered the plot against Emperor Francis. It would be criminal not to enlist his aid."

"Your mysterious source told you to trust no one."

"So now you believe my source?"

"I'm taking your advice not to reject any information out of hand."

"In the event the Austrians happen to be behind this, we'd be tipping our hand. But I think it's a risk we must take."

"In the event the Austrians prove to be behind an assassination plot at the Congress they're hosting—"

"You think it's impossible?"

"No, that's the devil of it. After the past two months, I think anything is possible."

"The tension across the conference table is frequently so thick one could cut it with a knife. Or a sword."

"Quite. But this is different." Castlereagh passed a hand over his face. For once he looked his forty-five years. "You think Vaughn's horse was deliberately tampered with at the Carrousel last night?"

"A shoe had been loosened."

"Where the devil does that fit into this?"

Malcolm reached for his own teacup for a diversion. He'd promised Fitz he wouldn't reveal his affair with Tatiana unless it became necessary. It wasn't necessary. Yet. "I don't know," he said. "It's even possible it's unrelated."

"Dear God, how much madness is in this city?"

"Do you really have to ask, sir?"

Castlereagh grimaced. "Get to the bottom of this, Malcolm. As soon as possible."

Fitz leaned back against the Bavarian lace–edged pillows piled high in his bed. "It doesn't make sense, Malcolm. Who would want to kill me?"

"Perhaps the same person who killed your mistress." Malcolm dropped down on the silk coverlet.

"But—"

"You were with her just before she was killed. Perhaps only a matter of minutes."

"But I didn't see anything."

"Someone may think you did. Or that Tatiana told you something. Or perhaps you saw or heard something and don't realize the significance."

"For God's sake—"

"I need to know everything that happened between you and Tatiana that last night. Word for word, if you can remember it."

Distaste twisted Fitz's face. "You can't—"

"This is no time to turn prude, Fitz."

Fitz glanced down at the tea and toast on his breakfast tray. "I told you—"

"I need you to go over it again. In more detail. Re-create what happened as best you can remember from the moment you arrived at the Palm Palace."

Fitz reached for his tea, then set the cup down untasted. "I told you, Tatiana was upset when I got there. Incoherent, actually, which was unusual for her."

"What did she say exactly?"

"That she'd never been spoken to in such a voice and the duchess had no right. Only it took me a while to make out that it was the Duchess of Sagan she was talking about. She kept saying 'treated me like a servant' and 'she has no right to judge.' Finally I realized she was talking about Wilhelmine of Sagan, and I got the story of the Courland casket. I tried to calm her down and tell her the Duchess of Sagan's opinion didn't matter, but she kept pacing. There was a wildness in her that night. As though she anticipated something. I couldn't make out what. I asked if she was afraid the duchess would publicly accuse her of dealing in art treasures. But then she said, 'she wouldn't dare,' quite coolly and with the greatest confidence. Almost as though—"

"She had a hold on the duchess."

"Yes." Fitz frowned and took a sip of tea. "Damned stuff. I swear they brewed the pot weak on purpose. Eithne insists on treating me like an invalid until Blackwell gives me a clean bill of health." A spasm crossed his face at the mention of his wife's name.

"She was very concerned last night," Malcolm said. "Terrified of losing you."

Fitz grimaced as though the tea was bitter rather than weak. "The shock made her forget for the moment. She'll remember." He put the cup down and pushed the tray aside. "We have more important things to talk about than the sorry mess I've made of my life. Tatiana started pacing again. I wonder now if perhaps her tension had nothing to do with the duchess. If it was because of whomever she was to meet later that night. Nothing I said seemed to calm her down, so finally I—" He swallowed. "I took her in my arms."

"And then? For God's sake, Fitz, I know she was your mistress. Did you make love to her?"

"No. She pushed me away, actually. She said she didn't—that is, that she hadn't—"

"That she hadn't taken the required precautions? She wasn't prepared with a sponge?" said Malcolm, whose own wife used them regularly.

Fitz flushed and nodded. Then he frowned, caught by memories he couldn't look away from much as he might wish to do so. "There was one thing. After she pushed me away, she said at least that was one mistake she'd never made. Finding herself with child. But that one couldn't be too careful. Malcolm—you don't think perhaps she did have a child long ago? Could that be why she was so careful to take precautions?"

Malcolm would like to have said he'd have known, but that was laughable. Tania's face swam before his eyes for a moment, bright with familiar mockery. "I don't know. She never said anything about it to me. But then there was a great deal she didn't tell me."

"Why the new questions about the night she died? Have you learned something?"

"Tatiana had discovered an assassination plot." Malcolm told him about the letter he'd received the previous evening.

"Good God."

"She said nothing about it to you?"

"No. But could that have been what she was so keyed up about that night? She was going to confront someone?"

"I'm beginning to think so."

* * *

Seated on the bed, Colin in her lap, Suzanne watched her husband as he recounted his conversation with Fitz. She nearly interrupted at one point, but she forced herself to stay quiet until he had done.

"I know that look in your eyes," he said. "Something Fitz told me means something to you."

"Possibly." Suzanne got to her feet, swinging Colin in the air. "I need to call on the Duchess of Sagan, darling. I'll explain if I'm right."

With Blanca's advice she chose a Vitoria cloak of Pomona green sarcenet and a French bonnet of green velvet and white satin (she was, after all, calling on one of the most fashionable women in Vienna, though the purpose of the visit was not social), kissed Colin, and then walked round to the Palm Palace.

After their last interview she wasn't sure Wilhelmine of Sagan would be at home to her. She hoped the duchess's anxiety about her letters would work in her favor. Sure enough, the footman who had taken her card to the duchess returned and showed her into a salon hung with rose-colored silk and bright with autumn sunshine.

"Madame Rannoch." Wilhelmine greeted her with a hand clasp and a light kiss on her cheek. "I'd have thought you would be lolling in bed this morning, relishing last night's triumph, as I trust Doro is doing." The duchess stepped back and scanned Suzanne's face. "How is Lord Fitzwilliam?"

"Chafing at being confined to bed on weak tea and toast. Dr. Blackwell says he should make a full recovery."

"I'm so glad." Wilhelmine's face showed genuine relief. "A piece of good news to share at my musicale this evening. I hope you and Monsieur Rannoch will be there. I've discovered a wonderful new talent to present."

"We look forward to it."

"Yet you had something to say to me that couldn't wait for this evening." Her gaze shifted over Suzanne's face. "Perhaps your visit isn't entirely social?"

"I'm afraid not. I've made a discovery I thought you would wish to hear."

Fear radiated from the duchess's petite frame, but she held her head high. "Sit down. Please." She waved Suzanne to a sofa carelessly strewn with cushions. The salon was elegant but furnished with an eye to comfort.

Suzanne sank down on the sofa and began to strip off her gloves. Half the trick to bluffing was stating one's case with the assurance of certainty. "Duchess, do the papers Princess Tatiana had that so worry you concern a child you bore out of wedlock?"

25

Wilhelmine slumped back in her chair, gaze shattered. "You found the letters."

"No." Suzanne laid a second amber-colored glove atop her reticule, beside the first. Blanca's careful inquiries at Princess Tatiana's dressmaker's had yielded no result. "Not yet."

"Then how—"

"I couldn't work out what it could be that so frightened you." Suzanne tugged at the ribbons on her bonnet and lifted it from her head. The lace edging obscured her view, and she needed all her senses to judge Wilhelmine's reaction. "With most women one would think the papers were love letters, but you're admirably comfortable with your love affairs. You have no husband whose jealousy to fear. And your birth and fortune give you an assured position in society." She set her bonnet on the sofa and smoothed the green velvet ribbons. "Then it occurred to me that a child was the one thing in your past you might want to hide away."

Wilhelmine got to her feet and strode to the window, her jaconet skirts whipping about her legs. "Hiding her away was what caused all the tragedy."

For a moment, self-hatred scalded Suzanne's throat at what she was doing to the woman across from her. "You have a daughter?"

The duchess nodded, gripping the window ledge. "When I was

eighteen—No, I should go farther back. My parents' marriage—it was not a love match. My father was a great deal older than my mother, and from the first he had other interests. My mother soon developed them as well."

"Not uncommon in aristocratic marriages."

"By the time Doro was born, they virtually lived separate lives. My mother's lovers were often part of our household. Not long after Papa died, Maman ended her affair with Doro's father and began a liaison with Baron Gustav Armfelt." Wilhelmine's voice turned flat as she said the name. "A former cavalry officer and quite as dashing as all one's images of cavalry officers. He could be wonderfully witty, and his smile shone as bright as his collection of medals. My sisters and I were entranced. All except Doro, though he was kindest to her. He said she was an exceptionally intelligent child. He taught her himself and encouraged Maman to engage tutors for her. With her he was quite paternal."

"But not with you."

Wilhelmine turned to face Suzanne, hands taut on the windowsill behind her. "One day I was pouring a cup of coffee in the morning room and caught him watching me. I met his gaze in the mirror and went hot all over. I think he was the first man who saw me as a woman."

Suzanne waited in silence, afraid to breathe for fear of stemming the confidences.

"To have a worldly, sophisticated man adore one at the age of eighteen—I was a fool, of course, but at the time I thought I was the most fortunate woman in the world, and no one had ever loved as we did." Bitterness dripped from Wilhelmine's voice. "Of course we were discovered. By my mother. In bed."

Suzanne could not control her indrawn breath.

"Quite," Wilhelmine said. "Late one night Maman noticed someone had taken a candle. She went to see who was abroad at such an hour and found her daughter in the arms of her lover. She slapped me. Her sapphire ring drew blood." Wilhelmine put a hand to her cheek, eyes dark with memories. "As I grow older, I begin to appreciate the horror it must have been for Maman. At the time, I was wholly focused on myself. I already suspected I was pregnant."

"And in an impossible situation."

Wilhelmine pushed herself away from the window and paced across the room. "Only the year before, my sister Jeanne had found herself with child. She was just sixteen. Her lover was a violinist from our father's private orchestra who taught us lessons. She fancied herself madly in love. They ran off together, but Jeanne was dragged back. Papa disinherited her in a fit of temper just before he died. She had to give the baby up, of course, though he's well cared for. I should have seen then—"

Suzanne had met Jeanne, now Duchess of Acerenza, and Pauline, the fourth Courland sister. Both were separated from their husbands and shared a house in Vienna. Jeanne and her lover of many years, Monsieur Borel, seemed more comfortable together than many married couples. "I don't think one learns from one's own mistakes at eighteen, let alone from a sister's," Suzanne said.

"No, I suppose not." Wilhelmine whipped her shawl closed about her. "After Papa died, our guardian had Jeanne's lover arrested and executed."

Suzanne drew a sharp breath.

Wilhelmine shot a look at her. "It sounds barbaric, doesn't it? But remember, we still have serfs in Courland."

"There are still slaves in British colonies."

"Very true. Our enlightened world isn't very enlightened in some ways." The duchess tugged at her shawl. "Gustav, being a baron, of course wasn't thrown in prison. Maman hastily contrived my marriage to Louis de Rohan, who had an ancient name but had been forced from France during the Reign of Terror. Like your family."

"And if he was like my family, he fled without much of his fortune."

"And spent the intervening years accumulating debts. He was so eager for my dowry he was quite willing to overlook my tainted state. I went to Hamburg alone to have the baby. Though Gustav was with me when she was born, I'll give him that. We named her Adelaide Gustava Aspasia, but we called her Vava from the first. Maman insisted we give her to Gustav's cousins in Finland to raise. I was too weak and tired to protest." Wilhelmine stared at a pink-skirted porcelain shepherdess on a nearby console table. "I haven't seen her since."

"She'd be—fourteen now?"

"Fifteen this January. She's supposed to be told the truth of her birth on her fifteenth birthday. At the time she was born, that seemed centuries in the future." Wilhelmine touched her fingers to the crystal girandoles on a candlestick, setting them tinkling against each other. "Louis had no objection to my continuing my affair with Gustav. The three of us drifted across the Continent indulging ourselves with my fortune. I was young enough to find it amusing until I got tired of watching them fritter away my money. I lost my patience with Gustav first. Or perhaps it was just that it was easier to get rid of him. Louis I had to actually divorce. It was years before I realized the enormity of the mistake I'd made in sending Vava away." She turned her gaze to the window. Tears glistened in her eyes. "I gave away the most important thing in my life."

Colin's soft skin and baby smell flooded Suzanne's senses. Her nails bit into her bare palms. "You were little more than a child yourself."

"I should have been stronger." Wilhelmine locked her hands on her elbows. "Doro doesn't know. Maman told my sisters I was recovering from a carriage accident."

"I won't tell Doro any of this if I don't have to."

"Thank you. That's more consideration than I deserve."

"You're too hard on yourself." Suzanne got to her feet and went to Wilhelmine's side. "Prince Metternich was going to help you get Vava back."

"He promised me. Gustav died recently, which seemed to simplify matters. Dear God, I sound heartless."

Suzanne touched Wilhelmine's arm. "You've little enough reason to mourn for him."

"To own the truth, at times I find it difficult to remember his face. But I'll never forget Vava's." Wilhelmine swallowed, eyes bright. "At first Metternich thought it would be easy." She gave a harsh laugh. "As though anything at the Congress has been easy."

"Austria has no control over Finland. Prince Metternich would have had to go to—"

"Tsar Alexander. Yes, one can't but appreciate the irony, though things weren't so bad between them then. The tsar had made Gustav governor of Finland. Prince Talleyrand once got Tsar Alexander to intervene with Maman to get Doro for his nephew." Wilhelmine passed her hand over her forehead. Strands of her burnished gold hair had slipped free of their pins and clung to her skin. "I thought—Metternich thought—that the tsar might use his influence with the Armfelts to get Vava returned to me."

"It must have seemed straightforward."

"Metternich genuinely did try. He even told me he would make the safety of Russia depend on it." Wilhelmine gave a twisted smile. "Yes, I know, quite shocking that my petty difficulties threatened to intervene in the business of the Congress. But in the end Metternich was unable to make progress, and his relationship with the tsar continued to deteriorate."

"So you went to the tsar directly."

Wilhelmine's mouth tightened. "Yes. Tsar Alexander offered his assistance."

"In exchange for your giving up Prince Metternich."

"He didn't say so in so many words. But he did say if I valued his friendship I'd have nothing to do with Metternich."

"And he began to visit you at eleven in the morning. The hour you had previously reserved for Prince Metternich." *Our hour,* Metternich had called it. Suzanne had been at Count Stackelberg's ball, where the tsar had made a very public point of telling Wilhelmine he would call on her at that hour. Suzanne could see Wilhelmine in her clinging red gown, a gold circlet set with a Courland heirloom emerald round her forehead, sinking into a curtsy before the tsar. Tsar Alexander seizing her hand and pulling her to her feet. Suzanne was not overly fond of Prince Metternich, but she had felt a stab of sympathy at the stricken look on his face that night.

"And with his encouragement I made some quite appalling criticisms of Metternich in public." Wilhelmine's hands fisted on the folds of her gown. "My actions were not honorable."

"How did Princess Tatiana learn of this?" Suzanne asked.

Wilhelmine paced back to the window. "After I broke with Metternich, his affair with Princess Tatiana resumed. I didn't realize it at first—I was too preoccupied with my own concerns—but I can understand. He was lonely, unhappy. They'd been lovers before. It never occurred to me she'd be so brazen as to form liaisons with him and the tsar at the same time. Even I wouldn't do that, and God knows I understand the allure of risk."

"Princess Tatiana found letters you'd written to Prince Metternich?"

"I never should have committed the words to paper, but I was so desperate to get Vava back, I threw caution to the wind. And I trusted him."

"Princess Tatiana stole one of the letters?"

"She must have done. I don't think Metternich would have knowingly betrayed me."

"How did you learn Princess Tatiana had the letter?"

"The last night I saw her. The night she was killed. I was furious over her refusal to return the Courland casket. As I told you, I lost my temper. Probably because my nerves were so worn from the anxiety about Vava." Wilhelmine pressed her fingers to her temples. "I threatened to make public that Princess Tatiana was dealing in looted art. I was arrogant enough to think that would put her in her place. Instead she laughed at me. That's when she told me she had the letter." The duchess's hand closed, hard, on the white-painted windowsill.

"You must have been terrified."

Wilhelmine met Suzanne's gaze directly, but the sunlight was at her back, leaving her face in shadow. "I told you it would have been a bit extreme to kill over the Courland casket. Now you're thinking that this is something one might kill for. And it's true. Protecting the secret of a child born out of wedlock. Knowing that if the truth became public I might lose all chance of ever getting her back. I was angry and frightened enough that perhaps I would have been capable of killing. But as it happens, I didn't."

"Have you told anyone about Tatiana having the letter?"

Wilhelmine glanced out the window and tapped her fingers on the ledge.

"Prince Metternich?" Suzanne asked.

"I went to him at the chancellery directly from Princess Tatiana's that night. I was so angry I accused him of giving her the letter deliberately to hurt me. He protested that I could think such a thing of him. He went to fetch the letter to prove I was wrong." Her gaze clouded. "He keeps my letters in a box in a secret compartment in his desk, tied with white ribbon." She shook her head at her former lover's actions. "He undid the ribbon and went through the letters. One was missing. He was so angry he hurled a crystal paperweight to the ground and smashed it. He swore she had stolen the letter. He promised upon his honor he would recover it for me."

"Have you spoken to him about it since?"

"At the opera the night before last. He again gave me his assurances that he would recover the letter. He said it was the least he could do."

Suzanne smoothed the Spanish fringe on her cloak. Some of the fine silk threads had twisted into knots. "I can't claim to know Prince Metternich well or to understand him. But it's obvious he's still in love with you."

"I almost wish—But one can't govern one's heart. I own, the depth of his rage surprised me. I was shocked when he smashed the paperweight. He's usually so fastidious."

"What time did you leave him the night of the murder?"

"About midnight." Wilhelmine's gaze jerked to Suzanne's face. "But—"

"You don't think he was angry enough to have killed Princess Tatiana."

"One doesn't like to think of a man one has been intimate with doing such a thing."

For a second, Suzanne was thrown back to the moment she had stepped into Princess Tatiana's salon, smelled the blood, seen

Malcolm kneeling over the princess's body. The haunted look in his eyes was imprinted on her memory.

"No," she said. "One doesn't."

Baron Hager tapped his fingers on the polished surface of his brass-bound desk. "A fascinating story, Monsieur Rannoch. You have a flair for the dramatic. And of course Princess Tatiana did as well."

"You don't believe me?"

The leather creaked as Hager leaned back in his chair. "I believe Princess Tatiana liked to put herself at the center of things. What better way to do that than by uncovering a mysterious plot that threatens to shake the Congress to its core?"

"If she'd made the whole thing up, she'd have had no reason to send me a note I'd only receive in the event something happened to her."

"Who's to say she didn't mean for you to discover the note as proof of the plot, knowing you would use just that logic? Princess Tatiana knew you well."

Malcolm could not deny the possibility had occurred to him. Even he could not unravel the inner workings of Tania's mind. "The attempt to run my wife and me down outside the Empress Rose yesterday was real enough."

"Yes. There is that." Hager flicked a finger through a stack of papers on his desktop. "It occurs to me, Rannoch, that all of this is quite convenient for you."

"Convenient?"

"All of a sudden every delegation at the Congress potentially has a motive to have killed Princess Tatiana. Which neatly diverts attention from the man intimately connected to her who discovered her body."

Malcolm kept his face expressionless. "It doesn't seem to have diverted your attention."

"I'll take the matter under advisement." Hager realigned the edges of the papers. "By the way, two of Baroness Arnstein's footmen have quite clear memories of your wife arriving at the Arnstein house the night of the murder, but none of them can say with certainty that they remember seeing you."

"I'm not surprised. My wife's much prettier than I am. Can they say with certainty that I didn't pass through the Arnsteins' doors that night?"

"No," Hager admitted. "Nor can Baroness Arnstein or her husband."

Malcolm leaned back in his chair and crossed his legs. "I didn't have a chance to speak with either of the Arnsteins. I arrived later in the evening than Suzanne, when the baroness's rooms were a good deal more crowded. Whether or not the Jewish community will be able to retain the full equality accorded them under Bonaparte remains a sadly open question, but that doesn't stop delegates to the Congress from flocking to the baroness's salon."

"I'm familiar with the crush at Fanny von Arnstein's." Hager set a bronze paperweight atop the papers. "I understand your friend Vaughn suffered an accident last night. While jousting with you."

"Someone had loosened a shoe on his horse."

"So I heard. You have a way of being close to potentially fatal accidents, Rannoch."

"Sometimes the accidents are directed at me. By the way, I'm sorry for leading your agents on. But it was a while before I realized what they were after, and still longer before I realized who they were."

Hager's brows lifted. "My agents?"

"The men who attacked Suzanne and me on our way back from the Palm Palace the night of the murder. And who then attempted to buy Princess Tatiana's papers from me. They were good at concealment, but I recognized the man I dealt with at the opera the night before last. Hoffmann, I believe his name is, or at least that was the name I knew him by. I do hope he didn't take serious hurt jumping out the window of the grand salon."

Hager's gaze remained steady on Malcolm's face. He played this game well. "As I said, Rannoch, your imagination is extraordinary."

"Of course, I presume it was Prince Metternich who gave you your orders. He must have been quite distressed to find the papers he wanted from Princess Tatiana weren't in her rooms."

"Have a care, Rannoch. These accusations are outrageous."

Malcolm pushed back his chair and got to his feet. "Not nearly so outrageous as the accusations you've leveled against me, my dear Baron."

Suzanne stepped into her bedchamber and closed the door. A rare moment of solitude. Blanca had taken Colin for a walk, and Malcolm wasn't back yet. She stooped to pick up a yellow block that Colin had left on the carpet the previous night while she was dressing for the Carrousel. As her fingers closed round the painted wood, her eyes blurred for a moment. Wilhelmine of Sagan's voice echoed in her head. To be forced to give up a child one has never been allowed to know or acknowledge. What was worse, to fear the past could destroy one's family, as she did, or, like Wilhelmine, to never have the family in the first place?

A piece of sheet music had fallen on the floor not far from the block. Malcolm must have dropped it. She picked it up, wondering if it was a code or just something he'd pulled out to try on the harmonium in the drawing room. Even in the midst of a crisis, Malcolm could find time for music. She studied the music for a moment, remembering a night a few weeks into their marriage when she woke to find he'd come in late and was playing Mozart's Piano Sonata no. 14 in C Minor—quietly, so he wouldn't wake her, but of course the music couldn't but draw her into the sitting room. It was one of the first moments she'd felt she caught a glimpse of who he was beneath the carefully constructed layers.

She moved to the dressing table to take off her bonnet and saw that Malcolm had left his shaving kit in the middle of the dressing table. He was tidier than most men, but he'd been accustomed to living alone for many years and to having his valet tidy up after him. Addison had been out making inquiries among tradesmen all day. Without him, Malcolm had a tendency to strew his possessions about. Just like Colin.

She picked up the shaving kit to move it to its place atop the chest of drawers so she had room to take off her bonnet and tidy her hair. But as she moved to the dressing table, carrying the shaving kit and the yellow block and the sheet music, she lost her one-handed grip on the polished walnut of the kit. It tumbled to her feet. The brass clasp came open, scattering shaving brush, soap, four razors, strop, and silver comb and mirror over the carpet. She knelt down to gather up the contents, wondering if she could train Colin to put his things away before he became too accustomed to having servants.

As she tucked the silver-handled razors back into their compartment, she noticed something shiny caught against the hinges of the box. A gold chain. Odd for a piece of her jewelry to end up there. Normally she'd never invade the sanctity of Malcolm's shaving things. She disentangled the chain and saw that there was a larger piece of gold attached to it, now dangling over the side of the box. She held the chain up to the light from the windows.

Her breath froze in her throat. It was an oval locket of antique gold on a slender chain, the metal mellowed with age. An *A* was engraved on one side in a curling script. She turned the locket over and saw a *P* in the same script. She pressed the catch on the side of the locket, and the case snapped open to reveal a lock of blond hair beneath the glass.

She closed the locket and stared at it for a long moment, her senses refusing to make sense of what was irrefutable. Malcolm had had Princess Tatiana's locket (for surely it strained the bounds of belief to think the locket could belong to someone else) in his possession. Which meant he must have taken it from round her throat the night she was killed. As to why—

The door swung open. "Suzanne—"

Malcolm's voice broke off. Suzanne looked up, the locket clutched in her hand, and met her husband's gaze.

For a moment his eyes held the horror of worst fears come true. Then his face went shuttered.

"I'm sorry." Suzanne got to her feet, her voice taut as a bowstring to her own ears. "I was moving your shaving kit, and I dropped it, and it fell open. Under normal circumstances, I'd never ask about your private possessions. But given that I'm your partner in the investigation—Malcolm, why did you take Princess Tatiana's locket?"

For a long moment he said nothing, and she feared he would

deny her an answer altogether. "I should have known," he said at last in a low, rough voice that held a trace of desperate amusement. "What hope do I ever have of keeping anything from you? I should have told you from the first. But it was never my secret to share."

"I already suspected you were lovers," Suzanne said quickly, compelled to put it into words herself before he could deliver the worst blow. "I was almost sure of it when I saw how her death affected you. That's not—"

"No," he said with sudden force. He crossed the room, sending the shaving brush and comb skittering across the carpet, and grasped her by the shoulders. "Sweetheart, it's not like that at all. Tatiana—"

The words seemed to catch in his throat. He looked down into her eyes, his own dark with conflicting loyalties. At last he drew a harsh breath, as though releasing an age-old burden. "Tatiana was my sister."

❧ 26 ❧

Suzanne stared up at her husband. She had been so armored against the words she expected to hear from him that for a moment she simply couldn't comprehend what he had actually said. "Your sister?" she repeated.

"Half sister, to be precise."

She took a step back and pressed her hand over her eyes. "Good God, this is a scene out of *The Marriage of Figaro*."

"Except that I've known who Tatiana was since I was twelve."

Malcolm spoke little about his family, but in almost two years of marriage Suzanne had learned the general outlines, many of them from Malcolm's soldier brother. In England and Scotland the previous spring and summer, she had met his father and his sixteen-year-old sister, the only other surviving members of his immediate family. His mother had died when Malcolm was nineteen. The night he proposed, Malcolm had told her that his parents' marriage had given him a poor impression of the institution.

"Your father had a child out of wedlock—"

"No." He bent down and picked up the silver comb. "My mother did."

The portrait of Lady Arabella Rannoch that hung in the Rannochs' Scottish country house shot into Suzanne's memory. A slender woman with a delicate, sharply boned face, thick fair hair, and restless, discontented eyes that blazed out of the canvas, as though seeking something she knew would always be denied her. "Your poor mother."

"You never met her."

"I can imagine the pain of giving up a child." Suzanne's hand went to her stomach as she recalled the feel of Colin tucked inside her. She saw Wilhelmine of Sagan's anguished expression when she told the story of giving up little Vava. "Tatiana was older than you?"

"Four years."

"So your mother was—"

"Eighteen when she was born. Seventeen when she was conceived." Malcolm stared at the silver comb clutched in his hand for a moment. "I was twelve when I first met Tania. When I first had the least idea she existed." He took a turn about the room, then crouched down and began to return the rest of the fallen objects to the shaving box with precise, controlled gestures. "It was the autumn of 1799. We were at war with France. My mother came to Harrow unexpectedly and took me out of school." He gave a bleak smile. "I hadn't seen her in two months. She was like that. Gone for weeks on end, and then she'd suddenly sweep one off and make one feel one was the center of the world."

Suzanne's throat tightened. For all she had been through, in some ways her childhood had been easier than his. "Darling—"

"She took me to the coast. She'd hired smugglers to ferry us to France when they went to pick up a load of brandy and champagne. I still remember her sitting among the barrels in a violet-striped gown and a cloak lined in white satin. It was on the boat that she told me the story."

He snapped the box closed with a rattle of the brass hinges, picked up the yellow block and the sheet of music, then got to his feet and returned them to the chest of drawers. "When she was seventeen, her father took her to the Continent. He was consulting with scholars, but of course she was thrilled by the delights of society."

Suzanne had only met Malcolm's ducal grandfather once. He had bowed over her hand, murmured that his grandson was a fortunate man, and then given her a sharper second look when she capped his quotation from *Measure for Measure* with one of her own. The duke was a reclusive scholar, kindly but detached. More so, Malcolm's aunt had told her, after the death of his wife, when his three daughters were still young. "I don't expect he gave her much supervision."

"No. And the governess they'd brought along as a chaperone was no match for my mother's determination." Malcolm leaned against the chest of drawers. "Despite all her liaisons, I don't think I ever saw my mother really in love in all the years of my growing up. But from the way she told the story, I think she did love this man."

Suzanne moved to the chest of drawers. "Who?"

"She didn't tell me. She made me promise never to ask and never to try to discover the truth on my own. My mother feared the revelation of the truth of Tatiana's parentage as she feared few things."

For a moment, his gaze held a weight of loss and unanswered questions. Suzanne took his hand. In two years of trying to sort out her feelings for Malcolm and struggling with her own deceptions, she had never properly seen him as a man who had left boyhood behind not so very long ago. She had failed to grasp that at times he was as much in need of comfort as she was herself.

He looked into her eyes and gave a quick smile. "The smugglers let us off on the coast near Dieppe. A coach was waiting for us. Mama was nothing if not resourceful. We went to a girls' school near Amiens. Tatiana had been moved there when she was eleven."

"Where was she before that?"

"Another school." Malcolm's mouth tightened in an angry line. "No one ever told me the full story, but from the bits I've heard, I think the drawing master forced himself on her."

Suzanne made a strangled sound and tightened her grip on his hand, her own memories sharp with cutting images.

Malcolm drew a breath that scraped against her skin. "The people at this new school seemed kind. My mother and I were shown into a sitting room. Tania—" He shook his head. "She wasn't called Tatiana then. Her name was Pierette. I still remember when she first came into the room, eyes defiant. My mother's eyes."

"Your mother had seen her during her childhood?"

"Every year or so. It had obviously grown more difficult with the war with France. She said she wanted Pierette and me to know each other, because one could never tell what the future might hold. We devised a code together that first day. We used it for years to send letters."

He turned toward her, still holding her hand. "At sixteen Pierette was growing old for school. She wore a muslin frock with a green sash and kept staring at my mother's silk gown and pearls. She was restless to spread her wings."

"So she ran away?"

"Not precisely." Malcolm drew her over to the armchair and pulled her down beside him. "Talleyrand was a family friend. My grandfather had known him before the Revolution. We saw a great deal of him when he was in exile in England during the Terror. What I didn't know, as a boy of five, when I first met Prince Talleyrand, was that my grandfather had enlisted Talleyrand's aid in arranging for my mother to go abroad and have her baby in secret and in finding a place for the child afterward. Except for his years in exile, Talleyrand had kept an eye on Pierette from the moment of her birth. Even in exile, he helped when she had to move schools."

"And then he recruited her."

"Yes." Malcolm stared down at their linked hands. "Or rather Pierette offered her services to him. Easier to pass her off as foreign than as a Frenchwoman. He crafted her identity as Princess Tatiana, daughter of Prince and Princess Sarasov, and arranged her marriage to Prince Kirsanov. The identity he created for her worked very well until Catherine Bagration's inquiries."

"And she could spy for Talleyrand in the Russian court."

"Bonaparte and the tsar teetered between enemies and allies in those days. As Tania told it she was very useful, and even allowing for her exaggeration, I suspect she was. My mother was furious at first—I remember her hurling a vase against the wall and dashing off an angry letter to Talleyrand. Then she went to meet him in secret on the French coast. When she came back, she told me she could understand a woman's need to find something to do with her life."

"You saw Tatiana in those years?"

"Not while she was in Russia. For several years we only wrote. Then Kirsanov died, and Talleyrand decided Tania could be more useful to him in Paris. In early 1807 I went secretly to Paris to tell her of our mother's death."

Suzanne touched her husband's arm. He pulled her tight against him and held her in silence for a long moment. "We could look at each other and see our mother. That meant a great deal."

"She was a French agent," Suzanne said, against his cravat.

"And within a year I was in the Peninsula, theoretically an attaché and actually a British agent. But by then Talleyrand was out of power and exploring alliances with Napoleon's enemies. He sent Tatiana to work with us in the Peninsula as a sort of peace offering."

"And so you became allies."

"We worked together closely for over a year." He paused, as though caught in a web of memories. "She returned to Paris shortly after I met you."

A grim note sounded in his voice on this last, but he drew her hand to his mouth and pressed his lips against her palm.

Suzanne looked down at the locket, which she still held in her free hand. "The locket was a gift from your mother?"

He nodded. "The *A* engraved on it is for our mother, the *P* for Pierette. The lock of hair inside is our mother's." He took the locket from her and held it to the light, the chain twisted round his fingers. "I'd put it in my pocket seconds before you came into the room the night of the murder. The old instinct to protect my family."

"And a keepsake of your sister."

"That, too." He ran his finger over the engraved *P*. "I should have told you. But—"

"You'd made a promise to your mother. It was a secret you'd been protecting more than half your life."

"Yes." For a moment she thought he meant to say more. She

could almost see the conflict in his gaze, the impulse to confide warring with some other claim she could not fathom.

Some other, stronger claim, for in the end he kept silent.

"I heard another story very similar to your mother's earlier today," Suzanne said. She told him about her visit to Wilhelmine of Sagan and the history of little Vava.

Malcolm grimaced when she mentioned Tatiana using the information against Wilhelmine but did not interrupt her. Nor did he seem surprised.

"I can imagine a lot," Suzanne concluded. "But to have to give up a child, not because it was what one wanted but because society's dictates would not allow otherwise, to have no access to her or him—"

Malcolm tightened his arm round her and bent his head to cover her mouth with his own. She tasted sorrow in his kiss and anger and a raw need. As though having finally told her the story, he had released himself to seek solace.

She slid her fingers into his hair, holding him against her as long as she could. When he lifted his head, she leaned against his shoulder.

"I feel for Wilhelmine of Sagan," he said. "Mama was at least able to oversee Tatiana as she grew up. And knowing my mother's fears, I can understand the duchess's panic if the story about her secret daughter became public."

"And why she is so desperate to recover the letter Princess Tatiana took," Suzanne said, letting her head sink into the hollow of his throat.

"So now we know what Metternich's agent was trying to buy from me at the masquerade and at the opera," Malcolm said, his voice muffled by her hair. "Which doesn't mean Metternich himself didn't go to the Palm Palace the night of the murder and try to force Tatiana to return the duchess's letter."

"But surely if the princess was the only one who knew where the letter was, he wouldn't have killed her?"

"He might have lost his temper," Malcolm said in a grim voice. "One of the games Tania was playing got her killed."

Suzanne shivered at the thought of Princess Tatiana, her life mired in intrigue, her past shrouded in mysteries the princess herself would not have understood. "Malcolm." She sat up so she could look her husband full in the face. "Was Tatiana curious about who her father was?"

"She could scarcely have failed to be so. When I first knew her, she kept trying to get me to reveal the truth. I think it was only when we worked together in Spain, after Mama died, that she finally believed I didn't know the truth myself."

"She told Schubert she now found herself identifying with Figaro. Figaro is a lost heir who discovers his parents. Could she have been trying to uncover the truth of her parentage in Vienna?"

His brows drew together.

"Important people are gathered here from all over the Continent. It's quite likely someone at the Congress is related to her. Perhaps her father himself is here."

Malcolm's face went still, but something in his eyes told her this was not an entirely new thought to him.

"You've wondered yourself," she said.

"How could I not? She stopped asking me after our time in Spain, but I'm quite sure she was still making inquiries from time to time. And you're right—living here, surrounded by people from across the Continent, she could hardly fail to wonder and therefore to ask questions."

"And if your mother was so desperate to keep the secret of Tatiana's parentage, perhaps her father was desperate to conceal it as well."

"You're suggesting my sister's father might be her murderer."

"The man who seduced and abandoned a seventeen-year-old girl and has had no contact with his child for over thirty years."

Malcolm's mouth tightened. "If that made for a murderer, the capitals of Europe would be crawling with them. But I take your point. While I know no details about the man in question, I've long had a desire to thrash him."

"It doesn't necessarily have to be him. It could be members of his family, being as protective of him—"

"As I am of my mother?" Malcolm gave a taut smile.

"Do you know where your grandfather and your mother traveled on the Continent?"

"Only from anecdotes. Paris certainly. Vienna. Berlin. St. Petersburg—my grandfather wanted to consult with a classicist there. The Italian Lake District—Mama talked about Lake Como. Possibly Milan. Given the way a certain set moves about the Continent, they could have encountered almost anyone in almost any of those places."

"Malcolm." Suzanne drew her feet up onto the chair. "You said Prince Talleyrand was a friend of your grandfather's. He helped look after Tatiana—"

"Don't imagine I haven't thought of it. I even asked my mother once. It was the one time I broke my promise and questioned her. She swore he wasn't Tania's father. With a dry asperity that rang true."

"If your mother was anything like you, she was an excellent actress."

"She was. I can only add that observing my mother and Prince Talleyrand together growing up, I never had the impression they were ex-lovers. Also, Talleyrand and my grandfather remained on good terms. My grandfather has his eccentricities, but I don't think he'd be so forbearing with the man who had seduced his daughter."

"Are you sure your grandfather knows the man's identity?"

Malcolm scraped a hand through his hair. "I always assumed—You're right. Mama might have refused to tell him."

Suzanne rested her chin on her knees. "Of course, if it was Talleyrand one would think Tatiana might have discovered the truth at any time these past ten years."

"And I can't imagine Talleyrand killing to keep an illegitimate child secret. He's already rumored to have several of them. But if he thought Tatiana had become a liability—"

"You like him," Suzanne said.

A faint smile flashed in Malcolm's eyes. "I still remember the first time I met him. I was riding in my mother's carriage in Hyde

Park. He treated a boy of five with surprising seriousness. Yes, I like him. That doesn't mean he didn't kill Tatiana."

Suzanne frowned over the puzzle of Tatiana's parentage for a moment, then shook her head. "It's still most likely Tatiana's death has to do with Otronsky's plot. Did Hager believe you?"

"He wouldn't admit that he did. I can only hope he believed me enough he'll be on his guard."

"Could—"

A rap on the door forestalled her. "Sir? I'm sorry, but this may be important."

It was Addison's voice. When Malcolm bade him come in, he nodded to Suzanne with his usual punctilious formality, then turned to Malcolm. "There's a message for you from Lisl at Café Hugel. She says she has an important package for you."

"Thank you. That could be important indeed." Malcolm got to his feet and stretched out a hand to Suzanne. "Come with me?"

She smiled into his eyes, warm and less guarded than usual, and put her hand into his own.

Malcolm led his wife to Café Hugel by a circuitous route. He kept his gaze on the cobblestones of the winding streets, but he was acutely conscious of the pressure of Suzanne's gloved hand curled round his arm. The pain of Tatiana's death still hung bitter in his throat, and a dozen different questions, including what awaited them at Café Hugel, clustered in his head. And yet—He had confronted the seemingly impossible choice between every warning engraved in his brain since the age of twelve, everything he owed to his family, and everything he owed to his wife. A choice he had feared would destroy him. Now he wondered how it had ever seemed to be any sort of choice at all.

Of course there were still things Suzanne did not know about Tatiana and his work with her in Spain. Perhaps—He cast a quick glance down at his wife. The green velvet brim of her bonnet, the dark ringlets curling against her cheek. She looked up at him, as though aware of his regard. He smiled, forcing back any further impulse to confide. He had to live with the choices he had made.

He might not deserve Suzanne, but they had bound their lives together for better or worse. What they had was still built on an unstable foundation. Some revelations would tear it down completely.

Instead of going in the café's main entrance, he led Suzanne round the side, and they slipped through a door to the kitchens. The smell of butter-rich pastry greeted them. Brigitta, a round-figured, fair-haired girl who was taking a tray out of the oven, nodded at him and called, "Lisl." A moment later Lisl, auburn-haired, disarmingly pretty, and brilliant at listening for information and passing messages along with discretion, emerged from the pantry, an enamel tin in one hand, a baking spoon in the other. "Thank God," she said. "I was afraid you wouldn't be in the Minoritenplatz."

She took them up a back staircase to a private room with white woodwork and violet trellis wallpaper. Two small figures sat at a gateleg table in the center of the room. One was Heinrich, the potboy from the Empress Rose. The other was a girl, a few years older and a few inches taller. Judging by her straight brown hair, wide cheekbones, and smattering of freckles, the two were related. Lisl had brought them cups of chocolate that appeared largely untouched.

"You'll be quite safe here," Lisl said, more to the children than to Malcolm and Suzanne, then withdrew and closed the door.

Heinrich and the girl sprang to their feet.

Malcolm crossed the room to them. "Thank you for seeking me out. You've learned something?"

Heinrich nodded. "This is Margot. My sister. She works at the Empress Rose, too."

Malcolm inclined his head. "I'm Malcolm Rannoch and this is my wife, Suzanne."

Margot dropped a curtsy. "Sit," Malcolm said. "Please."

"And don't let this lovely chocolate grow cold." Suzanne stepped between the children and touched them both on the shoulder with her usual disarming warmth. "Stories are always told better with fortification."

Heinrich gave her a shy smile, dropped into his chair, and

reached for the chocolate. The girl did likewise but cradled the cup in her hands instead of drinking.

Malcolm and Suzanne sat opposite them.

"Margot was out on an errand when you came to the tavern yesterday," Heinrich said. "I told her I'd talked to you. She waited on the gentlemen we were talking about in their private room. When she was in the room they didn't always speak German."

"Did you recognize the language?" Malcolm asked.

Margot shook her head.

"Was it this?" Malcolm tried a phrase in Spanish, then Italian, then Polish, then Russian.

"That's it," Margot said.

"You're sure?" Malcolm repeated the Russian again followed by Hungarian.

"No, the first one," Margot said.

Malcolm exchanged a look with Suzanne. A dozen thoughts and speculations raced through his brain. "What did the gentlemen look like?"

"There were four of them. It was hard to see much. They only lit a single brace of candles. They were about your age, sir. One had dark hair—thick and straight—and dark eyebrows. He seemed to be the leader, and I got the best look at him. One was short, with hair like straw. Two of them had brown hair, but one was thinner than the other."

"You have a painter's eye," Malcolm said.

"Or an agent's," Suzanne added.

Heinrich leaned forward, elbows on the table. "It's serious, isn't it?"

"Very, I'm afraid," Malcolm said.

Heinrich nodded, hesitated, then said, "The red-haired lady who came to the tavern—she's the princess who was murdered?"

"How do you know?"

"I saw a sketch in a newssheet. That's when I told Margot it was mortal serious."

Malcolm studied the young, intent faces before him and found himself thinking of his son. "You can't go back to the Empress Rose, either of you. My wife and I were attacked after we spoke with Heinrich. The people behind this won't leave any loose ends. Whom do you live with?"

"Ourselves," Margot said. "Mama died when Heinrich was born and Papa died of a fever last winter."

"I'm sorry." Suzanne reached across the table to touch Margot's hand. "But it makes matters easier."

Malcolm nodded. "We can find you both a place with the British delegation in the Minoritenplatz."

Margot cast an uneasy glance at her brother. "We don't need—"

"You've done us a great service," Malcolm said, "at considerable risk to yourselves. Let us at least repay you this far. You'll be paid well, and we can see that you're protected. Do you need anything from your rooms? If so, let me send someone to fetch them."

Margot studied him, then looked at Suzanne. "You're not an ordinary lady and gentleman."

"We'll take that as a compliment," Malcolm said.

27

"Rannoch." Adam Czartoryski looked up from his table in a window alcove at the Three White Lions Café. "You've learned something?"

"No. That is, yes. But not about the letters." Malcolm dropped into the chair across from Czartoryski. Even now he wasn't sure about the wisdom of this course of action. He was gambling a great deal on his sense that Adam Czartoryski was someone he could trust. If he was wrong, there were implications not just for himself but for the fragile peace on the Continent. God knows he'd been wrong to trust before. He'd trusted Tatiana.

Czartoryski's gaze flickered across his face. "What?"

Malcolm leaned back in his chair and regarded the Polish patriot who was Tsar Alexander's friend and adviser. And Tsarina Elisabeth's former—and perhaps current—lover. Through the years a number of people had tried to determine who Adam Czartoryski really was and where his loyalties lay.

A gust of wind from the opening of the door ruffled the stack of papers on the table. Adam slapped his hand down on them. "You're trying to decide whether to trust me."

"Isn't that what everyone in Vienna is trying to decide about everyone else? Except for the people they're actively plotting against."

Czartoryski frowned out the window. A calèche carrying two ladies in plumed bonnets was rolling over the cobblestones. "When I was sent to the Russian court as a virtual hostage, I spent my first months sure I could trust no one. Finally I decided I had to take the risk or my life would be unbearable."

"Whom did you risk trusting?"

"Alexander." Czartoryski reached for his cup and stared into the cooling coffee. "In the end, one could argue that I was the one who betrayed him."

"As I hear it, you betrayed him over something for which he had no proper regard himself."

"All too true. Loyalties can't be neatly aligned so they never collide. And one can feel the deepest friendship for someone and at the same time despise his actions in part of his life." Czartoryski took a sip of coffee and grimaced, though perhaps not at the bitter taste. "Castlereagh and Metternich and Talleyrand don't trust me. They think I have too much power over Alexander. That I'm pushing him to be intransigent on Poland. But to the Russians I'll always be an outsider, adviser to the tsar or no." He returned the cup to its saucer and wiped away a trace that had sloshed over the side. "For what it's worth, Rannoch, I've trusted you and your wife with secrets I'd share with few people."

A waiter brought Malcolm a cup of coffee and replenished Czartoryski's cup. Malcolm cast a glance about. The nearest tables were empty. A violinist had started up a Hungarian folk song, plaintive, poignant, and loud enough to drown out conversation.

Malcolm curled his hands round the warm porcelain of his cup and cast the die. "Apparently Tatiana got wind of a plot just before she was killed."

"A plot to do what?"

"To assassinate someone. She hadn't been able to discover who the target was. Or the identities of the plotters."

"Dear Christ." Czartoryski's gaze narrowed. "You wouldn't have come to me with this if you hadn't learned more."

"Apparently the plotters spoke Russian."

For several seconds the two men stared at each other, the implications thick as candle smoke in the air between them. Czartoryski picked up his cup, then set it down untasted. "You're asking me if my colleagues in the Russian delegation could be involved in a plot to assassinate someone."

"Yes."

Czartoryski picked up a small silver spoon and stirred his coffee, though he had added neither sugar nor cream. "You've considered that I might be involved in the plot myself?"

"Of course."

The spoon clinked against the porcelain. "And?"

"One can never be sure, of course. But I like to think I have some wit as a judge of character."

"I'm flattered." Czartoryski set down the spoon. Droplets of coffee spattered on the white tablecloth. "For me to even discuss this with you could be construed as treason."

"So could my bringing it to you." Malcolm blew on the steam from his own cup. The vapor dispersed in the air. "Have you read Shakespeare's *Winter's Tale*?"

"About a king driven insane by jealousy?"

"Yes. But I've always thought the real heroes of the play are the courtiers who prevent tragedy by going against the orders of two different kings."

Czartoryski gave a faint smile. "I'm a Pole first and foremost. I always will be. But while Alexander and I may not be the friends we once were, I owe him my loyalty."

Malcolm drew a breath, disappointment sharp in his throat.

"And," Czartoryski continued, "I'd hardly be serving him well if I didn't investigate the possibility that someone in his delegation was involved in a plot that might bring ruin to Russia. Not to mention to the entire Continent. Tell me what you know."

Malcolm spared a brief smile for Czartoryski and recounted Margot's description of the four men.

Czartoryski listened with a deepening frown. When Malcolm finished he sat back and took another sip of coffee. "The descriptions are vague. But the dark-haired one she calls their leader. It could be Dmitri Otronsky. Unlike many of the delegation, he actually is Russian by birth. I suppose any of us could have spoken Russian, thinking the tavern staff wouldn't recognize the language. But the hair and dark brows sound like him."

"I had the same thought. Do you have any reason to think—"

"That Otronsky's plotting to assassinate someone? Hardly; I wouldn't have kept quiet about it. But Otronsky's hungry for power. He prides himself on the fact that his family have served the tsars for generations, though they haven't been as powerful of late. He has dreams of Russian imperial glory. And personal advancement. He's worked his way into the tsar's inner councils in quick order. He's also made a point of pushing his very lovely sister in Alexander's way."

"Not precisely the actions of an honorable brother. But it's a leap from prostituting one's sister to assassination."

"It's more than that. Otronsky seems to grow more militant each day. He's become a close friend of the tsar's brother Constantine. In itself not an argument of stability or sense."

Malcolm nodded. Grand Duke Constantine had cut a belligerent swath through the Congress, going so far as to strike Alfred von Windischgrätz with his riding crop in the midst of a parade (which nearly led to a duel between the two men until cooler heads compelled Constantine to apologize). "I imagine Otronsky approves Grand Duke Constantine's new post."

"Quite," Czartoryski said with a look of distaste. The grand duke had recently left Vienna, sent by his brother to command the Polish army in Warsaw. "Constantine's one of the last people I'd have wished upon my poor country. His presence there makes it more likely Alexander will impose a military solution."

"Which might give you the closest thing you'll get to a free Poland."

"Under Russian military command. And it could well plunge the Continent back into war, which wouldn't be good for any of us. But I think Otronsky sees war as an avenue to power. If he had his way, Alexander would annex Poland, enforce Prussia's takeover of Saxony, and march out of the Congress daring Metternich, Castlereagh, Talleyrand, and the rest to do their worst."

"And you think Otronsky may have decided to help his case

along by taking action against someone he disagrees with? Or to push the tsar along the course he advocates?"

Czartoryski shifted his coffee cup on the tabletop. "If anyone in the Russian delegation is capable of it, he is."

"Who? Who would he further his cause by killing?"

Czartoryski cast a glance about. The Hungarian song had come to an end, followed by a smattering of polite applause. He waited until the violinist launched into a gypsy melody, filled with convenient bursts of fortissimo. "I think Alexander and Prince Metternich would have come to open blows more than once if it wasn't for Castlereagh."

It was Malcolm's turn to stare at his companion. "You think Otronsky might be planning to assassinate the British foreign secretary?"

"Without Castlereagh the Congress would lose one of the strongest forces against Russian expansion."

Malcolm reached for his coffee and took a sip, so quickly he nearly choked. Czartoryski's words made sense, though he wasn't used to thinking of Castlereagh as a victim. British arrogance, perhaps. "Of course, there's another man who has a way of turning every meeting of the Big Eight on its head. And who's been even more effective than Castlereagh at checking both the Russians and the Prussians."

"Talleyrand," Czartoryski said. "An interesting possibility."

Malcolm leaned back in his chair. "Addison, my valet, is skilled at tracking. I'll have him follow Otronsky. Perhaps we can learn whom he's meeting with."

"I could go to Alexander with what we have."

"Without proof? Based on the word of a British attaché? I fear the tsar would laugh in your face. Besides—"

"What?"

"There's another possibility." Malcolm chose his words with care. "That the tsar himself let Otronsky know he wanted someone got rid of."

Shock flared in Czartoryski's eyes. "That *is* treason, Rannoch."

"Not for me. He isn't my sovereign." Malcolm stared into the thick black liquid in his cup. "I don't know that the prince regent would be incapable on moral grounds of ordering an assassination—in fact, I suspect he'd be all too easily convinced of the rightness of his cause—but I'm not sure he has the wit for it."

Czartoryski scrubbed at the spattered coffee on the tablecloth. "There was a time when I'd have sworn I knew the inner workings of Alexander's mind better than anyone. Now—"

"Otronsky could have taken an angry outburst of the tsar's too literally. Like the knights who killed Thomas à Becket."

Czartoryski swallowed, gaze on the coffee-spotted linen. "You're saying we can't take this to anyone."

"Not yet. We don't know whom we can trust."

Geoffrey Blackwell pressed a cool hand against Fitz's forehead. "No headaches?"

"None," Fitz said in the heartiest voice he could muster.

"No dizziness?" Blackwell reached for his wrist and took his pulse.

"None at all. I slept like a log and ate all my breakfast. I'm right as rain except for a crippling case of boredom."

Blackwell snapped his medical bag shut. "Peevishness is a sign you're on the mend. You'll do."

Fitz swung his legs to the floor and reached for his dressing gown. "So my wife can stop fussing over me and feeding me bread and gruel?"

"Tea," Eithne said from the doorway.

"Weak tea."

Blackwell shot a glance between Fitz and Eithne. "Exercise is healthy. Provided you don't experience stabbing pains in your temples or start swaying on your feet, I see no reason you shouldn't return to your normal routine. No riding for a bit."

Fitz tied the belt on his dressing gown and got to his feet. To his relief, the bedchamber did not spin round him. Not that he'd have admitted it if it had. "You're a capital fellow, Blackwell."

Blackwell gave a grunt of acknowledgment, picked up his medical bag, and stopped to press Eithne's hand. "You're an excellent nurse, Lady Fitzwilliam. And admirably coolheaded."

"Thank you." Eithne kissed his cheek.

Blackwell colored, then touched her shoulder, nodded at Fitz, and left the room.

Eithne closed the door behind Blackwell and turned, leaning against it, to meet Fitz's gaze. The relief Fitz had felt at leaving his sickbed drained from him. He stared at his wife. Her pale blue gown fell in cool folds about her. A stiff white ruff framed her face. Her hair was drawn back into a simple knot, instead of the usual curls and twists. The light from the windows slanted across her face. He could trace her features from memory and yet—There were shadows in her eyes he had never seen before. And a hurt in the curve of her mouth that cut him to the quick. His familiar wife had become a stranger, and he had only himself to blame.

"Blackwell spoke true," he said. "I had no right to expect you to take such good care of me. I had no right to expect you to take care of me at all."

"Don't be silly, Fitz." She took a step away from the door, her dress rustling. "You're my husband."

"I rather think I've abrogated a husband's rights."

Eithne adjusted the vase of autumn roses that stood on the table in the center of the room. "No more so than most of the husbands in Vienna. Or London. I never thought to find us such a fashionable couple."

Who would have guessed simple words could carry such a sting? "When I recovered consciousness and found you kneeling over me—I was sure you'd never look at me in that way again."

She snapped off a drooping rose with a quick flick of her fingers. "I was in shock."

"Shock can make one forget. I have no illusions that the amnesia will continue."

She turned to look at him. "Would you want it to?"

"I don't want you to be other than you are."

She jabbed the broken rose into the vase. "*I'm* not sure who I am anymore. Last summer in London Lady Sefton told me I was the perfect wife, and I fear I was fool enough to believe her. I thought I was that rare woman whose dreams had come true." She tugged at a rose, then drew her hand back as though she'd pricked her finger.

"I'm almost glad you know. I couldn't have borne living with the lies. I respect you too much."

She gave a wintry smile. "That's something."

He took a step forward, then checked himself. "Eithne, I love you. Surely you realize that."

Eithne walked over to the bed and smoothed the coverlet. So close he could smell the violet of her perfume. "When you fell from your horse and I saw you lying on the ground unmoving, all I could think was that I couldn't bear a world without you in it. It seems feelings have a way of persisting. Even when one doesn't want them to."

He swallowed, tasting the bitterness of everything he had lost.

"It will never be the same again, Fitz. We can't go back."

"No. Of course not."

She stared down at the ivy pattern on the coverlet. "I can't forget, and I don't think you can, either. I hope you can't. If you could, you'd be far shallower than the man I believe you to be. But—"

Hope sprang hot within him. He strode to her side and caught her hand in his. "What?"

"But I think perhaps we might go forward. That even if I know you aren't the man I loved, I might come to love the man you are."

His breath caught in his throat. "I don't deserve you—"

Her gaze settled on his face, signaling warning like an armed sentry. "Might. With time. We'll have to see what the future holds. For both of us."

Malcolm surveyed Prince Metternich across the desk from which the Austrian foreign minister managed the business of an empire. "You're a good actor, Prince. Better than I credited. I had no notion how angry you were at Tatiana the night of the murder."

Metternich dipped his pen in the inkpot and signed his name to a document with a flourish. He hadn't given Malcolm the compliment of stopping work during their interview. "Why on earth should I have been angry at Tatiana? We always maintained a very cordial relationship."

"Because you'd just learned she'd stolen a letter from the Duchess of Sagan that revealed the truth about the duchess's illegitimate daughter."

The prince surged to his feet. "What the devil have you done, Rannoch?"

"Searched for what we all want. The truth behind who killed Tatiana."

Metternich slammed his hand down on the desk, spattering ink. "How dare—"

"Spare us both the denials. The duchess admitted the truth to my wife."

"By God, if you've distressed her—"

"Wilhelmine of Sagan is made of sterner stuff than that. What distresses her is the letter being missing in the first place."

Metternich spun away from the desk and strode across the room. "Tatiana had no right. I trusted her."

"With Tatiana that was more than one man's fatal mistake." Malcolm crossed the room after the prince. "You were protecting the woman you love. I'd do a great deal to protect my wife. I'd have done a great deal to protect Tatiana if I could. Though I'd argue attempted murder is going over the line."

Metternich stared at an oil landscape hung against the robin's-egg blue wall. "I had nothing to do with Tatiana's—"

"I meant the attack on Suzanne and me on our way back to the Minoritenplatz the night of the murder. Oh, I'll do you the credit of thinking you didn't directly order your people to try to kill us. There wouldn't have been time to be so specific. You simply made it clear you wanted them to recover what you thought we possessed."

Metternich cast a sidelong glance at Malcolm. "You're an impertinent bastard, Rannoch."

"If the truth is impertinent."

The foreign minister turned to face Malcolm directly, hands clasped behind his back. "I knew Tatiana was a mercurial woman. But we'd managed to stay friends through everything. I'd turned to her for comfort when I was sorely in need of it. It never occurred to me—"

"That she'd betray you."

"Why in God's name she could be so petty as to turn on Wilhelmine—"

"Knowing Tatiana, I suspect she had her reasons."

"Blackmail?" Metternich's voice turned harsh.

"Possibly. Though I suspect it was more complicated."

"I never got the chance to ask her." Metternich crossed back to his desk and balled up the document ruined by spattered ink. The paper crackled in his fist. "When I received her note asking me to call at three in the morning, I thought she wanted to see me to make some sort of demand."

"So when you went to the Palm Palace the night of the murder—"

"I was going to confront her. I walked into her salon to find her dead on the floor, with Tsar Alexander hurling accusations at you." Metternich lifted his head. His gaze slammed into Malcolm's own. "And your wife conveniently coming to your defense."

28

Malcolm wound a length of starched linen round his throat. "You're sure you'll recognize Otronsky?"

Addison tucked Suzanne's sketch of Count Otronsky inside his coat. "Mrs. Rannoch's likenesses are always invaluable."

Malcolm glanced at the closed dressing room door. Suzanne was reading a story to Colin before they left for dinner at the Prussian embassy, followed by the Duchess of Sagan's musicale. "Don't try to intervene, whatever you see. Otronsky isn't a man to trifle with." Malcolm wrapped one fold of fabric over another. "Note where he goes and whom he talks to and come back with a report."

"No unnecessary risks."

"Quite."

"Because you wouldn't run them yourself."

"Er—just so." Malcolm tugged at the cravat.

Addison stepped in front of him and adjusted the folds of linen. "A Mathematical should have a tighter knot, sir."

"What would I do without you?"

"I have no doubt you'd manage." Addison held out an ivory silk waistcoat. "But perhaps it's as well we don't have to find out."

Malcolm slid his arms into the waistcoat and did up the buttons. "Precisely my point about being careful with Otronsky."

Addison gave a faint smile and lifted Malcolm's coat from the chairback.

"Addison," Malcolm said, as he slipped into the black cassimere.

"Sir?" Addison smoothed the coat over Malcolm's shoulders.

Malcolm cast another glance at the white-painted panels of the dressing room door. "The compartment in the bottom of my dispatch box has travel documents and letters to my aunt and David Worsley. Should anything happen to me, I trust I can count on you to get Mrs. Rannoch and Colin safely back to Britain."

Addison's hands froze on Malcolm's shoulders. "Sir—"

Malcolm turned round and did up the buttons on his coat. "This has become a bit more dangerous than I at first anticipated. And I'm afraid I've managed to make an enemy of Prince Metternich as well as of Baron Hager. I only think it's wise to be prepared."

"Naturally." Addison spoke in the voice of one treading on glass. "But I hope I do not presume too much when I say that you would be sorely missed should such an event occur."

"Thank you, Addison. But I have no doubt you'd get on with your life admirably. And you'd probably find yourself in a good deal less danger."

"But sadly at risk of boredom. I should also add that your loss would be a blow from which your wife and son would find it difficult to recover."

For a moment, Tatiana's lifeless blue eyes flickered in Malcolm's memory. "Don't overexaggerate. At this age Colin wouldn't even remember me. Suzanne would mourn, and she'd find it difficult to be in a strange country. God knows England can be insular. But she'd have the protection of my name and fortune, and my family and friends would help her."

"The letters to Lady Frances and Lord Worsley." Addison's gaze didn't flicker from Malcolm's face.

"Quite. With their help, Suzanne would build a new life. I expect she'd marry again." And perhaps make a wiser choice.

"With all due respect, I think you underestimate the strength of Mrs. Rannoch's feelings."

Malcolm stared at the man who had been his valet since he went up to Oxford. A man's valet knew him as few people did. Addison knew details from his hat size to the nights he had trouble sleeping. He had seen sides of Malcolm that Malcolm hoped he never revealed to another human being. Malcolm would risk his life for Addison without question, and he knew Addison would do the same for him. Yet they rarely spoke of personal matters.

"I never took you for a romantic, Addison."

"Just an observer of my fellow creatures. One can care deeply without showing it in an overt way. I would have thought you of all people would understand that, sir."

"And there are layers beneath the surface that it's difficult to glimpse from the outside." Malcolm recalled the warmth of Suzanne's lips beneath his own only a few hours before, and the trust in her eyes. And then he reminded himself of the things she still did not know. "I'd have thought you would understand that, Addison."

"Quite. The question would seem to be who's overlooking what. I've had a great deal of leisure to observe Mrs. Rannoch. I don't think she guards her feelings as well round me as she does with you."

Malcolm reached for his evening gloves. "To the extent there's anything in what you say, it merely proves the inadvisability of a man in my position taking a wife."

"That wasn't my intention."

"No. I didn't think it was." Malcolm tugged on a glove. "You're far too considerate to point out my inadequacies."

"To an outside observer, sir, it's plain that Mrs. Rannoch enjoys working with you."

Malcolm pulled on the second glove. "That doesn't change the fact that I've been gone too bloody many weeks out of the hundred some weeks we've been married. That I missed Colin's first word and his first step. Not to mention that I—"

He broke off. Addison was silent and statue still.

"As I explained, I'm merely taking precautions," Malcolm said.

"Sir."

Malcolm looked up from smoothing the gloves over his knuckles.

"No one could fault you for grieving for Princess Tatiana," Addison said.

"Perhaps not. But there doesn't seem to be time for it."

Talleyrand watched his niece—his nephew's wife—descend the limestone staircase at the Kaunitz Palace. She wore a gown of ivory tulle embroidered with silver acorns that caught the candlelight. Pearls gleamed in her rich dark hair. A creature of sunshine and spring, even in the chilling air of autumn. For an unexpected moment he was reminded of Tatiana at the same age, vibrant and not quite grown into her beauty. Though even then Tatiana had had a cynical shell he hoped Dorothée never acquired.

He moved to the base of the stairs to greet her. "You look particularly lovely this evening, my dear."

Dorothée laughed, gaze on the diamond bracelet she was fastening. "I was in a shocking hurry dressing. I stayed out much too long riding in the Prater."

"With Suzanne Rannoch?"

"No." Dorothée hesitated on the bottom step, tugging at the clasp of the bracelet. "With Count Clam-Martinitz."

A chill passed through Talleyrand that had nothing to do with the hall's high ceiling. "Ah. His admiration for you was plain last night at the Carrousel."

"He was my cavalier for the evening, so he felt obliged to dance with me."

"A bit more than that, I think. Here, let me do that." He took the bracelet and fastened it round her slender wrist, then immediately released her. There were times it was best not to give in to temptation or one might be burned. "There's no need to be embarrassed, my dear. You have every right to an admirer. Surely you realize I have no illusions about the state of your marriage."

Dorothée fingered a fold of her skirt. "I—"

He reached out and lifted her chin. So much for resisting temptation. "I owe you an apology for saddling you with Edmond. At the time, I thought—"

"That you could secure the Courland name and fortune for your family?" Her tone was more matter-of-fact than bitter. Which made it worse.

"In a word, yes." He dropped his hand. "I was thinking strategically. I didn't know you then, you see."

"So you'd be justified in playing dice with my life if I'd been a different sort of person?"

"My dear child. I've never claimed anything I do is morally justified. It's one reason I never made a good priest. In any case, after my role in your unfortunate marriage, I could hardly blame you for seeking consolation."

She turned her head away. "You make it sound—"

"I had no intention of making it sound anything, Dorothée. You've earned the right to make your own decisions."

She lifted her chin. There was a decisiveness to the set of her jaw that was new. "I'm not my sister."

"No. You're very much yourself. More so every day." He studied the proud lift of her chin, the determination in her eyes. He had always thought Dorothée would grow into a formidable woman. It occurred to him now that she already had. A woman who could fall in love in a quite different way from her adolescent infatuation with Adam Czartoryski.

She was right, she wasn't her sister. Talleyrand suspected that when she gave her heart she might well continue the rest of her life without swerving from her choice.

"You deserve happiness, my dear. And I hope you've found the courage to take it."

"Uncle—" She twisted her bracelet round her white-gloved wrist. "I've been happy here. Happier than I've been all my life. Thank you for bringing me."

He watched her for a moment, imagining what it would have been like if he hadn't brought her, what it would be like now to return to the Kaunitz Palace and not hear her laugh or anticipate her light step on the stair. "To hear you say you've been happy, Doro, is the greatest gift you could give me." He held out his arm. She hesitated a moment, then curled her fingers round his elbow and leaned into him with her old ease.

The familiar camaraderie between them was a great deal. He should learn to be grateful for what he had.

But of course he wasn't. Talleyrand bit back a curse. With the fate of the Continent hanging in the balance, it was a sad thing to discover that he was every bit as capable of foolery as a callow youth of five-and-twenty.

"Champagne, sir?"

Malcolm accepted two glasses from Wilhelmine of Sagan's footman and found a piece of paper slipped into his hand, closed with a pin. He opened it to see his valet's writing.

> *O. stopped in the Graben. He exchanged words with a cloaked man I couldn't identify and received a note that he tucked into his shirt cuff. I don't believe he's had time to dispose of it.*
> *A.*

Malcolm tucked the note into his own shirt cuff and made his way across the duchess's crowded salon. Fans of painted silk and carved ivory stirred the air, crystal clinked, words like "Saxony," "Carrousel," and, inevitably, "Tatiana" flew back and forth in the conversational volley.

His wife, unmistakable with her dark hair and pomegranate silk gown, was standing by the velvet-curtained windows, laughing with Dorothée, Count Clam-Martinitz, and Aline.

"Champagne, darling?" Malcolm said, putting a glass into Suzanne's hand. "Will you excuse me if I borrow my wife for a moment?"

Dorothée smiled at him with approval.

"What is it?" Suzanne murmured, head close to his own as he took her arm.

"What makes you think it's anything?" he murmured into her glossy dark curls. A silk flower brushed against his cheek.

"You never call me darling in the general run of things. It's practically an alarm code."

That, he realized, was all too true.

"A very effective one," Suzanne added as they stopped in front of the porcelain stove.

Malcolm took a sip of champagne and dug his shoulder into the gilded molding, a pose calculated to radiate casual ease. "I heard from Addison. Otronsky has a note tucked in his shirt cuff. Can you get it?"

She lifted her brows. "Need you ask?"

He touched his glass to hers. "Purely a formality."

A few moments later, his wife off on her mission, Malcolm passed the open door to the music room to see a slight young man leaning over the piano, wire-rimmed spectacles slipping down his nose as he sorted through scores.

"Schubert." Malcolm stepped into the room and walked toward the young composer.

"Herr Rannoch." Schubert looked up with a quick smile.

"You're to play for us? A pleasant surprise."

"A great opportunity." Schubert pushed his spectacles up on his nose. "I owe it to the princess."

"Tatiana arranged for you to play for the Duchess of Sagan's guests?"

"In a manner of speaking." Schubert grinned. "Princess Tatiana sang my praises to the duchess so much and made such a point of how impossible it was to engage my services that the duchess made me a quite extravagant offer."

"That's Tania."

"Yes." The smile faded from Schubert's eyes. "I owe her more than I can say."

Malcolm glanced at the scores spread on the glossy rosewood of the piano and touched the young man's shoulder. "If there's any debt, your music will more than repay it."

"Doro." Suzanne slid her arm through her friend's. "Walk across the room with me. You'll excuse us, Count Clam-Martinitz?"

The count gave a smile that was as warm as it was dazzling. "How could I fail to grant so charming a lady anything she asked for, Madame Rannoch? So long as you promise to return her."

"I suspect she'll do that on her own, Count." Suzanne drew Dorothée across the room. "The Carrousel produced some interesting results," she whispered to her friend.

Dorothée flushed. "The count thinks it's still his duty to fuss over me because he was my cavalier."

"I think it's a bit more than that."

"That's what my uncle said."

"Prince Talleyrand is a perceptive man."

Dorothée twisted her diamond bracelet round her wrist. "He—" She shook her head. "He's very understanding."

"Count Clam-Martinitz is an exceedingly handsome man."

Dorothée flushed, gaze fastened on the sparkling flower links of her bracelet.

Suzanne cast a sideways glance at her friend. "Doro, surely after everything your husband's done, you don't feel qualms—"

"No. I don't feel qualms about betraying Edmond." Dorothée's glance flickered infinitesimally to the side.

Suzanne turned, aware of a gaze upon them, and found herself looking at Prince Talleyrand. He was deep in conversation with Baron Hardenberg, but his gaze slid to the side for a moment and rested on Dorothée with a look that made Suzanne suck in her breath. Dear God. Why had she thought Talleyrand more immune than any other man in Vienna? Yet in his case it was more complicated than the usual intrigues. That look held not lust but a longing for the unattainable that she recognized all too well.

Talleyrand turned back to Hardenberg with an air of perfect unconcern.

Dorothée flashed a quick smile at Suzanne. "I've never been very good at flirting, is all."

"I'd say you're managing admirably." Suzanne squeezed her friend's arm. "You deserve happiness, Doro. Wherever you decide to seek it."

"Oh, Suzanne. Who says love has anything to do with happiness? Unless you can manage not to take it seriously, but even Willie can't do that properly."

Her gaze moved to Wilhelmine of Sagan, who stood laughing

with Alfred von Windischgrätz, her cheeks flushed too bright, her eyes glittering like cut glass.

Suzanne remembered the desolation in those brilliant dark eyes when Wilhelmine had spoken about her lost daughter only hours before. Now she appeared to be doing her best to forget.

Otronsky stood by the door with Julie Zichy and Count Nesselrode. "Help me distract him," Suzanne murmured to Dorothée.

Dorothée scanned her face, then nodded. She was beginning to understand the life Suzanne and Malcolm lived.

"Count Otronsky, settle an argument between the Comtesse de Périgord and me," Suzanne said. "Does the summer palace at Tsarkoe Selo have an English garden or a French garden?"

Otronsky inclined his head, dark brows lifted with amusement. "The grounds at Tsarkoe Selo include both an English garden and a garden *à la française*, Madame Rannoch. Never let it be said we Russians are anything but international in our tastes."

"How splendidly diplomatic of Catherine the Great. You see, Doro, we're both right."

A footman was moving toward them with a tray of champagne glasses. "Oh good," Dorothée said. "There's seemed to be champagne everywhere but where I am."

Otronsky sketched a bow and procured glasses for both of them.

"What a gallant man. It's so insufferably hot. Champagne is just the—Oh dear." Suzanne stumbled and fell against Otronsky, spattering champagne over both of them as well as the Savonnerie carpet.

"Are you all right, Madame Rannoch?" Otronsky steadied her with firm hands.

"Yes, so silly of me. The room started to spin."

"It's this dreadful heat," Dorothée said. "You'd never know it's November."

"I've never done well with the heat since I had the baby. Oh dear, I'm so sorry about your coat." Suzanne brushed a hand over Otronsky's coat and stepped back, the note that had been tucked into his cuff now in the palm of her hand.

29

"Dr. Blackwell. Thank goodness." Aline crossed to his side as he stepped into the duchess's salon. "Does it sound dreadful to say I'm longing for a few moments of conversation where I don't have to remember the map of Europe every time I open my mouth?"

"Entirely understandable. Though I have no doubt you have the map of Europe memorized. It seems to run in the family."

She took his arm, and they moved to the relative privacy of a window embrasure. Aline dropped down on the window seat and glanced across the room where Malcolm was in conversation with Gregory Lindorff. "Dr. Blackwell, has Malcolm talked to you?"

Blackwell gave a dry smile. "I know my advanced years, but you're getting to be quite grown-up yourself. Don't you think you might bring yourself to call me Geoffrey?"

Aline returned the smile. "Much more egalitarian."

"So I was thinking."

"Your flexibility is impressive, D—Geoffrey. Most people have the hardest time acknowledging that one has grown up."

"I may be a bit slow at times, Aline, but some things are unavoidably obvious." Blackwell—Geoffrey—put out a hand, as though to touch her wrist, then drew it back. "Has Malcolm talked to me about what?"

"Everything. Well, Princess Tatiana, really." Malcolm's face was turned to the side, but Aline had memorized the wasteland in his eyes. "He's taken it hard."

"Malcolm tends to take things hard. He makes everything his responsibility."

"Yes, I know. But this is different. Was Princess Tatiana—"

Geoffrey turned to look her full in the face.

"His mistress," Aline finished.

Geoffrey's face was like a notebook page with all the ink jottings smudged to illegibility. "If so, he'd hardly confide it to me."

"I thought gentlemen were always talking about their women."

"Malcolm isn't the sort for that kind of talk." He gave a bleak smile. "And God knows I'm not."

"No," she said, "you're sensible that way. As I am. But you've neatly avoided answering my question."

"About Malcolm and Princess Tatiana? All I could do is speculate. As a good scientist I deplore theorizing without data."

Aline's gaze shifted to her cousin's wife, crossing the room, her arm linked through Dorothée Périgord's. "I was quite put off by Suzanne at first when Malcolm brought her to England last spring. To own the truth, I'd always thought Malcolm would be like me and never marry. It was a sort of—"

"Solidarity?" Geoffrey asked.

There was an odd note in his voice, but Aline was too intent on what she was trying to say to examine it. "I suppose so, yes. And then suddenly there he was with this Paris fashion plate on his arm, jacket and petticoat cut just so, satin straw hat with a veil worn at precisely the right angle, pearl-trimmed gloves without a smudge. She seemed entirely too perfect to be approachable. Or to be the sort of wife Malcolm needed, assuming he needed a wife at all. But I quickly discovered she's every bit as eccentric as the rest of us and blessedly practical as well."

Geoffrey's gaze followed her own. "I still remember her kneeling over Malcolm on a camp bed, six months pregnant and cool as a cucumber as her husband lay wounded. But you could see the fear in her eyes. And her smile when he woke up was brighter than a dozen wax tapers."

"Well then. And Malcolm—"

Geoffrey frowned down at the reflection of the flame from the candle sconce in the polished parquet floor. "I was at their wedding at the embassy in Lisbon. They hadn't even known each other a month. Malcolm was distinctly white about the mouth, and Suzanne—" He shook his head, as though even now he could not make sense of what Suzanne had felt on her wedding day. "They took their vows seriously. But they were no Romeo and Juliet." He turned his gaze back to Aline. "You've always been refreshingly free of romanticism. And God knows you saw enough of the world growing up in your family. You must know that what's at the heart of most marriages is far more complicated than a fairy tale."

"Is that why you've never married?"

He gave a short laugh. "I never married because I never found anyone who would put up with me."

"Or who you thought worth putting up with?"

A smile pulled at his mouth. "Perhaps."

Aline pleated the orange blossom crêpe of her frock between her fingers. She had a lowering feeling she wasn't quite as free of romanticism as Geoffrey had confidently stated. "I'm not a fool. I know their courtship wasn't moonlight and roses. But I can't believe Suzanne doesn't *mind*."

"Marriages aren't equations, Aline. One can't always solve for the unknown variable. Take it from one who's observed far too much and learned the hard way. It doesn't pay to meddle."

Aline studied Suzanne, who was now laughing up at Count Otronsky, head thrown back, ringlets stirring above her bare shoulders, a perfect study in flirtation. "I can't help it," she said, aware that her scientist's detachment had quite deserted her. "I care about them both too much."

"Rannoch." Frederick Radley clapped a hand on Malcolm's shoulder. "Hard to get used to seeing the same people night after night."

"The society in Lisbon was even more confined."

"But that seems centuries ago." Radley leaned an arm against a pillar that supported a bronze of Persephone. "Where's your lovely wife?"

"Amusing herself."

"You don't dance attendance upon her, do you?"

"What sensible husband does?"

"Yes, but I never thought you were the sort to follow society's dictates." Radley's gaze skimmed round the room and settled on Suzanne. "Flirting with Otronsky. You're a brave husband indeed. Or a complacent one."

"My wife can take care of herself."

"Like Princess Tatiana?"

Malcolm's gloved fingers clenched. "What the devil's that supposed to mean?"

Radley ran his fingers down the clinging folds of Persephone's gown. "Merely that Vienna's a dangerous place in a number of ways. A woman can slip through one's fingers. As Prince Metternich has learned to his sorrow. If you'll excuse me, Rannoch, I need to pay my respects to our hostess."

Geoffrey Blackwell came to stand beside Malcolm as Radley moved off. "I was going to rescue you from the good colonel, but then I realized you might be in the midst of investigating. No, don't answer, I wasn't fishing for information." Blackwell surveyed the crowd. The salon grew more closely pressed by the minute as guests continued to stream through the door. "Until I came to Vienna I never spent so many evenings in a row in company."

"Enough to strain your patience with the human race?"

"My dear boy, surely you realize I never had much patience to begin with."

"A trait with which I am much in sympathy. And yet you do a remarkable amount of good. I haven't yet thanked you for what you did for Fitz."

Blackwell waved his hand. "It's my job."

"That's what I mean."

"Vaughn will do well enough. His recovery owes more to how he fell and the fact that the horse didn't trample him than to any efforts on my part. And to Lady Fitzwilliam's good nursing."

Blackwell's gaze strayed across the room to where Fitz and Eithne stood talking with Paul and Thérèse Esterhazy. "Vaughn is fortunate in his marriage."

As they watched, Fitz turned to look down at Eithne, like a man staring at a precious jewel that hovers just out of reach. As if aware of his regard, Eithne looked up at him with a quick smile. "Sometimes it takes a shock to make one realize all one has to lose," Malcolm said.

"Quite." Blackwell's gaze shifted from Fitz to Malcolm, as acute as a lancet guided by a surgeon's hand. "You told me a few days ago that it might have been a mistake for you to marry Suzanne. You were under a great deal of strain at the time. I hope it was the strain speaking. No one observing you and Suzanne together could think it a mistake."

Malcolm forced himself not to look away from that keen gaze. "You don't know how it seems from Suzanne's perspective."

"No. But I may have a more objective view of the matter than you do, lad."

Malcolm glanced down at the bronze Persephone, burnished by the candlelight, her head tilted down to study the half-eaten pomegranate she clutched in one hand. "I told Suzanne about Tatiana this afternoon."

Blackwell's sharp breath cut the air. "Thank God."

Malcolm shot him a sideways look. "You think I should have done it years ago."

"I think everyone is entitled to their secrets. But sometimes keeping them causes more damage than sharing them. And what you and Suzanne have is strong enough to withstand most revelations."

"You seem damned sure of what Suzanne and I have."

Blackwell frowned into his champagne glass and then looked up at Malcolm's face. "For God's sake, Malcolm, she loves you. She'd be lost without you."

Malcolm gave a laugh that grated against the rose-scented perfection of the air. "Have Viennese waltzes addled your brain? You're the last person on earth I'd have thought to find turning into a romantic."

"One doesn't need to be a romantic to recognize the bond between two people."

For a moment Malcolm had an intense memory of the pressure of Suzanne's hand in his own. There was a bond between them. But it was a bond built of necessity, shared danger, and the sins of the past, not romantic yearnings. He studied Blackwell, whom he'd known since childhood and whom he trusted and respected far more than his own father. "Bonds you've successfully avoided your entire life."

"Good God, surely you wouldn't expect me to advise you to follow my example. Besides—" The cynicism faded from Blackwell's eyes, and he looked as perhaps he had in his undergraduate days, younger and more vulnerable than Malcolm had ever seen him. He was silent for a long moment, and then a faint smile played about his lips. "We can all change."

"Lord Fitzwilliam. Lady Fitzwilliam." Wilhelmine of Sagan swept toward them with a rustle of rose tulle over blue satin and a waft of subtle perfume. What was it about Continental women, Eithne wondered, that was so effortlessly sophisticated? "I'm so sorry I didn't greet you when you came in. And so glad to see you recovered from your injury last night," the duchess added as Fitz bowed over her hand.

Eithne stiffened instinctively, but she could detect nothing beyond polite gallantry in the brush of her husband's lips against the duchess's white-gloved fingers.

"It's kind of you to come," Wilhelmine said, touching her cheek to Eithne's. "I know I've no hope of enticing Lord and Lady Castlereagh. They don't approve of my being a divorcée."

Fitz gave her one of his dazzling smiles. "As my friend Rannoch could tell you, Duchess, there are a number of matters upon which we do not agree with our chief."

"Showing admirable good sense." The duchess looked from Fitz to Eithne. "I do like watching the two of you. It's so refreshing to see a married couple who actually enjoy each other's company."

Eithne gave the sort of practiced smile she had long since perfected as a diplomat's wife. "I fear we're dreadfully unfashionable."

"No one with your dress sense could be called unfashionable, Lady Fitzwilliam." The duchess cast a glance round the room. "I see my sister is enjoying herself. Count Clam-Martinitz is quite charming. Poor Prince Talleyrand. If you'll excuse me. I must talk to our musician. A new talent. I think you'll be impressed."

Eithne watched the duchess sweep off. She could feel Fitz's gaze upon her. "Will you ever trust me again?" he said in a quiet voice.

She cast a quick glance at him. "What—"

"I could see the look in your eyes when I greeted the duchess. It's no more than I deserve. Will you possibly believe me when I tell you she's nothing more to me than a charming woman who happens to be our hostess?"

"*She* isn't."

She saw the flinch in his eyes. "If I tell you that never again—"

"You can't promise that, Fitz." Eithne's gaze drifted round the room. The crystal and gilt and soft rose walls created the picture of fairy-tale romance. The light had that soft glow that comes from the best wax tapers sparkling off jewels and cut glass and shimmering against silk and velvet, superfine and cassimere. Everywhere couples leaned close together, warm laughter rippled through the air, fans hid whispered conversations. "Any more than I can promise I'll never fall in love with another man."

She didn't risk a look at Fitz, but she could feel the shock that ran through him.

She let herself wait a few moments, breathing in the scent of beeswax and hothouse roses, before she turned back to him. A small measure of revenge. Unworthy, but she could not deny the satisfaction. "I didn't say it would happen. I don't think it will."

"If you—"

"No." She lifted her face to his. They were as close as the flirtatious couples who thronged the salon. "I wouldn't do it in revenge. But a few months ago I'd have said it would be impossible. I don't believe that anymore."

He swallowed. "I'll never forgive myself for doing that to you."

Eithne pulled the folds of her Grecian scarf tighter about her shoulders. "If you're human, I am as well, my dear. Whatever the duchess said about us, our life isn't a fairy tale. We can't know we won't be tempted or make mistakes. All we can do is promise to try."

Music and candlelight shimmered in the air. The silk-hung walls of the music room reverberated with the sound. Sparkling, effervescent, then suddenly poignant. As intricate as one of Aline's equations, but with the power to cut straight to one's heart. The lights of Vienna shone beyond the windows, the lights of the chandelier were reflected back in the glass. The cascade of melody seemed to wash over the city.

For a moment Suzanne forgot Otronsky's letter tucked into her bodice, forgot the shadowy plot, forgot Princess Tatiana, forgot even her questions about her husband. The clear, crystalline sound transported her.

When the last note drifted away, Count Nesselrode leaned forward from the row behind to speak with Malcolm. Suzanne rose and moved to the pianoforte. "That was exquisite, Monsieur Schubert. I'd give a great deal to sing some of your songs one day."

"I'd be honored if you did," he said in French. He closed his sheet music and glanced round the salon. The guests had got to their feet and were milling about, accepting fresh glasses of champagne from the footmen who had begun circulating with silver trays as soon as the music ended. "It's an odd world. I never thought to find myself here."

"One never quite grows accustomed to it, no matter how long one lives among its numbers. But they're quite harmless for the most part."

Schubert grinned and continued to tidy his music. "Odd that I owe this to Princess Tatiana. I knew she moved in these circles, but I never really saw her in the heart of her world." His gaze strayed across the room, then stilled. "Though I saw that man with her once."

"Who?" Suzanne glanced round. Nearly every man in the room would have known Princess Tatiana, at least in the less salacious use of the word.

"The man talking to Monsieur Rannoch."

"Count Nesselrode?" No, Suzanne saw, Nesselrode had moved off, and Malcolm was talking to—Damnation. "Colonel Radley?"

"I never heard his name. I saw them leaving her dressmaker's. I waved, but they were deep in conversation, and she didn't seem to see me."

"When was this?"

Schubert frowned. "Six days ago. So it would have been—Two days before she died."

A chill spread through the shot silk of Suzanne's gown. Schubert had seen Frederick Radley with Tatiana three days before Radley had supposedly arrived in Vienna. Radley had lied.

And she was going to have to find out why.

30

Malcolm struck a flint to the tapers on the escritoire in their bedchamber. "Very adroitly done. Even I wasn't quite sure when you took the paper."

Suzanne reached inside her ruched bodice, where the paper she had taken from Otronsky was tucked into her Circassian corset. "I should hope not. A good agent should be able to deceive a good agent."

He grinned as the second taper sparked to life. "A good agent should be able to see through a good agent."

"We're well matched." Her fingers clenched on the paper for a moment at the reverberations in the words. Malcolm gave no sign he had noticed either the reverberations or her reaction. But then, as he'd said, a good agent could conceal things from another agent. Or from his or her spouse.

The paper Otronsky had been so carefully concealing was a half sheet of hot-pressed writing paper, folded in quarters and closed with a pin. Suzanne removed the pin and spread the paper in the glow of the candlelight. A few words, not in code.

Confirmed for 10 December.

She and Malcolm exchanged glances. "The gala night at the opera," she said.

Malcolm nodded. "So we know when. And who is behind the plot. But not who the target is."

All the royalty and heads of delegations would be at the glittering concert at the Kärntnertortheater on 10 December. "Is it enough proof?" she asked.

Malcolm stared down at the paper and shook his head. "The note's not in Otronsky's hand. There's only our word for it that we took it from him. And he could claim it's merely from a mistress arranging a liaison."

"So if you take it to Baron Hager—"

"He may very well call me a liar. Not for the first time."

"But if we don't warn him—"

"It's criminal negligence. We have to try." He pocketed the note. "I'll talk to Castlereagh tomorrow and call on Hager."

"While I'll have a quiet day with Colin. And I need to see my dressmaker."

Malcolm blew out the tapers and turned to the bed. She caught his arm. A smile curved his mouth, but he looked down at her for a long moment, as though seeking the answer to an unvoiced question. As though for all today's revelations, something still held him in check. For a moment, she returned his gaze, searching for a way past the barriers that still existed between them. Then she closed the distance between them and put her lips to his, reaching out to him in the one way that never failed.

A shudder ran through him. He brushed his mouth lightly across her own. She caught his lower lip between her teeth, deepening the kiss. But as he lifted her against him and she wound her arms round his neck, she was aware that her fingers were not quite steady.

Foolish. This was hardly the first time she had lied to her husband. But for some reason the lie bit her in the throat with the pain of a fresh betrayal.

Castlereagh stared down at Otronsky's paper in the cloudy light from his study windows. He had risen early and had already been at his desk for a while by the time Malcolm sought him out. "How did you get this?"

"Suzanne got it."

Castlereagh looked up from the paper, brows lifted. "How on earth—?"

"Last night, at the Duchess of Sagan's musicale. Simple enough for a lady to stumble and catch a gentleman's arm. I believe a glass of champagne was spilled."

"I hadn't realized quite how much you'd taught her."

"My wife is a very resourceful woman. I can't take credit for her talents."

"But you brought her into the world of espionage."

Malcolm grimaced. "Yes, I know."

"Don't look so guilt-stricken, lad. From what I've seen she enjoys it, and we certainly have cause to be grateful for her help, here and in Spain." Castlereagh looked down at the paper again.

"You can't deny it's proof," Malcolm said.

"Proof that Otronsky intends something the night of the opera gala. Hardly proof of what that something is."

"Put together with Tatiana's information and what Heinrich and Margot reported—"

"Yes." Castlereagh moved to his desk. "It seems more likely now that Princess Tatiana was telling the truth." He stared down at the piles of papers on the gilt-embossed Spanish leather of the blotter. "God help us."

"At least we're starting to learn what we're up against."

"And it puts us in the devil of a mess." Castlereagh gripped the edge of the desk. "I'm sorry, Malcolm. I know you're relieved to find Princess Tatiana was telling the truth, but I'd have much preferred it if she'd been lying through the teeth. Apparently one of the tsar's closest advisers is involved in a plot we can't prove, against an unknown target."

"I'll talk to Hager. I doubt he'll believe me, but perhaps it will at least put him on his guard on the tenth."

"It isn't enough." Castlereagh reached for a pen, then tossed it down as though it burned him. "We need more details."

"I intend to discover them."

The foreign secretary fixed Malcolm with a hard stare. "Accusing Otronsky without sufficient proof could cause as much of an international incident as whatever this attack is. Go carefully, Malcolm."

"I always do, sir."

Suzanne tightened the Barcelona handkerchief that held her satin straw hat in place and adjusted the folds of her Cossack mantle. The bow windows that flanked the shop door before her displayed a profusion of hats and bonnets and caps, and a swansdown-trimmed crimson velvet evening cloak that might have made her take a second look in different circumstances.

She hesitated before the curved glass of the window, recalling the first time Malcolm had taken her shopping in Lisbon. They hadn't been married yet or even betrothed. She'd come to the British embassy a refugee, with no wardrobe and no funds to purchase one. Malcolm had shown surprising patience, cooling his heels on a fragile gilt chair while she was fitted for new gowns, though she suspected a modiste's was the last place he'd choose to spend an afternoon. He'd even selected a bonnet for her. She stared at a plum-colored bonnet in the window and remembered him setting the sarcenet-lined velvet on her head, and the brush of his fingers as he tied the ribbons.

For a moment the silk and lace and straw in the window wavered before her eyes. She had woken this morning in Malcolm's arms, his skin warm beneath her cheek, his fingers twined in her hair. He'd turned his head and brushed his lips across her forehead, and she'd looked into his eyes, knowing the ghost of Tatiana Kirsanova didn't stand between them.

At least not in the way she had once feared. Schubert's revelations about the link between Tatiana and Frederick Radley had introduced a new danger. It seemed the closer she came to the truth of Princess Tatiana's murder, the closer she came to disaster. Her marriage might be half compromise, half illusion, but she had never valued it so much as she did now, when she saw how easily it could crumble to bits before her eyes.

Damnation. She was being a fool. She had got herself into this, and she had no one to blame but herself. She turned the brass knob at the center of the shiny blue-painted door and stepped into a world of hats and bonnets clustered on stands, bolts of velvet and silver tissue spilling from shelves, ribboned and beaded gloves laid out on countertops, fashion periodicals stacked on fragile gilt tables. The smell of lavender and violet was instantly recognizable. The scent of a fine dressmaker's was the same in Vienna as in Lisbon or London.

A dark-haired woman in her midtwenties stood behind the counter, showing fashion plates to three ladies, a mother and two daughters by the look of it. When Suzanne stepped into the shop, the woman paused in her monologue on the merits of moss green satin over sapphire shot silk.

Her gaze took in the cherry-striped Italian sarcenet of Suzanne's gown, the Chinese binding on her mantle, the sparkle of the diamonds in her ears, and the gleam of the pearls round her throat. She turned to the back of the shop. A moment later, a slender woman with dark red hair and an angular, interesting face came through the blue velvet curtains behind the counter.

"I am Madame Girard," she said. Unlike many dressmakers with French names, her accent was unmistakably Parisian.

"I am Countess Irina Derevna." Suzanne spoke in French with a Russian accent. Not enough to deceive a Russian, perhaps, but hopefully enough to deceive a French dressmaker who had immigrated to Vienna.

"You are in need of a new gown, Countess?"

"No, of information. Princess Tatiana Kirsanova was my cousin."

Madame Girard's gaze flickered from side to side. "My deepest sympathies, Countess. Your cousin was a favorite client. Perhaps it would be best to speak in private." She led Suzanne through the blue velvet curtains into a workroom stacked with bolts of fabric. A girl of about ten with long red hair sat sewing at a long table by the window.

Suzanne smiled at the girl. "Your daughter?" Though in fact she knew as much from Blanca's report after her earlier inquiries at Madame Girard's.

"Charlotte. Countess Derevna, Charlotte."

Charlotte got to her feet and dropped a graceful curtsy.

"You must have known my cousin," Suzanne said. "Princess Tatiana."

Charlotte's eyes widened. "She brought me chocolates the last time she was here. Are you trying to find out who killed her?"

"Charlotte," Madame Girard said.

"It's all right. That's precisely what I am trying to do," Suzanne told Charlotte.

Charlotte nodded solemnly.

Madame Girard conducted Suzanne through the sewing room to a fitting room lined with mirrors and furnished with a blue velvet chaise longue and spindle-legged chairs. She struck a flint to an oil lamp that stood on a small round table covered with a shawl.

Suzanne sank down on one of the chairs. "I understand my cousin was here only two days before she died."

"For a fitting." Madame Girard adjusted the pink silk shade of the lamp.

"I know how she admired your designs. I have only recently come to Vienna, but Tania was always writing to me about your exquisite creations and what a stir she made in them."

"Thank you, Countess. But I don't believe you came here to flatter me." Madame Girard sank into a chair across from Suzanne.

Madame Girard was a shrewd woman with a keen understanding. Which could either make this easier or more difficult. "I believe on this particular occasion Tatiana may have come here for more than a fitting." Suzanne opened the steel clasp on her reticule and drew out a sketch. "Madame Girard, do you recognize this man?"

Madame Girard's gaze flickered over the sketch Suzanne had drawn of Frederick Radley. Suzanne saw the swift calculation in her gaze. The risks of lying and the risks of telling the truth.

"I came to Vienna during the Revolution, Countess," Madame Girard said. "I was only sixteen. My father had been killed. I had to look after my mother and sisters." She smoothed her hands over her skirt, pressing the twilled silk taut. "I worked as an assistant to a modiste. In time, I opened my own shop. Then war came to Vienna as well. Charlotte's father was killed. It was no longer so fashionable to be a Frenchwoman, though people still crave French gowns. I have learned to live carefully."

"No one could blame you for anything that occurred." Suzanne leaned forward. "Madame, I, too, understand the difficulties a woman alone faces making her way in the world. My cousin faced those same difficulties, and in making her way in the world she lost her life. I want to find out who did this to her."

Madame Girard returned Suzanne's gaze, then gave a faint smile. "You're a persuasive woman, Countess." She glanced down at the sketch. "This gentleman came to see the princess during her fitting. He called at a side door and asked for her. The princess indicated that she wished to see him."

"They spoke in private?"

"In a fitting room."

Suzanne suspected this was not the first time a gentleman had come into the shop through the side entrance and enjoyed a private tête-à-tête with a client. Licentious as Vienna might be, it was still more difficult for ladies to arrange their liaisons than it was for their husbands. "How long did this interview last?"

"A quarter hour. Perhaps twenty minutes."

"And then?"

"They left the shop together."

"How did they seem?"

Madame Girard frowned. "As though they'd reached an accommodation. They didn't appear—"

"To be lovers?"

"No. They evidently knew each other well, but I wouldn't have said they were lovers."

A scratch sounded at the door. "Maman?"

"A moment, *ma chère*."

"No," Suzanne said, "let her come in."

"You're talking about Princess Tatiana?" Charlotte asked as she slipped into the room.

"Yes." Suzanne held out her hand to the girl. "Your *maman* was telling me that this gentleman spoke with my cousin the last time she was here. Do you remember him?"

Charlotte glanced down at the sketch her mother still held. "I was in the sewing room hemming a gown for Countess Zichy. Their voices got loud. I wasn't spying."

"Of course not, *chérie*," Suzanne said. "What did you hear?"

"At first I could just hear voices, not the words. Then the gentleman's voice got louder. I heard him say—"

Charlotte hesitated. Her mother put an arm round her. "It's all right, *ma petite*. Just tell us what happened."

Charlotte drew a breath and spoke in a rush. "I heard him say 'this is blackmail.' And then she said something about 'be reasonable.' Then their voices got quieter. When they came out of the room, he held the door open for her, and they seemed to be friendlier." She looked at Suzanne with anxious eyes. "Does that help?"

"Very much. My thanks to you both." Suzanne got to her feet and pressed the hands of mother and daughter. A surprisingly successful interrogation.

Which took her one step further down a path that seemed to lead inexorably to ruin.

"Monsieur Rannoch." Baron Hager put aside his newspaper and got to his feet. "Do you have another flight of fancy for me? I've had my fill of the *Wiener Zeitung*. I could do with some entertaining fiction."

"This isn't fiction." Malcolm held out Otronsky's note and recounted Margot's description of Otronsky, Addison following Otronsky, and Suzanne recovering the note.

Hager listened in a silence that gave nothing away. "You're an enterprising family."

"Thank you."

The baron folded the note. "Monsieur Rannoch, surely I don't have to tell you that this proves nothing. The note could be from anyone, about anything. It's no crime for Count Otronsky to have frequented the Empress Rose tavern with his friends. The only evidence of wrongdoing still comes down to Princess Tatiana's word."

"And mine."

"Just so." Hager slid the newspaper to cover the files on his desk.

"Baron, if there's even a chance this is true—"

"I should be doubly on my guard at the opera gala. But I like to think I always am, Monsieur Rannoch."

"Suzanne." Frederick Radley got to his feet and crossed his sitting room toward her. "I confess I didn't expect this. Though I can't deny that I hoped."

He took her hand and raised it to his lips. Suzanne let him do so, despite the wash of memories. "We haven't had a chance to talk properly, Freddy. For all the things one may say in a Viennese salon, so much remains unvoiced."

"How true." He moved to the drinks table and poured two glasses of Madeira.

Suzanne sank down on a tapestry sofa. Lodgings were hard to come by in Vienna these days, but Lord Stewart had provided Radley with a handsome suite of rooms overlooking the Minoritenplatz. Through the window she could see the plaster moldings of the British delegation's lodgings across the square. The smells of tobacco and brandy hung in the air. Radley had a way of landing on his feet.

She pulled off her gloves, then undid the cords on her mantle and let it slither about her in a stir of cherry-colored shot sarcenet and white silk. She had deliberately chosen a gown that was cut low and had not worn a tippet or kerchief. She felt Radley's gaze linger on the lace-edged bodice.

"I confess my hope of a private tête-à-tête with you brightened when I encountered your husband." He crossed to her and gave her one of the glasses. "I may not be the best judge of character, but it's obvious to the meanest observer that he doesn't appreciate you as you deserve."

"You've scarcely seen either of us."

Radley touched his glass to hers. "It didn't take a great deal of time to form a conclusion. Don't forget, I have rather more knowledge than the average observer of the sort of attentions you deserve."

"Old knowledge."

"You're no Princess Metternich, content to pour tea and give parties and run the nursery, Suzanne. You're a passionate woman. You'll have to seek passion somewhere."

She took a sip of wine, remembering the first time he'd given her a glass of Madeira. The wine cloyed on her tongue, but she forced it down. "Perhaps I've learned the dangers of passion."

He shook his head. "The dangers only make it more seductive, my darling."

She stretched an arm along the curved back of the sofa. He was really very easy to play. Strange to remember that he had once sent a thrill through her that was equal parts fear and excitement. But then she had been a different person in those days.

Radley dropped down on the sofa beside her, his Hessian-booted foot inches from her Spanish slipper, his buckskin-covered knee brushing her striped sarcenet skirts. "My poor sweet. I think you're fonder of him than he is of you. Have you made the mistake of falling in love with your own husband?"

Suzanne took another sip of wine. Odd, the sense of power that came with the knowledge that Tatiana was Malcolm's sister. "I thought you knew me better than that."

"You've always had a knack for surprising me. It was one of the things that made you endlessly intriguing."

"Not endlessly, as I recall."

He gave a brief laugh. "We all make mistakes."

"In our dealings we both made them."

Radley laid his hand over her own. His fingers were warm. She remembered them tugging at the laces on her corset, parting her thighs, pinning her hands over her head. "It can't be easy watching your husband mourn Princess Tatiana," Radley said. "Even with a man as cold as Malcolm, one can see the grief."

"Yes, I didn't realize until recently quite how deep Malcolm's grief over the princess went. I only hope I've been able to offer him the support he needs."

Radley gave an incredulous laugh. "My dear Suzanne—"

She forced herself to keep her hand still beneath his own. The smell of his shaving soap choked her. "But then a number of men are grieving the princess. I had no idea you knew her so well."

She felt his fingers stiffen. "Hardly well. I attended her salon once or twice in Paris last spring. But I could scarcely fail to appreciate her."

"But you also knew her in the Peninsula?"

He removed his hand from her own and took a swallow of Madeira. "I told you. Our paths crossed."

"And yet the acquaintance was strong enough that you came to see her in Vienna three days before you officially arrived."

Radley's face froze. Then he gave a shout of laughter. "My darling. Aren't we living with enough drama without your inventing it?"

"It's not an invention, Freddy. You were seen with Princess Tatiana leaving Madame Girard's in the Graben."

"That's—"

"Undeniable."

His gaze hardened. "What the devil do you want?"

"An explanation."

"Damn it, Suzanne." Radley pushed himself to his feet and stood over her. "You're accusing me of murder."

"I don't have enough of the facts yet to do so. But I do know you quarreled with Princess Tatiana in the fitting room at Madame Girard's. You accused her of blackmail."

He tossed down the last of his Madeira. "I don't have to justify myself to you."

"A few moments ago you seemed quite ready to seduce me."

"Old habits." He stalked over to the drinks table and filled his glass with brandy.

"It was once your habit to confide in me. A simple explanation, Freddy. Surely that isn't so very much to ask."

"You have no right to ask anything of me."

"Princess Tatiana knew something about you. She was threatening you. But by the end of the interview you were on friendlier terms." Suzanne studied Radley. His shoulders were taut beneath the red fabric of his jacket. His hand shook as he lifted the glass of brandy to his mouth. Surely what she had discovered thus far was not enough to explain this degree of fear. "But there's more, isn't there?" She took a sip of Madeira and tossed off her bluff. "You went to see Princess Tatiana the night she died. I saw you leaving the Palm Palace."

He spun round. His gaze locked with her own. "You can't possibly know that's true."

She got to her feet. "Do you really think after all that's passed between us, I wouldn't recognize you?"

He drew a breath, then set his glass on the drinks table as though he wished he could smash it. "You're playing with fire, my sweet. You always were drawn to danger. But in the end you won't tell anyone. Not even your cold bastard of a husband."

"You seem very sure."

"Oh, I am." He crossed to stand a handsbreadth away from her. "I told you I had no wish to disrupt your marriage, Suzanne. Which is true. But if you go to Malcolm with this, I shall be compelled to tell him precisely how well you and I knew each other. And under what circumstances. He's always been a damned Radical, but he's still a duke's grandson. Whatever the terms of your marriage, I don't think he'd care to have a wife who's damaged goods."

Suzanne took a sip of wine, willing her hand to be steady. "I could hardly fail to anticipate that you'd say that. As obvious as moving a pawn to defend one's queen."

"Well then. We have each other neatly in check."

"Sometimes the only way out of check is to sacrifice one's queen." She tossed off the last of her wine and set the glass on the sofa table. "Say whatever you must to Malcolm, Freddy. I'll do the same."

His harsh laugh rang off the polished woodwork. "You're bluffing."

"Am I?" She reached for her mantle and flung it round her shoulders. "It will be interesting to see."

"Damn it, Suzanne." He seized her arm.

She jerked away from his grip and picked up her gloves and reticule. "Good day, Colonel Radley."

"My God." Radley's gaze bored into her own. "You're in deeper than I realized. Do you really think you can make him love you by discovering who killed his precious Tatiana?"

"On the contrary." She tugged on her gloves, still feeling the imprint of Radley's fingers on her arm. "I have no illusions that I can make Malcolm do anything at all."

❧ 31 ❧

As she turned into the Minoritenplatz, Suzanne met Eithne, in a Dresden blue pelisse and a willow-shaving bonnet, pushing Colin in a baby carriage. Eithne looked up, autumn sunshine slanting across her face. Suzanne suspected it wasn't only the golden light that had driven the shadows from her friend's eyes.

"It seemed a shame not to get him out for a walk before it rains again," Eithne said. "And truth to tell, I've been missing my own little ones."

"That was kind of you." Suzanne bent over the carriage. Colin dropped his rattle and stretched up his arms to her. Children could trust so unconditionally, she thought as she scooped him up and felt him snuggle into her. She couldn't remember a time when trust had been so simple. "How's Fitz?"

Eithne gave a wry laugh. "One would never know he'd suffered an accident. At least from his behavior. He and Malcolm have gone to a meeting at the chancellery."

Colin's hands had fisted round Suzanne's pearls. She disentangled them and settled him on her hip. "It's good to see you smiling."

Eithne shot a quick glance at her. "Do you quite despise me?"

"Dearest. Of course not."

Eithne's primrose-kid-gloved hands tightened on the bar of the baby carriage. "I suspect everyone must think me a fool."

"What matters is what you think."

"I had all sorts of satisfying revenge thoughts. Quite beastly, the sort of imaginings I'd not have thought myself capable of. But the thing is, I love him. If I doubted that, I changed my mind when I saw him lying unconscious at the Carrousel."

Suzanne had a clear memory of sitting beside a camp bed in which Malcolm lay wounded, not long into their marriage. She'd stared at his pale, bruised skin and thought that she might never have a conversation with him again. Fear and loss had choked her. Loss of something she hadn't begun to value properly. "I understand."

"Do you?"

"I've faced losing my husband. It has a way of putting things in perspective."

Eithne stared down at the cobblestones. "Sometimes I'm still angry. He isn't the man I thought he was in my girlish delusions. But he's still the father of our children. He's still the boy who lost his mother at ten and held things together for the younger ones while his older brothers were off at school and his father was busy with politics. He's still the stepbrother who made sure his new stepmother's children were welcomed into the family. Who dutifully danced with his sisters and stepsisters at their coming-out balls and pays his stepbrother's gambling debts. He takes his responsibilities so seriously."

"He and Malcolm are much alike in that."

Eithne looked up at Suzanne. "I know it will never be the same. But if what we have is flawed, it's more honest than my romantic imaginings. And I'd rather have it, flaws and all, than lose it altogether."

Colin had tugged loose the cords on Suzanne's mantle. She smoothed his hair. "I can understand that."

"Last night I saw him being charming to the Duchess of Sagan, and I couldn't help but wonder—He said I'd never trust him again."

"Perhaps not never. But it takes time."

Colin wriggled in Suzanne's arms. "Down."

Suzanne set her son on his feet and reached down to take his small hand.

Eithne touched her fingers to Colin's dark hair. "Does it sound mad to say that I almost love Fitz more, knowing his flaws?"

"Perhaps knowing the truth makes the feelings deeper." Even as she framed the words, Suzanne wondered how they applied to the conversation she was about to have with her husband. Of course Eithne had entered the marriage loving Fitz, unlike the prosaic start of her marriage to Malcolm. That made a difference.

"I keep thinking how dreadful it would be to lose everything."

Suzanne tightened her grip on Colin's hand. "I know precisely what you mean."

"There are times when putting forward Castlereagh's talking points sticks in my throat." Fitz scowled across the bustling traffic of the Ballhausplatz as he and Malcolm emerged from the chancellery, where they had been meeting with Friedrich von Genz, Metternich's assistant and the secretary to the Congress.

"Arguing strenuously for the partition of Poland does rather tarnish Britain's image as a defender of constitutional liberties." Malcolm drew a breath. The crisp autumn air was welcome after two hours shut in a room with an overly warm stove and overly circumscribed ideas. "Of course, so did handing Genoa over to Sardinia a mere eight months after Bentinck marched in with British soldiers and proclaimed the republic restored."

"A buffer against French incursions in Italy," Fitz said, parodying Castlereagh's accents to the like.

"'Republic' is a dangerous word in a lot of minds. I don't think it even occurred to anyone Venice should be turned back into one." Malcolm drew up to avoid a four-in-hand tooled by a side-whiskered man in Hungarian uniform. "But no matter how hard Castlereagh and Metternich try, they can't erase it entirely."

"What?"

"The French Revolution. They're doing everything they can to put it back in the box. Quite ignoring the fact that the box broke twenty years ago. You can't take ideas out of people's minds."

They moved forward across the cobblestones, stopping to exchange greetings with an Austrian undersecretary hurrying back to the chancellery with a sheaf of documents under his arm.

"We've lost any moral high ground we had when we came to Vienna," Fitz said. "It's got to the point where even when we argue against the slave trade, people think we're doing it for advantage in the colonies."

"Do you really think that has nothing to do with it?"

Fitz shot a look at him, eyes narrowed against the slanting late-afternoon sun. "I can't even attempt to say no. It'll be good to be out. To be able to frame one's own opinions instead of always arguing someone else's."

"You're still going to stand for Parliament?"

"Yes. That is—" Fitz paused as they were about to turn out of the Ballhausplatz. "I don't know. I don't know about Eithne's father. I don't know about anything."

Malcolm studied his friend's set profile. "You'd make a good MP, Fitz. Nothing that's happened has changed my view of that."

Fitz turned to look him full in the face. A bitter smile twisted his lips. "You're such a good agent you can even lie convincingly to those who know you best, Malcolm."

"It's no lie. In my optimistic moments, I'll even acknowledge you might make a difference."

Fitz returned his gaze, swallowed, turned away abruptly. "You don't know how much that—Thank you." He tugged at the curling brim of his hat and resumed walking toward the Minoritenplatz. "I don't suppose there's any chance you'd consider returning home and standing for Parliament with me?"

Home flashed into Malcolm's mind. Granite cliffs, salt spray, candlelit drawing rooms. The black metal railings and leafy plane trees in Berkeley Square. Secrets and lies he had been running from for six years. Perhaps longer. "Ask me again the next time Castlereagh instructs us to argue an untenable case."

Fitz touched him on the shoulder but said nothing further. They returned to the Minoritenplatz in a silence more amicable than anything that had passed between them for the past five days.

"Darling." Suzanne's voice stopped him as they stepped into the British delegation's lodgings. Musical as always, yet there was a note in it that sent a chill through him. "Can you come into the library for a moment?"

Malcolm nodded to Fitz and followed his wife through the double doors to the library. Papers littered the long table in the center of the room, but the book-lined chamber was empty. A branch of candles burned on the table against the lengthening afternoon shadows, as though Suzanne had lit them in readiness. "What's happened?"

"I need to talk to you." She paced to the far end of the room, putting an expanse of green and gold Aubusson carpet between them. Her cherry-striped skirts whipped round her legs. "I thought it would be easier with more space than in our bedchamber. And I suppose I didn't want to do it with Colin right next door."

Her tone now was quite unlike his wife's usual matter-of-factness. Malcolm studied her face. She was parchment pale, but it was her eyes that frightened him. They looked as though she'd seen into hell and was convinced she'd never escape.

"What is it?" His voice came out more sharply than he intended.

She walked halfway toward him, then stopped, hands locked together. The candlelight struck sparks from her diamond earrings and hollowed out the bones of her face. "Schubert told me last night that he'd seen Colonel Radley with Princess Tatiana. Leaving Madame Girard's. Her dressmaker's. Two days before the murder. Three days before Radley supposedly arrived in Vienna."

Malcolm leaned against the library table, hands braced on the marble behind him. "You wanted to talk to Radley before you told me?"

"How did you know?"

"You didn't tell me last night. And I know Radley was acquainted with your family in the Peninsula. It makes sense you'd want to get his version of events first."

She swallowed. "Before I talked to Radley, I went to Madame Girard's. Radley and Princess Tatiana had a private interview that sounds as though it was prearranged. Madame Girard's daughter heard Radley say 'That's blackmail.' But they left the shop together and seemed on better terms."

"Did Radley admit to any of this?"

"No. He seemed even more panicked than one would expect. I had a mad thought, and I voiced it. I accused him of being the man I saw in front of Princess Tatiana's the night of the murder. From his reaction, I think I was right."

"That was probably over an hour after she was killed. After Czartoryski was there."

"But Radley could have killed her and stayed nearby. Or come back." Her voice was level but her gaze remained racked by demons he didn't understand.

"Perhaps. We'll have to discover what hold Tatiana had on him."

"Malcolm, there's more. Radley tried to blackmail me into not revealing any of this to you."

The bastard. His hands tightened. The brass edging on the table cut into his palms. "Blackmail you with what?"

She drew a breath. "Darling—"

"Suzanne." He stepped forward and took her hands. They were ice cold in his grip. "I shouldn't have asked. You don't have to tell me any of this."

"I do." She jerked her hands from his touch. "I want you to hear this from me rather than Radley. I did know Frederick Radley in the Peninsula but not when my parents were alive. Just after they were killed."

He frowned, sorting out the chronology. "Before—"

"Before I met you. There was a bit more time between when my parents were killed and when you found me in the Cantabrian Mountains than I allowed you to think."

He nodded, his gaze steady on her face. He'd never pressed her for the details. But he'd held her numerous times when she woke, shaking and sweat-drenched, from nightmares she never described. Nightmares he was sure went back to that time. "Go on."

"I did what I could for the servants and tenants and then Blanca and I left the estate. We were making our way toward Galicia when we met an expeditionary force of British soldiers. Radley was their leader. He offered me his protection. In every sense of the word."

"Good God." This would have been only a short time after she'd been raped by French soldiers and seen her parents killed. "You'd just been—"

The candlelight flickered over her face, so it was half blue-shadowed, half washed by golden warmth. "My world had been torn apart, and I needed comfort. I was desperate to find something to hold on to. Radley can be very charming. I think—" She hesitated, as though searching for the right words. Her eyes held echoes of nightmare memories she had never fully described to him. "I think I wanted to lose myself in that charm. To be so dazzled I'd forget. Radley didn't ravish me or seduce me."

"He took advantage of you." The rage Malcolm was trying to control shook his voice.

"I couldn't think beyond the moment."

"But he should have been able to."

"He took us to Léon. And then it became clear he didn't find it convenient to continue our involvement." Her hands locked on her elbows. "He had another mistress there. He set Blanca and me up at an inn, but it turned out he hadn't paid the reckoning. He constantly overspent his income. He complained his brother had cut back on his allowance when his father died."

"I'm not surprised. By all reports Radley's father left the estate heavily encumbered."

"Apparently it's a family failing. Radley's resources were strained, and I was a financial burden he couldn't afford."

Malcolm's fists tightened. "He damn well—"

"So Blanca and I left to look for my relatives in Galicia. We got lost in the mountains and were attacked by bandits. That's when you found us."

Malcolm saw the fragile, defiant woman who'd run out of the underbrush on a mountain road and stumbled into his arms, face smeared with dirt and dried blood. "Dear God."

"Malcolm, I'm sorry. I should have told you from the first. If not when we met, the moment you offered for me."

"I never asked—"

"You offered me your protection, but you should have known what you were getting in a wife." She stood before him, hands locked together, head high. "You knew I wasn't a virgin, but you thought I was a victim of war. Instead I was a cast-off mistress."

He heard the words, but it was a moment before he made sense of them. "God in heaven, Suzanne. How could you possibly think—" He crossed to her side in two steps and folded her in his arms. "Sweetheart," he said, his voice muffled by her hair, "how could you think so poorly of me as to imagine any of this would matter?"

She drew back and took his face between her hands. Her fingers trembled against his skin. "Because you're still a British gentleman, darling. And your world has rules."

"And you didn't think I could see beyond them." He kissed her forehead, then her cheek, then her lips, but lightly. She seemed as fragile to him as she had on their wedding night. "I'm only sorry I didn't find you before Radley did, so you wouldn't have had to go through this."

She clung to him for a moment with the abandon of the girl she had ceased to be before he met her. "How could I be sure? In so many ways we don't know each other."

He tightened his arms round her as though he could anchor her to safety and erase the past. Then, because his impulse was to crush her in his arms and cover her mouth with his own, he did just the opposite. Her story had served as a reminder of his own secrets, and why he didn't deserve her trust or anything approaching love.

He pressed his lips to her forehead, then released her. "I need to report to Castlereagh about the meeting with Genz this afternoon. We'll talk later. About what Tatiana might have known about Radley. About—what to do next."

Suzanne rubbed her arms. He could feel the confusion in her gaze, but he couldn't meet it. Not now. Too much was roiling inside him. He turned to the door.

"Malcolm—"

Heavy footsteps cut short her words. A single knock sounded, and then the library doors were flung open with scarcely a pause. Castlereagh stepped into the room, followed by Baron Hager.

The foreign secretary's gaze went to Suzanne. "I'm sorry you're here, my dear. Though perhaps it's as well."

"Madame Rannoch." Hager inclined his head. "Rannoch." He turned to Malcolm. "I regret to say I am here on unhappy business. I have a warrant for your arrest for the murder of Princess Tatiana Kirsanova."

32

Suzanne heard the scrape of her own breath. Beside her Malcolm had gone absolutely still. "Naturally I am at your disposal, Baron. But might I inquire as to what has changed since I saw you this morning?"

Hager met Malcolm's gaze, his own impassive. "As I just explained to Lord Castlereagh, I have received evidence that Princess Tatiana was blackmailing you."

"*What?*" Malcolm's voice ricocheted off the fretted ceiling with the force of a pistol shot.

"A letter from the princess to you came into our possession this afternoon." Hager's gaze flickered toward Suzanne. "And a reliable witness saw Madame Rannoch enter the Palm Palace alone, a quarter hour later than the time she had indicated. Which means you were alone with Princess Tatiana for an undetermined length of time and have no alibi."

Suzanne started to speak. Malcolm's fingers closed round her wrist.

"I'm afraid I am not at liberty to say more, Monsieur Rannoch," Hager continued. "You must understand that we have had considerable interest in you from the moment you discovered the body. So often the person who reports a murder proves to be the culprit.

With this new information we had no choice but to act. If you will come with me, sir?"

"Certainly." Malcolm might have been agreeing to a game of billiards. "Might I beg the indulgence of going up to say good-bye to my son first?"

Hager hesitated, then gave a quick nod. "One of my men will accompany you."

Four of Hager's men stood at attention outside the library doors. At Hager's signal, one followed Malcolm and Suzanne upstairs, though he waited outside the dressing room door. "Listening in case I make a run for it over the roofs," Malcolm murmured as he closed the door behind them.

"It wouldn't be the first time you'd done it." Suzanne forced herself to match the lightness in his voice.

Blanca got to her feet and looked from Malcolm to Suzanne. "Mr. Rannoch?"

"I'm afraid I'm going to have to go away for a bit, Blanca," Malcolm said. "Baron Hager requires my presence. He's under the mistaken impression that I murdered Princess Tatiana."

"*Madre de Dios.* The man is a fool."

"Certainly he is grossly mistaken." Malcolm moved to the cradle. He went very still, one hand on the flower-painted rail. For a long moment he stood looking down at their sleeping son. Then he bent and brushed his lips over Colin's forehead, lightly so as not to wake him.

He straightened up quickly and turned to Suzanne. For all the cheerful mockery in his voice, his face was very pale and his eyes darker than usual. "We haven't much time. Blackwell may be able to help you with questions about Tatiana's childhood. He knew my mother. Talk to Czartoryski. He's our best ally in the Russian delegation."

"Malcolm—" Suzanne put her hands on his chest. "Adam Czartoryski could tell Hager Princess Tatiana was dead before you arrived at the Palm Palace."

"Assuming Hager believed Czartoryski. And even if he did, they'd argue I could have left after I killed her and come back."

He pulled his signet ring off his finger and pressed it into her hand. "If you need to communicate in my name."

She nodded, her fingers closing tight over the metal. "Malcolm—"

"You can use the ring to open the false bottom in my dispatch box. You'll find papers to get you and Colin and Blanca to Britain in case of emergency. Addison knows about them."

She caught his hand in her free one. "Darling, for heaven's sake, I wouldn't leave you here."

"Only as a last resort." He bent his head and gave her a quick, hard kiss. "Take care of yourself, sweetheart."

His lips were cool and there was a tang of good-bye that frightened her. She clutched the superfine of his coat for a moment. Then she forced herself to release him, because fears and imaginings wouldn't help the situation.

Malcolm stepped back and smiled at Blanca. "Look after her for me."

"I always do, Mr. Rannoch." Blanca returned his smile, though her eyes were shadowed.

Malcolm touched her arm and turned to the door. "We'd best go, or our friend outside will think I've escaped."

He cast one last look at the still sleeping Colin, as though imprinting the image on his memory, then held the door open for Suzanne. Hager's man followed them downstairs, bootfalls heavy on the marble stairs.

Lady Castlereagh had joined Lord Castlereagh in the entrance hall. Tommy Belmont was also there, a puzzled look on his normally insouciant face.

Malcolm nodded at Castlereagh and gave Suzanne's hand a quick squeeze. Suzanne watched the men march her husband out the door. Before he stepped through the door he turned back and gave her a brief, warming smile. An unvoiced cry choked her throat.

Lady Castlereagh put an arm round her. "Oh, my dear, I am so very sorry. But you must be brave for him."

"Suzanne's always brave. It looks as though Rannoch needs

more than bravery." Tommy stared at Castlereagh. "What the hell happened, sir?"

"Apparently new information came into Hager's possession," Castlereagh said in his colorless voice.

"And he seriously thinks that Malcolm—"

"So it seems."

Suzanne pulled away from Lady Castlereagh's comforting arm. "Thank you, ma'am, but I knew this might happen." She moved to the foreign secretary. "I need to speak with you, my lord."

Castlereagh inclined his head and held open the library doors. He followed her into the room and pulled the doors to behind them with a quiet click. "Suzanne, I know this comes as a great shock—"

"Not so very great." She could feel the pulse beating in her temples. She clasped her hands behind her back, Malcolm's trick when his shaking fingers threatened to betray him. "As I told Lady Castlereagh, we knew Malcolm being arrested was a risk from the night of the murder. Metternich and the tsar made no secret of their suspicions. My lord, this letter Baron Hager supposedly has that shows Princess Tatiana was blackmailing Malcolm. Have you seen it? Where did it come from?"

Castlereagh drew a breath. "Suzanne—"

"For God's sake, sir, we're talking about my husband." She crossed to him and barely checked herself from gripping his arm. "A man who has served you loyally for over six years. A man who has risked his life for Britain countless times. You at least owe me this."

Castlereagh moved to the library table, frowning at the medallions on the carpet, then turned to face her. "Hager allowed me a brief look at the letter. In it Princess Tatiana said she knew she could count on Malcolm to act as she wished over an unspecified matter because if he did not she would reveal certain information."

"What information?"

Castlereagh slapped closed a book that lay open on the table. "The letter doesn't specify."

"But—?"

He stared down at the gilt-embossed book cover. "It does say 'certain information you would not wish your wife to obtain.'"

Suzanne swallowed. Unvoiced fears clogged her brain. "Where did Hager get this letter?"

Castlereagh added the book to a stack on the table. "The letter came from a source I have reason to trust."

Realization washed over her in an icy rush. "Frederick Radley."

Castlereagh's gaze jerked to her face. "I never said—"

"You didn't need to. I can put puzzle pieces together." She crossed to the table in two impatient steps. "Radley saw me go into the Palm Palace alone because he was there himself."

"So you admit you went in alone?"

"Would you believe me if I denied it?" Suzanne gripped the brass-trimmed edge of the table. "Radley took this letter from Princess Tatiana's rooms the night of the murder. Before Malcolm arrived at the Palm Palace. Which means the princess hadn't yet sent the letter and Malcolm never saw it."

"My dear—" Castlereagh stretched out a hand across the table and then let it fall. "You can't possibly be sure of any of that."

Suzanne stared at the foreign secretary. "You aren't certain he's innocent."

For a moment Castlereagh's cool gaze held genuine regret. "I'm very fond of Malcolm. I owe him a great deal, as you said. But in the course of my career, I've seen all sorts of good people commit acts of which I would have sworn they'd be incapable."

"Malcolm isn't—"

"My dear Suzanne, if Malcolm went into the Palm Palace without you, even you can't be sure he didn't kill Princess Tatiana."

"But I am." The sterling certainty in her voice surprised even her. In so many ways she still didn't know her husband, and yet she was sure of this. She'd stake her life on it.

Castlereagh gave a sad smile. "Malcolm will have the best legal assistance possible. You have my word on it."

"But you can't be seen to intervene yourself. It could upset the balance of the Congress if it looked as though you were interfering with justice to save one of your attachés, who had killed the woman who'd been mistress to the tsar and Prince Metternich." And yet Malcolm had probably loved Princess Tatiana more than either of those two gentlemen had done.

Castlereagh put up a hand to the pristine folds of his cravat. "You know what a critical pass we are at just now. Tsar Alexander could storm out of the Congress, and without Russia any agreement we manage to come to is unstable. We could find ourselves in the midst of armed conflict in a frighteningly short time." He touched Suzanne's arm with awkward sympathy. "Malcolm may yet be safely returned to you. And I assure you that that is the outcome I hope for."

"Thank you, my lord." Suzanne gave a contained smile. "But surely Malcolm's arrest—even Malcolm's guilt—doesn't negate the need to learn who is the target of Count Otronsky's plot."

"No." Castlereagh strode back to the doors and opened them. "Belmont. Vaughn," he called.

Tommy, who had apparently been waiting outside the doors, stepped into the room, closely followed by Fitz.

"I know this is difficult, my dear," Castlereagh told Suzanne, "but I fear we have no time to waste. I want you to brief them on what we know of Otronsky's plot. They'll need to take over the investigation."

"Count Otronsky's plotting?" Tommy said. "To do what?"

"We don't know," Castlereagh said between gritted teeth.

Suzanne quickly outlined the bare bones of the Otronsky plot. The fragment of a letter Princess Tatiana had discovered, the secret meetings at the Empress Rose, Margot's identification of Otronsky, the note she herself had taken from Otronsky (was it only last night?) at the Duchess of Sagan's musicale.

"You think Count Otronsky is planning to assassinate someone at the opera gala?" Fitz said in disbelief.

"Cleverer than I'd have given Otronsky credit for," Tommy said. "Think of the havoc he could wreak."

"Precisely," Castlereagh said. "I'm putting you two in charge of learning the truth of the plot before December tenth. With Malcolm gone, you're the best I've got."

"Thanks," said Tommy. "Nice to know where we stand."

"Don't, Tommy," Fitz said. "There's too much—" He turned to Suzanne. "I'm sure you can't even consider—"

"Don't be ridiculous. Of course I'll work with you."

Tommy grinned, and Fitz pressed her hand. They both knew her too well, thank God, to treat her like a creature of porcelain. They asked brisk questions, which she answered in equally brisk tones. But when she left the library, Fitz followed and caught up with her in the hall.

"Suzanne." His voice was low and urgent. "I'll do everything I can to help you. To help Malcolm. We'll get him out of there somehow. I can't believe Hager was mad enough to make this accusation."

She turned at the base of the stairs and put her hand over his on the newel post. "You're a good friend, Fitz. But even you must have doubts. Castlereagh does."

"Castlereagh can be a cold-blooded pragmatist. And while he's known Malcolm a long time, it's not the same as being friends from university as we—" He broke off. His gaze clouded, then turned away from hers altogether.

"It's all right, Fitz," Suzanne said. "Malcolm had doubts about you. He'd understand your feeling the same."

Fitz gave a bleak smile. "Malcolm had learned I'd betrayed my wife. He had a right to wonder who and what else I'd betrayed."

"And you aren't wondering the same about Malcolm?"

Fitz drew a breath as though to make a quick denial, then shook his head. "Any fleeting thoughts I may have had don't lessen my friendship for him. We're all capable of nightmare imaginings. I suppose I'm still a suspect myself."

She swallowed. She couldn't deny it.

He shook his head. "Perhaps one day when all this is over, and we're safely back in England, we'll be able to trust each other again."

"Fitz—" Suzanne reached out and hugged him, taking comfort from his brotherly embrace as his arms closed awkwardly round her.

"I meant what I said," he told her, hands on her shoulders. "I'll do anything in my power."

Aline was waiting for her in her bedchamber. "Suzanne." She sprang up from the edge of the bed. "Lady Castlereagh told me. Well, I confronted her. I overheard one of the footmen saying Malcolm had been arrested. What in God's name is going on? And don't fob me off with reassurances. This is my cousin."

Suzanne drew Aline down on the edge of the bed beside her, searching for how much she could safely say. "Baron Hager received a letter Princess Tatiana wrote to Malcolm, which makes it sound as though she was blackmailing him."

"About what?"

Suzanne swallowed, a raw taste in her mouth. "I don't know. But I'm quite sure the letter was taken from Princess Tatiana's rooms the night she died and that Malcolm never received it."

Aline stared at the floorboards for a moment, then fixed Suzanne with a firm stare. "Was Princess Tatiana Malcolm's mistress? I'm sorry, it's a beastly question, but we've rather lost the time for tact."

Suzanne felt a smile break over her face. "No. She wasn't."

"You seem very sure."

"I am. Now."

Aline's taut expression relaxed into a smile. "Good. That's something, at least." She glanced at the silver gauze evening gown draped over the dressing table bench. "I suppose we won't be dining at the French embassy after all."

"On the contrary." Suzanne had forgot the engagement, but now she knew it was just the thing. "It's more imperative than ever that we put in an appearance. I count on you for moral support, *chérie*."

"Then I'd best dress. As Mama says, it's the trivial rituals of life that get one through the bad times."

Alone in her room at last, Suzanne leaned against the closed door and pressed her fingers to her forehead. She was shaking so badly she felt the door panels rattle. She had confided bits and pieces of the truth to Castlereagh, Tommy, Fitz, and Aline, but she could tell none of them the whole of it.

She had seen Malcolm wounded. She had seen him with his back to the wall, using all his wits to protect them both. But never, in the over two years she had known him, had she seen him removed completely from the field of play. He had offered her his protection and then become her comrade. But except when he had been wounded, never had he been so vulnerable and dependent on her. The foreign, émigrée bride with the tarnished past was going to have to rescue her aristocratic husband.

She recalled his matter-of-fact words about taking Colin to Britain. Cold terror washed over her. He had brought her into this alien world and now she was alone in it. But it wasn't the prospect of making her way as an outsider in the mysterious labyrinth of British society that truly terrified her. It was the thought of being without him.

She hadn't realized how necessary he had become to her happiness. Perhaps that was the true measure of love. Not a racing pulse or dizzy rapture or a rush of physical longing. Knowing one would be in a desolate world without the other person.

Talleyrand turned round at the opening of the door to the private stairs. "What's happened?"

"Devil take it, I don't know how you do it," his visitor said. "I swear I remember every trick you taught me about moving silently."

"I would be a sad failure if I weren't able to see past tricks I myself taught you." Talleyrand set his glass of calvados on the gilded boulle cabinet. "I trust this is serious for you to risk coming here in daylight."

"I wasn't followed or seen. I learned my lessons that well." His visitor dropped into a damask chair. "There's been a complication. Malcolm Rannoch's been arrested."

Every so often, a move in the chess game that was Continental politics took Talleyrand completely by surprise. "Interesting. Why?"

"Apparently Hager got information that Rannoch arrived at the Palm Palace alone the night of the murder, contrary to his wife's version of events. And if I have it correctly, there's also evidence Tatiana was blackmailing Rannoch."

"Ah." Talleyrand picked up his glass and wiped at the condensation on the lacquered mahogany of the cabinet. "I should have thought of that."

"Do you know why?"

"I can guess."

"So help me, if he hurt Tatiana—"

"Spare me the theatrics. One can never be sure of another's actions, but I very much doubt Malcolm Rannoch killed Tatiana. Not given how he felt about her."

"So they *were* lovers?"

"Or something closer." Talleyrand sank into his favorite chair. "The important thing now is what this does to our plans."

"Upsets them completely. Rannoch's no use to us in prison."

"No, but his wife's still free, and unless I've misjudged her, she won't rest until she has him out of prison. Nor will she let his investigation flag in the meantime."

"Madame Rannoch is a lovely woman with a keen understanding, but—"

"My dear boy, by the time you've got to be my age you've learned not to make the mistake of underestimating women."

"So what do you suggest?"

"We count on her to do what Rannoch would have done. We may be able to make use of Czartoryski as well. We know Malcolm was working with him." Talleyrand settled back against the chair cushions. "Suzanne Rannoch is to dine with us tonight. Fortuitous."

"She won't attend. Not after today."

Talleyrand smiled. "Oh, I think she will. If I've judged her correctly. It will be very interesting to see how events unfold."

"Damn you, do you have to find everything amusing? Aren't you the least bit worried?"

"One must take one's amusements where one can. Otherwise life would quite fail to be worth living." Talleyrand swirled the calvados in his glass. "And for what it's worth, the last time I was this worried my hôtel shook with cannon fire and the allies were at the gates of Paris."

❧ 33 ❧

Dorothée's salon in the Kaunitz Palace glittered with scented candles, a multitude of jewels, and the hum of bright, brittle talk. Talk that dimmed perceptibly when Suzanne and Aline stepped into the room.

"*Chérie.*" Dorothée swept toward them in a swirl of primrose crêpe over white satin and kissed Suzanne's cheek. "I'm so glad you came. We've heard the news, and of course everyone knows there's been a shocking mistake. Aline, what a lovely gown—amber is so pretty with your hair. Come and sit by the fire."

Count Clam-Martinitz came forward and bowed over Suzanne's and Aline's hands as though on cue. Talleyrand followed at a more leisurely pace, his gold-headed cane glinting in the candlelight.

"Madame Rannoch." His shrewd gaze held genuine kindness. Or at least seemingly genuine kindness. With Talleyrand one could never tell the counterfeit from the reality. Suzanne doubted if he knew himself. "I hope you know you may count me a friend."

He didn't, Suzanne noted as he bowed over her hand, say Malcolm could count him a friend. But perhaps, like Castlereagh, he didn't think it politic to offer public support for the accused murderer of the woman who had been mistress to the tsar and Metternich.

Dorothée led Suzanne to a seat beside Wilhelmine on a Grecian sofa.

"It's your name day today, isn't it, Duchess?" Suzanne said in a bright voice as she sank down on the sofa. "Your given name is Catherine?"

"How kind of you to remember. Yes, something else I share with Princess Bagration. As a Protestant, I'm not in the habit of celebrating my name day, but people seem to keep remembering it today. Metternich sent me a very handsome portfolio with gilt embossing. Perhaps because I remembered his name day two days ago." She frowned, as though considering the implications of the gift. "Or perhaps he'd have sent it in any case. He's much more thoughtful than I am. Though I can't say he's been very thoughtful when it comes to your husband." The duchess turned an apprais-ing gaze on Suzanne. "I was right. You do love him."

Suzanne's pearl bracelet caught on a fold of gauze as she settled her skirt. She disengaged it, forcing herself not to tug. "And here I prided myself on my abilities at deception."

"Don't tease her, Willie," Dorothée said. "Of course she's over-set. He's her husband."

Wilhelmine let her cashmere shawl slither lower on her arms. "There were any number of times I'd have quite liked to see both my husbands locked up." Her gaze drifted across the room to Count Clam-Martinitz, who was handing Aline into a chair. "I thought you felt the same about your own, Doro."

Dorothée frowned. "I may not wish to share a roof with Ed-mond, but I wouldn't wish him—" She shook her head, her glossy dark side curls stirring about her face. "Suzanne and Monsieur Rannoch are a different case entirely."

"Precisely my point." Wilhelmine touched Suzanne's hand. "I'm sorry, Madame Rannoch. It's quite obvious what's going on. The powers that be are desperate to tidy the crime away, and as an attaché Monsieur Rannoch is conveniently expendable. I imagine even Castlereagh knows he dare not come too strongly to his de-fense. I must say, I'd have hoped Metternich would show more fortitude."

"Anyone may be misled by the evidence."

"Particularly when they desire to be misled."

When Dorothée rose to indicate that it was time to go in to dinner, Suzanne caught Wilhelmine's gloved wrist. "I haven't found what you're looking for. But Malcolm's imprisonment doesn't mean I'm giving up."

Wilhelmine turned her head to look Suzanne directly in the eye and gave a quick, genuine smile. "Thank you. Suzanne."

Four silver candelabra ran the length of the table in the elegant dining room, shedding soft light over the jewels and medals of the assembled guests. Chairs scraped discreetly against the carpet, gowns rustled, and Suzanne felt a crossfire of gazes shot in her direction.

She found herself seated beside Count Clam-Martinitz. Aline was partnered by Wilhelmine's lover Alfred von Windischgrätz, who appeared to be making her laugh over a military story. Suzanne hadn't seen her husband's cousin so at ease with anyone but Geoffrey Blackwell. As she pulled off her gloves, Suzanne cast a glance at Wilhelmine, who gave a faint smile. Dorothée coming to their rescue was no surprise. She was more surprised about Dorothée's eldest sister. One could find one had friends in unexpected places.

"I was with your husband at the Carrousel after Vaughn was wounded," Count Clam-Martinitz said in a low voice, as bewigged footmen poured a fine Hungarian wine. "One can take a man's measure quickly in a moment like that. I'm sure the Comtesse de Périgord is right that this is a terrible mistake."

Suzanne took a sip of wine. "My husband is fortunate in his friends."

"Besides," Clam-Martinitz added with a smile, "I can't imagine a man married to such a beautiful woman having any other interests."

"If that were true, my dear Count, a number of women in this room would have very different marriages."

"Touché." Clam-Martinitz risked a brief glance at Dorothée, presiding with elegant insouciance at the foot of the table.

Carême, the renowned chef Talleyrand had brought with him

from Paris, had outdone himself. Rich dish followed rich dish with delicately flavored sauces and the finest wines. "Monsieur Carême had the truffles sent from Paris by diplomatic courier," Clam-Martinitz told her as they sampled a beef vol-au-vent.

"You're very at home at the French embassy."

"Yes." He cast an almost imperceptible glance down the table at Talleyrand. "Everyone has been most kind."

After dinner they returned to the salon. Talleyrand carried a cup of the coffee Dorothée was pouring out over to Suzanne, who was sitting on the bench built into the porcelain stove. "I'm sorry," he said in a different voice from the one he'd used earlier. "I'm sure of few things in life, but I'm quite sure Malcolm didn't kill Tatiana."

"I'm glad you can at least admit that to me."

"Neutrality has its uses, my dear Madame Rannoch. Besides, I have every faith Malcolm can extricate himself from this predicament without me. Though I suspect he will rely on your help."

Suzanne took a sip of coffee. Strong and as exquisitely flavored as everything else that came from the embassy kitchens. "Malcolm told me you were friends with his grandfather."

Talleyrand eased himself down beside her on the bench. "The Duke and Duchess of Strathdon came to Paris fairly often before the Revolution. The duchess was French by birth, a Lisle. Charming woman. The duke had his head in his books, but perhaps that's a sensible place to be. They both offered rational conversation, which I sometimes find in short supply."

"You stayed close to the family through the years."

"With letters, at least. The duke and his daughter Arabella, Malcolm's mother, were very kind to me when I was forced to take refuge in England. To a certain extent, to me Malcolm will always be the five-year-old boy I met then."

"Prince Talleyrand." Suzanne settled her cup in its saucer. "Malcolm told me. About his mother's predicament thirty-some years ago and Princess Tatiana's birth."

The firelight seemed to leap in Talleyrand's hooded eyes. The shadows sharpened his face. "Interesting."

"A comment that admits nothing."

"But of course." He regarded her for a moment. "What I find most interesting is that he told you. Malcolm held that secret even closer than Tatiana did. He's never trusted easily. There is evidently more to your marriage than I realized."

"It's never wise to think one knows what goes on inside any marriage, Prince."

"In the case of most marriages, the inner workings are of less interest than the average laundry list. But then Malcolm has always been unconventional."

Suzanne turned so she could look Talleyrand full in the face. "Who do you think was Princess Tatiana's father?"

"If I knew, don't you think I'd have told Tatiana? And Malcolm?"

"No."

Talleyrand flung back his white head and gave a shout of laughter, letting loose a cloud of hair powder. "You're very likely right, though it would have depended on who the father was. But Arabella was a master at keeping secrets." His gaze shifted to the fire for a moment. "She was a formidable woman."

Suzanne thought it was more than the glow of the firelight that softened the prince's voice and eyes. "Malcolm believes you weren't Tatiana's father," she said.

He lifted his gaze to her face without hesitation. "And you?"

"I'm not sure."

He twitched a satin cuff smooth. "If Tatiana had been my daughter, I'd have been proud to own her. I said Arabella was a remarkable woman, and I meant it. But she was never mine. Not in that sense."

The faint regret in his voice was faultless. But Prince Talleyrand was as skillful an actor as any who graced the stage of the Comédie Française. "Do you know any reason why Princess Tatiana would have been blackmailing Malcolm?" Suzanne asked.

Talleyrand lifted his brows.

"Over something he didn't wish me to discover?"

She expected another light denial. Instead, Talleyrand regarded her in silence for a long moment. "I suggest you ask your husband about that, Madame Rannoch. I'll be very interested to hear what he chooses to tell you."

Despite the warmth from the stove, a chill coursed through her. She subdued the impulse to pull her shawl about her shoulders. "Of course she might have been blackmailing others, as well. By any chance was she blackmailing you?"

"A bold attack. My compliments. No, she wasn't. Though if she had been, I doubt I'd have admitted it."

"My thoughts precisely. Of course it also occurred to me that you might have been the person orchestrating her blackmail of Malcolm."

Talleyrand's gaze stilled for a moment, steady on her face. "My dear Madame Rannoch. To what end?"

"I don't know."

"Even if I could bring myself to do such a thing to Arabella's son, do you really think I would employ Malcolm's sister in the matter?"

"That, my dear Prince, would depend on what you expected to get out of it."

Geoffrey Blackwell dropped into a gilded chair beside Suzanne in her box at the Burgtheater an hour later. "I was working on an experiment all afternoon. Didn't hear the news until I arrived here. To find us all under a different sort of microscope." He cast a glance round the theatre. One could almost feel the pressure of the opera glasses turned in their direction. "How are you holding up?"

Suzanne forced a smile to her lips. "I'm not the one in prison."

"No, but you're the one having to put up with the intense scrutiny of Vienna, or at least a certain segment of Viennese society. All of whom seem to be in this theatre tonight. I never thought to see Malcolm the center of a scandal."

"Malcolm has a way of taking one by surprise."

Geoffrey grimaced. "You're too sensible a woman to take gossip seriously, Suzanne."

"With Malcolm I've learned not to make assumptions."

He scraped a hand through his thinning black hair. "Tell me what I can do to help."

Suzanne shifted her chair toward him. "You knew Lady Arabella Rannoch well, didn't you?"

Geoffrey's gaze went straight to her own. The buzz of conversation seemed to fade away about them. "I'm glad Malcolm finally saw sense and told you about Tatiana. You're better off without secrets."

"How long have you known?" Suzanne asked.

"Almost from the first. I grew up with Malcolm's mother and her sisters. When Arabella returned from her trip abroad with her father, she confided her predicament to me. I was a year her junior—just starting at Oxford at the time."

"She trusted you a great deal."

He glanced away for a moment, staring out over the heads in the audience below—jeweled, feather-trimmed, combed into stylish disarray or shiny with pomade. "I like to think she did. Though I confess to an unfair advantage. I found Arabella being sick into an orange tree in the conservatory at a ball. I was already interested in medicine, and I noticed other changes in her. I guessed, and she could tell I had."

"Did she—"

"Confide the identity of the father to me? No." Anger at the man in question shot through Geoffrey's eyes. "She refused to do so. She said the truth would do too much damage. Arabella was—" His ironic gaze turned unaccustomedly soft, much as Prince Talleyrand's had done. "Restless. Mercurial. But something changed in her in those months. It was as though she stopped believing in the possibility of happiness." Geoffrey stared at the royal blue swags of curtain veiling the proscenium. "I sometimes think she married Alistair Rannoch because he was a man who could be calculated not to touch her heart."

During the first interval in Schiller's *Don Carlos*, Suzanne pressed a note for Adam Czartoryski into the hand of an obliging footman and went in search of Aline. Her cousin-in-law had found Schubert in the passage behind the boxes. He bowed to Suzanne.

"I've heard, like the rest of Vienna. I've been telling Fraulein Dacre-Hammond that I can't believe it of Herr Rannoch."

"So many people are saying that this evening," Suzanne said. "But I have the sense you really believe it."

A smile crossed his serious face. "I saw how he cared for Princess Tatiana." He bit back the words and his gaze slid to the side with confusion. "That is—"

Suzanne touched his hand. "No. You're right, Malcolm did care for her."

Schubert turned his gaze back to her and gave an awkward smile. "I keep remembering things she said to me. She was quite fearless. That last day I saw her, I stopped by to deliver some music for some new songs. She was in her salon writing letters. I asked if she was writing to a friend, and she laughed and said she wasn't sure."

"Do you know whom she was writing to?"

He shook his head. "She drew a book over the letter when she got up to greet me. But then she glanced back at the writing desk and said the oddest thing. That sometimes enemies could be more useful than allies."

"Madame Rannoch." Adam Czartoryski stepped into the salon in the Burgtheater that Suzanne had appointed in her note.

"Thank you," Suzanne said. "I needed to see you. This seemed the safest way."

"If you hadn't sent me a note, I'd have sent one to you."

"You heard about Malcolm?"

He moved toward her and paused, one hand resting on a gilded chairback. "The talk is all over the city, I'm afraid. I'm so very sorry."

Suzanne looked at the man who had seemed to be beginning to trust her husband. "It's true Malcolm got to the Palm Palace before I did the night of the murder. But I'm sure he didn't kill Princess Tatiana."

"Of course."

"You sound very certain."

"I've learned to choose my allies carefully and believe in them once I've made the choice." Czartoryski touched her arm. "Sit. You look exhausted." He pressed her into a chair, poured a glass of wine from a decanter on a console table, and put it in her hand.

Suzanne cupped her hands round the glass and took a quick swallow. She was shaking, which was absurd. "Too many hours of not knowing whom I can trust."

Czartoryski stood watching her, leaning against the table. "And you aren't even sure about me."

"Perhaps not entirely. But I confess I find you surprisingly trustworthy, Prince."

He gave a brief laugh, pulled up a chair, and sat beside her. "I'm glad to hear it."

She took another sip of wine. "I'm sorry to be such a fool."

"There's no shame in being overset because the person you love is in danger."

She stared into the red-black of the Bordeaux. "I don't want to fail him. I'm not used to him needing me."

Czartoryski squeezed her shoulder. "Well, perhaps it's not bad to realize that he does."

She gave a quick smile, one of her habitual masks. "He'll stop needing me once this is resolved."

"Do you really think so?" An answering smile, far less defensive, played about Czartoryski's mouth. "Don't make the mistake of underestimating your husband."

"Underestimating him?"

"Or the depth of his feelings."

She shook her head. "Malcolm and I don't have illusions. It's one of the advantages of our marriage."

He was silent for a moment. "There are different types of illusions, Madame Rannoch."

She cast a quick look at him. The regret in his eyes spoke volumes about the risks of loving.

"But I wouldn't take back a moment of it," he said, as though she had spoken. "Don't make the mistake of not grasping hold of what you can, when you can. There may come a time when all you have are the memories."

She touched his gloved hand where it lay on the arm of the chair. "I think the tsarina is a fortunate woman for all her difficulties."

He shook his head. "We'd best talk about what's to be done next. We're no closer to knowing whom Otronsky is plotting against. If—"

They both went still at a creak and stir from the side door. "You have all my sympathies, Madame Rannoch," Czartoryski continued in a comforting voice as the door swung open and Tsarina Elisabeth stepped into the room.

They both sprang to their feet.

"Lisa!" Czartoryski said, caution forgot.

"It's all right, Adam." The tsarina closed the door behind her. "I left my box with my lady-in-waiting. She'll cover for me. Safer to meet under everyone's noses. And I think it's high time I spoke with Madame Rannoch."

The tsarina walked forward, unbound ash blond hair stirring over her shoulders, the gold embroidery on her azure satin gown glinting in the candlelight. "I'm so very sorry, *chérie*." She took Suzanne's hand. "From what Adam has said of your husband and what I have seen, I am sure Baron Hager is under a misapprehension."

"Thank you, Your Majesty."

The tsarina sank into a chair and indicated that Suzanne and Czartoryski should do likewise. "And from what Adam has told me of you, I make no doubt you will continue the investigation in your husband's absence." She smoothed her hands over the shimmering fabric of her skirt. "You still don't know how it all fits together. Princess Tatiana's murder. This plot of Count Otronsky's. The papers she took from me. And of course you're hampered because you don't know the contents of those papers."

"Lisa." Czartoryski gripped the arms of his chair.

"She already knows enough to destroy us both, Adam. You're the one who told me we could trust Monsieur and Madame Rannoch."

"That was—"

"Dear Adam." A sad smile curved the tsarina's mouth. "You've always been quicker to trust with your own safety than with mine."

He stared at her for the length of several heartbeats. When he spoke, his voice was low and rough. "I'd give my life for you, Lisa."

She reached out and put her hand over his own. "I know it, beloved. That's why if you trust Madame Rannoch, I trust her as well."

"Lisa—"

"We owe it to Tatiana Kirsanova, much as I never thought to hear myself say so." Elisabeth shivered. "Dear God, I was so angry at her that night. I'll never forget—"

"There's no need to go into details," Adam cut in, a note of warning in his voice.

"No more half-truths, Adam." The tsarina turned her gaze to Suzanne. "I went to Princess Tatiana's rooms with Adam the night of the murder. We were going to demand the return of my letters. Instead we saw the woman for whom I was sure I could never feel a shred of sympathy, crumpled on the floor like a child's doll. We knelt beside her to make sure she was dead. Her blood got all over my gown—"

She pressed her hand to her mouth. Czartoryski got to his feet and took a step toward her, but she forestalled him with an outstretched hand. "No, Adam. I've let myself become distracted. It isn't the details of that night Madame Rannoch needs. It's why we were there in the first place."

"Lisa, I beg you—"

"This is my problem, Adam. I need to be part of solving it."

"If anything goes wrong—"

"That's been true from the first. I've spent too much time hiding and being frightened. Now pour me a glass of that wine with the lovely color, while I explain matters to Madame Rannoch."

34

Tsarina Elisabeth turned her almond-shaped blue eyes to Suzanne. "If you've heard any gossip about me at all, Madame Rannoch, you know my marriage has not been a happy one. Politics brought my husband and me together. At the beginning, I had a young girl's illusions that there could be more between us. But I soon learned my folly. My husband already had a mistress. I found comfort with Adam."

Czartoryski slammed the decanter down on the drinks table.

"The world knows that much, Adam," Elisabeth said. "We were recklessly indiscreet in those days. No amount of pretending now will sweep it under the carpet."

He put into her hand the glass of wine he had poured, a grim look about his mouth.

"My husband was remarkably understanding in those days. But in the end, my father-in-law had suspicions." Her knuckles showed sharp beneath her glove as she held the wineglass. "Tsar Paul was not a comfortable man to cross. He sent Adam off to Sardinia as ambassador. After my father-in-law died, my husband recalled Adam." She risked a glance at Czartoryski, who was staring fixedly at drops of red wine spattered on the tabletop. "But I fear I had finally learned the ways of the Russian court. Those very things that had once appalled me. When I was little more than a bride Catherine the Great's young lover tried to seduce me. I couldn't imagine I would ever play those games myself." She took a quick sip of wine as though steeling herself.

Czartoryski splashed wine into a third glass, snatched it up, and tossed down the contents.

"There was another man," Suzanne said.

"Alexis Okhotnikov. A staff officer." Memories drifted through Elisabeth's eyes. "He wasn't Adam, but for a time—" She shook her head and shivered. "There's no need to dwell on that." She set the wine on the table beside her chair and fixed her gaze on its gilded rim. "Seven years ago, Alexis was knifed leaving the theatre. He died of his wounds."

"I'm so sorry." Suzanne reached out instinctively to touch the tsarina's hand.

Elisabeth gave a sweet, sad smile. "Thank you. It was—" Her fingers curved inward. "I shall always blame myself. But for the purposes of this story, the important thing is that I don't believe his death was an accident. I'm almost sure my husband's brother, Grand Duke Constantine, was behind it."

Czartoryski thunked down the decanter again as he refilled his glass.

"You think Constantine would be incapable of orchestrating murder?" Elisabeth asked.

"No." Czartoryski's voice was as hard as the thud of the crystal. "That's just the point."

"Why?" Suzanne asked.

Elisabeth drew a breath. Czartoryski had gone still. The candle-warmed air seemed to tremble with danger, as though the answer to this question held the real risk. Secrets more dangerous than the love affairs the tsarina had just revealed.

"You must know that my husband's father, Tsar Paul, was an unstable man," Elisabeth said. "And that he was killed in a coup by his own officers." For a moment, beneath the sapphires, the gold-embroidered satin, and the polished sophistication of two decades of court life, the stark terror of the young Grand Duchess Elisabeth showed through. "We could hear the screams through the floorboards. My husband crouched with his hands over his ears, but I don't think he'll ever forget the sound. I know I won't."

The tsarina drew a sharp breath. Czartoryski watched her, as though her next word might be a dagger thrust to her own heart. "Even when it was over, when the terrible sounds stopped, Alexander wouldn't move. I had to take his hands, had to remind him what he owed his people, before he'd go out on the balcony and show himself. If he hadn't—"

Her gaze shot to Czartoryski's face. For a moment the horror of what might have been hung between them. "Some say Alexander collapsed with guilt because in killing his father the officers had done what he would have done himself had he been brave enough," Elisabeth continued. "But there always have been whispers that it was more. That my husband was part of the plot. Or at least knew about it and kept silent." Elisabeth folded her arms and pressed her fingers against the gathered satin of her bodice. "I fear Constantine thought I had confided my own suspicions about Tsar Paul's death to Alexis."

"Dear God." Suzanne could hear the wind hissing through gaps round the windowpanes, feel the cool draft of air and the warmth of the candle flame.

Elisabeth loosed her hands with deliberation and spread them over her lap. "The papers Princess Tatiana got hold of are letters I wrote to Alexis. Letters I retrieved after his death. Letters I should have burned."

Czartoryski moved to her side and put a hand on her shoulder. His gaze now held a tenderness that was more intimate than an embrace.

"I understand your fears," Suzanne said. "And your desperation."

"Alexander can live with the rumors. Letters in his wife's hand would be another matter entirely." Elisabeth squeezed her eyes shut for a moment, as though she would blot out her imaginings. "You see why I would do almost anything to recover the letters."

Suzanne frowned at the wineglass in her hand. "As would your husband, presumably."

"If he knew of them. Which, thank God, he doesn't."

"Are you sure?"

The tsarina cast a quick glance at Czartoryski. "You think Princess Tatiana told Alexander?"

Suzanne took a sip of wine and let it linger on her tongue. Smooth but with a sharp bite beneath. "My husband wasn't arrested just because of his broken alibi. Baron Hager had come into possession of a letter that implies Princess Tatiana was blackmailing Malcolm. Or was about to blackmail him."

Czartoryski and Elisabeth exchanged an involuntary glance.

"Yes, I know," Suzanne said. "I think the letter was taken from Princess Tatiana's rooms before she could send it. I don't know what it was about, and I haven't had a chance to ask Malcolm yet. But I'm beginning to think—Perhaps the princess really did invite Malcolm and Prince Metternich and Tsar Alexander all to come to her rooms at the same time the night of the murder."

Czartoryski's hand tightened on the tsarina's shoulder. "To what purpose?"

Suzanne looked between the couple. For whatever Elisabeth had said about their love affair ending, now the bond was unmistakable. It radiated between them. Suzanne wondered what it would be like to know another person so intimately. Whether or not they were sharing a bed, Adam Czartoryski and Tsarina Elisabeth were a couple.

Suzanne drew a breath. "I take it I may count on your discretion when it comes to the secrets of another lady?"

"Of course," Czartoryski said, with a simplicity Suzanne believed, where more fervent assurances would have rung false.

"I would not wish to put anyone through what I fear myself," Elisabeth added.

"Princess Tatiana had come into possession of papers which could damage Wilhelmine of Sagan. Papers Prince Metternich would go to great lengths to recover. She could have used those papers to blackmail Prince Metternich. She was apparently going to try to blackmail Malcolm. And she could have planned to use your letters to compel the tsar to do as she wished."

Czartoryski's eyes widened. Elisabeth gasped, a dozen scenarios racing through her gaze.

"You think Princess Tatiana was planning to blackmail Metternich, the tsar, and your husband?" Czartoryski said. "To what purpose?"

"I don't know," Suzanne said. "Yet."

Malcolm stared at the cloudy light trickling through the barred window set high in the wall of his cell. Mildew clung to the rough stone walls and clogged the air. A single tallow candle burned on a three-legged table beside a narrow bed covered with a gray blanket.

He'd known worse. Mud huts in Spain. Field tents that leaked like a sieve. Patches of snow-covered ground with only his greatcoat for a blanket. On more than one occasion he'd known his odds of death were more than even. Several times he'd not been sure he cared very much. But he'd never been deprived of his liberty by his supposed allies. And he'd never had so much leisure to dwell on the sins of his past and their implications for his future.

A key rattled in the iron lock. Hinges groaned.

"Malcolm?"

He turned toward the familiar voice. His wife stood just inside the open door. She wore a dark hat and spencer, but the meager light clung to the white stuff of her gown. The jailer pulled the door to behind her and slammed the bolt home.

Malcolm stood frozen. Less than twenty-four hours and he was parched with longing for the sight of her. And for all the reasons that had been echoing through his head since he'd been brought to the prison, she had never seemed more out of his reach.

She hesitated a moment. He could feel her gaze moving over his face. Then she rushed forward. His arms closed about her with a need stronger than any qualms. He slid his fingers into her hair, pushing her hat and half her hairpins to the floor, and sought her mouth with the hunger of one who'd feared he might never touch her again.

When he lifted his head, she took his face between her hands. Her fingers trembled against his skin. "Darling. Are you—"

"I'm treated much better than the poor bastards in Newgate."

"I was afraid—"

He covered one of her hands with his own. "Odd, the tricks one's mind can play."

"Frightful." She gave a quick, defensive smile, and he knew she felt as awkward as he did at their unwonted display of emotion. "Radley must have lingered outside the Palm Palace after I glimpsed him," she said. "He told Baron Hager he saw me going in alone. Which takes away your alibi."

He bent to retrieve her fallen hat. "I should never have put you in this position."

"I put myself in it." She took the hat from him and smoothed its brim.

"What about the letter that supposedly proved Tania was blackmailing me?" Malcolm took her hand and drew her over to the bed.

She sat beside him and continued to speak in a matter-of-fact voice, though she retained hold of his hand. "I think Radley took it from Princess Tatiana's room the night of the murder. So she never sent it, and you could never have seen it."

"Unfortunately we have no way of proving that. And the contents?"

"Hager showed it to Castlereagh. I haven't seen it, but I got a few details from Castlereagh." She looked into his eyes, as though searching for the right words. "Apparently Tatiana threatens to reveal something if you don't do as she wishes." She brushed the mulberry velvet of her hat with her free hand. "Something you would not wish me to learn."

"Dear Christ." He jerked his hand from her hold and turned his head away.

"Malcolm." She touched his back with cautious fingers. "I'd have no right to pry under ordinary circumstances, but I need to know. I assume Tatiana wasn't just talking about the secret of her birth?"

"No." He turned back to face her and brushed his fingers against her cheek. Those wonderful sea green eyes held a concern that cut him like broken glass. "In some ways, it might be better for you if I don't get out of here."

She grabbed his wrist. "Don't be ridiculous, Malcolm."

"You don't know, sweetheart. And it was criminal of me not to tell you before you married me." He pulled the table closer, so the light from the tallow candle fell between them. "As I said, Talleyrand sent Tatiana to work with us in the Peninsula. I was her chief contact." Late nights sketching decoding tables. Laughing as they devised aliases. An exchange of glances across a room to agree on an escape plan. "Our minds seemed to work in a similar way."

"Your mother's legacy."

"I suppose so. It made for good teamwork." His fingers tensed on the coarse gray wool of the blanket. "In the late summer of 1812, Wellington had scored a victory at Salamanca and was meeting with other allied leaders in Madrid to try to coordinate our next moves. As usual, gold to pay the army was sorely needed. A shipment was being sent overland from Rothschild's in Vienna. Tatiana and I were on our way to rendezvous with a contact near Palencia when we intercepted a letter. One of the most challenging pieces we ever decoded." He could still hear his sister's crow of delight when they unlocked the final piece. "It told us the French had got wind of the shipment of gold. It was critical that the gold get through. The only solution seemed to be to deceive the French as to the route of the shipment."

He could still remember the exhausting discussions, the plans made and discarded, the hours poring over maps of Spain. "We wrote another message that supposedly revealed the path of the shipment. Tatiana, posing as the vengeful ex-mistress of a British officer, dropped a hint to a French agent. Later that evening I allowed my pocket to be picked."

"Clever. It worked?"

Guilt squeezed his throat. "All too well. Our false message sent a French patrol to Acquera."

Suzanne, usually five steps ahead of him, hadn't seen it coming. He forced his gaze to remain steady on her face, watching as realization dawned in the eyes that had looked on him with such trust.

"The French captain must have been angry when he failed to discover the gold. He torched the village. He attacked the family that lived on a nearby estate."

"My family," Suzanne said. The words were flat as tempered steel.

"Yes." Images flooded his brain and cut at his soul. "It wasn't until I stumbled across you in the Cantabrian Mountains and heard the story of your family's death and the destruction of your home that I realized what must have happened. It was criminally negligent of Tania and me not to have foreseen how events might play out."

A cool mask settled over his wife's features. She sat very still, as though afraid if she breathed she'd shatter in pieces. "You couldn't have known the French officer would react so violently. You had to do something to protect the gold."

"The actual gold shipment ended up falling into the hands of bandits, so it never reached Wellington. Irony on top of bloody irony."

"Civilian casualties are a fact of war."

"One should never learn to tolerate them." He saw Suzanne as he'd first seen her in the Cantabrian Mountains, hair tangled, eyes vibrant, face smeared with blood. "It shouldn't have taken seeing you to bring home the truth. The truth of those nameless victims who suffer every time Castlereagh and Metternich redraw a border. There's real blood behind the bloodless decisions being made in Vienna's council chambers."

"Dear Malcolm." Her gaze moved over his face as though he were retreating into the distance. "Always so compassionate. So that was why—"

He studied her drawn face. "Why what?"

She drew a breath that had the scrape of a dagger against rock. "Why you asked me to marry you so chivalrously when you found me. You were trying to make amends."

"No. That is, yes, in a way, but that wasn't—" He looked at the woman he had taken under false pretenses. "What's the use? I should never have offered for you without telling you the truth. It was criminal of me to entrap you in a marriage to a man you had good reason to hate."

"Malcolm." She curled her hand over his shoulder. A dozen unspoken words raced through her eyes. "Surely you know I could never hate you."

"That's because you're much too good a person, sweetheart. It doesn't lessen my crime. I should have told you the truth, seen that you were looked after, and let you make a life for yourself. Instead I behaved no better than Radley."

She gave a harsh, incredulous laugh. "You can't compare yourself to—"

"No? Radley took advantage of your predicament to get you in his bed. I did much the same by making you my wife. I had no right to take advantage of you."

"*Take advantage of me*—" Her fingers tightened on his shoulder. "You gave me your name, your fortune, your protection. All when by your own admission you'd never thought to marry."

"Because I knew what a poor bargain I made."

"Dozens of matchmaking mothers and their daughters would disagree with you. Clever, handsome, wealthy, connected to Britain's most powerful families—"

"Liable to disappear in the middle of the night at a moment's notice, ill-equipped to share a home, let alone a life, dangerously likely to disappoint—"

"You've never disappointed me, Malcolm."

He stroked his thumb against her cheek. "Liar." He'd seen the look in her eyes when he retreated behind his habitual mask.

She squeezed his hand and pulled it away from her face. "No time to dwell on that now. None of this explains why Tatiana was threatening to reveal to me that you were behind the attack on Acquera. What did she want?"

He shook his head.

Suzanne fingered the brim of her hat. "Tsarina Elisabeth came in last night when I was talking to Adam Czartoryski. She told me what's in the letters Tatiana took." She leaned forward, put her lips to his ear, and whispered a short account of what she'd learned from the tsarina.

A few brief words that could shake a nation. "No wonder she and Czartoryski were so desperate to recover the letters," Malcolm said.

"And if Tsar Alexander had known, he'd have been desperate as well. Darling. I don't think you were the only one Tatiana was blackmailing. I think she summoned you and Metternich and the tsar that night because she was planning to blackmail all of you."

"Why in God's name would she—"

"Not for money. For something she wanted."

He checked his instinctive denial and forced himself to sift through the facts. "Dear Christ. I should have seen it."

"Easier to see the pattern when one's standing a few feet off. Could Talleyrand be behind it?"

"You think Talleyrand was using Tania to blackmail Metternich, the tsar, and me?"

"You have to admit, he'd have a great deal to gain from all of you. Or—" She twisted the satin ribbons on her hat between her fingers. "We know she was still in contact with Bonaparte."

"God in heaven." For a moment Malcolm heard his sister's silvery, mocking laughter echo in his ears.

"You don't think it's possible?"

"I think it's entirely possible—that's the hell of it. Difficult for a man who's ruled so much to accept that he's powerless. If Bonaparte thought he had a way to force concessions on Metternich and the tsar and Castlereagh, if he even had delusions about a return to power—"

"You don't think he could be successful—"

Malcolm drew a breath. "With Metternich's tendency to think kingdoms are clay when it comes to the Duchess of Sagan and what you told me about the tsar—God knows. The one thing I'm sure of is that even if I'd acceded to Tania's demands, I could have brought no influence to bear on Castlereagh." He clasped his hands together and stared down at them, rubbing the place where he normally wore his signet ring. "I knew she was capable of blackmail. But somehow I never thought—"

"That she could use it against you?"

He could hear his sister's ironic, affectionate voice. *Dear Malcolm, your illusions will be the death of you. I think you even have illusions about me.* "Utterly deluded of me. Blackmailing me is no worse than blackmailing anyone else. But I thought—"

"That she cared for you." Suzanne gripped his hand, her touch warm and firm. "I think she did, Malcolm. I saw you together, remember. If what was between you hadn't been so palpable, I wouldn't have been—" She bit the words short. "But that's hardly of any account now. Your sister was a complicated woman, but I do think in her fashion she loved you."

"Perhaps. We'll never know."

"You don't know what pressure she was under when she wrote you this blackmail letter."

"Pressure from Bonaparte?"

"Well, no, I suppose in that case she'd have been driven by dreams of glory."

"Very like Tatiana."

"Bonaparte gave her the Courland casket. Perhaps there's more to it than an art treasure. Something hidden inside it?"

"It's probably with her papers."

"Which we have to find. Addison and Blanca are still checking all the tradesmen she might have trusted, talking to the servants of the friends we've been able to think of—"

Malcolm stared at the circle of light the candle cast on the stones of the wall. "I keep trying to think which of her friends we could be forgetting—"

Suzanne froze. "I saw Schubert last night. He said the last time he saw Tatiana she told him sometimes enemies could be more useful than allies. She was about to blackmail two of the most powerful men in Vienna. Two of the most powerful men on the Continent. And her brother, who she was well aware could be a formidable antagonist. She'd know you'd all try to recover the papers. She'd know you'd think of all her friends, anyone obviously connected to her. She'd be too clever to hide it with them. But her enemies—"

The triumph of a puzzle piece locked into place glinted in his wife's eyes. "Darling, I think I know where to look."

35

"Madame Rannoch. Suzanne. Thank goodness." Wilhelmine of Sagan, clad in a jaconet muslin round gown, came forward as the footman showed Suzanne into the duchess's rose and gold salon in the Palm Palace. She pressed her scented cheek to Suzanne's own. "You find us quite running out of sisterly confidences."

Dorothée stood behind her sister. Her face was shadowed as though she had received difficult news, but she came forward and gave Suzanne a hug as well.

Wilhelmine waved her sister and Suzanne to the sofa. "We owe you a debt of gratitude," the duchess said, pouring Suzanne a cup from the Meissen chocolate service that stood on the sofa table. "If it weren't for you, I doubt Doro and I would ever have had the conversation we were just engaged in."

"Willie—" Dorothée said.

"A bit late for caution, Doro. Suzanne already knows more of my secrets than you do. Or more than you did, at any rate." Wilhelmine handed Suzanne a pink-flowered cup. "I've told Doro about Vava." Her voice was steady, but the cup rattled against the saucer in her grip.

"I'm glad." Suzanne took a sip of the rich drink. It lingered, bittersweet, on the tongue. "Troubles are sometimes more easily borne when shared."

"I can't believe I *liked* Baron Armfelt." Dorothée scowled into her own chocolate cup. "It's beastly that you had to bear this alone, Willie. Though I don't suppose I'd have understood it properly until I had children of my own." Her gaze darkened. Suzanne could see her remembering her little daughter, who had died last spring. "There's nothing worse than losing a child."

Wilhelmine reached across the sofa table and squeezed her sister's hand. "At least Vava is still alive."

Dorothée looked up and met Wilhelmine's gaze. A silent understanding passed between the sisters. Despite the painful subject matter, there was an ease between them that Suzanne had not seen in all her weeks in Vienna.

"But I don't imagine this is a social call any more than the last time you called on me, *ma chère* Suzanne." Wilhelmine settled back against the cushions on the sofa across from the one Suzanne and Dorothée occupied. "Have you been to see your husband?"

"Earlier this morning."

"He's well treated?" Dorothée asked. "That is—"

"He's not kept in a dungeon." Suzanne set her cup on the table. "Duchess—"

"Wilhelmine."

"Wilhelmine. I don't think you were the only one Princess Tatiana was holding information over. And I think I know where to look for it."

Wilhelmine went still. "Where?"

"When was Princess Tatiana last in your rooms?"

"What's that to say to—Good God, you don't think she hid them *here?*"

"I think Princess Tatiana knew that a number of very powerful people would be trying to discover where she'd hidden the papers. And the Courland casket. She'd know they'd look in her rooms. She'd know they might think to search the lodgings of any of her friends."

"So where better to hide them than with an enemy," Wilhelmine said.

"That was my thinking."

"Princess Tatiana was at your salon the Wednesday before she was killed," Dorothée said. "I remember her standing there, by the stove, talking with my uncle."

Wilhelmine sprang to her feet, the light of the chase in her eyes. "Where to begin?"

"It would have to be somewhere she could hide it easily in company," Suzanne said. "But somewhere she could count on being secure."

They opened the cabinets, turned back the carpet, pulled the cushions from the sofas, looked in the stove. Suzanne reached up the chimney, scraping her knuckles and turning her arm quite sooty. In the library they pulled the books from the shelves and removed every drawer from the desk. Wilhelmine snatched up a crumpled paper stuck behind a drawer and muttered that it was a good thing *this* letter hadn't fallen into the wrong hands. In the duchess's bedchamber—"She could have slipped in here during the evening, it was empty," Wilhelmine said—they pulled the feather bed from the bedstead, rummaged through the wardrobe and chests of drawers, turned open hatboxes and portmanteaux.

"Damnation." Wilhelmine dropped down on the edge of the bed, face flushed, hair slipping from its pins. "I was so sure you were right."

"So was I." Suzanne rubbed her hands, still not quite clean of soot. "I was so proud of my own cleverness. Princess Tatiana even told Schubert that sometimes enemies could be more useful than allies."

Dorothée flopped down on the chaise longue. "Of course, it isn't as though Willie is the only person the princess might have thought of as an enemy. Though it does seem so convenient. This way her box would have been in the Palm Palace within easy reach."

Wilhelmine sat up straight. "Oh, good God. Could the wretched woman—I'm not the only resident of the Palm Palace Princess Tatiana might have considered an enemy."

"Princess Bagration," Suzanne said.

Wilhelmine stirred the fringed bed curtains with her kid-slippered toe. "The question is how the devil we're going to manage to search her rooms."

Suzanne frowned at her black-tinged nails. "Clearly a diversion is called for. Do you think—?"

"That I could outwit Catherine Bagration?" A smile curved Wilhelmine's mouth. "Can you doubt it?"

"Willie." Dorothée went to her sister's side. "If Princess Bagration realizes what you're after—if she finds the papers herself—you'll have to be careful."

"I always am, *chérie*."

"You always say that. But I don't know that the stakes have ever been this high."

Half an hour later, hair pinned and combed, gowns smoothed, scent plashed on, faces rouged and powdered, the three ladies crossed the Palm Palace to Princess Bagration's rooms.

The princess's footman had mastered the mask of impassivity required by his profession, but even he could not entirely conceal his surprise at seeing his mistress's rival at the door, accompanied by her sister and the wife of the man whose arrest was the talk of Vienna. In a world of diplomatic intrigue, the Duchess of Sagan calling on Princess Bagration was as daring a move as any made by Metternich or Talleyrand.

The footman left them in an elegant entry hall and went to speak to his mistress. Suzanne was already considering what to do if Princess Bagration was not at home to visitors. (While they'd been repairing the damage to their hair and gowns, Wilhelmine had said she gave even odds on it.) To her surprise and relief, the footman returned after less than five minutes to say that the princess would be pleased to receive them.

The Naked Angel, as she was called in Vienna on account of her low-cut gowns, greeted them in a salon filled with jewel-toned Turkey carpets and gleaming mahogany furniture, rich with the smells of lemon oil and spicy potpourri. She came forward in a soft stir of signature white India muslin, trimmed with Valenciennes lace. Shaking the princess's well-groomed hand, Suzanne was keenly aware of the hastily pinned tear in the cuff of her spencer and the soot marks concealed by a zephyr scarf Wilhelmine had lent her.

Wilhelmine shook the hand of the woman who was her rival for the affections of two of the most powerful men in Vienna. "I know. I'm the last person in Vienna you expected to have call on you. Very likely I'm the last person in Vienna you *wanted* to have call on you. No sense pretending this isn't awkward. But I find myself in the hellishly uncomfortable position of being in need of your help."

Princess Bagration gave a rich laugh. "Hardly the last person, Duchess. Think of how crowded Vienna is just now. You must know your words could not but intrigue me. Please do sit down."

The ladies disposed themselves about the room, Suzanne and Dorothée on the sofa, Wilhelmine and the princess in matched green and gold damask armchairs, like a pair of rival queens met to negotiate a treaty.

"Whatever our differences, we know each other too well to prevaricate," Wilhelmine said. "You must have heard that Madame Rannoch's husband was arrested yesterday."

"Duchess—" Suzanne protested on cue, flushed with embarrassment.

Wilhelmine waved her hand. "My dear Madame Rannoch, you must permit me to handle this. I am far wiser than you in the ways of the world."

"I was never more shocked than by the news of Monsieur Rannoch's arrest." Princess Bagration turned her gaze to Suzanne. This, Suzanne realized, was the reason the princess had received them. Like the rest of Vienna, she was agog at the news of Malcolm's arrest. "My deepest sympathies, Madame Rannoch."

"Thank you," Suzanne said. "I can only hope the misunderstanding is cleared up quickly."

"People are being dreadful," Wilhelmine said in her blunt way. "You could cut the tension with a knife at Doro's dinner last night, and at the Burgtheater the gossips were doing their worst. Whatever you think of Monsieur Rannoch's possible guilt—and I for one am convinced he's innocent—poor Madame Rannoch deserves none of this. It is already difficult enough for her to have her husband facing these accusations." Wilhelmine fixed Princess Bagration with the gaze that could command salons and drawing rooms across the Continent. "I have come to enlist your aid."

Princess Bagration adjusted a fold of her gold-embroidered shawl. "You find me most sympathetic. But I'm afraid I don't see what I can do."

"Oh, come, Princess. Let us dispense with any pretense that either of us wields less power than we do. If we are both seen to publicly support Madame Rannoch and to dismiss rumors and idle speculations, the buzz of comment will dim to a whisper. Do you doubt we can do it?"

A gleam of challenge entered the princess's light blue eyes. "I must say, you intrigue me."

"But of course. What could be more a triumph than diverting all Vienna from the topic of the day? Especially from such a particularly intriguing scandal. And who would have guessed that we would do it in concert? Of course, if you don't wish to assist me, I shall have to do it on my own. I can understand that you might fear to risk your reputation."

"On the contrary." The princess straightened her spine, her aquamarine earrings flashing. "I never shrink from a challenge."

Wilhelmine smiled. "I thought not. I have always admired that in you. Now we must put our heads together about how best to handle this. If you will grant me a moment in private, Princess, I have some thoughts to put to you, and I know Madame Rannoch will be embarrassed if we speak in her presence."

"Duchess—" Suzanne protested.

"No, no." Wilhelmine waved an imperious hand. "You must allow more experienced heads to consult over this matter. I know you survived a war, but Vienna is its own battlefield, and Princess Bagration and I are veterans. I'm sure you and Doro can amuse yourselves while the princess and I talk."

Two of the greatest rivals in Vienna left the salon arm in arm. Dorothée stared fixedly at the pink satin ribbons on her slippers.

The moment the door clicked closed, she burst into laughter. "Dear God." She pressed her fingers over her mouth. "I forget quite how masterful Willie can be."

"No time to be wasted." Suzanne was already on her feet. "I'll do the stove. Check beneath the sofa cushions."

She managed to get less soot on her hands this time, but the stove yielded nothing. Nor did the sofa or the striped satin chaise longue by the windows.

"This is the room Princess Bagration entertains in," Dorothée said, "but perhaps Princess Tatiana slipped out during the reception and hid the box in a different room."

"Perhaps." Suzanne stood in the center of the room, recalling Princess Bagration's reception three days before the murder—what a lifetime ago that now seemed. She could see Tatiana Kirsanova in blood red sarcenet trimmed with jet beads that flashed in the candlelight. Tatiana and Malcolm had sat in the chairs by the window, their heads close together, the fringed edge of her skirt trailing over the gleaming black leather of his shoe, her leg just brushing his own. Odd to remember the dagger stab she had felt at the sight, in light of what she now knew about their relationship.

The princess had had a richly worked shawl of black and red draped over her arm. Its generous folds could easily have concealed the box. The chairs Tatiana and Malcolm had been sitting in had oval backs and spindle legs—no possible hiding places. But then Count Nesselrode had joined them and fallen into conversation with Malcolm. Tatiana had got to her feet and strolled across to the window. She had paused by the pianoforte, unoccupied for the moment. She'd leaned across to look at the sheet music—

Suzanne ran to the pianoforte and reached into the compartment beneath the folded-back lid. Nothing on the right.

"Suzanne," Dorothée said. "I think I hear footsteps."

Suzanne could hear them, too, and a buzz of conversation. Wilhelmine had her voice raised to warn them. Suzanne darted round the side of the pianoforte and reached into the compartment on the left. Her fingers touched cool wood that did not belong to the piano. She pulled out a rectangular box and dropped it in the capacious reticule Wilhelmine had lent her, seconds before the door opened to admit the duchess and the princess.

"Splendid," Wilhelmine said, sweeping into the room as though it were her own. "I think we have hit upon a plan that will work admirably. I hope you two have managed to amuse yourselves."

"To own the truth," Suzanne said, "after yesterday, a quarter hour of peace and quiet was bliss."

They were obliged to stay a half hour longer, sipping tea that Princess Bagration served from a samovar and making conversation about tomorrow's Beethoven concert. The concert had been postponed several times—once, Princess Bagration pointed out, because the English objected to holding it on a Sunday. At last, they were able to take their leave without arousing suspicions and return across the Palm Palace to the duchess's apartments.

Wilhelmine slammed the door of her salon shut behind them. "You found it, didn't you? Suzanne is a masterful actress, but I could read it in Doro's face."

Suzanne unclasped the reticule and drew out the box. Despite her words, Wilhelmine's gaze widened with wonder, fear, anticipation. They clustered round a game table, the box on the green baize top. It was of polished rosewood, warm with a patina of age, inlaid with cedar.

"Is it a box or a piece of wood?" Dorothée said. "There doesn't seem to be a way to open it."

"Not an obvious one. Could you bring a lamp over, Wilhelmine?" Suzanne pulled a pin from her hair. In the glow of the Argand lamp Wilhelmine lit, she probed the inlaid wood. She could hear the tense breathing of the Courland sisters as she worked. There were four cedar flowers with onyx centers on the top of the box. She pressed each, then all four in succession, then tried a different sequence. With the third sequence she pressed, the top of the box sprang open.

Dorothée gasped. Wilhelmine remained absolutely still, as though she didn't dare breathe.

Two sheets of paper tied with white ribbon lay on top. Below was another, larger bundle tied with buff-colored ribbon. Suzanne held them both out. "Do you recognize one?"

Wilhelmine reached for the two sheets with the white ribbon but did not take them. Suzanne pressed the letter into the duchess's hand without looking at it further.

The papers crackled as Wilhelmine's fingers closed round them. "Thank you." Her voice was raw.

"Whom do the papers with the buff ribbon belong to?" Dorothée asked.

"Tsarina Elisabeth, I think." Suzanne set the papers to the side. Beneath them in the box was a single sheet of paper, water stained and seemingly torn from a notebook, filled with a string of block capitals. The jagged red wax remnants of a broken seal clung to both ends of the paper.

"Is that a coded letter Princess Tatiana wrote?" Dorothée asked. "Or something she took from someone else?"

"I'm not sure," Suzanne said, ignoring for a moment the implications of the handwriting and what she could discern of the crest on the seal.

Beneath all the papers was a square shape, wrapped in a soft cloth. Suzanne lifted it carefully and set it on the green baize tabletop. She felt the pressure of Wilhelmine's and Dorothée's gazes locked on the object in her fingers. With the care one keeps for fragile memories that are not one's own, she unwrapped the cloth.

Dorothée and Wilhelmine both drew in their breath. The light sparked and danced. The sides of the miniature casket were inlaid with mirrored glass etched with roses. Bands of silver leaves divided the glass on the lid into triangles with an exquisitely wrought silver rose at the center. The lamplight played off the silver, bounced off the mirrored glass, and turned the whole into a sparkling confection out of a fairy tale.

Wilhelmine touched the casket with a reverence Suzanne suspected she rarely showed. "I thought we might never see it again."

Dorothée brushed her fingers over the letters scratched into the metal in one corner: *PBC*. "Papa carved his initials there. I remember tracing them with my fingers after he died, trying to remember his face."

"It stood on the desk in his study," Wilhelmine said. "I was fascinated by it." She looked up at Suzanne, an unvoiced question in her eyes.

"Princess Tatiana obviously valued it," Suzanne said. "We think it was a gift to her from Napoleon Bonaparte."

Dorothée's eyes widened, but Wilhelmine nodded. "It disappeared when Napoleon went into Poland the first time. We've never been sure who took it, but I'm not surprised it found its way into Bonaparte's hands. I didn't realize Princess Tatiana's reach extended into the bedchamber of the conqueror of Europe."

"Nor did we, until recently." Suzanne lifted the lid of the casket with the same care she had taken when unwrapping it. At first glance it appeared empty. Then she saw that there was actually a slim pocket to one side into which something had been tucked. She tugged at it with the hairpin she had used to open the box. A folded piece of paper. She spread it out carefully, for it was yellowed with age, to see that it was a page of handwritten music. "Does either of you recognize this?"

Both Courland sisters shook their heads.

"I don't think I ever actually saw inside the casket," Dorothée said.

"Nor did I," Wilhelmine said. "We were always told to be careful because it was so fragile. Though one could have looked inside and quite missed that." She stared down at the casket. "You think Princess Tatiana may have kept the casket for reasons beyond that it was a memento of one of her most illustrious lovers?"

"She hid it along with her most valuable information. It may be important to the investigation."

"So you want to keep it." Wilhelmine's voice was devoid of inflection.

"Only until the investigation is completed."

"Of course—" Dorothée cast a quick glance at her sister. "Willie, we can trust them."

A faint smile curved Wilhelmine's mouth. "Not a word much in my vocabulary. My sister can be a bit naïve, Suzanne, but in this case I believe she is right." She cupped her hands round the casket and put it in Suzanne's hands. "I owe you this, and more, for returning my letter to me."

* * *

Suzanne returned to the Minoritenplatz to the delicate, haunting sound of the glass harmonium. Schubert had called and was sitting with Aline in the drawing room on the ground floor, playing one of his songs for her. He broke off as Suzanne entered the room. He and Aline both scanned her face.

"You found something," Aline said, springing to her feet. "I'm sorry, I know I shouldn't ask questions—"

"On the contrary." Suzanne closed the door. At this hour it was unlikely anyone else would come into the drawing room. "As it happens, I have something I'd like you to look at. Both of you."

Suzanne set Princess Tatiana's box on a porcelain-inlaid table. She pressed the sequence to open it and took out not the Courland casket, but the sheet of music that had been tucked inside it. She smoothed the yellowed paper and held it out to Schubert. "Do you recognize this? Could it have had special significance to Princess Tatiana?"

He took the sheet music in his hands. "I don't think I've ever seen it. It doesn't look like the princess's hand. I saw some songs she'd written. Is this something she composed?"

"I don't know. It was tucked inside something important. I thought perhaps it was important as well."

"There are an awfully lot of notes crowded together." Aline ran her fingers over a bar of quarter notes. "It looks familiar somehow, but I can't think from where."

"May I?" Schubert said to Suzanne. At her nod, he carried the sheet music over to the harmonium and picked out the tune on the tinkling keys. A fast-paced march with a lot of flourishes and trills. Suzanne had never heard it before, but Aline's eyes lit up.

"I knew I recognized it, and I think it *is* important. Suzanne, could this be a code?"

"Why?"

"My Aunt Arabella was brilliant with numbers. She used to devise codes for Malcolm and sometimes for me. Once she did one concealed within a piece of music. It looked and sounded quite like this. A lot of notes and all those trills and flourishes. Suzanne, did Princess Tatiana take this from Malcolm?"

"I don't know. Let's work on the code."

Suzanne took a sheet of paper from a drawer in the escritoire, mended a pen, and dipped it in ink. "Don't turn the notes into letters right away," Aline said. "If it's like the other one, you have to transpose everything up a key first. Be careful to note the sharps and flats—they'll correspond to different letters. Schubert?"

He was already rewriting the music. They turned the transposed notes into letters and then sketched a table according to Aline's instructions.

At last, Suzanne copied down the plain text with Aline and Schubert reading to her.

> *My dearest P.,*
>
> *Just a few words to let you know I am well. How long it seems since I have seen you. The weeks drag on leaden feet. The world seems so dull, as though it had been drained of all its color and taste and fragrance. I think perhaps it was always like this before I met you, but I didn't, couldn't understand how gray and bland life was. Strange to think how clever I thought I was six months ago, and how little, I now realize, I knew of anything.*
>
> *You said once that I might have regrets someday, but I'm sure I never will. How could I? I wasn't properly alive until I met you.*
>
> *Write to me soon.*
>
> *I am yours always,*
>
> *A.*

Aline frowned. "Perhaps it is from Aunt Arabella. But I can't imagine why it should have mattered to Princess Tatiana."

Suzanne stared at the words and remembered Dorothée tracing the letters carved on the casket. A chill shot through her. A chill of recognition and of the myriad consequences of the connection she had just made.

Because if she was right, this changed everything.

36

"You found the papers?" Malcolm grinned at Suzanne over the light of the tallow candle in his prison cell. "Castlereagh should turn intelligence operations over to you."

Suzanne smiled back at her husband. She had left him only a few hours before, but simply seeing him sent relief coursing through her the way whisky warms the blood. "I couldn't have done it without Wilhelmine and Doro."

He lifted his brows. "Wilhelmine?"

"We seem to have become friends." Suzanne smoothed the cuff of her velvet spencer. She could see a smudge on the mulberry-colored fabric, probably acquired somewhere in their searching. "I gave Wilhelmine back her letter."

He nodded. "Her friendship can be useful."

"Yes. But that isn't why I did it."

His mouth curved in a smile. "I didn't think it was, sweetheart."

"Malcolm." Suzanne studied her husband in the greasy candlelight. In the half hour since she and Aline and Schubert had broken the code, she hadn't been able to determine how to break her theory to him.

"What is it?" He stepped toward her and took her hands.

She drew a breath, taking in the odors of dust and damp and candle grease. "I think I know who Tatiana's father was."

His hands went still and cold in her own. "How—"

"There was a piece of sheet music tucked inside the Courland casket. Aline recognized it as a code of your mother's." She opened her reticule and took out the sheet music.

Recognition leapt in Malcolm's gaze. "That is my mother's hand. I didn't know she wrote to Tania in code."

"She didn't. At least this wasn't written to Princess Tatiana." Suzanne pulled the plain text from her reticule and handed it to him. "Doro showed me her father's initials carved on the casket: *PBC.*"

"Peter von Biron, Duke of Courland."

"Malcolm, on their journey across the Continent, did your mother and grandfather meet Peter of Courland?"

His gaze froze on her face, though she knew his thoughts were miles and years away. Sifting, analyzing, combing through the evidence. "They must have. But—" He stared down at the papers as though looking for clues to his mother's past.

"Peter. Pierre in French, which is the language your mother would have used with him. For whom a daughter might be named Pierette. I don't think the *P* on Tatiana's locket was her own initial. The *A* was for your mother. I think the *P* was for Tatiana's father."

Malcolm's gaze jerked to her face. "Peter of Courland was almost forty years my mother's senior."

"He was a powerful, charismatic man. You only have to look at Doro with Talleyrand to understand the fascination a brilliant older man can hold for an intelligent young woman. The kind of young woman who is likely to be bored by boys her own age."

Malcolm closed his eyes. "A man who was almost a sovereign in his own right. A man connected to the royal families of Russia and Austria. No wonder Mama was so determined to keep it quiet. If she'd so much as breathed Peter of Courland's name to anyone, the gossip would have spread like wildfire."

"He must have kept the paper tucked into the casket. Tatiana must have discovered it when Bonaparte gave the casket to her."

"So Peter of Courland cared enough to keep a memento of my mother tucked into a bit of silver." Malcolm's voice cut with bitterness. "But not enough to help her. Or to seek out their daughter."

If Peter of Courland had stepped into the jail cell in that moment, Suzanne suspected her restrained husband would have slammed his fist into the duke's jaw and sent His Grace of Courland flying into the stone wall.

"If it's true," Suzanne said, "it would mean—"

"That Wilhelmine and Dorothée and the other Courland princesses are Tania's sisters."

"Or at least that Wilhelmine and Pauline and Jeanne are. Doro freely admits that by the time she was born her parents lived separate lives, and that Alexander Batowski was her actual father. But she still feels the weight of the Courland heritage."

"One of the most powerful families in Europe, and Tania was outside with her nose pressed to the glass."

"It must have been galling. Especially since she and Wilhelmine of Sagan were already rivals in so many ways."

Malcolm stared at the shadow patterns the window bars made on the stone floor. "I don't think Tania was trying to blackmail the tsar and Metternich and me under orders from Bonaparte or Talleyrand. I think it was personal. I think she wanted to force Metternich and Tsar Alexander and Castlereagh, through me, to give her her heritage."

"The Courland estates?" Even after weeks of friendship with Dorothée, Suzanne could scarcely conceive of the fantastical wealth the Courland family possessed.

"Part of them. We're redrawing the map of Europe. Why not carve out a bit for Peter of Courland's fifth daughter? A daughter who might be illegitimate, but who at least could boast that the duke had actually fathered her."

"Which would mean, if Wilhelmine and Doro and their sisters knew—"

"They'd have a motive to get rid of her," Malcolm said in a voice stripped of expression.

"Or at least Wilhelmine and Doro and Pauline would. Jeanne was disinherited."

"Do you think the duchess and Dorothée knew?" Malcolm asked in the same voice.

"Nothing in their actions thus far would make me think so. But we both know the power of deception." Suzanne stared at yellow wax trickling down the side of the candle. "Malcolm, there's someone else it gives a motive. If Talleyrand knew what she was planning—"

"You think he'd have tried to silence Tania to protect Dorothée?"

"I think there's very little Prince Talleyrand wouldn't risk for Doro."

Malcolm's fingers clenched. "If only Tania had told me, I'd—"

Suzanne scanned his face. "What?"

"God knows." He strode to the high, barred window. "I still remember her grilling me about the family history that first day my mother took me to meet her in France. Tania got me to sketch her a family tree. We had to burn it before I left, but she memorized the names. A family she couldn't acknowledge, who couldn't acknowledge her." He stared up at the damp-spotted iron bars of the window. "The only family she could lay claim to were the Sarasovs Talleyrand appropriated for her. While I grew up with all the comforts of rank and fortune and legal legitimacy. And the truth is, Tania and I were no different."

It was the closest Malcolm had ever come to admitting to Suzanne a fear he had danced round in the past. That though acknowledged as the legitimate son of his mother's marriage to Alistair Rannoch, he, too, might be a bastard, born of one of his mother's many love affairs after her marriage. A bastard who happened to exist on the right side of the blanket in the world's eyes.

Suzanne went up behind him and put her arms round his shoulders. She could feel the shudder of his breath through the silk of his waistcoat. "You have no control over the circumstances of your birth or how those circumstances are viewed. You were the best brother you could be to Tatiana once you knew the truth."

He turned in her embrace and took her face between his hands. "You're a good liar, sweetheart."

"That was no lie."

"Perhaps not to you. All I can see are the things I might have done differently. If I could have made her believe she belonged—"

He spun away and slammed his fist into the wall. "Damn this world we live in."

"I frequently feel the same myself."

He turned and gave her a crooked smile, though his gaze remained bleak. "Recognition. Power. It was all within her grasp."

"If the tsar and Metternich and you had refused her demands, would she have made the papers public?"

"In spite?" He rubbed his knuckles. "I don't think so. But if she thought releasing some of the truth would push us to give her what she wanted—Oh yes. I think that's why she wanted you there."

"She asked you to arrive before Metternich and Tsar Alexander and me."

"I think she was going to lay out her plan in detail to me first and tell me what she was threatening. She wouldn't have revealed what she was holding over each of us during the actual meeting. She'd just have mentioned that she had information that could make matters difficult for all of us. Metternich and the tsar would have been able to guess what she meant." Malcolm stared down at the blood welling to the surface of his skin. "With you there, I'd see how very real her threat was. I'd merely need to look at you to be reminded of everything I had to lose."

Suzanne pulled a handkerchief from her reticule and wrapped it round her husband's torn knuckles. "In some ways Tatiana didn't know you very well."

Malcolm flinched, and she wasn't sure it was because she was pulling at his hand. "On the contrary," he said. "Tania was damnably acute when it came to reading me. She always warned me my marriage was a chimera. It took her deception to force me to be honest with you. In some ways my sister and I are remarkably alike."

Suzanne knotted the handkerchief. "There are different types of deception, darling. Tatiana was acting in her own interests."

"Hard to say that's worse than deceiving people in the name of a country that's quick enough to turn its back on those it should be helping."

Suzanne looked up at her husband in the gray light slanting in through the bars of the prison window. Clouds were massing outside and the air held the promise of rain. She considered and abandoned a number of possible responses. "We need to get you out of here. You have too much time to brood."

"You're right. I'm leaving all the work to you and burdening you with my self-pity on top of it."

"Never that. Malcolm—" She laid her hand against his face. "We don't know that she died because of this."

"No. Tania had herself in a web of danger. Not for the first time." He took her hand and squeezed her fingers before he released it. "What about the other coded paper you found in the box?"

"I gave it to Aline."

He frowned.

"She isn't a child anymore, Malcolm. And she'll be faster at it than either of us."

"No, it was a wise choice. Allie has a good head on her shoulders. What are you going to do with Tsarina Elisabeth's letters?"

"You're leaving it up to me?"

"You found them. The investigation's in your hands now."

"Darling—" She tugged at one of her gloves and saw that the ivory silk was smeared with black, though she had put on a fresh pair before she left the Minoritenplatz. The grime of the prison rubbing off on her. "I don't know that we're going to be able to keep your mother's secrets."

"I know it." His voice was low and rough.

Her gaze flew to his face. "Malcolm—"

"We're beyond personal considerations." He took her hands in his and looked down at them. "This all comes down to deciding whom we can trust. Like most of diplomacy."

"And a mistake can be fatal."

His fingers tightened over her own. "Quite."

Adam Czartoryski shook the rain from his beaver hat and bowed to Suzanne across a private parlor in the back of Café Hugel.

"Thank you for coming on such short notice," she said. "This was the safest place I could think of. I knew there'd be talk if you came to the Minoritenplatz. And we can't even be sure we're safe from Baron Hager's agents there, despite Castlereagh's care in choosing the servants. Hopefully if we're noticed here, they'll only think we're having an assignation."

"Which would merely cause me to be the subject of envy," Czartoryski said with a smile.

"And me as well, Prince."

He shook his head. "You flatter me, Madame Rannoch."

Suzanne moved to the gateleg table in the center of the room and opened her reticule. "I asked you to meet me here because I have something for you." She held out the letters tied with buff-colored ribbon.

Czartoryski strode to the table and seized the letters. The silk ribbon shimmered in the candlelight in his shaking fingers. "Where—"

"She hid them in Princess Bagration's piano."

"Good God."

"She correctly assumed it was the last place we'd think to look."

Czartoryski tugged loose the ribbon. He unfolded the first of the letters with great care, as though he could still not quite believe it.

"Is it the tsarina's?" Suzanne asked.

He nodded, staring down at the paper as though he were seeing into his beloved's heart. Then he lifted his gaze to Suzanne's face and inclined his head with the formality of a gentleman at court. "Words cannot express my gratitude to you, madame. I know full well you had no need to return these to me once you discovered them."

"And you have no need to continue to help us now you have them back."

"But you know that I will."

"I think I've come to read you that well, Prince."

He smiled. "I'm relieved to hear it."

"Sometimes the honorable course of action is also the prudent one."

"You have the sense of a diplomat and the courage of a soldier,

Madame Rannoch." Czartoryski tucked the letters inside his coat. His hand lingered, pressing the letters against his chest. "There's no way, of course, to know if Princess Tatiana showed these to anyone. Or if she took them in the service of one of her masters."

"I think she took them in service of her own ends. And because of that, I don't think she showed them to anyone."

Czartoryski frowned.

A light rap sounded on the door. "Ah," Suzanne said. "Good. It's all right, Prince. These are expected visitors. And we all have reasons to keep each other's secrets."

The door opened to admit two slender, cloaked figures. Raindrops clung to the dark fabric of their cloaks. The smell of wet wool filled the air. "I thought I'd got used to all the intrigues in Vienna, but this is like something out of a novel." Wilhelmine of Sagan put back the hood of her cloak to reveal the burnished coils of her hair.

Dorothée tugged at the ties on her own cloak. "I don't think we were seen."

"Even if we were, it will only enhance Prince Czartoryski's reputation," Wilhelmine said. "An assignation with three ladies at once."

"Willie," Dorothée protested.

"You flatter me, Duchess." Czartoryski bowed to her and then turned to do likewise to Dorothée. "Madame la Comtesse. It's some years since we've had an opportunity for private conversation. I always knew you'd grow into a rare woman."

Dorothée flushed in the candlelight under the gaze of her first love. "I wasn't sure you remembered me."

"I could scarcely forget." Czartoryski took their rain-splashed cloaks and draped them over the bench built into the red-tiled stove.

Wilhelmine moved toward the table. "I can see by your face that Suzanne has returned to you what Princess Tatiana took. What I suspect she hasn't told you is that Princess Tatiana was also in possession of a letter of mine that I would not have wished to fall into the wrong hands. Which I suspect is why we're all here."

Suzanne moved to stand between Czartoryski and the Courland sisters. "I think I know why Princess Tatiana was in possession of these papers and what she meant to do with them. And it concerns all of you."

Wilhelmine regarded her with an odd smile. "And you're trusting us with your theory?"

"As Prince Czartoryski once said to my husband, at some point one needs to trust someone."

They drew up chairs and sat round the circle of light cast by the brace of candles on the table. Dorothée's gaze was wide with curiosity and apprehension, Wilhelmine's appraising. Czartoryski held himself as though in check, waiting for what was to be revealed.

"Princess Bagration was correct at the Metternich masquerade. Princess Tatiana was not the daughter of Prince and Princess Sarasov."

"I suspected that was the case," Wilhelmine said. "But how the devil did she pull it off?"

"Prince Talleyrand helped her."

Dorothée frowned. "He—"

"He turned her into his agent."

Wilhelmine nodded. "Well, we always knew they were—"

Dorothée shook her head. "I don't think she was his mistress."

"Doro—"

"No, she's right," Suzanne said. "Prince Talleyrand was looking after Tatiana for family friends. My husband's family, as it happens." She explained about Lady Arabella's travels on the Continent with her father and her subsequent pregnancy but said nothing about Peter of Courland.

Wilhelmine squeezed her eyes shut. "That poor woman. Of course she was compelled to give the child up."

"But she did see her from time to time. And when Malcolm was twelve, his mother took him to meet his sister." She explained about Prince Talleyrand recruiting Tatiana as an agent and setting up her identity as Princess Tatiana Sarasova and her subsequent marriage to Prince Kirsanov.

"And so she came to Vienna to spy on us all," Dorothée said.

Wilhelmine shot a glance at her sister. "Half the people in Vienna are spies for one power or another."

"She certainly deceived the court of St. Petersburg brilliantly." Czartoryski studied Suzanne. "But—"

Dorothée finished the thought for him. "There's a reason you're telling us all this. It has something to do with the papers she was concealing?"

"I think she was planning to use them to claim her heritage."

"From Monsieur Rannoch's mother?" Dorothée said. "But what—"

"No. From her father."

"But who—"

Wilhelmine's hand closed into a fist on the linen tablecloth. "Dear God. The bastard."

"Who—" Dorothée stared at her sister, then at Suzanne. "Was it something to do with the paper in the Courland casket? But—"

The patter of rain against the casement echoed in the suddenly still room.

"Suzanne," Wilhelmine said, "are you trying to tell us Tatiana Kirsanova, or whatever her name really was, was our sister?"

Suzanne met her gaze. "I believe so." She opened her reticule again and took out Arabella Rannoch's letter and the plain text version, as well as Tatiana's locket.

Dorothée leaned close to her sister to read the letter, brows drawn.

Wilhelmine gave an incredulous laugh. "I thought our parents were beyond the ability to shock me."

Dorothée stared at the papers as though they were in a foreign tongue. "Lady Arabella would have been—"

"Scarcely more than a child," Wilhelmine said in a flat voice. "Though I'm sure she thought of herself as quite grown-up. The attentions of an older man can be so flattering."

Dorothée touched her sister's hand. "Papa—"

"Was a selfish man who took what he wanted." Wilhelmine picked up the locket and ran her finger over the engraved *P*. "I don't know why I thought he'd have caviled at this."

"Princess Tatiana was our sister. That is—" Dorothée cast a glance at Wilhelmine. "I suppose she wasn't really my sister. Not by blood. She was more a Courland than I am." She looked at

Suzanne. "Is that what Princess Tatiana wanted, to be acknowledged?"

"Or a piece of the Courland fortune?" Wilhelmine set down the locket and turned her gaze to Suzanne. "That's why she was accumulating all the information she had in that box, wasn't it? She was going to blackmail Metternich and the tsar into giving her a piece of the Courland estates."

"I think so."

Dorothée frowned at the tabletop. "She had more right to them than I do."

"In this world, rights come with legal acknowledgment, not paternity," Suzanne said.

"Or they used to." Wilhelmine tented her gloved fingers beneath her chin. "Under Bonaparte the rules rather changed. And despite Prince Talleyrand's talk about legitimate rulers, it isn't quite clear what the new order will be."

"Willie," Dorothée said, "Princess Tatiana was—"

"Yes, I know." Wilhelmine pressed her fingers to her temples. "No, I suppose I don't properly. It hasn't sunk in. I wish—" She shook her head. "I don't know what I wish. Except that I'd had a chance to talk to her."

"Did she actually make these demands of Prince Metternich and the tsar?" Czartoryski asked.

"I don't think so. I think she meant to tell them the night she was killed."

"But there's no way to be sure," Wilhelmine said. "If they knew, it gives them a whole new set of motives to have killed Princess Tatiana. And of course if we knew, it gives us motives as well."

"Willie," Dorothée protested, "we wouldn't—"

"There's no way anyone could be sure from the outside, *chérie*. Imagine how it looks. Especially since my spendthrift husbands have rendered my share of the vast Courland fortune not quite so vast as it once was."

"Don't be silly, Willie, it's madness to think—"

Wilhelmine's sharp gaze cut short her sister's words. "Can you even be sure about me, *m'amie?* Despite our charming reconciliation this morning we haven't exactly been close these past years."

"You're my sister."

"So was Tatiana Kirsanova." Wilhelmine touched her fingers to the locket that lay on the table.

"I know you that well."

Wilhelmine squeezed her sister's hand. "I'm flattered, *ma chère.* But it doesn't change the way it will appear to others. Or what Suzanne cannot but be pardoned for wondering."

"I never said—" Suzanne began.

"No, you're much too polite. And tactful."

Dorothée rubbed her arms through the thin cambric of her sleeves. "Did Tatiana try to blackmail my uncle as well?"

"We haven't found anything to indicate that's the case."

Wilhelmine cast a sidelong glance at her sister. "Prince Talleyrand would have been furious if he'd known Tatiana was trying to get her hands on the Courland fortune."

"Because of Edmond, you mean? It's true that's why he wanted me as Edmond's wife, but—"

"Not because of your sad fool of a husband. Because of you. Prince Talleyrand is ridiculously protective when it comes to you. I think you're the one person he'd protect for reasons other than politics."

Dorothée tugged at her high-standing lace collar. "Don't be ridiculous, Willie. He's fond of me, but everyone knows what a pragmatist he is."

"Would Tsar Alexander have acceded to Princess Tatiana's blackmail?" Suzanne asked Czartoryski.

"I don't know." His voice was that of a commander weighing the odds of a battle plan.

"And I'm not sure about Prince Metternich, either," Wilhelmine said. "But there's one thing I can do." She looked at Suzanne. "I don't know what suspicions you may have about me. But your husband and I apparently share a sister, which makes us stepsiblings of a sort. And I think I can get my newfound brother out of prison."

❧ 37 ❧

The rain had let up and the clouds were breaking apart by the time Suzanne and Wilhelmine arrived at the chancellery. Patches of autumn sunlight cut like diamonds through the oriental windows of Prince Metternich's study. Bars of light shot across the intricate pattern of the carpet and bounced off the gleaming furniture. The smells of wood polish and good ink hung thick in the air.

The Austrian foreign secretary surveyed Suzanne and Wilhelmine from behind the polished ramparts of the desk.

"An unexpected pleasure, ladies." His dazzling, practiced smile was as much armor as a steel breastplate. "What may I do for you?"

"Klemens." Wilhelmine stripped off her gloves with brisk tugs of her fingers. "Even a diplomat of your skill can't pretend the circumstances are anything approaching normal."

Prince Metternich twitched a brilliant shirt cuff smooth. "There is, of course, a great deal of business before me. But not so much that I don't have time for an old friend."

"You must know we're here about Madame Rannoch's husband."

Metternich's hands stilled on the ink blotter. "No, as it happens. I didn't realize you had interested yourself in Malcolm Rannoch's fate, my dear Duchess."

"There's a great deal you don't know about me, Klemens. Just as there's a great deal I don't know about you. But I can't believe you wish to keep an innocent man in prison."

Metternich's gaze locked with Wilhelmine's across the desk. Memories shimmered in the shaft of sunlight between them, as gleaming and sharp as a naked blade. One recalled that only a few scant weeks before, these two people had been in each other's arms.

Metternich wrenched his gaze away from Wilhelmine and turned to Suzanne. "Madame Rannoch." His expression was veiled, but his fingers curled inward on the desktop, manicured nails cutting into his palms. "I am of course sympathetic to your predicament, but you must understand that I cannot intervene with the course of the law."

"Rubbish." Wilhelmine slapped her gloves down on top of her reticule. "You are the law."

"You overrate me."

"Never."

Metternich put up a hand to the immaculate folds of his cravat. "You are naturally concerned for your husband, Madame Rannoch, but you must have faith in the course of justice."

Wilhelmine drew her gloves through her ringed fingers. "Klemens, I'm sorry. I know you're angry with me. I'll even admit you have a right to be angry with me. I never wished to cause you pain, but I—" She shook her head. "This isn't the place to dwell on that. Madame Rannoch and I deserve more than platitudes."

"Wilhelmine—"

"She was trying to blackmail you."

Prince Metternich's polished façade shattered into shards of confusion. "Who?"

"Tatiana Kirsanova."

"What—"

"And she was my sister. Oh good, I'm glad to see we've got your attention." Wilhelmine rested her shoulders against the chairback. "Suzanne, why don't you tell Prince Metternich what you've discovered."

Suzanne launched into an abbreviated version of the story. Tatiana's birth, her relationship to Malcolm, the revelation that Peter of Courland was probably her father.

"We think she wanted to have a share of the Courland lands carved out for her," Wilhelmine said. "That that's why she took my letter from you."

Metternich shook his head. "You're saying Tatiana took your letter—"

"To force your hand," Wilhelmine told him. "Evidently she believed you'd be concerned for me."

"Of course I'm—" Metternich drew a breath and spread his hands on the ink blotter. His fingers were very white against the green leather. "Go on."

"Princess Tatiana also had information that Tsar Alexander would not wish to become public knowledge," Suzanne said. "And information which my husband would wish to keep private."

"And you think—"

"We think that that's why she summoned you all the night she was killed," Wilhelmine said. "To convince you to give her her heritage."

Metternich pushed his chair back from his desk with a rough scrape. He strode to the nearest window and stood staring through the glass for a moment, then turned to face them. Against the sunlight, his handsome face was drained of color. "This is—"

"The only logical explanation for a seemingly illogical series of events." Wilhelmine got to her feet and walked toward him. "We think she was planning to make her demands of all of you the night she was killed. You, Tsar Alexander, and Monsieur Rannoch, whom she wanted to intercede with Castlereagh." She took his hand. Metternich's expression froze at her touch. "Klemens, Monsieur Rannoch never received Princess Tatiana's blackmail letter, any more than you or the tsar heard her blackmail demands. He was as much a victim as you."

Metternich looked into her eyes. For a moment, Suzanne knew he was seeing not his former mistress but the woman whose political instincts he had learned to count on. "If this is true—"

"Tsar Alexander won't want to believe it, of course. He's been eager from the first to put the blame on Monsieur Rannoch. And he doesn't have your subtlety."

A faint smile pulled at Metternich's mouth. "Rank flattery, Wilhelmine."

"It's no more than the truth. Birth gave Tsar Alexander power. An unconscionable amount of power. You've earned your place in the world. You have ten times the understanding the tsar possesses, and you have to walk in the room after him and let him speak first. To own the truth, I don't know how you manage it."

Metternich detached his hand from her own. "You've seemed to find his company agreeable enough these past weeks."

Wilhelmine tilted her head back, her dark gold curls catching the sunlight, her gaze steady on his own. "I needed him. Because of Vava."

Metternich cast a quick glance at Suzanne. Suzanne stared fixedly at the red and gold frieze that ran round the top of the walls.

"It's all right," Wilhelmine said. "Madame Rannoch knows. She's been a good friend to me. It's times like these when we learn who our friends are."

Metternich leaned against the window frame, holding her gaze with his own. "What are you asking, Wilhelmine?"

"For you to be the man I know you can be. To stand up to Tsar Alexander and do what's right."

"Are you so sure you know what that is?"

"Think, Klemens. If Malcolm Rannoch didn't kill Tatiana, her killer is running free."

"And that bothers you?"

Wilhelmine's hand closed on the window frame. "She wasn't treated well by my family. A family she should have been a part of."

"I can't believe—"

"Your pride is hurt. It's understandable. But you're not a man to turn your back on a woman you've cared for, *mon ami*." Wilhelmine touched his arm. "You want her killer brought to justice. The longer Malcolm Rannoch stays in prison, the longer her killer runs free."

"Assuming Rannoch is innocent." His gaze locked with Wilhelmine's, Metternich seemed to have quite forgot Suzanne was in the room.

"If you learn Monsieur Rannoch isn't innocent, you can rearrest him. Castlereagh won't let him go anywhere. Meanwhile, I think Malcolm Rannoch is far more likely to discover the truth than Baron Hager." Wilhelmine paused for a moment. "Unless you don't want to go against the tsar."

For the length of several heartbeats Metternich's gaze remained steady on Wilhelmine's face. He lifted a hand, then let it fall. "How well you know me, *mon amie*."

"I have faith in the man you are."

Metternich turned to Suzanne. "Madame Rannoch, would you accompany me to pay a call upon your husband?"

Footsteps echoed through the gaps round the scarred door. Malcolm closed the copy of the *Wiener Zeitung* he'd been endeavoring to read and pushed himself up from the edge of the narrow bed. The key rattled in the lock and the hinges creaked. Suzanne stepped into the room as he expected, followed by the Duchess of Sagan and the foreign minister of Austria.

"Rannoch." Metternich moved to stand in the center of the room. The shafts of light cut by the window bars clung to his brilliant shirt collar and cravat. "Your wife and the duchess have been telling me an extraordinary story."

"Prince." Malcolm inclined his head in a gesture that stopped short of a bow. "I would offer you a chair or a drink, but I fear my resources are somewhat strained."

Metternich crossed the remainder of the cell to look him in the eye. "Tatiana was your sister."

"Yes."

"And she was going to blackmail you and me and Tsar Alexander."

"So it appears from the evidence. I'm still finding it hard to believe she could turn on me."

For a moment he saw an echo of his own pain in the Austrian foreign minister's usually veiled gaze. "It's difficult to face betrayal from a woman one cares for," Metternich said.

"Tatiana was a complicated woman. She'd had to make her own way in the world, and she'd learned that the way to do so was to put her own interests first. For what it's worth, I don't think it meant she didn't care for people. Simply that she looked beyond her personal feelings."

Metternich's gaze locked with his own. In that instant there was greater understanding between them than at any point in all the weeks of negotiations. "What about this supposed plot of Count Otronsky's that you claim Tatiana had stumbled upon?"

"Baron Hager told you?"

"You have so little respect for our attention to duty?"

"I wasn't sure you'd listen to the word of an imprisoned murderer."

"Alleged murderer." Metternich brushed at a smudge of prison grime on the tan leather of his glove. "It now appears you never received Tatiana's blackmail letter. The rest of the evidence was circumstantial. I've spoken to Hager. Pending further information coming to light, we agree it is appropriate for you to be released. Of course you will remain in Vienna."

"Of course. I'm a member of the British delegation. Prince—" Malcolm looked into Metternich's cool blue eyes. "I cannot thank you enough."

"Your wife and the duchess are persuasive women."

Malcolm cast a quick, grateful glance at Suzanne and the Duchess of Sagan, standing in the shadows by the door, then looked back at Metternich. "Otronsky's plot—"

"We'll take extra precautions the night of the opera gala."

"If—"

"I think you may leave Vienna's security to the Austrian government, Rannoch."

"Sir."

Metternich moved to the door, then turned to look back at Malcolm with the gaze of the man who ran an empire. "And Rannoch—"

"Yes."

"Go carefully. The investigation isn't closed."

The heavy door closed behind the foreign minister. Malcolm

stared at the thick wood for a moment, scarcely able to comprehend that it was no longer barred against him, that he could walk out into the cool autumn sunlight.

He took a step forward. Suzanne moved at the same time, and then she was in his arms in a stir of roses and vanilla and soft velvet. He hugged his wife to him and spun her round in a circle, as though they were the heedless young lovers they'd never been. "You're a remarkable woman."

Suzanne laughed up at him, cheeks flushed with color, hat slipping back from her face. "It was mostly Wilhelmine."

Malcolm turned to the Duchess of Sagan, who was regarding them with a smile of surprising warmth. He took her hand and lifted it to his lips. "Duchess. I don't know how to thank you."

"We appear to share a sister, Monsieur Rannoch." The duchess's dark gaze shifted over his face, as though searching for something. "I'm sorry. About Tatiana."

Their eyes met with the understanding of two people who share the same burden of guilt. "Thank you," Malcolm said. "So am I."

The duchess fingered the cuff of her pelisse. "I keep wondering what I'd have done if she'd simply come to me with the truth."

"And?"

She stared at the black braid on her cuff, as though the answers lay in the twists of silk thread. "I'd like to say I'd have offered to make generous provision for her. Even acknowledged her paternity if she'd insisted. But the truth is, I've had my own preoccupations. My finances aren't what they once were. Princess Tatiana and I hadn't been the best of friends. I have a tendency to lose my temper. Depending on how the scene had played out—" She shook her head, eyes heavy with self-knowledge. "I don't know."

"You're an honest woman, Duchess."

She gave a twisted smile. "I try to be. Your mother is owed an apology, Monsieur Rannoch. On my family's account."

"If we were responsible for our parents' misdeeds, Duchess, God help us all."

This time her smile was full and surprisingly sweet. "You're a generous man, Monsieur Rannoch." She lifted her gaze to his face.

"I don't know what I'd have done if I'd known Tatiana was my sister, but I wish I'd had the chance to try."

"Rannoch. Thank God." Adam Czartoryski sprang up from his chair in a private parlor at Café Hugel. He gripped Malcolm's arms. "I confess I didn't think Wilhelmine of Sagan could do it."

"The duchess is not a woman to underestimate. Nor is my wife."

Czartoryski smiled at Suzanne, who stood beside the door. "That I already knew." He looked between them. "Metternich believed the story?"

"I wouldn't quite say that," Malcolm said. "But he had enough doubts to let me out of prison for the moment."

"And Otronsky?"

"Metternich claims he and Hager have the matter in hand and will be on their guard at the opera gala."

Czartoryski grimaced. "We can't let it wait until then. Or trust them with it."

"My thoughts exactly. Do you think you could help me break into Otronsky's rooms in the Hofburg?"

"If necessary. But it may not come to that." Czartoryski reached inside his coat. "I received this today."

He drew out a sheet of plain writing paper, folded in four and sealed with a pin. The writing was in French.

> *If you want to know more about Otronsky's plans, be in the library at the Zichys' tonight, at eleven-thirty. Be sure you're there in time to take cover. Remember to trust no one.*

"It could be a trap," Suzanne said, reading over Malcolm's shoulder.

"Possibly," Malcolm said. "But the last bit sounds as though it's from our friend who spoke to me at the opera."

"That doesn't mean it isn't a trap."

"If so, he's taking his time about springing it."

"But you'll be careful."

The urgency in her voice startled him. "When am I not, sweetheart?"

"Surely you don't expect me to take that seriously." Her hands tightened on his shoulders. "Look after him for me, Prince Czartoryski."

"I'll do my best, madame."

Suzanne curled her fingers round the superfine of her husband's sleeve as they stepped out of the café. It was a ridiculous relief to be able to touch him.

Malcolm paused for a moment. A gust of wind had come up, rattling the sign of the café on its iron chains. He looked down at her, his breath warm on her face. "I haven't said thank you yet. It seems quite inadequate."

"I only did what you'd have done."

"And perhaps not pulled off."

She smoothed his cravat, crumpled from his night in prison, aware that her fingers were not quite steady. "False modesty doesn't become you, darling."

He lifted a hand and brushed his fingers against her cheek. "I don't know how I ever managed to muddle through without you."

"Very handily." Her throat had turned thick.

"No. I was just too blind to realize how lost I was."

Something in his gaze made her look quickly away. Because in that moment something she wanted desperately seemed so close she could feel its warmth, while at the same time she knew with a pang of certainty that it would always be out of reach. "We should get back to the Minoritenplatz and reassure Aline. And you must want to see Colin."

Blanca nearly woke the sleeping Colin with her cry of excitement when Malcolm stepped into their dressing room. Malcolm squeezed her hand and bent to kiss his son. Then he and Suzanne went to the ladies' sitting room, where they found Aline hunched over the escritoire.

She sprang to her feet and threw her arms round her cousin in an uncharacteristic display of affection. "I don't think I've ever been more glad to see you."

"Well, there was the time I helped you get the ink and Bordeaux out of the drawing room carpet just before Aunt Frances got home."

"There is that." She stepped back and studied his face. "Is everything all right now?"

"For the moment."

"Not precisely reassuring. I know the sort of life you lead." Aline glanced at the escritoire. "I decoded the paper. It was much more complicated than Aunt Arabella's code. Pages of tables. I finally turned it into plain text, but I'm not sure what it means."

Malcolm and Suzanne moved to the escritoire and stared down at the words copied in Aline's quick, scrawling script.

> *A map of the route is attached. My emissary will go with you to make sure all goes according to plan. You'll deliver the items in question to him after the operation, and we'll go our separate ways.*

A rough map of a section of northern Spain was sketched below.

"The coordinates and place names were in code," Aline said. "Very clever. But I think I've got it right."

Malcolm drew a sharp breath. "Good God—"

"I think I know who sent it," Suzanne said. "He'll be at the Zichys' ball tonight. You aren't the only one with work to do, darling."

38

The buzz of conversation and clinking glasses in the Zichys' salon stilled to silence as the British delegation entered the room. "I see what you mean," Malcolm murmured to his wife. Her accounts of the attention she had drawn while he was in prison were nothing compared to the attention he himself drew, now that he had been released without being officially cleared of involvement in Princess Tatiana's murder.

Castlereagh advanced into the room with an air of complete unconcern. Lady Castlereagh began chattering to Julie Zichy about tomorrow's Beethoven concert. Malcolm had never thought to be so grateful for the good-natured prattle of his chief's wife.

"Monsieur Rannoch." Dorothée Périgord swept toward them in a cloud of gauzy draperies and pale pink satin. "It is so good to see you. You've been missed."

"Thank you, Madame la Comtesse." Malcolm bowed over her hand. "I have cause to be very grateful to you and your sister."

Dorothée grinned, turning from woman of the world to schoolgirl in an instant. "One should always help one's friends."

"Diplomacy would be so much easier if everyone followed that maxim."

Fitz and Eithne joined them, having exchanged greetings with the Zichys. "It's like stepping into a play," Fitz said. "I swear I don't think I've had so many people looking at me since I ran the wrong way on the cricket field at Eton."

"Poor Castlereagh." Malcolm glanced at the foreign secretary, in earnest conversation with Count Nesselrode. "No one thought to find the staid British the center of such attention."

"One simply has to brazen it out." Eithne tucked her arm through her husband's own. "Like Mary Feversham sweeping into Almack's in scarlet silk after the business with Phillip Stanhope."

Suzanne and Dorothée were claimed by Marie Metternich, who had been asked to play the pianoforte and wanted help choosing music. Fitz and Eithne drifted into conversation about tomorrow's concert with Beethoven's patron, Count Razumovsky, and Malcolm found himself standing beside Talleyrand.

The French foreign minister surveyed Malcolm with a shrewd gaze. "I thought you wouldn't remain in prison long."

"I'd say I was touched by your faith in my innocence if I didn't think you meant something else entirely."

"I have faith in your ingenuity, my boy, which is far more important. And in your wife's. You're to be congratulated. I caught a glimpse of her mettle while you were behind bars."

Malcolm glanced across the room. Suzanne's gown, the color of a midnight sky, stood out in the crowd. She had moved to a knot of people by the windows. As he watched, she lifted a white-gloved arm, circled by a gleaming pearl bracelet, and touched Frederick Radley on the shoulder. An unaccountable chill ran through him. "Yes," he said, "I know it full well."

"Drink some champagne and stop frowning." Geoffrey Blackwell put a glass into Aline's hand.

Aline's fingers closed automatically round the chilled crystal. "You seem to be telling me to drink a lot lately. I wonder if Mama would approve."

"Fanny?" Geoffrey laughed and touched his glass to hers. "She'd probably say you ought to drink more. You aren't a child any longer, Allie."

"Thank goodness you're finally beginning to notice," Aline said. Oh dear, had her single sip of champagne gone right to her head?

Instead of glancing away as she expected him to, Geoffrey regarded her for a moment, his gaze unreadable. "I'm not as blind as you may think me, Aline."

"I never thought—" Aline took a sip of champagne, a rather bigger sip than she intended, and choked it down.

"I saw you frowning," Geoffrey said. "While I grant there's still more than enough worry to go round, matters aren't quite so dire as they were a day ago."

"I'm happier than I can say that Malcolm is out of prison. But nothing's resolved."

"Not yet."

"Malcolm won't let up until he learns the truth. But I can't see the truth making anyone very happy."

The light faded from Geoffrey's keen gaze. "No. But it will at least end the questions."

"And perhaps open a whole new set of them."

"You're a scientist, Allie. You understand about the need to keep pursuing the truth."

"But people aren't equations, as you pointed out. So much harder to predict. And so much more vulnerable." She rubbed her arms, bare between her puffed sleeves and the top of her evening gloves. "Part of me wants to run home to London and bury myself in my books. And part of me thinks I'll never be able to bear being safe and solitary again. So much that's happened here has been unpleasant, but I don't think I've ever felt more alive." She thought of her mother's house and the familiar comfort of her study. Why did it suddenly seem so desolate? "I don't know what I'm going to do with myself after Vienna."

Geoffrey turned his head and watched her for a moment, his gaze even more intent than usual. "You could marry me."

The candlelight and clink of crystal and strains of a ländler faded away about her. The candle-warmed air pressed against her skin. "Are you that sorry for me?" she said, tightening her grip on her glass before she could drop it.

"Sorry for you? Haven't I told you I'm not so altruistic, Allie? I'm not in the least sorry for you. I have no doubt you'll make a splendid life for yourself under any circumstances. Perhaps a better life than I can offer you. In scrupulous fairness, I should advise you to consider your answer carefully."

His voice was even more brisk than usual, but she had the oddest sense he was holding his breath. Her own breath seemed to have got bottled up in her throat. "You still haven't told me why you made the offer."

His gaze moved over her face. She felt it like the brush of fingertips. "Do you remember when I came home on leave last Christmas?" he asked.

"Of course. We put Christmas riddles into codes that could only be read under the microscope."

"We spent a day locked in your mother's yellow parlor and drank three pots of coffee. And I looked at you across those stacks of paper and twists of red ribbon and realized I was in love with you."

Her heart, which had gone still, now seemed to be hammering in her throat. "You never—"

"And I've spent the last year telling myself it's ridiculous and would never work, that I'm much too old for you, and I couldn't give you the life you deserve. Or perhaps that's merely been an excuse for my own cowardice." His gaze lingered on her own. "Sometimes we have to take a risk, Allie."

Aline leaned forward and let herself curl her fingers round his arm. "A year is nothing." She lifted her face to his, close enough that she could feel his breath on her skin. "I think I fell in love with you when I was twelve years old."

Malcolm slid his hand into his breeches pocket and eased his pistol into his palm as he and Adam Czartoryski took up positions behind the long velvet curtains in the Zichy library. The heavy fabric tickled his nose and cold air leaked round the glazing, but as hiding places went it ranked considerably higher than prickly underbrush in the Cantabrian Mountains, icy water in a cave off the Douro River, or precarious oak branches in a forest north of Toulouse.

Beside him, Czartoryski controlled even his breathing. He was a man bred up in intrigue.

The mantel clock struck half-past eleven with delicate chimes. After an interval that was probably less than a minute, though it dragged at his nerves, the barest creak of well-oiled hinges indicated the opening of the door. Soft-soled evening shoes brushed over the Aubusson carpet. The clink of crystal indicated a glass being poured.

The door eased open again.

"You're late." The voice, speaking slightly accented French, belonged to Otronsky. Malcolm had paid careful attention to his tones in recent days.

"Only a few minutes," the second man said. "Wouldn't do for us both to disappear from the ballroom at the same instant."

"This isn't a game."

"Lord, everything in Vienna's a game. This just happens to be one that could get us killed. Pour me one of those, will you?"

The second voice was lighter than Otronsky's, with an edge of mockery. It tugged at Malcolm's memory, but he couldn't identify the speaker.

Crystal clinked again and liquid sloshed. "They've released Malcolm Rannoch from prison," Otronsky said.

"So I heard." Footfalls indicated the second man crossing the room. "A surprise move on Metternich's part."

"He'll start investigating again. Which makes it all the more imperative we recover the papers."

"Rannoch hasn't been able to find them, either."

"Yet," Otronsky said.

"We could try following him and bash him over the head when he finds them."

Something in the ironic tones tugged at Malcolm's memory. Foils clashing. A glass of beer on a scarred tabletop. Sunlight shooting through the amber liquid. Gregory Lindorff, Tatiana's former lover. And, it seemed, Otronsky's fellow conspirator.

"It isn't funny," Otronsky said.

Lindorff was silent for a moment. The footfalls and the change in the direction of his voice indicated he'd moved across the room. "If we could recover the papers Princess Tatiana took, would it change anything?"

"No." Otronsky's voice was sharp. "We proceed with the plan one way or another. Not turning squeamish, are you?"

"The risks—"

"The risks are far greater if we don't act."

"Greater than treason?" Lindorff's voice turned harsh.

"There are worse things than treason."

"That's all very well to say over a glass of brandy, but if we're caught—"

"We have no choice," Otronsky said. "She's become too much of a liability."

Malcolm frowned at the folds of bronze damask. *She?*

Suzanne studied Frederick Radley across the polished rectangular table in one of the Zichys' salons. His face was flushed with one too many glasses of champagne. Or brandy. Or both. His eyes glittered with overconfidence. Difficult to believe that face had once genuinely fascinated her.

"So," he said. "We're back where we were when you did me the honor of calling on me."

"Not quite. More information is on the table. I know you saw me going into Princess Tatiana's room alone on the night of the murder. And that you saw the letter Princess Tatiana wrote to Malcolm but never sent. And Malcolm knows about my past association with you."

He raised his brows. "You told him?"

"You left me little choice."

Radley's gaze darted over her face. "And?"

She smiled, though her lips trembled. "I owe you my thanks."

"For?"

"Making me realize my husband is less a prisoner of the rules of his world and upbringing than I had thought."

Radley folded his arms across his chest. The gold braid on his dress uniform shimmered in the candlelight. "You went to great lengths to get him out of prison. It begins to appear your marriage is less bloodless than I thought. Or was it gratitude?"

"My marriage is no concern of yours."

"Your happiness will always be my concern, my darling."

Suzanne let herself indulge in a deep laugh. "It's a bit late for that, Freddy. Much easier to fight with the gloves off." She walked round the side of the table and paused where the candlelight fell full on her face. "I know why Tatiana was blackmailing you."

Radley controlled his shock of surprise to only a faint flash in his eyes. "Really? Then you know more than I do."

"To achieve her objectives, Tatiana needed the support of the chief players at the Congress." Suzanne moved toward Radley. "She thought she had ways to get Prince Metternich and Tsar Alexander to go along with her. But Castlereagh was more of a challenge. She was trying to force Malcolm to intercede with Castlereagh on her behalf. But though Castlereagh values Malcolm's abilities, Malcolm can't even persuade him to show more consideration for the self-determination rights of the Poles and the Saxons, let alone to accede to Princess Tatiana's demands. So she needed other ways to reach Castlereagh. And who better than a man who is both a war hero and a crony of Castlereagh's beloved half brother?"

Radley hitched himself up on the edge of the table. "You flatter me. But Princess Tatiana and I never had the sort of relationship for her to have that type of influence over me." He lifted a hand and brushed it against her side curls. "I've always preferred brunettes to redheads."

"That wasn't the type of influence she wielded." Suzanne rested her fingertips on the table edge and looked sideways at him. "Tatiana knew about what you'd done in Spain."

This time the flash of fear in Radley's eyes was more pronounced. "You intrigue me. Do, pray, enlighten me about these mysterious actions of mine."

"In the summer of 1812, Malcolm and Tatiana were working together in the Peninsula."

Radley gave a rough laugh. "If you're gullible enough to believe that's all—"

"My dear Freddy, anything else that was between my husband and Princess Tatiana is no concern of yours. The French had intercepted word of a shipment of gold from Rothschild's to Wellington's forces in Spain. Malcolm and Tatiana fed the French misinformation about the route the gold was traveling. That misinformation led to a village being destroyed." She controlled her voice. She would not let Radley see her vulnerability. "But in the end, the gold fell into the hands of bandits and never reached the British army. Surely you remember?"

Radley swung his foot against the table leg. His dress shoe gleamed in the candlelight. "A lot was going on then, but I remember something of the sort. Old Hookey was damned hard-pressed to pay the men's wages."

"And you were pressed for funds yourself at the time. But in your case, the lack of wages was more than compensated for by the gold that came into your possession."

Radley pushed himself to his feet and paced round the table. "What the devil—"

"Remember I knew you then, Freddy. You even borrowed from your batman. You constantly complained about your debts and the stinginess of your allowance from your brother. Even in bed, as I recall."

"That's a damn—"

"I expect that's what drove you to do it."

"Do what?"

"Must I spell it out for you? The gold that was intended for the British army came to you, Freddy. Except for whatever percentage you had to pay to the bandits you hired to steal it for you."

He spun to face her across the table. "If you were a man, I'd call you out for that."

"You still can. I'm an excellent shot. Or would you prefer swords?"

"Don't be ridiculous, Suzanne." His voice had the force of a hand slapped against her mouth.

"No sense in pretending you cavil at hurting women. We both know you quite enjoy it under the right circumstances."

"You can't possibly prove—"

"Tatiana had a coded letter and map you sent to your confederates. Malcolm and I found it with her other blackmail items. I wonder if she stole it from the bandits or if they sold it to her. The coordinates of the map are damning. Malcolm says they point to exactly where the bandits' attack took place. Despite the block capitals, I thought I recognized your hand. I definitely recognized the seal. Risky to use it, but I suppose you had to have some way to prove to the bandits that the instructions really came from you. You probably counted on the code being too difficult to break in the event it fell into the wrong hands."

His skin turned ashen in the warm candlelight. "None of this proves—"

"Even a war hero from one of Britain's best families can't get away with treason, Freddy. Tatiana had you in a devilishly difficult position. Who was the emissary you employed as liaison with the bandits, by the way?"

"Damn it to hell, you don't—"

"Tatiana must have mentioned something of what she knew in the letter she sent that got you to come to Vienna early. I know she arranged to meet you in secret at Madame Girard's." Suzanne fingered the silver filigree clasp on her pearl bracelet. "How much did she tell you then? The whole of what she wanted? Or did she just ask you to intervene with Castlereagh over an undefined matter?"

"She didn't—" Radley turned his head away and bit back the words.

"I don't think she'd have told you the whole. She was waiting to spring it on Metternich and the tsar. I think she just said she required your assistance." The finger of her glove snagged on her clasp. She tugged it free. "You accused Tatiana of trying to blackmail you. Don't deny it, Charlotte Girard heard you. But then you thought about all you had to lose—treason is a nasty accusation."

"Devil take it, I'm not—"

She leaned forward across the table. "What else do you call stealing the army's pay? If the truth came to light, at best it would mean the loss of your career and reputation. At worst the loss of your life. You thought it over and decided it might be wisest to come to a compromise with Tatiana. Charlotte said when you left the shop you were on better terms, and Schubert saw you together in the street afterward. Tatiana must have asked you to call on her two nights later so she could explain what she wanted you to do. You were bargaining that whatever she was going to ask of you was something you could deliver on. At least well enough to persuade Tatiana to keep your secret."

"You can't—"

"Of course that was before you knew what she actually wanted you to do. When she told you, you may have decided the only way out was to get rid of Tatiana herself."

"Damn it, Suzanne." Radley slammed his hands down on the table. One of the tapers fell from the candelabrum and hissed against the polished wood. "She was dead when I got there."

Suzanne picked up the taper and pinched the wick to make sure it was extinguished. Hot wax spattered against her fingers. "I see." She set the taper down.

"You don't see *anything*. Stop being so goddamned superior." Radley strode round the table and grabbed her wrists. "You bloody bitch, you've always been too clever for your own good. So sure you know everything. I went into the room, and the smell was enough to choke me. The blood was everywhere. I got it all over my shoes."

His breath was hot on her face. She made no effort to pull away from him. "You went through her desk."

"She was already dead. People were going to be pawing through her things. I couldn't leave the papers for anyone to find. But the bloody things weren't there."

"But you found her letter to Malcolm. And took it as insurance."

"If I hadn't taken it, Malcolm would only have been suspected sooner."

"And then you left?" She scanned his face. She could see the pores in his skin and the golden hairs he'd missed with his razor.

"I went downstairs, but I heard the door opening."

"Malcolm."

"I hid in the stairwell and saw him go up. Then I slipped out."

"Stopping to look up at the window. But you didn't leave right away."

"I was at the corner when I heard footsteps. I turned and saw—"

"Me."

His gaze blazed down on her own. "Yes."

She jerked her hands free of his grip. Red marks showed round her wrists. Not the first time he'd left marks on her. "It's a good story, Freddy. But it doesn't prove you didn't kill her."

Malcolm stepped out from behind the enveloping folds of the curtains and drew a welcome breath of fresh air. "*She's become too much of a liability.* Their target is a woman. But who—"

Czartoryski pushed free of the curtains and strode across the room. "The bastard. The spineless, contemptible—I wouldn't have thought even Otronsky would go this far."

"How far—"

Czartoryski stared into the fire, his face ashen. "I should have seen it. God help me, I'm a fool."

"I very much doubt that, but I can't help unless you enlighten me. Do you know who the target is?"

"I'm afraid so." Czartoryski lifted his head, his mouth hardened into a harsh line. His hands were balled into fists. His voice trembled with shock and rage. "It seems Otronsky is planning to assassinate Elisabeth."

❧ 39 ❧

"You think Otronsky is plotting to assassinate *his own sovereign's wife?*" Malcolm was used to surprise moves in the world of diplomacy, but this revelation befuddled even his chess-player's instincts.

"Otronsky is a crony of the tsar's brother, Grand Duke Constantine." Adam prowled the length of the room. "There are rumors that Otronsky orchestrated the murder of Elisabeth's lover, Alexis Okhotnikov, on Constantine's orders. If Otronsky learned that Lisa's letters to Okhotnikov were missing and guessed at the contents—"

"He might have decided she'd become too much of a liability."

"Quite." Czartoryski's hand closed into a fist. He brought it down hard on the marble mantel, sending a tinderbox crashing against the andirons.

"And if he could blame it on the representatives of another country, he could push the tsar further down the path to war."

"Precisely. Not to mention that he's been putting his sister in Alexander's way. I thought he had dreams of her being the tsar's mistress. But he may have gone so far as to think she might become Alexander's wife."

Malcolm moved to the fireplace. "Will the tsar take your word over Otronsky's for what we just overheard?"

"He'll have to." Czartoryski sounded as though he would physically force the Tsar of all the Russias to take action if necessary.

For a moment Malcolm saw Suzanne the victim of a sniper's bullet or a knife in the back and felt the force of the other man's fury. "We may be able to get more proof. I think the second man was Gregory Lindorff."

Czartoryski drew a breath, as though swallowing his rage. "So do I." He bent down and picked up the tinderbox. "I'm surprised to find Lindorff caught up in this. He's a drinking companion of Otronsky's, but I never thought he was—"

"A killer."

"And so totally devoid of honor."

"I think we can break him. He was Tatiana's lover in Paris. He gave her the looted art treasures she was selling. It's leverage of a sort."

Czartoryski's fingers tightened on the blood red enamel of the tinderbox.

"Killing Otronsky won't solve anything, satisfying as it might be," Malcolm said. "The plot has already been set in motion. It would go forward without Otronsky. And we don't know whom he hired."

Czartoryski set the tinderbox on the mantel with the care of one whose every impulse is under iron control.

"We have time," Malcolm added. "The opera gala is still a fortnight away."

"Lindorff's in the ballroom." Czartoryski moved to the door. "We can confront him tonight."

"No." Malcolm crossed to Czartoryski's side and caught his arm. "Not with Otronsky so close. If he bursts in, we'll lose all chance of getting Lindorff to talk. We can find Lindorff tomorrow at the fencing academy. Or at the Beethoven concert. Without Otronsky breathing down our necks."

Czartoryski's muscles bunched beneath Malcolm's hand, but he nodded. "Tomorrow. We'll get Lindorff to talk. If necessary, I'll make him talk."

Tsarina Elisabeth studied Suzanne Rannoch as she came through a side door into the ballroom. She wore a gown that suggested moonlight and shadows, indigo crêpe fastened with silver clasps over a cool white satin slip. Her head was held high and she moved with deliberate grace, but Elisabeth caught the tension in the set of her mouth. The tension of feelings ruthlessly suppressed. Elisabeth knew a great deal about that sort of tension.

Elisabeth swept her demi-train to the side and crossed the room to stand beside the younger woman. "Madame Rannoch. I can't tell you how pleased I am to see your husband a free man."

Suzanne Rannoch's armor broke to reveal a swift, genuine smile. "Thank you, Your Majesty."

The tsarina dropped into a chair and gestured for Madame Rannoch to sit beside her. "You look—forgive me, but you look as though something has disturbed you."

Madame Rannoch's hand stilled, settling the rich blue of her skirts. "Old ghosts."

"Ghosts you've managed to lay?"

"I hope so," Suzanne said. "It's hard sometimes, looking back, to realize how foolish one's been."

Elisabeth scanned the young woman's face. Difficult to believe her past could be too tangled at her age. Yet Suzanne Rannoch didn't have the eyes of a young girl. And at her age, Elisabeth had been seven years a wife and had loved and lost Adam Czartoryski.

Elisabeth allowed her gaze to drift over the company, circling the floor in a waltz, sipping champagne, wielding fans, taking snuff. Diamonds and crystal glinted in the candlelight with a brilliance that could cut like a knife. The elite of Europe. Clever, brilliant, and oh, so dangerous. "For my own selfish sake I'm very glad you and your husband came to Vienna. But if you will permit me to say so, as your friend, I realize this can't be the easiest place for a young marriage. Dangers of all sorts abound."

Suzanne Rannoch gave a faint smile. "Believe me, Your Majesty, Vienna is no more dangerous than the other worlds I've lived in. Before and after my marriage."

The young woman's sea green eyes were like clear water that masks secrets fathoms beneath the surface. The words fit with what Elisabeth knew of the Rannochs' life, and yet she had the oddest sense that Suzanne Rannoch had just confided in her, much as she had trusted Madame Rannoch with her secrets at the Burgtheater the previous night.

Elisabeth pressed her hands over the beaded satin of her skirt. "When I was fourteen I was sent away from everything I knew to a strange country and given a new name. In the two decades since, I haven't been sure who I am or whom I can trust. For all those years, Adam's been the one constant in my life, even when we were apart." She laid her hand over Suzanne's own. "I know what you went through with the fear of losing your husband. Don't let yourself be caught by ghosts. Hold on to what you have, *chérie*. You won't—"

"Suzanne." Young Aline Dacre-Hammond slipped through the crowd, then drew up short when she saw Elisabeth sitting beside her cousin's wife. "Your Majesty." She sank into a curtsy.

"Please, mam'selle. You clearly have something to tell your cousin. I will leave you in privacy."

"No, don't go." Mademoiselle Dacre-Hammond gave a smile that seemed quite uncharacteristic of the reserved young woman Elisabeth had seen her to be. "I should like to tell everyone." She held out her hand to Suzanne Rannoch. "I'm engaged to Geoffrey Blackwell."

Eithne accepted a slice of orange Fitz held out to her. "It may be horribly unpatriotic of me, but I confess I prefer Herr Beethoven's musical tribute to Bonaparte to the piece we just heard in Wellington's honor."

Schubert smiled at her. "I think that shows admirable musical taste, Lady Fitzwilliam. Though the audience seemed to enjoy it."

Malcolm grinned at the young composer. He, Suzanne, Eithne, Fitz, Schubert, Aline, and Geoffrey were standing in a corner of a crowded salon during the interval in the concert. The concert itself was being held in the larger of the two Redoutensaals or Redouten Halls, court ballrooms adjoining the Hofburg Palace. Malcolm had positioned himself with his back to a pillar so he could scan the crowd for Gregory Lindorff. He hadn't been able to find Lindorff at the fencing academy before the concert, which was to take most of the afternoon.

"At least we get a new symphony in the second half." Aline curled her fingers round Geoffrey's arm. Odd how strangely intimate such a simple gesture seemed between two such reserved people. Malcolm was still reeling from the news of their betrothal, yet looking at them together it seemed so very right.

"An almost new symphony," Schubert said. "It was actually performed last December. The musicians complained at how fiendishly difficult the music was. But it's his seventh symphony. He needs to keep trying new things."

"What a crush." Dorothée joined them, her arm tucked through Count Clam-Martinitz's, her cheeks flushed with color, dark ringlets escaping a crimson bonnet. "I do love Beethoven's music. I always feel as though it takes me to the most unexpected places."

Malcolm had caught sight of a tawny head and gold epaulettes. "Excuse me."

He moved across the hall, keeping his gaze on Lindorff. Lindorff caught his eye but didn't dodge to the side as Malcolm expected. In fact, he seemed to be coming right at him. When they met, Lindorff seized his arms before Malcolm could speak. "Rannoch."

"Lindorff. I was looking for you."

"No time for explanations." Lindorff's voice was rough, his gaze that of a soldier who's spotted enemy snipers. "I need your help. He has to be stopped."

"He?" Malcolm said, wondering what smoke screen Lindorff had constructed.

"Otronsky. For God's sake, don't pretend you didn't hear the whole from behind the curtains last night."

"What the devil—"

Lindorff's fingers bit into Malcolm's arms. "He's moved up the attack. It's to happen today. I need your help to stop him."

"You were willing enough to help him last night."

"It was never supposed to go this far."

Malcolm stared at the desperate eyes of the man before him. "You're the one who sent me the notes. Why—"

"Later."

"When's the attack set for?"

"During the second half of the concert."

"How?"

"Originally it was supposed to be a sniper. Now—God knows what else Otronsky's changed along with the date."

"Will you recognize the assassin?"

"I've never seen him."

Some six thousand people were packed into the Redoutensaal for the concert. Malcolm took Lindorff's arm and dragged him across the room to Suzanne, whose aubergine velvet gown was blessedly easy to spot, and the others.

"Lindorff's just informed me of an impending attack on the tsarina," he said, breaking into an anecdote Fitz was telling. "Suzanne, go to the tsarina. Get her somewhere secluded. Don't let her eat or drink anything."

Dorothée stepped to Suzanne's side. "I'll go with you. They'll be certain to let me into the imperial box."

"It could be anyone," Malcolm said. "A footman, a waiter, a seeming friend."

Suzanne gave a quick nod.

Malcolm cast a glance at the others, who had all gone admirably still. "The rest of you fan out round the hall. The greatest threat is a shooter, but the attack could come in any form. Fitz, Clam-Martinitz, go to the box opposite the Russian imperial one. Schubert, can you get me backstage? Good. That's the likeliest place for a sniper to shoot at the boxes."

"Willie." Dorothée seized a fold of her sister's violet lustring skirts as she and Suzanne passed her on the stairs to the boxes. "Come with us. No time for discussion. Alfred, there may be an armed man in the hall. Planning an attack on the tsarina. Monsieur Rannoch and Karl and others are searching for him. Go to the box opposite the Russian one."

Alfred von Windischgrätz blinked, but nodded and set off in the direction she indicated.

"Good God," Wilhelmine said, permitting her sister to pull her along. "You're serious."

"It's the plot Princess Tatiana uncovered," Suzanne said as they pushed through the suffocating crowd. "We think Count Otronsky is behind it."

Instruments could be heard tuning from the hall. The crowd surged toward the doors in a press of silk, velvet, cassimere, and superfine, expensive scent and overheated flesh. Three slender ladies were able to slip through the throng with comparative ease, but it still took maddening minutes to negotiate the masses clogging the stairs and corridors. Suzanne's sarcenet slipper skidded on an orange peel. She would have fallen had the Courland sisters not caught her by both arms.

At last they reached the gilded door of the box allotted to the Russian imperial party. Two footmen in powdered wigs stood outside. Wilhelmine stepped between them with an unshakable air of authority and opened the door.

They passed through the box's antechamber and stepped through rose-colored curtains into the box itself as the first notes of Beethoven's Seventh Symphony crashed from the orchestra.

The tsar and tsarina sat in chairs at the railing. The tsar's sister, Grand Duchess Catherine, had left the box, probably to join the Crown Prince of Württemberg, whom she was earnestly pursuing. Adam Czartoryski had positioned himself protectively just behind the tsarina. Count Otronsky sat in the back row beside Count Nesselrode.

All eyes turned to the curtains as the three ladies stepped through. A smile crossed Tsar Alexander's face at the sight of Wilhelmine. Czartoryski's gaze went to Suzanne, dark with worry.

Suzanne positioned herself between Otronsky and the tsarina.

"Forgive the intrusion," Wilhelmine said, as a plaintive phrase gave way to another crescendo. "Your Majesties, might we have a word in private?"

Alexander frowned. "After the concert, surely—"

"We have reason to believe the tsarina may be in danger."

Elisabeth got to her feet. So did Otronsky. Czartoryski hurled himself at the count. "You bastard, what you have you done?"

"Here." Schubert directed Malcolm through a side door and up a narrow flight of stairs. For today's concert, a stage had been set up at one end of the large hall. The crash of the symphony's opening notes echoed down the stairs.

"If we see him, try to draw his attention," Malcolm told Schubert as they pounded up the stairs.

A blaze of candlelight bouncing off chandelier crystals greeted them as they reached the top of the stairs. In the shock of light, the musicians were a dark-coated blur. Brass and cymbals sounded, answered by strings. Malcolm paused at the head of the stairs, trying to make out shapes.

There. As the man moved he was caught against the light, a rifle in his hands. At the same moment Malcolm saw him, Schubert let out a whistle in a break in the music. Malcolm hurled himself forward and tackled the man from behind. The shot went wide, pinged off a chandelier, and buried itself in the white and gold plasterwork, the report drowned out by a crescendo.

☙ 40 ☙

Tsar Alexander took a half step toward Czartoryski and Otronsky. "What the devil—"

"Lisa," Czartoryski said, gripping Otronsky's shoulders, "I suggest you go into the anteroom. Alexander, I advise you to accompany your wife."

"In God's name—"

"Your Majesty." Wilhelmine's lilac-kid-gloved fingers closed round the tsar's arm with a command few would have dared.

They moved into the anteroom, Czartoryski gripping Otronsky. Otronsky made no effort to escape, but he fixed the prince with a hard gaze. "Czartoryski, have you taken leave of your senses?"

The door to the corridor opened to admit a footman with a bucket of champagne.

"Not now," the tsar said. "Leave it and go."

The footman set down the champagne bucket. The tsarina twitched her amber silk skirts out of the way. The footman straightened up. Then he collapsed to the floor as Suzanne pulled the trigger on the pistol she'd taken from her reticule.

Dorothée screamed. For a moment after, it seemed no one moved or even breathed. Music spilled through the curtains, a riot of quickening, insistent melody. Blood dribbled from the footman's mouth. His eyes already had the fixed glassiness of death.

"In God's name—" The tsar broke off, his gaze on the lethal knife clutched in the dead waiter's hand.

The tsarina put her hand to her throat. "It seems I owe you my life, Madame Rannoch." The knots of cinnamon-colored ribbon on her gown trembled as she drew a breath. "Might we prevail upon you to explain?"

Czartoryski, still holding tight to Otronsky, had his gaze on Elisabeth. Wilhelmine had put her arm round her sister. Tsar Alexander stared in stupefaction from the dead man to his wife. Count Nesselrode stood silently by the curtains.

"Count Otronsky hired an assassin to kill the tsarina," Suzanne said, lowering the pistol. Acrid smoke lingered in the air.

Otronsky pulled away from Czartoryski's grip. "I won't even dignify that with a response. We all know your husband very likely murdered Princess Tatiana. And with this man conveniently dead, you can't possibly have any proof."

The door opened. Malcolm stepped into the anteroom, propelling a slight, nondescript man in a dusty coat. He had a pistol pressed to the man's side. "Your Majesties." Malcolm inclined his head to the tsar and tsarina. "I caught this man—" He broke off, staring down at the dead footman.

"You were right about not trusting the footmen," Suzanne said.

His gaze went from her face to the smoking pistol in her hand. The nondescript man stared down at the dead man, eyes gone wide.

"He wasn't acting alone," Malcolm said. "I caught this man taking aim at your box from the wings, Your Majesty." He tightened his grip on the nondescript man's shoulder. "Do you see the person who engaged your services?"

The man hesitated, gaze still on his dead confederate.

Malcolm pressed the pistol closer to the man's side.

"Him." The nondescript man jerked his head at Otronsky.

Otronsky stared at the man for a fraction of a second, then gave a shout of incredulous laughter. "How much did Rannoch pay you to say that? Or is the pistol pressed to your side sufficient incentive?"

The nondescript man glanced down at the blood spilling from

his dead confederate onto the gold swirls of the rug. "I've kept every communication you sent to us."

The candlelight from the wall sconces jumped in Otronsky's eyes. "Any proof you claim to have must be a fabrication."

"Oh, you didn't put any details in writing, I'll grant you that. But the communications prove you were in contact with us. And I think His Majesty there will recognize your hand."

"That's preposterous—"

The door was jerked open on his words. Gregory Lindorff stepped into the room. His gaze went to the tsarina, then froze on the dead footman. "I'm sorry I wasn't sooner."

"What do you know about this, Lindorff?" Tsar Alexander demanded.

"Enough to tell you Malcolm Rannoch is speaking the truth."

Otronsky jerked toward Lindorff. "You damned liar—"

Tsar Alexander's arm shot out, cutting Otronsky off midsentence. "How can you be sure?" he asked Lindorff.

Lindorff kept his gaze steady on his sovereign. "Because I was his confederate."

Violins from the hall cut into the stunned silence that followed. Otronsky lurched at Lindorff. "You can't drag me into your plots."

"Silence." Alexander grabbed Otronsky by the back of his coat. "We will go somewhere better suited to talk."

"I believe there is a salon across the corridor," Malcolm said.

They progressed across the corridor to the larger chamber, Malcolm keeping the pistol pressed to the nondescript man. Alexander held Otronsky's arm. Czartoryski walked close to the tsarina. Suzanne, Dorothée, and Wilhelmine clustered close together. Count Nesselrode brought up the rear, closed the door and set his slight shoulders against it.

Alexander fixed Lindorff with a hard stare. "You claim you and Otronsky were involved in a plot to assassinate me?"

"To assassinate the tsarina."

Alexander's gaze jerked to his wife. "Why—"

"Otronsky seemed to feel she represented a danger. I was never able to determine precisely why."

"And you went along with it—"

"To uncover proof." Lindorff was very pale but his gaze remained unwavering. "I never felt I had enough to bring the matter to Your Majesty. I knew I would get just the questions I'm getting now. I was hoping for some tangible evidence. I thought I had time. Then Otronsky moved up the date of the attack and urgent action was required."

"That's a tissue of arrant lies." Otronsky stepped toward the tsar.

"Your word against mine," Lindorff said.

"You were the one who came to me—"

Lindorff folded his arms and surveyed Otronsky. "Yes?"

"You were at the Palm Palace the night of the murder, Otronsky," Malcolm said. "You went to search for papers you thought Princess Tatiana had in her possession. The only thing I'm not sure about is whether or not you killed her."

"For God's sake, she was dead when I got there."

The silence was deafening. Otronsky seemed to be the last person in the room to realize what he'd said.

"Nesselrode," the tsar commanded in clipped tones, "you will escort Count Otronsky back to the Hofburg. He is to remain in his rooms until further notice. Place a guard outside the doors."

"Your Majesty—" Otronsky's voice was hoarse.

The tsar turned his back to his former favorite. "I have nothing further to say to you for the present. Lindorff, I will speak with you in private." He glanced at the would-be assassin. "Rannoch, you will deal with this person?"

"I still can't believe it." Dorothée looked from her sister to Suzanne and Malcolm. They were in a side salon at Count Stackelberg's. The afternoon's near tragedy had gone unnoticed by the majority of those at the concert and had not put an end to Stackelberg's evening reception. "Even after everything else we've been through, I never thought to find myself in the midst of such a fantastical scene."

"Nor did Talleyrand," Wilhelmine said.

Talleyrand had met them in the corridor when they left the salon at the Redoutensaal. He'd obviously heard rumors of something being amiss. He'd moved with a quickness that belied his clubfoot, and his gaze had fastened on Dorothée with the sort of heartfelt relief that comes only after bone-crunching fear. Shock had washed through Malcolm and an unexpected welling of kinship.

"Good God," Wilhelmine said, staring across the salon, "there's Gregory Lindorff. I was certain he was about to be clapped in irons."

Malcolm excused himself and crossed to meet Lindorff. Once again, Lindorff made no effort to evade him.

"We need to talk," Malcolm said without preamble.

"By all means. I believe there's quite a cozy anteroom through that door that's stocked with cognac."

Malcolm closed the door to the anteroom behind them. "You're a man of great ingenuity, Lindorff."

"You thought I'd be under guard like Otronsky?" Lindorff splashed cognac into two glasses. "I'd have given even odds on it as well. The tsar grilled me for over an hour. I gave him the names of the other conspirators. He dispatched men to round them up. He seems to have decided I'm an ally."

"Baron Hager seems to have decided the same about me. I turned the surviving assassin over to him. He thanked me and had the decency to admit he'd been mistaken."

Lindorff crossed the room to give Malcolm the other glass. "What's the title of that play of your Shakespeare's? *All's Well That Ends Well*?"

Malcolm's fingers closed round the crystal. "The tsarina could have been killed."

"Otronsky was caught."

"It was a damn near run thing."

Lindorff tossed down a swallow of cognac. "You must believe I never thought Otronsky would change the date of the attack or—"

Malcolm scanned the other man's face. The guilt was plain and seemingly genuine. So was the fear that lurked in the back of Lindorff's usually ironic gaze. "Or what?"

"It doesn't matter. Suffice it to say I'm not proud of many of the choices I've made."

Malcolm turned his glass in his hand. The candlelight bounced off the crystal and turned the amber liquid to gold. "You faced up to what you'd done. I acknowledge that, at least."

Lindorff moved to the red-tiled stove. "I didn't have much choice."

"You could have let the attack go forward instead of risking exposing yourself."

Lindorff's gaze snapped to Malcolm's face. "If you think I'd have let the tsarina be killed—"

"Quite. And once the attack had been foiled you could have run. There was only my word to connect you to it."

"You have a way of making your word listened to, Rannoch." Lindorff stared down at the burning coals. "Besides, I couldn't risk Otronsky getting away with it. That would have made it all for naught."

Malcolm studied Lindorff's thin, intent face. "What game are you playing?"

Lindorff looked up with a crooked grin, but his eyes remained bleak. "The same game we're all playing in Vienna. Survival. And redrawing the map to our liking."

"You can't convince me you decided to entrap Otronsky entirely on your own."

"You don't think I'm so brave? So clever? So ruthless? I wouldn't argue with you on any of those counts. But there's no proof otherwise."

"How did Tatiana get the tsarina's letters?"

"Tatiana was a very enterprising woman."

"With an ex-lover in the Russian delegation."

"Rannoch—" Lindorff studied him for a moment, as though weighing trust in the scales against an incalculable weight of risk. "I haven't been my own master for so long I've forgot how it feels. And I've seen the risks of trying to go one's own way."

"In Tatiana's example."

"Yes."

"And you think your master—"

"Oh no, Rannoch. I've given you a great deal already. Far more than I should, I suspect. But you can be dangerously persuasive. Tatiana warned me about that."

"You may face more questions from the tsar."

"That's my lookout. I'll manage. I'm more worried about Czartoryski deciding to wring my neck."

Malcolm swallowed the last of his cognac. "Czartoryski may be a romantic, but he's also a pragmatist. And ultimately he knows who stopped the attack on the tsarina."

"And who instigated it. But I take your point."

Malcolm turned to the door. "As you said, you've told me a great deal. What's left for me now is to confront your master."

❧ 41 ❧

In the gray morning light, the lines in Talleyrand's face appeared harsher and more deeply scored than usual. The habitual sangfroid was still there, but something else was visible beneath. Emotions unexpectedly stirred and not quite under control. The man showing through the mask. "I understand we all have to thank you and your charming wife for your heroics last night," he said, waving Malcolm to a chair. "While I didn't entirely understand what was happening at the time, I confess to feeling a certain degree of alarm on Dorothée's account."

"Your nephew's wife is an intrepid young woman. As is her sister."

"Dorothée has blossomed in Vienna. But I would never forgive myself if she came to harm."

"Particularly as this particular harm was at your instigation."

Talleyrand's brows shot up. "I'm accustomed to making leaps of thought with you, Malcolm, but this is beyond even me."

"I should have seen it sooner. I forget sometimes how ruthless a strategist you can be. You think Tsar Alexander is the greatest threat to stability on the Continent at present."

Talleyrand smoothed a lace ruffle over his fingertips. "You disagree?"

"On the contrary. You also saw Count Otronsky as the most dangerous influence on the tsar, pushing him toward extreme views that would lead down the road to violent confrontation with the other Continental powers."

"I suspect many at the Congress would agree with that analysis."

"But you were willing to take action."

"By helping Otronsky assassinate the tsarina?" Talleyrand eased his clubfoot straight and regarded the diamond buckle on his shoe. "My dear Malcolm. Your grasp of chess strategy used to be better than that."

"By entrapping Otronsky into a plot that would expose the extent of his propensity to violence and lose him the tsar's favor."

Talleyrand's eyes narrowed. His face was admirably under control. "Interesting. Do, pray, continue."

"You knew the tsarina had papers in her possession that Otronsky would kill to keep secret. Letters she'd written to Alexis Okhotnikov in which she confided her suspicions about her husband's role in his father's assassination. You had Tatiana steal the papers with the help of another of your minions. And then you had the minion tell Otronsky Tatiana had taken them and suggest that the tsarina had become too dangerous a liability. How long has Gregory Lindorff been in your employ?"

Talleyrand gave a low laugh. "You overestimate my reach, my dear boy."

"I think not."

"My dear Malcolm, you're suggesting I would risk the tsarina's life—"

"Oh, the attack was never meant to succeed. The whole idea was for the plot to be uncovered."

"How?"

"By me." Malcolm leaned back in his chair. "Tatiana was supposed to feed me information. I'm an outsider whom Alexander would be far more likely to believe than Lindorff if he denounced Otronsky directly. It was quite clever, really. Lindorff acted as *agent provocateur* with Otronsky. He kept Tatiana advised of the plot. Tatiana fed me information. I'm flattered that you placed such faith in my deductive abilities. Tania even wrote a note to be given to me at the Carrousel in the event something happened to her. At the time she wouldn't have thought anything *would* happen to her, but she must have planned to use the note in case she needed further evidence that she'd been investigating the plot. Only, as it happened, harm did befall Tania. With her out of the picture, I wasn't quick enough, so Lindorff had to start feeding me information himself."

Talleyrand crossed one leg over the other. "Ingenious."

"But you reckoned without Tatiana's determination to claim her heritage. Once Tania saw what the tsarina's letters contained, she decided she could make use of them for her own ends. And you realized you'd unwittingly given her the power to take part of Dorothée's heritage away from her."

"You've lost me again."

Malcolm slapped his hand down on the marquetry tabletop. "For God's sake, sir. I suspect you knew Peter of Courland was Tatiana's father from the moment you learned of my mother's pregnancy."

Talleyrand drew a breath. "No. But your mother did tell me. When I was in Britain."

The admission caught Malcolm off guard. Which perhaps was why Talleyrand had made it. "So you always knew Tania could pose a threat to Dorothée."

"If every sibling born on the wrong side of the blanket posed a threat, no one in the aristocracy would be safe."

"But Tatiana had the ear of Metternich and Tsar Alexander and leverage over them." Malcolm pushed himself to his feet. "If she'd been compensated with Courland lands, they'd have had to come from Peter of Courland's legitimate children. I can't imagine you wouldn't have been distressed. And then there's the fact that you knew Tatiana could no longer be relied upon."

"My dear boy, Tatiana couldn't be relied upon at the age of five."

"But she could do incalculably more damage now. Especially if she became financially independent and no longer needed you."

Talleyrand flicked a bit of lint from the lapel of his frock coat.

"We could dance round this for hours, or you could ask me straight out."

Malcolm leaned over Talleyrand, gripping the arms of his chair. "Damn it, sir, did you order my sister killed?"

"To protect myself?"

"And Dorothée."

He expected a blanket denial, but as so often, Talleyrand surprised him. "I won't deny Tatiana had become a liability. I sent Lindorff to deal with her that night."

"*Deal with her?*" Malcolm's fingers bit into the damask of the chair.

"His orders were to get her out of Vienna."

"Alive?"

"For God's sake, Malcolm, I've known her since she was a baby."

"And that would stop you?"

"It would certainly have an influence upon me." A smile played about Talleyrand's lips. "When I saw you talk with Lindorff last night at Count Stackelberg's, I suspected you'd have reasoned things through this far. But I'm not the one who can give you details of what happened that night."

"Don't think you can fob me off—"

"On the contrary. As Tatiana was your sister, I agree you have the right to as much of the truth as may be uncovered. It's the least I owe to your mother. A woman of whom I was very fond." Talleyrand hesitated a moment. When he looked at Malcolm, his eyes were more hooded than usual. "I don't expect you to believe this, but I will regret what happened to Tatiana until the day I die. Now if you will permit me to reach for my walking stick, I will summon someone who can give you answers."

Malcolm straightened up and stood, arms crossed, before Talleyrand's chair. Talleyrand lifted his walking stick and pounded three times on the floor.

A few moments later, Gregory Lindorff stepped into the room. He glanced at Talleyrand, who inclined his head. "As predicted, Malcolm has worked most of it out. I think it's time you told him what you saw the night of Princess Tatiana's murder."

Lindorff met Malcolm's gaze directly. "I got there after you did. I could see people in Tatiana's salon through the bay window. I questioned a servant and heard she'd been murdered. What I didn't realize at the time is that Otronsky had had the bright idea of trying to force Tatiana to give up the papers that night."

Malcolm's pulse quickened. "He said as much yesterday. Do you know when?"

"He arrived just before two o'clock, as near as I can tell. He told me Tatiana was dead when he arrived. As he confessed yesterday, he searched the rooms but couldn't find the tsarina's letters."

"And he suspected I had them."

"He thought you were the likeliest person for Tatiana to have given them to. Especially after he had one of his agents break into Tatiana's rooms and search again the following night, without success. His agents got wind of the fact that Metternich's agents were trying to buy Tatiana's papers from you."

"So Otronsky tried to take the papers at gunpoint that night at the opera. That was Otronsky himself who put a knife to Suzanne's throat, wasn't it?" Malcolm regretted not planting Otronsky a facer the previous night when he'd had a chance.

Lindorff nodded. "He wouldn't have trusted something so delicate to anyone else."

"And when Metternich's agent jumped out the window with the papers, Otronsky followed. Did he catch him?"

Lindorff gave a wry smile. "Otronsky is nothing if not efficient. He recovered the papers from Metternich's agent, and saw they were fakes."

"So he realized I didn't have the letters and turned his attention elsewhere."

"He had his agents searching other places he thought Tatiana might have hid them. Meanwhile, he was preoccupied with fresh concerns. I'm sorry about Vaughn."

"Fitz?" Malcolm cast a glance between Lindorff and Talleyrand, who was looking on with the detached interest of a spectator at a fencing match. "What about him?"

"The accident at the Carrousel," Lindorff said. "I didn't know what Otronsky had planned."

"Otronsky was behind Fitz's accident—" A pulse pounded in Malcolm's head. "Why, in God's name?"

"Otronsky saw Vaughn leaving Tatiana's rooms the night of the murder. Otronsky was afraid Tatiana might have told Vaughn about the tsarina's letters and what they contained. He wondered if she could have given Vaughn the letters, but he couldn't manage to infiltrate the British delegation's lodgings to search, and he suspected Tatiana wouldn't have entrusted them to a lover who wasn't an agent. His real fear was that Vaughn had seen him going into the Palm Palace the night of the murder. He was worried about what Vaughn might let slip, particularly because Vaughn is a friend of yours, and you were poking your nose into things. When he heard Vaughn was to compete in the Carrousel, he seized on the chance to remove him from the field of play."

"But—" Malcolm stared at Lindorff, while in his mind he saw Fitz smiling at Eithne in the antechamber of Redoutensaal the night before. Every drop of blood in his body seemed to turn to ice. "Thank you, Lindorff. That explains a number of things."

Suzanne stared at her husband. His fingers were pressed to his temples and there was a look in his eyes she had never seen before. "But why—"

Malcolm shook his head. Unanswered questions clustered behind his gaze, each one a potential killing blow. "There's no sense in speculating until we confront him."

"We?" Despite the circumstances, his words warmed her. And yet—"Malcolm, are you sure—"

"I need you with me. I need your judgment and your cool head." He drew a breath that scraped like granite against granite. "And I need you to make sure I don't murder Fitz." He held out his hand. When she put her own into it, his fingers closed tight on hers. "The truth is, I need *you*, sweetheart."

"Malcolm. Suzanne." Fitz looked up from the paper-littered surface of the writing desk in the attachés' sitting room. "No rest at the Congress. Castlereagh thanked me for my efforts at the Beethoven concert and gave me a mountain of dispatches to draft before dinner." He pushed back his chair and got to his feet. "Have you recovered from yesterday, Suzanne? I still can't believe—" He shook his head.

Suzanne advanced into the room where she had a good view of Fitz's face. His gaze was as seemingly open, his smile as quick and warm as they had always been. "Unfortunately it isn't the first time I've shot someone. We all lived through the war."

His eyes clouded with the memories. "We just never expected it to follow us here."

Malcolm pushed the door of the sitting room to. The panels rattled against the frame. "Being surrounded by killing changes one. Even when one isn't a soldier."

Outside the windows, rain dripped from the plaster moldings and ran in rivulets down the sash windows. The sound echoed through the room.

Fitz stared at Malcolm. "What is it?"

Malcolm walked forward and faced his friend across the desk. "Count Otronsky saw you leaving Tatiana's rooms the night of the murder."

"Good God. Otronsky was there, too?"

"At two in the morning. Nearly an hour after you claim to have left."

For a moment, Fitz simply stared at Malcolm with numb, vacant eyes. "I—"

"Damn you." Malcolm slammed his hands down on the desk, sending a hail of papers fluttering to the floor. "Were you so desperate to keep your sordid little affair a secret?"

"You think that's why—" Fitz turned away. "Oh God, what does it matter now?" He sounded unutterably weary.

"She tried to blackmail you, didn't she? She demanded you use your influence on Castlereagh, as she demanded of me and of Radley."

"No." Fitz looked back over his shoulder. "That is—Revealing the affair wasn't what she threatened. I could have withstood that. God, I hope I could have withstood that."

"What, then?" Malcolm said, hands taut on the edge of the desk.

"Christopher. My stepbrother."

Suzanne drew a sharp breath. "Radley."

Fitz's gaze flew to her face. "How did you know?"

Malcolm looked between them. "Christopher was Radley's confederate in stealing the gold?"

"He must have been the emissary Radley sent to the bandits to make sure they carried out the mission according to his orders," Suzanne said, her gaze on Fitz.

"I didn't know at the time." Fitz squeezed his eyes shut and pressed his hands to his face. "Christopher was always a bit feckless, always with pockets to let, but I never thought—I refused to believe it until Tatiana showed me papers in his hand."

Suzanne exchanged a glance with Malcolm. Tatiana must have not put those papers in the box she hid at Catherine Bagration's because she'd needed them to convince Fitz of Christopher's perfidy.

"You burned the papers?" Malcolm asked.

Fitz nodded, meeting Malcolm's gaze without flinching.

"It was to show you those papers that she summoned you the night of—" Malcolm bit the words back. He was very white about the mouth. "That night."

"I think she—" Fitz's face twisted. "I think that was the whole reason she began our involvement. To be close to another Englishman she could force to do her bidding. When she told me, I couldn't—I knew even if I tried my damnedest, I'd never be able to persuade Castlereagh to do anything to give her a share of the Courland lands. If she carried through on her threats—Christopher's only five-and-twenty. It's always been my job to protect him. He'd have been ruined."

"Tatiana's dead."

The reality hung in the air between the two men. Layers of the past—Oxford lectures, chess games in the British embassy library, missions in the Spanish mountains—overlaid by this stark fact that changed everything.

Fitz shuddered and looked away first. "I know."

"To save your sorry brother you killed my sister."

Malcolm's voice shook. Some part of him, Suzanne realized, hadn't really accepted this fact until now.

Fitz shook his head in confusion. "Tatiana was your sister?"

"My mother's daughter."

Silence gripped the room for a moment. A gust of wind rattled the windowpanes. Then Malcolm lurched across the room, grabbed Fitz by the throat, and slammed him against the wainscoting. Two tapers tumbled from wall sconces.

"She left me no choice." Fitz's voice was a harsh rasp.

"There's always a choice." Malcolm tightened his grip. A porcelain clock fell from the wall to shatter on the floorboards.

"Malcolm." Suzanne ran forward and grabbed her husband's arm. Fitz's face was losing color. "Not that way."

His muscles were like iron beneath her hand. She wasn't sure he heard her. Yet after a moment he relaxed his grip and flung Fitz against the wall.

Fitz put his hand to his throat and drew a rough breath. "I'll meet you anywhere you please."

"For God's sake." Malcolm slumped against the desk. His own breath was harsh. "Firing pistols at each other across a stretch of green is no answer."

Fitz wiped his hand across his mouth. "There isn't any answer to this, is there?"

"None that I can see."

The broken shards of a friendship littered the room. Fitz straightened his shoulders. He had the eyes of a man staring into an abyss and knowing he has no choice but to jump. "I'll go to Hager and make a full confession to Tatiana's murder. But I'll tell him it was a lovers' quarrel. I'll keep Christopher out of it."

His tone made the last not quite a question. Malcolm inclined his head.

Fitz met his gaze for a moment. "Thank you." He took a step forward. "If you'll permit me, I'd like to speak to Eithne first."

Malcolm nodded again. Then, as Fitz crossed to the door, he took a half step toward him. "Fitz—"

Fitz looked back at Malcolm over his shoulder. "Don't worry. Putting a bullet through my brain would be by far the simplest solution, but that would leave the question of who killed Tatiana unresolved, and the least I can do is make a full confession. My word on it. Though I realize you've no reason to take my word."

Malcolm looked directly into the gaze of the man who had killed his sister. "I don't discount it."

Fitz held Malcolm's gaze a moment longer, then turned to Suzanne. "Eithne will need friends."

Suzanne swallowed. Her mouth felt scalded. "Eithne will always be my friend."

"That means a great deal to me."

The door closed behind Fitz with a click of finality. Suzanne went to Malcolm and touched his arm. He reached out and pulled her tight against him as though he would meld his body into her own. "I suppose that passes for justice," he said, his voice rough against her hair.

She drew back and looked up at him. "You know the truth. And he won't escape without consequences."

"So why does it have such a hollow ring?"

42

Metternich slapped his Córdoba leather gloves down on Castlereagh's desk. "Lord Fitzwilliam Vaughn just presented himself at Baron Hager's office and tried to make a confession to Princess Tatiana's murder."

Castlereagh glanced across the desk at Malcolm, then looked back at Metternich. "Tried?"

Metternich's gaze shot between them. "Surely we can agree that a trial is the last thing we need at the moment. Men summoned to give testimony when they're wanted in council chambers, private lives turned public, questions asked—"

"You said you wanted her killer brought to justice," Malcolm reminded him.

"There's more than one type of justice." Metternich picked up his gloves and ran them through his fingers. "He's yours. Deal with him."

Castlereagh watched the door close behind the Austrian foreign minister. "I thought this might happen."

"Feared or hoped?" Malcolm asked.

"A bit of both. Metternich's right, a trial would have been difficult." Castlereagh studied Malcolm's face as though looking for clues to his future behavior. "You claim not to believe in capital punishment, Malcolm. I'm asking you to put your unorthodox opinions to the test and not exact retribution on Vaughn yourself."

Anger, frustration, and a small measure of relief tightened Malcolm's chest. "What will happen to him?"

"I haven't decided yet." Castlereagh took a sip of tea from the cup beside the inkpot. "You've done well, Malcolm. I'm aware this hasn't been easy on you. And that I haven't perhaps seemed as understanding as I might." He returned the cup to its saucer and stared into the milk-laced tea. "For what it's worth, you have my sincere thanks. The question of the princess's murder would have hung over the Congress if we hadn't received an answer, however painful that answer may be."

Malcolm nodded, his throat clogged with feelings he doubted he'd ever be able to put into words. "Tell me one thing, sir. Did you really think I'd killed her?"

Instead of giving the quick, facile denial Malcolm more than half expected, Castlereagh was silent for a long moment. "No. I found it hard to imagine you turning on a woman like that. Particularly Princess Tatiana. But I—"

"Couldn't rule it out."

"Precisely."

Malcolm nodded. "I don't suppose I could, were I in your position. After all, I've been trained to kill. And we've both known good men to commit unspeakable acts."

Castlereagh regarded him across the desk piled high with papers relating to the fate of numerous countries and peoples. "It's going to take you time to get over this. Both Princess Tatiana and Vaughn. Unfortunately, time is just what we don't have. This regrettable business with Otronsky may give us a much-needed opening with the tsar. The next days and weeks are going to be critical to the Congress. Which means critical to the future of the Continent. I need you, clearheaded and focused."

"I'm flattered. But Belmont or another of the attachés could just as easily take notes."

"I need you for a lot more than note taking, as well you know."

Their gazes met, a moment of shared acknowledgment between two men who disagreed about many things but recognized each other's worth.

"I'll manage," Malcolm said.

"Yes, I expect you will. I'd be a deal more worried if it weren't for Suzanne. She won't let you lose perspective. If nothing else, I hope these past days have made you realize what a fortunate man you are, Malcolm."

Malcolm felt an unexpected smile break across his face. "That, sir, I know full well."

Two days later, the tsar and tsarina called in the Minoritenplatz. It was not the first time Tsar Alexander had come to the British delegation's lodgings, in blatant defiance of the rules of etiquette that forbade a sovereign from calling upon the foreign minister of another country.

Six weeks ago, the tsar had got round the problem by ostensibly calling on Lady Castlereagh. He had drunk tea with Lady Castlereagh, Suzanne, and Eithne, paid them some very pretty if overblown compliments, chatted about the latest offering at the opera and Marie-Louise's arrival at the Schönbrunn, and even made a few comments about Prince Metternich being the sort of cold fish of a man who could not love. Then Castlereagh had come in with Malcolm. A suitable interval later, the ladies had withdrawn, and the tsar had had his private conference with Castlereagh.

On this occasion, the tsar and tsarina made it plain that they had called to see Monsieur and Madame Rannoch. Castlereagh and Lady Castlereagh were present as well.

Tsar Alexander accepted the gilt-rimmed cup of tea Lady Castlereagh held out to him and settled back in his shield-back chair with the casual ease of a commander in a field tent. His tall form overflowed the delicate chair.

"The tsarina and I wished to personally offer our thanks to Monsieur and Madame Rannoch. I still have not unraveled all the details of this plot of Otronsky's, but it's plain your quick thinking averted a great catastrophe."

Elisabeth returned her own cup to its saucer. "What my husband means is that I undoubtedly owe my life to the quick thinking of you both. There are no words to express my gratitude."

"I'm only glad you are unhurt, Your Majesty," Malcolm said. "And profoundly sorry you came as close to harm as you did."

"You are not to blame for that," Elisabeth said.

"Otronsky and his confederates have been sent back to Russia under military escort," the tsar said. "I understand Lord Fitzwilliam Vaughn has also left Vienna abruptly."

Castlereagh took a sip of tea. "He's been assigned to India. The nature of the mission required him to leave at once."

"And Lady Fitzwilliam?" Elisabeth said. "Such a kind woman and so devoted to her husband."

"She is returning to her children in England," Suzanne said.

Lady Castlereagh coughed and made a great fuss of refilling the teacups. Droplets of tea spattered over the silver tray.

The tsar tossed down his second cup as though he wished it contained something stronger. "Castlereagh, might I have a word with you before we go."

Castlereagh got to his feet. "I am at your disposal, Your Majesty. Malcolm, you will accompany us."

Even the attempt on the tsarina's life became an excuse for negotiation.

The tsarina leaned toward Suzanne. "Perhaps you would permit me to see your little boy, Madame Rannoch? Such a charming child. I do so love children."

Elisabeth did not attempt conversation as they climbed the stairs. Colin had just finished his midafternoon refreshment and was covered in toast crumbs but in a very agreeable mood. Suzanne lifted him in her arms. He consented happily to being handed to the tsarina and closed his fist round the velvet ribbons at the neck of her pelisse.

"No, it's all right, let him play." Elisabeth waved aside Suzanne's efforts to intercede. She touched her fingers to Colin's dark hair. "You're a fortunate woman, Madame Rannoch."

"I know it. I've always known it—at least ever since I met Malcolm. But perhaps never more so than now. Danger has a way of focusing one's priorities."

"So I find." Elisabeth smiled down at Colin as he twisted his hands in the plum-colored ribbons. "I'll always be grateful for the time I've had with Adam. To my shame, I'm even grateful for the events of the past few weeks because they brought us back together."

"Your Majesty—" Suzanne hesitated. "You needn't ever fear—"

"No." Elisabeth looked up and gave her a full, sweet smile. "I know it. As Adam said, one has to trust sometimes."

"Trust is a great gift."

Elisabeth reached out and squeezed Suzanne's hand. "So is knowing one may safely bestow one's trust."

43

"You're setting a new fashion, Doro. They're calling it Christmas Berlin style." Wilhelmine of Sagan looked over the balustrade at the fir tree that stood beside the limestone staircase in the Kaunitz Palace, gleaming with candlelight and hung with garlands of gold and silver. The fragrance of fresh pine drifted up the stairwell.

"Always one of my favorite parts of the season." Maroon velvet skirts swirling round her, Dorothée took her sister, in dark green velvet, and Suzanne, in peacock crêpe, by the arm and drew them into the salon, where her Christmas Eve party was underway. Above the babble of conversation, the strains of "Stille Nacht" came from the piano where Schubert was playing, Aline turning the pages of his music.

Wilhelmine accepted a cup of spiced wine from a passing footman. "A month ago I'd have sworn any sort of Christmas cheer would be quite impossible."

"Only a month." Dorothée ran her gaze over the company assembled in her salon, sipping spiced wine and champagne, sampling marzipan and butter cookies, exchanging quips and laughter.

"And all the questions answered, more or less." Wilhelmine blew on the steaming wine. "But sometimes the answers are less satisfactory than the lingering questions."

Dorothée frowned into her own cup. "Poor Lady Fitzwilliam. How is she, Suzanne?"

Suzanne hesitated, but she knew the Courland sisters too well now for easy reassurances. "Her life has been completely shattered. I think it's only the thought of her children that keeps her going." She saw Eithne's pale face, thin and drawn beneath her deep-brimmed bonnet, when Malcolm had handed her into a carriage in the Minoritenplatz a fortnight since. Castlereagh had sent Tommy Belmont to escort her home. "I hope it will be easier for her in England."

"I can't imagine—" Dorothée shivered and pulled her paisley shawl closer over her velvet gown. "I keep seeing Lord Fitzwilliam with Lady Fitzwilliam at the Carrousel. I still can't imagine him doing such a thing."

"Who's to say what any of us is capable of, if pushed to it?" Wilhelmine said.

"And I think of Princess Tatiana. To trust a man, to share such intimacy with him, and then—"

"Not all men are untrustworthy, Doro." Suzanne touched her friend's hand.

"I know that. I can't imagine Adam Czartoryski turning on the tsarina. Or Malcolm not being everything he could be to you."

Wilhelmine turned an appraising gaze on Suzanne. "I was wrong about your husband. I can understand why you took the risk of falling in love with him. Of course, loving's always a risk, one way and another. I don't imagine Malcolm Rannoch is an easy man to know. But I don't think he'll ever turn away from you."

Suzanne breathed in the cloves and cinnamon of the wine, thinking of her husband and of the risks that still lay in their relationship. "We've learned a lot about each other these past weeks."

"Then that, at least, is something."

Dorothée stopped a footman and asked him to open more champagne, then turned back to her sister. "I can't imagine Alfred turning away from you, Willie."

Wilhelmine's mouth curved in a reluctant smile. She glanced toward the smoking salon to which Alfred von Windischgrätz had retired to enjoy a cigar. "Alfred's a good man. Better than I deserve."

"You still don't believe love can last, do you, Willie?"

"Well, perhaps sometimes. For the right people. In the right circumstances." Wilhelmine's gaze drifted across the salon to Count Clam-Martinitz. "You're a fortunate woman yourself, Doro. I don't say this about many men, but I don't think you need doubt your count."

Dorothée smiled and lifted a white-gloved hand to wave to Clam-Martinitz. Her diamond bracelet sparkled in the candlelight. "I know."

Her sister shot her a look. "You don't sound as though you believe it. I didn't mean to turn you into a cynic."

"It's not that." Dorothée fingered the clasp on her bracelet. "I do trust Karl, as much as I trust anyone. I just—"

Wilhelmine stared at her sister. "Dear God. I knew he was in love with you, but I didn't realize you were more than half in love with him."

"Of course I'm in love with Karl, or I wouldn't—"

"Not Karl."

Dorothée glanced away. "Then I don't know whom you're talking about."

"Don't you?" Wilhelmine's ironic gaze had gone dark with concern. "I've seen the way he looks at you. He never even looked at our mother that way. But speaking of men one can't trust—"

"That's just it, Willie." Dorothée looked her sister full in the face. "I do trust him. Sometimes I think I've never trusted anyone more."

"So now we can get back to the business of the Congress." Adam Czartoryski took a sip of spiced wine.

Malcolm let his gaze drift over the crowd. The buzz of conversation in the embassy salon created as effective a cover as if they were in an enclosed room. More so. One didn't need to worry about who was listening behind the door or hidden in the draperies. "One can only hope it will seem tame after recent events."

Czartoryski's gaze went to Tsar Alexander, holding court by the stove, flanked by Catherine Bagration and Julie Zichy. "You're afraid Alexander will storm out over Poland and Saxony? He might have done, with Otronsky still in the picture. The odds are considerably improved now. Interesting how that worked out."

"Quite." Malcolm's gaze drifted toward Talleyrand, engaged in a tête-à-tête with Castlereagh by the windows. "And Poland?"

Czartoryski gave a twisted smile. "No one really wants a free Poland. No one in power, that is. Alexander half thinks he does, but that's nine-tenths lust for power and one-tenth self-satisfaction at his own benevolence. And perhaps a small fraction of remembrance of ideals past."

The pain of lost friendship in Czartoryski's voice brought a memory of Fitz so keen it was like acid in his throat. Malcolm forced it down, as he had done so often these past weeks. "So you will—?"

"Try to get the best result for Poland that I can. Stability is the order of the day with the men making the decisions in Vienna. I have no quarrel with stability—we could use more of it—but it doesn't equal equality."

"We have a number of master chess players in Vienna. But the problem with treating countries like chess pieces is that one tends to forget each piece contains scores of people with their own thoughts and dreams and ideas about shaping the future."

Czartoryski twisted his wine cup between his hands. "Not exactly Lord Castlereagh's view."

"No." Malcolm cast a glance at Castlereagh and Talleyrand. "My chief and I are in disagreement about a number of matters. I don't think quashing dissent is the way to avert revolution. Quite the reverse, in fact. But I fear I'm in a distinct minority." Even more so with Fitz gone to India, and their friendship in ashes.

"One must muddle through and take what gains one can, Rannoch. When you're my age, you'll have learned to take pride in small successes."

"Assuming I've managed not to lose my temper and destroy my career. In some ways, I'm a very undiplomatic diplomat."

Czartoryski grinned and clapped him on the back. "At least we have Smith's feast next week. Quite something to see so many of the sovereigns in Vienna agreeing on anything, let alone the freeing of slaves."

"Almost enough to restore one's faith in humanity." British admiral William Sidney Smith, at the Congress to represent the dethroned King of Sweden, was holding a banquet in the Augarten on 29 December. The cost of tickets to the banquet and the ball at the palace afterward would all go to ransoming slaves. "Of course we still can't get all the good monarchs who'll dine to ransom slaves to agree to abolish the slave trade."

"Small steps, Rannoch. If—" Czartoryski went still. Malcolm saw that the tsarina had come in from the adjoining salon and was speaking with the King of Denmark. The candlelight shimmered off her smooth, pale hair and the ivory satin of her gown.

"In my foolish youth, I used to think I couldn't go on without her," Czartoryski said in a low voice. "Now I know that's nonsense. One doesn't die of a broken heart. One sinks into everyday trivialities and muddles through. It's just that there's a void that's never quite filled."

What could one say to a man separated from his beloved? Especially when one professed not to believe in love oneself.

"But we've regained something I thought we'd lost," Czartoryski said. "And now I know there's something worse than being separated from her. I'm forever in your debt, Rannoch. Should you ever stand in need of my services—"

"That goes both ways."

Czartoryski gripped Malcolm's shoulder. "Despite the pain, it's worth it, you know. Every moment, however imperfect."

The lively, incongruously British tones of "Deck the Halls" came from the pianoforte. Aline and Schubert were laughing as she showed him the English carol. Geoffrey had joined them at the pianoforte, smiling at Aline with a look Malcolm had never thought to see on his face.

"I do know," Malcolm said. "Or rather I didn't, but I'm beginning to grasp it. Hopefully not too late."

Later in the evening, Malcolm found himself standing beside Talleyrand. Not, he thought, an accident. Talleyrand's chess-playing talents worked in the salon as well as the council chamber.

"Tsar Alexander is in a more temperate mood," Malcolm observed.

"With Catherine Bagration and Julie Zichy beside him, who wouldn't be?"

"I didn't just mean tonight."

Talleyrand shifted his weight, his fingers flexing on the diamond handle of his walking stick. "Despite the regrettable events of the past days, there have been some happy outcomes. Part of the trick of staying in power is taking advantage of fortuitous situations, you know."

"I thought it was making your own luck."

Talleyrand smiled. The candlelight glinted in his eyes. "That, too."

Malcolm studied the man who in some ways knew more about his family than he did himself. "Was it worth the risk?"

"One never knows that when one takes a risk. One simply weighs the odds and acts accordingly." Talleyrand regarded him for a moment from beneath half-closed eyelids. "Your mother would be proud of you, Malcolm."

Bitter gall rose up in Malcolm's throat. "Doing it much too brown, sir. My mother was a clear-sighted woman. At the moment all she'd be able to see is my failure."

"You were a good brother to Tatiana. Probably the one person she permitted herself to genuinely care for."

A knifepoint twisted between his ribs as surely as if he held the knife himself. "I couldn't—"

"Save her? But you brought her killer to justice."

Malcolm gave a harsh laugh. "I'm not sure I understand the meaning of justice."

"The search for the truth can take one to uncomfortable places, my dear boy. But then you've never been one to shy from discomfort. Your mother would appreciate that. She wasn't one to hide from difficult truths herself. And then some truths are inescapable, however hard one tries to hide from them."

Talleyrand's voice had shifted into a different key. His gaze had gone across the room to Suzanne, who was standing between Dorothée and Wilhelmine. "Your wife was invaluable throughout the whole."

"My wife is invaluable in many ways."

Talleyrand's gaze remained on the three women, framed beneath a red-ribboned pine garland, their ringleted heads close together, their gowns spots of vibrant color. "It's an odd thing to realize one wants something one never even thought one believed in. And to realize it's entirely out of reach."

Once again Talleyrand surprised him. The naked longing in his face and voice was very like that shown by Adam Czartoryski when he'd looked at the tsarina. Malcolm hesitated, then touched Talleyrand's arm.

"Oh, don't worry," Talleyrand said. "I'll muddle along."

As though aware of his regard, Dorothée turned and met his gaze. A smile crossed her face and was reflected in Talleyrand's eyes.

Suzanne and Malcolm stayed after most of the guests had filtered out, drinking a final cup of wine with Dorothée, Count Clam-Martinitz, Wilhelmine, Alfred von Windischgrätz, and Talleyrand. Perhaps it was the spiced wine, but Suzanne could almost feel the peace of the holiday begin to steal over her.

When they finally took their leave, Wilhelmine pressed a kiss to Malcolm's cheek. "Happy Christmas." She squeezed his shoulders and stepped back. "By the way, Annina Barbera is a wonderful addition to my staff. She has a splendid fashion sense. Thank you for recommending her."

Suzanne knew how pleased Malcolm had been to find a place for Annina, just as he was pleased young Heinrich and Margot had settled in well in the Minoritenplatz.

Malcolm smiled at Wilhelmine, the warm, unguarded smile Suzanne knew he reserved for those he trusted. "Thank you for taking her on. I'm glad it's working out."

Wilhelmine met his gaze in her frank way. "I'm sorrier than I can say that I never had the chance to acknowledge my sister. But I'll always be grateful that I got to know her brother."

Malcolm bowed over her hand. "The feeling is mutual, Wilhelmine."

Talleyrand had offered to send them home in his carriage, but Malcolm suggested they walk. Dorothée and Talleyrand waved to them from the doorway, Dorothée clinging to Talleyrand's arm and holding her shawl against the chill.

Malcolm and Suzanne emerged from the Kaunitz Palace to find a light snow falling, dusting the courtyard and the cobblestones of the street beyond and the tiled roofs above. Suzanne raised the hood of her cloak. Malcolm tucked her arm through his own, and they stepped forward into the still, white world.

"The first Christmas Colin will be able to appreciate," Suzanne said. "He loved the tree when I brought him to see Dorothée this afternoon. I think he would have climbed it if I hadn't kept hold of him."

"Perhaps one day we'll have a settled enough home that we're able to have a tree for the holidays ourselves," Malcolm said.

Suzanne pressed her cheek against the snow-dampened wool of his greatcoat. The thought seemed not as madly laughable as it once would have.

Malcolm stopped walking suddenly and swung round to face her. Snowflakes dusted the shoulders of his greatcoat and the curling brim of his hat. He hesitated, as though searching for a way to step over a divide. "I love you."

Simple words. Words he'd said once before, but only, she was convinced, because they'd been under sniper fire and he'd thought one or both of them was about to be killed. Words she'd thought she'd never be able to believe from him. Yet, to her own amazement, she believed his declaration without question. She put her hands on his shoulders to pull him to her, and felt a smile break across her face. "I know."

Historical Notes

In combining real and fictional characters and events, I have, of course, had real historical people do and say things that are not part of the historical record. I have tried to stay true to things these people *might* have done, based on my research into the complex and fascinating individuals they were. Count Otronsky is fictional, as is his plot against the tsarina and Talleyrand's attempt to manipulate him. But Tsar Alexander was increasingly belligerent in his dealings with the allies at the Congress in October and November. Talleyrand was particularly concerned with the dangers posed by Alexander's positions on both Saxony and Poland. Talleyrand was also a master manipulator throughout his career.

Tsar Alexander was rumored to have had a role (from advance knowledge to outright complicity) in his father's assassination. Tsarina Elisabeth's lover Alexis Okhotnikov was knifed to death outside the theatre in 1807. Alexander's brother, Grand Duke Constantine, was rumored to have been behind his death. When a third brother, Nicholas, succeeded Alexander as tsar, he destroyed the letters between Elisabeth and Okhotnikov and some of her diaries. From these facts I have constructed the story of the letters stolen by Tatiana and Gregory Lindorff.

Wilhelmine of Sagan did have a secret child by her mother's lover Gustav Armfelt. In 1814, Wilhelmine was desperate to have Vava restored to her. Metternich was determined to help her. They corresponded freely and many of their letters concern their attempts to recover Vava. Their letters, tied with white ribbon, were discovered by Maria Ullrichová in a fake well on one of Metternich's estates in Bohemia in 1949.

For the purposes of the story, I have compressed the timeline of historical events slightly. Prince and Princess Metternich did give a ball on 21 November, two days before the Carrousel, but the Venetian-themed masquerade that occurs in *Vienna Waltz* on 21

November actually took place on 8 November. Beethoven's gala concert at the Redoutensaal took place on 29 November. In the chronology of *Vienna Waltz*, it occurs on 27 November.

Lord Castlereagh brought a large staff to the Congress, including three plenipotentiaries, his private secretary, and ten young assistants from the foreign office. In the events of the novel, I have involved only my three fictional attachés (Malcolm, Fitz, and Tommy) and Castlereagh's half brother, Lord Stewart. Some of the British delegation stayed in the twenty-two-room suite in the Minoritenplatz; others were scattered in lodgings about the city.

The Courland casket is fictional, as is Maddalena Verano, but Cellini was imprisoned in the Castel Sant'Angelo, on charges of embezzling jewels from the pope's tiara.

Wilhelmine of Sagan and Princess Catherine Bagration both lodged in the Palm Palace during the Congress. I have taken the liberty of giving Tatiana rooms there as well.

Dorothée was very involved in the Carrousel, but I have enhanced her role in orchestrating it, and involved Suzanne in the planning as well. My apologies to Felix Woyna and young Trautmansdorff, to whom I gave fictional cases of the mumps to allow Malcolm and Fitz to participate in the Carrousel.

Schubert was in Vienna at the time of the Congress, teaching in his father's school and studying with Salieri. His first mass premiered in October 1814. He did not play at a musicale given by Wilhelmine of Sagan or at Dorothée's Christmas party at the Kaunitz Palace (which she did give on Christmas Eve 1814). But perhaps if he had met Tatiana, Malcolm, and Suzanne, he would have done so.

Selected Bibliography

Alsop, Susan Mary. *The Congress Dances.* New York: Simon & Schuster, 1985.

Brion, Marcel. *Daily Life in the Vienna of Mozart and Schubert.* New York: The Macmillan Company, 1962.

Dino, Dorothée de Talleyrand-Périgord, Duchesse de. *Souvenirs.* Middlesex: Echo Library, 2008.

Erickson, Raymond (editor). *Schubert's Vienna.* New Haven & London: Yale University Press, 1997.

King, David. *Vienna, 1814.* New York: Harmony Books, 2008.

La Garde-Chambonas, Auguste, Comte de. *Anecdotal Recollections of the Congress of Vienna.* London: Chapman & Hall Limited, 1902.

McGuigan, Dorothy Gies. *Metternich and the Duchess.* New York: Doubleday & Company, Inc., 1975.

Nicholson, Harold. *The Congress of Vienna.* New York: Harcourt Brace and Company, 1946.

Pradt, Dominique Georges Frédéric. *The Congress of Vienna.* London: Samuel Leigh and Messrs. Bossange and Masson, 1816.

Zamoyski, Adam. *Rites of Peace.* New York: Harper Perennial, 2008.

A READING GROUP GUIDE

VIENNA WALTZ

Teresa Grant

About This Guide

The suggested questions are included to enhance your group's reading of Teresa Grant's *Vienna Waltz*.

DISCUSSION QUESTIONS

1. Before Malcolm told Suzanne the truth about his relationship with Tatiana, what did you think had transpired in the past between Tatiana and Malcolm?

2. How does being in Vienna at the Congress constrain the characters' actions and/or free them to act in ways that might not be possible were they at home in London, St. Petersburg, Paris, or wherever their homes may be?

3. Both Malcolm and Suzanne keep secrets from each other. How might their marriage have been different if they had told each other the truth from the start? Or would they have married at all in that case?

4. Tatiana sets in motion an elaborate plot to regain what she sees as her rightful heritage. What are the parallels between the game she is playing and the more overtly political games being played at the Congress?

5. Do you think Malcolm would ever have told Suzanne the truth about Tatiana if Suzanne hadn't found the locket?

6. Do Castlereagh, Metternich, and Talleyrand remind you of any present-day politicians? If so, in what ways?

7. Suzanne and Malcolm both frequently are playing a part, whether they are in disguise (as at the Empress Rose), or playing their roles as a diplomatic couple, or at times even (or perhaps especially) when they are alone together. At what points in the novel do you think each of them is the most wholly her- or himself without masks or deception?

8. How are Suzanne's, Dorothée's, Wilhelmine's, Elisabeth's, and Tatiana's attitudes toward marriage and love shaped by their experiences in childhood and adolescence?

9. Compare and contrast Suzanne and Malcolm's marriage with Fitz and Eithne's, from their reasons for marrying, to their secrets and betrayals.

10. Several of the characters in *Vienna Waltz* fear the revelation of secrets about their personal lives. Do you think they have more or less to fear from their secrets being revealed than present-day public figures?

11. Did you suspect Fitz of killing Tatiana before the end of the book? Why or why not?

12. Malcolm says to Fitz that Castlereagh and Metternich are doing everything they can to put the French Revolution "back in the box. Quite ignoring the fact that the box broke twenty years ago." How does this idea parallel some of the characters' efforts to erase the past on a more personal level?

13. Suzanne and Malcolm struggle to balance their roles as agents and their duties in the diplomatic corps with being parents and husband and wife. How are the difficulties they face juggling all this similar to or different from those of a present-day couple?

14. Many of the characters claim not to believe in love or not to believe love lasts, yet a number of them do things that are motivated by love. Which actions, by which characters, do you think most strongly convey love for another character?